I CROUCH AND LEAN OVER the edge. "Ailesse?" I shout.

The water stirs. Nothing surfaces.

Seventy-five.

My racing pulse can't be keeping correct time. She hasn't been down there this long. Maybe thirty seconds. Possibly forty.

Eighty-six.

"Ailesse!"

Ninety-two.

I watch for the blue water to turn bloodred. But whose blood will it be?

One hundred.

I curse all the gods' names and throw myself off the cliff.

BONE CRIER'S MOON

KATHRYN PURDIE

KATHERINE TEGEN BOOKS
An Imprint of HarperCollins Publishers

Katherine Tegen Books is an imprint of HarperCollins Publishers.

Bone Crier's Moon
Copyright © 2020 by Kathryn Purdie

Library of Congress Cataloging-in-Publication Data
Names: Purdie, Kathryn, author.
Title: Bone Crier's moon / Kathryn Purdie.
Description: First edition. | New York, NY : Katherine Tegen Books, [2020] |
    Audience: Ages 14 up. | Audience: Grades 10-12. | Summary: "When her friend
    Ailesse is kidnapped, Sabine must embrace her bone magic to rescue her"—
    Provided by publisher.
Identifiers: LCCN 2019040565 | ISBN 978-0-06-279878-7 (paperback)
Subjects: CYAC: Magic—Fiction. | Friendship—Fiction. | Kidnapping—Fiction. |
    Fantasy.
Classification: LCC PZ7.1.P93 Bon 2020 | DDC [Fic]—dc23
LC record available at https://lccn.loc.gov/2019040565

Typography by Joel Tippie
21 22 23 24 25 PC/LSCC 10 9 8 7 6 5 4

First trade paperback edition, 2021

To Sylvie, Karine, and Agnés
for four life-changing summers

Eight Years Ago

FINGERS OF MIST CURLED AROUND Bastien's father as he walked away from his only child. The boy lifted up on his knees in their stalled handcart. "Where are you going, Papa?"

His father didn't answer. The light of the full moon shone on Lucien's chestnut hair, and the mist swallowed him from sight.

Alone, Bastien sank back down and tried to be quiet. Stories of cutthroat robbers on forest roads ran rampant through his ten-year-old mind. *Don't be afraid,* he told himself. *Papa would have warned me if there was any danger.* But his father was gone now, and Bastien began to doubt.

Outside the city walls, the idle cart offered little shelter. Bastien's skin crawled at phantom whispers. His breath caught when the branches around him formed claws.

I should follow Papa right now, he thought, but the nighttime chill seeped into his bones and filled them with lead. He shivered, pressed up against the limestone sculptures in the cart. Tyrus, god of the Underworld, stared back at him, his mouth chiseled in a wry line. Bastien's father had carved the figurine months ago, but it never sold. People preferred the sun god and the earth goddess, worshipping life and disregarding death.

Bastien turned his head, hearing a song without words. Lilting. Primal. Sad. Like the soft cry of a child or the plaintive call of a bird or a harrowing ballad of lost love. The song swelled inside him, achingly beautiful. Almost as beautiful as the woman standing on the bridge, for Bastien, like his father, soon followed the music there.

The mist settled, and a thick fog rolled in from the Nivous Sea. The breeze played with the ends of the woman's dark amber hair. Her white dress swished, exposing her slim ankles and bare feet. She wasn't singing. The music poured from a bone-white flute at her mouth. Bastien should have recognized her for what she was then.

She set the flute on the parapet when Lucien met her in the middle of the bridge. The hazy moonlight cast them in an unearthly glow.

Bastien faltered, unable to take another step. What if this was a dream? Perhaps he'd fallen asleep in his father's cart.

Then his father and the woman started dancing.

Her movements were slow, breathtaking, graceful. She glided through the fog like a swan on water. Lucien never looked away from her midnight-dark eyes.

⚜ X ⚜

Bastien didn't either, but when the dance ended, he blinked twice. What if he *wasn't* dreaming?

The bone-white flute caught his eye again. Dread dropped hot coals in his stomach. Was the flute *really* made of bone?

Legends of Bone Criers rushed back to him and clashed warning bells through his mind. The women in white were said to stalk these parts of Galle. Bastien's father wasn't a superstitious man—he never avoided bridges during a full moon—but he should have, for here he was, enchanted like all doomed men in the tales. Every story was alike. Each had a bridge and dancing . . . and what happened afterward. Now was when—

Bastien sprang forward. "Papa! Papa!"

His father, who adored him, who carried him on his shoulders and sang him lullabies, never turned to heed his son.

The Bone Crier withdrew a bone knife. She leapt straight into the air—higher than a roe deer—and with the force of her descent, she plunged the blade deep into his father's heart.

Bastien's scream raged as guttural as a grown man's. It carved his chest hollow with pain he would harbor for years.

He ran onto the bridge, collapsed beside his father, and met the woman's falsely sorry eyes. She glanced behind her at another woman at the bridge's end, who beckoned with a hasty hand.

The first woman lifted the bloody bone knife to her palm, like she meant to cut herself to complete the ritual. But with one last look at Bastien, she cast the knife into the forest and fled, leaving the boy with a dead father and a lesson seared forever in his memory:

Believe every story you hear.

1
Sabine

IT'S A GOOD DAY FOR shark hunting. At least that's what Ailesse keeps telling me. I pant, climbing behind her as she springs from one rock outcropping to the next. Her auburn hair gleams poppy red in the morning sunlight. The strands whip wildly in the sea breeze as she effortlessly scales the cliff.

"Do you know what a true friend would do?" I grab a handhold on the limestone and catch my breath.

Ailesse pivots and looks down at me. She doesn't mind the precarious ledge she's standing on.

"A true friend would toss me that crescent pendant." I nod at the grace bone that dangles among the small shells and beads on her necklace. The bone came from an alpine ibex we hunted in the far north last year. He was Ailesse's first kill, but I was the one who fashioned a piece of his sternum into the pendant she wears. I'm the better bone carver, a fact Ailesse encourages me to gloat about. I should, because it's the *only* thing I'm better at.

She laughs, my favorite sound in the world. Throaty, full of abandon, and never condescending. It makes me laugh, too, even though mine is self-deprecating. "Oh, Sabine." She climbs back down to me. "You should see yourself! You're a mess."

I smack her arm, but I know she's right. My face is hot, and I'm dripping sweat. "It's very selfish of you to make this look easy."

Ailesse's lower lip juts in a humorous pout. "I'm sorry." She places a supportive hand on my back, and I relax onto my heels. The thirty-foot distance to the ground doesn't seem so vast anymore. "All I can think about is what it will feel like to have a shark's sixth sense. With its grace bone, I'll be able to—"

"—discern when someone is nearby, which will make you the best Ferrier the Leurress have seen in a century," I drone. She's talked of little else all morning.

She grins and her shoulders shake with merriment. "Come, I'll help you up. We're almost there." She doesn't give me her crescent pendant. It wouldn't do any good. The grace can only belong to the huntress who imbued it with the animal's power. Otherwise, Ailesse would have given me all her bones. She knows I loathe killing.

The journey to the top is easier with her at my side. She guides my feet and takes my hand when I need a little lift. She prattles on about every fact she's gleaned about sharks: their enhanced sense of smell, their superior vision in low light, their soft skeletons made of cartilage—Ailesse plans to select a hard tooth for her grace bone, since it won't decay over her lifetime. The defining mineral in real bone is also abundant in teeth, so the shark's graces will imbue it in the same way.

We finally reach the summit, and my legs tremble while my muscles unwind. Ailesse doesn't pause to rest. She races to the opposite side, plants her feet at the extreme edge of the drop-off to the sea, and squeals in delight. The breeze ripples across her short, snug dress. Its single strap complements her shoulder necklace, which wraps in strands from her neck to below her right arm. The dress is the perfect length for swimming. Before we set off this morning, Ailesse removed the longer white skirt she usually wears on top.

She spreads her arms wide and stretches her fingers. "What did I tell you?" she calls back to me. "A perfect day! There's scarcely a wave down there."

I join her, though not as close to the edge, and peer downward. Forty-five feet below, the lagoon is encircled by limestone cliffs such as this one. The wind can only skip across the skin of the water. "And a shark?"

"Just give me a moment. I've seen reef breeds here before." Her burnt umber eyes sharpen to see what I can't, deep beneath the water. Ailesse's second grace bone, from a peregrine falcon, gives her keen vision.

The salt spray tingles my nose as I warily lean forward. A heady breeze tips my balance, and I scuffle back again. Ailesse holds steady, her body still as stone. I know that predatory, patient set of her jaw. She will wait like this—sometimes for hours—for what she wants. She was born to hunt. Her mother, Odiva, *matrone* of our *famille*, is our greatest huntress. Perhaps Ailesse's father was a skilled soldier or a captain. Mine was probably a gardener or an apothecary, someone who healed or helped things grow. Paltry skills for a Leurress.

I shouldn't wonder about our fathers. We'll never know them. Odiva discourages our *famille* from speaking about dead *amourés*, the select men who perfectly complement our souls. We novices will have to make our own sacrifices one day, and it will be easier if we don't grow attached to those destined to die.

"There!" Ailesse points to a darker spot of water, close to the cliff wall below us. I don't see anything.

"Are you sure?"

She nods, flexing her hands in anticipation. "A tiger shark—a king predator! How fortunate is that? I was worried you'd have to dive in after me and scare away the other reef sharks attracted to the blood." I swallow hard, imagining myself as bait. Gratefully, no creature will come near a tiger shark. Except Ailesse. She heaves a sigh of admiration. "Oh, Sabine, she's beautiful—and large, even taller than a man."

"She?" Ailesse may have far-reaching vision, but she can't see *through* the shark to its underside.

"Only a female could be that magnificent."

I scoff. "Says someone who has yet to meet her *amouré*."

She smirks, ever amused by my cynicism. "If I get this bone, I'll have all three and get to meet him on the next full moon."

My smile wavers. Every Leurress must choose and obtain three grace bones in order to become a Ferrier. But that's not the only requirement. It's the thought of the final achievement that renders me silent. Ailesse speaks so casually about her rite of passage and the person she'll have to kill—a *human*, not a creature who can't scream when its life has ended. But her tolerance is natural; I'm the anomaly. I must accept, like the other Leurress do without flinching, that what we do is necessary, a price demanded by the gods for the safety of this world.

Ailesse rubs her palms on her dress. "I have to hurry. The shark is turning back for the mouth of the lagoon. I'll never catch her if I have to fight against the current." She points to a small, sandy beach below. "Meet me down there, all right? I'll drag her to the shore when I'm finished."

"Wait!" I catch her arm. "What will happen if you fail?" I sound like her mother, but it must be said. This is my friend's life. This risk is different from those Ailesse has taken before. Maybe graces from a shark aren't worth the danger. She could still choose a bone from another animal.

Her expression falls. I usually support her in everything. "I can take a shark. Most are docile unless threatened."

"And a dive attack off a cliff isn't threatening?"

"Better than a slow swim from the shore. I'd never gain any momentum on her."

"That isn't the point."

Ailesse crosses her arms. "Our hunting *should* involve danger.

That *is* the point. The animals with the best graces *should* be difficult to kill. Otherwise we'd all be wearing squirrel bones."

A wall of hurt slams into me. My hand closes around the tiny skull resting above my heart. It hangs from a waxed cord, my only grace bone.

Ailesse's eyes widen. "There's nothing wrong with your bone," she stammers, realizing her mistake. "I wasn't making light of it. A fire salamander is worlds better than a rodent."

I look down at my feet. "A salamander is even smaller than a rodent. Everyone knows it was an easy kill."

Ailesse takes my hand and holds it for a long moment, even while her shark swims away. "It wasn't easy for *you*." Our toes are almost touching, her creamy skin against my olive. "Besides, a fire salamander has the gift to heal quickly. No other Leurress had the wisdom to obtain that grace before."

She makes me sound so clever. The truth is Odiva was pressuring me to make my first kill, and out of desperation I chose what wouldn't make me weep. I chose wrong. My eyes were red for days, and I couldn't bear to touch the dead creature. Ailesse boiled the flesh off his bones and made my necklace for me. She suggested I use the vertebrae, but to her surprise, I chose the skull. It reminded me of the salamander's life and personality the most. It was the best homage I could pay him. I couldn't bring myself to carve any pretty designs onto the skull, and Ailesse never asked me why. She never makes me talk about anything I don't want to.

I wipe my hand under my nose. "You better get your shark." If anyone can do it, she can. I'll stop fretting about the danger.

She smiles my favorite smile, the one that reveals all her teeth and makes me feel like life is one long adventure, large enough to keep even Ailesse satisfied.

She unstraps a spear from her back. We fashioned it from a sapling and her bone knife. Like all ritual weapons, it's made from the bones of a stag to symbolize perpetual life. Ailesse backs up several steps and grips the spear's shaft. With a running start, she launches herself off the cliff.

Her leap is tremendous. Her falcon's wing bone can't make her fly, but it definitely makes a jump impressive.

She shrieks in the thrill of the moment and brings her arms together, one hand over the other, to break the water. Her body aligns, her toes point, and she plunges in headfirst.

Her dive barely creates a splash. I creep closer to the edge of the cliff and squint, wishing for Ailesse's vision. Won't she come up for a breath? Maybe she means to strike the shark first. That would be the smartest way to catch it off guard.

I wait for her to emerge, and my heart thrums faster. I count each beat. *Eight, nine . . . thirteen, fourteen . . . twenty-one, twenty-two . . . forty-seven . . .*

Ailesse has two grace bones, the ibex and the falcon. Neither can help her hold her breath for long.

Sixty-three.

I crouch and lean over the edge. "Ailesse?" I shout.

The water stirs. Nothing surfaces.

Seventy-five.

My racing pulse can't be keeping correct time. She hasn't been down there this long. Maybe thirty seconds. Possibly forty.

Eighty-six.

"Ailesse!"

Ninety-two.

I watch for the blue water to turn bloodred. But whose blood will it be?

One hundred.

I curse all the gods' names and throw myself off the cliff.

In my panic, I jump feetfirst. I quickly straighten my body and pull my flailing arms to my sides—almost. They still slap the water. I gasp with pain and release a spray of bubbles—air I need. I clamp my mouth shut and glance around me. The water is clear, but the salt stings my eyes; my salamander was a freshwater creature. I twist in a circle, searching for my friend. I hear a faint sound of struggle.

Several feet beneath me, Ailesse and the shark are locked in combat.

Her spear is in the shark's mouth. The beast doesn't appear injured and bites on the shaft Ailesse is holding. Ailesse is thrown about like a reed in the wind, refusing to let go.

I scream her name and lose more breath. I'm forced to swim to the surface and gulp in air before I swim back down again.

I charge forward with no plan in mind, only viciousness in my veins and desperate fear in my heart. *Ailesse can't die. My best friend can't die.*

The tiger shark's face is ferocious. Serrated teeth. Lidless eyes. An oversized snout that makes her look even hungrier. How did

Ailesse think she could defeat her? Why did I allow her to jump?

Her spear snaps in two between the shark's jaws. The bone knife sinks. Ailesse is left with a three-foot pole. She jabs the shark's mandible and narrowly dodges a vicious bite.

The shark doesn't notice me. I reach for my dagger, but the blade is caught in my bloated sheath. Weaponless, I use all the force I can muster and kick the shark in her side. Her tail whips, but nothing more. I grab her gills and try to tear them. I can't. At least I've disturbed her. She bites once at me—barely missing my arm—and darts away behind a coral reef.

Ailesse floats nearby, her energy spent. The broken spear slips through her fingers. *Go!* I mouth, and point to the surface. She needs air.

She struggles to kick. I grab her arm and kick for her. Her eyes close just before we break the surface. She coughs up a mouthful of water, and I hit her back, pounding out the rest.

"Sabine . . ." She gasps and blinks salty drops from her lashes. "I almost had her. But she's so strong. I wasn't prepared for how strong." Ailesse looks below. I don't need her keen vision to see what she does—the shark circling and drawing closer. She's playing with us. She knows she can kill us any moment she wishes.

I kick madly toward the shore. "Come on, Ailesse. We have to go." I drag her behind me. "We'll find a better kill another day."

She coughs again. "What's better than a shark?"

"How about a bear? We'll travel north like we did last year." I'm rambling, trying to urge her to swim. She's still dead weight in my arms, and the shark's circle is tightening.

"My mother killed a bear," she says, like it's the most ordinary animal in Galle, even though Odiva's bear was a rare albino.

"We'll think of something else, then. But for now I need your help." My breaths fall heavier. "I can't swim for you the whole way."

I feel Ailesse's muscles gather strength. She starts paddling, but then her eyes narrow, her jaw goes stiff. She rotates around. *No, no, no.* "I remember where the spear tip sank," she murmurs.

"Wait!"

She dives underwater again.

Dread seizes me. I plunge in after her.

Sometimes I really hate my friend.

My eyes burn before they focus. Ailesse zips forward in a sharp line. The shark stops circling and faces her squarely. Ailesse is probably smiling, but she'll never fetch her spear quickly enough. Tiger sharks are brutes. This one will attack first. She needs a distraction.

I swim faster than I thought possible. My one grace bone proves helpful; salamanders move through the water with more ease than falcons, ibexes, or even humans. That's my only advantage.

I pass Ailesse and briefly meet her gaze. I pray sixteen years of friendship will help her understand my intentions.

She nods. We separate. I dive for the coral reef, and she dives for the spear.

The shark stalks her, not me. Ailesse is the one who started this fight.

I reach the coral and scrape my palms against it, then both my arms for good measure. My skin stings like fire. My blood swirls like smoke. I struggle to free my dagger, but its blade is still stuck in my sheath. I spy a large rock in the coral. It's sharp and jagged, freshly fallen from the cliffs. I pull it loose.

Three feet from Ailesse, the shark turns, her dead eyes fixing on me through the blood-veined water. For a moment, all I fathom is the terrifying beast and the twenty feet between us. I barely notice Ailesse swimming toward the seafloor.

The shark comes for me. Lashes through the water like lightning.

I brace for impact. I'm fierce. Strong. Fearless.

I'm like Ailesse.

An instant later, the shark's hideous face is before me. I bash my rock against her snout with a muted whimper. I'm nothing like Ailesse.

My strike barely cuts her face. She jerks sideways and hits my hand with her head. The rock fumbles out of my grip. She doesn't dart away this time. She circles me twice. So near her fin grazes my shoulder. So fast her head and tail blur together. She tries to bite. I drop below her with salamander speed and grope for the rock. It's out of reach.

I look up and startle. Right above me, I stare at the shark's open jaws and countless blades of teeth. I punch her blunt nose. She doesn't back off. I don't frighten her.

Her jaws snap. I don't roll away fast enough. Her teeth snag on my dress. She hauls me closer, chomping up more cloth. I twist and kick as her mouth yawns open again. I see into the cavernous tunnel of her belly. I'm out of air, out of options. Desperately, I wrestle with the hilt of my dagger. At last, the blade pries free.

I swing it up and stab the shark's snout, then one of her eyes. She thrashes madly, half-blind. My sleeve rips away, and one of her serrated teeth along with it. I wish to the gods it could be the bone Ailesse needs, but an animal must die to impart its graces.

As the shark pitches and reels, I zoom to the surface and gasp for air. Three breaths later, I'm underwater again.

Save Ailesse, save Ailesse, save—

I stop kicking as a cloud of red blooms beneath me. My throat tightens. Just when I fear the worst, Ailesse swims up through the blood, her spear shaft in her teeth. I hurry after her to the surface.

I push wet black curls from my face and search my friend's eyes. "Did you kill her?"

She pulls the shaft from her mouth. Her hand is bleeding. She hurt herself during the fight. "I couldn't reach far enough to stab her brain, so I cut off her dorsal fin."

Nausea pools inside me. The red in the water fans wider. The shark is down there, horribly injured, but still alive. She could rush up any moment and end us both. "Ailesse, we're done. Give me the spear."

She hesitates and looks below with longing. I wait for it, that stubborn set of her jaw. But it never comes. "She's yours if you want," she finally says.

I recoil. "No, that isn't what I meant."

"I've given her a fatal wound, Sabine. She's weak and partially blind. Take her." When I say nothing, only continue to stare at her, Ailesse swims closer to me. "I'm giving her to you—another grace bone. Surely killing that monster won't break your heart."

I picture the shark's grotesque face. I see her trying to wring the life out of Ailesse. She isn't majestic like the alpine ibex or beautiful like the peregrine falcon. She isn't even charming like the fire salamander. I won't mourn to see her dead.

But does that mean she deserves to die?

"I . . . I can't." I'm freezing in the water, but shame still flushes my cheeks. "I'm sorry."

Ailesse looks at me for a long moment. I hate myself for turning away the most generous gift she's ever offered to me. "Don't be sorry." She manages a small smile as her teeth chatter. "We'll find you another grace bone when you're ready."

With a sure grip on her knife, Ailesse descends below.

2
Ailesse

THE CHILL OF CHÂTEAU CREUX brushes my skin as Sabine and I walk down its crumbling stone staircase and through the entrance of the ancient castle's ruins. Long ago, the first king of South Galle built this fortress, and his descendants ruled here until the last of his line, King Godart, died an unnatural death. The locals believe he still haunts these grounds. Sabine and I hear them speak of the old days as they travel the rutted roads outside the city walls. They don't see us perch in the trees or hide in the tall grass. But we don't have to hide near Château Creux. The locals never venture here. They believe this place is cursed. The first king worshipped the old gods—our gods—and the people do their best to pretend Tyrus and Elara never existed.

My bandaged hand burns and throbs. I accidentally sliced my palm with my ritual knife when I sawed off the shark's fin. I'm still upset with myself for its drawn-out death. I feared the gods wouldn't find the kill honorable, but they must have; I received the shark's graces when I chose a bone and pressed it into the blood of my wounded hand.

At my side, Sabine totes a sack of shark meat over her shoulder. She grips the cinched rope with ease. Her injuries from the coral reef have almost healed. She dismisses her salamander skull as a pitiful grace bone, but it was a clever choice. What she really regrets is killing the creature. One day she will see she is meant for this life. I know Sabine better than she knows herself.

We duck under fallen beams and a collapsed archway. The Leurress could fortify the castle if my mother so desired, but she prefers it to look desolate and disturbing. If our home were beautiful, it would attract people. And a Leurress should only attract someone once in her life.

I adjust my shoulder necklace and trace the largest shark tooth, my newest grace bone. The other teeth are only ornamental, but they'll make me look formidable when I ferry the dead. After my rite of passage, I can finally join the Ferriers in their dangerous work.

"Are you nervous?" Sabine asks me.

"Why should I be?" I flash her a smile, though my heart drums. *My mother will approve of my kill. I'm just as clever as Sabine.*

My friend's presence behind me tickles my spine. Now she's ten feet away. Eight feet. Seven. As the vibrations grow stronger, the sixth sense I wanted so badly begins to annoy me. I prance farther ahead so Sabine can't see the frustration on my face. If she thinks I'm nervous, she'll be nervous, too.

We descend to a lower level of the château, then plunge deeper. The manmade stone corridors, carved with King Godart's crest of the crow and the rose, give way to tunnels shaped by tides of the sea. No water remains here, but pearlescent shells shimmer, embedded in the walls like ghosts clinging to the past.

Soon the tunnel opens to an enormous cavern. I blink against the sunlight bouncing off the limestone ground. A magnificent tower used to rise above this place, but it couldn't withstand the gales of the sea. After Godart died, the tower fell. It crushed and demolished the cavern ceiling. The Leurress chose this château as our home for that very reason. A clear view of the skies is necessary. Half our power comes from the bones of the dead, but the other half flows from Elara's Night Heavens. Our strength diminishes if we spend too long sheltered away from the goddess's moon and starlight.

Twenty or so women and girls mill about the cavern, the vast space we call the courtyard. Vivienne carries a freshly tanned deer hide. Élodie hangs rows of dipped candles on a rack to harden. Isla weaves white ceremonial cloth on her loom. Little Felise and Lisette carry baskets of garments to be washed. Two of the elders, Roxane and Pernelle, are off in a corner, training with their quarterstaves. The rest of the Leurress must be hunting for meat, gathering berries and herbs, or tending to chores within the depths of the château.

Isla moves away from her weaving loom and steps in my path. Her ginger brows lower as she scrutinizes my shoulder necklace. I purse my lips to keep from smiling. She can't identify the beast I killed from its teeth. "I see you've had a successful hunt," she says. "It certainly took you long enough. You girls have been gone almost a fortnight."

Girls, she calls us with her nose in the air. She's only three years older than me and four years older than Sabine. Isla completed her rite of passage when she was eighteen, but I'll do so in my seventeenth year—and with better graces.

I thrust my shoulders back. Until now, no Leurress has ever killed a shark. Probably because they never had help from a friend like Sabine. "The hunt was exceptional," I reply. "And more so because we took our time."

Sabine sneaks a wry glance at me. We were really gone so long because I kept changing my mind. I needed an awe-inspiring grace bone to complete my set of three and rival my mother's five— which only a *matrone* is allowed.

Isla wrinkles her nose at Sabine's sack of raw meat. The stink is terrible. After I greet my mother, I'll wash the scent out of Sabine's dress. That's the least I can do. She insisted on carrying the meat because of my wounded hand, but I know she won't eat it with the rest of us.

"Another long trek with Ailesse and no new grace bones?" Isla's eyes drop to Sabine's salamander skull.

My teeth grind together. "Do you wish you could have come in her place, Isla?" I turn to Sabine. "Tell her how much you enjoyed wrestling a *tiger shark*." My raised voice echoes through the courtyard and turns heads.

Sabine lifts her chin. "I've never had a more pleasurable swim in the sea."

I hold back a snort and link arms with her. We leave behind a speechless Isla as the women of our *famille* flock to us in a flurry of gasps, congratulations, and embraces.

Hyacinthe, the oldest Leurress, takes my face in her aged hands. Her milky eyes twinkle. "You have your mother's fierceness."

"I will be the judge of that." Odiva's silky voice ripples with authority, and I temper my smile. The women clear a path for the *matrone*, but when Sabine moves to do so, I touch her arm and she stays with me. She knows I'm stronger with her by my side. "Mother," I say, and bow my head.

Odiva glides forward, her huntress feet silent on the stone floor. Dust motes sparkle about her sapphire dress like stars in the sky. What's more breathtaking are her grace bones. The bone pendant of an albino bear, carved in the shape of a claw, dangles among the bear's real claws on her three-tier necklace, along with the tooth band of a whiptail stingray. Talons and feathers from an eagle owl form epaulettes on her shoulders. One of the talons is also carved from bone, like the bear claw pendant. And then there's my mother's crown, crafted from the vertebrae of an asp viper and the skull of a giant noctule bat. The bones are offset by her raven hair and chalk-white skin.

I hold my posture to perfection while her black eyes drop to my necklace. She slips a finger under the largest tooth. "What graces did you gain from a tiger shark that were worth endangering yourself to such a degree?" She speaks in a casual manner, but her red lips tighten with disapproval. Her *famille*—the only *famille* in this region of Galle—has dwindled over the years to forty-seven women and girls. While we seek the best graces, the hunt to obtain them shouldn't compromise our lives.

We had numbers to spare until fifteen years ago, when the great plague struck the land. The fight to ferry its countless victims killed half of those who died among us; the rest perished from the disease. Ever since then, we've struggled to manage the population of South Galle. But despite our size, we're still the founding *famille*, chosen of the gods. The other Leurress throughout the world can't ferry their dead without us. Our power is linked.

"A greater sense of smell, good vision in the dark, and a sixth sense to detect when someone is nearby, even without looking," I say, reciting the answer I've prepared.

I'm about to add *swimming, hunting, and ferocity,* when my mother replies, "I possess the same from a stingray."

"Except for vision in the dark." I can't help but correct her.

"Unnecessary. You have the wing bone of a peregrine falcon. That's all the enhanced vision you need."

Some of the Leurress whisper in agreement. Each Ferrier among them wears a bone from an animal—mostly fowl—that gives her the eyesight to see an additional color. The color of the dead.

I cross my arms and uncross them, fighting a flare of defensiveness. "But the shark was strong, Mother. You can't imagine how strong. She even took *us* by surprise." Surely Odiva can't argue the fact that I needed to add more muscle to my graces. Now I have it—with an extra measure of fierceness and confidence, as well. But she's only caught on one word.

"*Us?*"

I briefly lower my eyes. "Sabine . . . helped." My friend stiffens beside me. Sabine hates drawing attention to herself, and now all the Leurress are staring at her, my mother's gaze the heaviest.

When Odiva looks back at me, her expression is as smooth as the waters of the lagoon. But something fiercer than a shark churns beneath. I'm the one she's angry with, not Sabine. She's never angry with Sabine.

The Leurress grow quiet. The distant sounds of the sea funnel through the cavern like we're caught in a giant shell. My heart pounds in time with the crashing waves. Receiving the assistance of another Leurress during a ritual hunt isn't strictly forbidden, but it's frowned upon. No one cared a moment ago—the incredible kill overshadowed that fact—but my mother's silence makes them all reconsider. I hold back a sigh. What will it take to impress her?

"Ailesse didn't ask for my help." Sabine's voice is small but steady. She sets down her sack of shark meat and clasps her hands together. "I worried she might run out of air. Out of fear for her life, I dived in after her."

Odiva's head tilts. "And did you find that my daughter's life was truly in danger?"

Sabine chooses her next words carefully. "No more than your own life was threatened, *Matrone*, when you confronted a bear with only a knife and one grace." No cynicism drips from her tone, only gentle but powerful truth. Odiva was my age when she took on the bear, no doubt to prove herself to her own mother, the grandmother I scarcely remember.

My mother's brows lift, and she suppresses a smile. "Well spoken. You could learn a lesson from Sabine, Ailesse." Her eyes slide to mine. "A better way with words might curb your penchant to provoke me."

I square my jaw to mask my hurt. Sabine casts me an apologetic glance, but I'm not upset with her. She was only trying to defend me. "Yes, Mother."

No matter how hard I try to prove my worth as the future *matrone* of our *famille*, I fall short of the simple virtues that come naturally to my friend. A fact my mother never fails to make known to me.

"Leave us," she commands the other Leurress. With a sweeping tide of bows, they scatter back to their work. Sabine starts to follow, but my mother holds up a hand for her to stay. I'm not sure why, because her words are for me: "The full moon is in nine days."

My ribs ease against my lungs, and I inhale a deep breath. She's speaking of my rite of passage. Which means she's accepted my grace bones—all of them. "I'm ready. More than ready."

"Hyacinthe will teach you the siren song. Practice it only on a wooden flute."

I nod fervently. I know all of this. I've even learned the siren song by heart. Hyacinthe plays it at night. Sometimes I hear her cry afterward, her soft sobs flowing with the echoing tides of the sea. The siren song is that beautiful. "When can I receive the bone flute?" My nerves thrill at the thought of being able to touch it. I'm on the cusp of a dream I've had since I was little. Soon I'll stand among my sister Leurress, each of us using our graces to guide departed souls through the Gates of the Beyond, the very realms of Tyrus and Elara. "Do I really need to wait until the full moon?"

"This isn't a game, Ailesse," my mother snaps. "The bone flute is more than an instrument to call forth your *amouré*."

I roll back to my heels from my toes. "Yes, I know." The music of the bone flute also opens the Gates on ferrying night, which in turn opens all the other Gates around the world. Wherever people live, people die and must be ferried. And without the bone flute, none of the dead, near or far, can move on to the afterlife.

Odiva gives the smallest shake of her head, as if I'm still the impossible child who ran around Château Creux badgering each Ferrier to let me try on her grace bones. That was years ago. I'm fully grown now, fully competent, with three bones of my own. I'm prepared to make my final kill.

She steps closer, and my sixth sense hammers. "Have you decided whether or not you will try to bear a child?"

Heat scalds the tips of my ears. A quick glance at Sabine reveals she's just as red in the face. This conversation has taken a mortifying turn. My mother never discusses intimacy with me. I've learned what I know from Giselle, who spent one passionate year with her *amouré* before she killed him. Unfortunately, that year never produced another daughter Leurress—or a son, for that matter, although conceiving a boy is unheard of. The Leurress look at Giselle differently now, like she's a failure or someone to be pitied. She takes it in stride, but I don't envy her.

"Of course I will," I declare. "I know my duty as your heir."

Sabine fidgets beside me. I've told her the truth. I have no intention of providing another successor in our line. My mother will be forced to accept my decision after I've killed my *amouré* on the bridge. And when the day comes that I am *matrone*, I'll choose an heir among our *famille*. I'll be the first to break the chain of my mother's ruling bloodline, but the Leurress will go on. They'll have to, because the thought of getting to know a young man—for surely Tyrus and Elara wouldn't summon me an old one—and possibly falling in love with him, then killing him, is a cruelty I can't face. I'll do what is necessary. I'll sacrifice my promised lover, nothing more. Like all Ferriers before me, my rite of passage will be my oath to the gods, my promise to sever my last ties of loyalty to this world and dedicate myself to ushering souls into the afterlife. If I can resist my *amouré*, I'll have the strength to resist the ultimate siren call—the song of the Beyond.

My mother's hands fold together. "Then heed my advice, Ailesse. Conceive a child without forming a lasting attachment to your *amouré*, no matter how handsome, clever, or amiable he turns out to be." Her eyes look through me, lost to somewhere I can't follow. "You cannot escape the consequences of time spent in passion."

Is she thinking of my father? She never mentions his name. When she does speak of him, it's indirectly like this.

"He won't break me," I reply, steadfast in my answer. One day

I will rule this *famille* with Odiva's fierceness and dedication, but I'll also show each Leurress deep and unconditional affection. Perhaps my mother once intended to do the same, but killing my father built a wall around her heart. She isn't the only Leurress who suffers from the loss of her *amouré*. It may be the real reason Hyacinthe cries at night. After playing the siren song on her wooden flute, she whispers the name of her beloved.

Odiva hesitates, then places a hand on my shoulder. I startle at the contact. Her warmth tightens my throat with a surprising rush of emotion. "Without the Leurress," she says, "the dead would wander the land of the living. Their unmoored souls would wreak havoc on the mortals we are sworn to protect. Our task is to keep the balance between both worlds, the natural and unnatural, and therefore it is our privilege to be born a Leurress and our great honor to become Ferriers. You will make a fine one, Ailesse."

My mother's serene face swims in my tear-blurred vision. "Thank you." My voice is a croak, barely an utterance. It's all I can manage. All I want is for her to fold me in her arms. If she's ever embraced me, I've lost the memory.

I'm about to shift closer when she abruptly pulls back. I blink and collect myself with a quick swipe under my nose. My mother turns to Sabine, who hangs back a step, uncomfortably present during our conversation. "You will be Ailesse's witness at her rite of passage."

A small gasp escapes Sabine's mouth. "Pardon?" I'm equally stunned. The elder Leurress always serve as witnesses.

Odiva lifts Sabine's chin and smiles. "You have proven

unwavering loyalty to my daughter, even in the face of death. You have earned this right."

"But I'm not ready." Sabine shrinks back. "I only have one grace."

"That doesn't matter," I say, my stomach fluttering with excitement. "You just need to watch me. Witnesses aren't allowed to intervene." I must be tested on my own.

"Ailesse is my heir," Odiva adds. "The gods will protect her." Warmth surges through my limbs, even though my mother doesn't look at me. "Your role is to bear sacred record, Sabine. You might find the ritual inspires you to finish earning your own grace bones." My friend's strained expression says she seriously doubts that. Odiva releases a quiet sigh. "I have been patient with you, but the time has come for you to accept who you are—a Leurress, and very soon a Ferrier."

Sabine tucks a loose curl behind her ear with trembling fingers. "I'll do my best," she murmurs. Earning graces, completing a rite of passage, and becoming a Ferrier are supposed to be choices, but the truth is they're expected of us. No one in our *famille* has ever dared to shun the life we lead. Not unless she dies along with her *amouré*, the way Ashena and Liliane did.

Odiva stands taller, looking back and forth at us. "I want you both to prepare for the full moon in earnest."

"Yes, *Matrone*," Sabine and I answer as one.

"Now take that shark meat to the kitchen and tell Maïa to prepare it for supper."

"Yes, *Matrone*."

With a skeptical arch in her brow, Odiva leaves us. I wait, lips pressed together, until she's deep in conversation with Isla on the other side of the courtyard. Then I turn to Sabine and release a squeal of happiness. "You're my witness!" I grab her arms and shake them. "You're going to be there with me! I couldn't wish for anyone better."

She grimaces as I rattle her. "Far be it from me to deny anyone the chance to watch you slaughter the man of your dreams."

I giggle. "Don't worry, I'll make it clean and quick. You'll barely see it happen." I shove the image of the de-finned tiger shark from my mind.

"What if your *amouré* is more than you bargained for?" Sabine squirms. "I'm not convinced you'll be able to resist him. You swoon at even the ugliest boys we spy on the roads."

"I do not!" I slug her arm.

She finally laughs with me. "Your *amouré* will probably be a foot shorter than you and smell of sulfur and bat dung."

"That's better than the scent rolling off you."

Her mouth falls open, but then she smirks. "That was low, Ailesse. It was your idea to harvest the shark meat."

I grin and heft up the sack from the floor, ignoring the flare of pain in my hand. "I know. Come on."

She begrudgingly joins me as we walk toward the east tunnel to the kitchen. "I hope that rope cuts your wounds wide open." She nods at the handle of the sack, then bumps my shoulder with hers. We both giggle again.

As we trail away into the tunnel and out of earshot of the other

Leurress, Sabine slows her footsteps. "Are you sure you don't want to bear a daughter? What if you grow old and regret your one chance?"

I try to picture becoming intimate with a man. How much could my graces help me? And then to feel his offspring growing inside me until she's so large she has to rip out. "I can't . . ." I shake my head. "I'm just not maternal."

"That's not true. I see how you are with Felise and Lisette. They adore you."

I smile, thinking of the youngest girls in our *famille*. They fight over who gets to sit on my lap while we pluck quail feathers. When the clover blooms, I weave them through their hair. "I'll be a better aunt. We're practically sisters, right? Why don't you have a child one day, and I'll dote upon her?"

"I don't know." Sabine places a hand over her stomach. "The rite of passage should happen when we're . . . thirty-seven." She throws out a random age, well removed from her own sixteen years. "Right now it's hard to imagine any of *that*."

The word "that" speaks volumes and hangs heavy in the air. "That" is the hardest path a Leurress can choose. If she decides to live with her *amouré*, she's given exactly one year from her rite of passage to do so. Regardless of what happens afterward, the man's life is forfeit. If she doesn't kill him by the year's end, they're both cursed. The magic of the unfinished ritual will cut his life short *and* hers. It is how Ashena died. It is how Liliane died five years before her. It's the ultimate disgrace.

I push my shoulders back. "If I'm going to die, I'd rather do so ferrying the dead."

"Like *my* mother?" Sabine's brown eyes shine in the darkness.

I stop and squeeze her hand. "Your mother died a hero."

Her expression falls. "I don't find any glory in death."

Sabine's sadness is a dull knife sawing through me. I'm desperate to cheer her. Her mother died two years ago, but the pain is still fresh and strikes without warning. The departed soul of a wicked man—a Chained soul—killed Sabine's mother on the land bridge leading to the Gates. The nearness to the Beyond turned his spirit tangible—a form all souls keep for the rest of eternity, where they are rejoined with their bodies, and a form they can use to fight Ferriers. Only the Chained attempt to do so, resisting their punishment in the depths of Tyrus's Underworld, unlike the Unchained, who will live in Elara's Paradise. "That settles it, then," I say brightly. "We'll never die."

Sabine sniffs and cracks a smile. "Deal."

We walk into the darkness, our shoulders pressed together. "Let's pray that Tyrus and Elara send me a ghastly man," I say. "Then even *you* won't regret his death."

Sabine's silent laughter shakes me. "Perfect."

3

Bastien

Nine days until I kill her.

I climb into the rafters in the blacksmith's shop, the best place
to practice when Gaspar has spent a late night in the tavern. The
old man will be sleeping off his ale for at least another hour.

Nine days.

I steady my feet on a sturdy center beam and throw the hood
of my cloak over my eyes. When I meet her, the moon will be full,
but the night could be cloudy or rainy. Dovré and the surrounding
parts of South Galle can be fickle like that.

I pull two knives from my belt. The first I stole right under
Gaspar's nose as it was cooling from the forge. The second is
unremarkable. Cheap. The hilt isn't balanced with the blade. But

the knife was my father's. I wear it for him. I'll kill with it for him.

Half-blind, I lunge forward. Dust meets my nostrils as my feet strike the beam. I parry back and forth, my knives slashing the air as I begin my exercises. I've done these formations a thousand times, and I'll do them a thousand more. Being too prepared is impossible. I can't leave anything to chance. A Bone Crier is unpredictable. I won't know what animals she's stolen magic from until I meet her. Even then, I'll only be guessing. She might have twice my strength, probably more. She could leap right over me and stab me from behind.

I pivot on the beam and adjust my grip on both knives. I throw one after the other, and hear a satisfying *thunk, thunk*. I race to my target—a vertical crossbeam—and grab the hilts. I don't withdraw them yet; I use them as handholds and climb to a higher rafter.

I picture a bridge and the girl I'll kill there. Any Bone Crier will do. They're all murderers. I'll take what they stole from me, my father's life for one of their own.

Nine more days, Bastien. Then my father will be at peace. I'll be at peace. I can't imagine the feeling.

I drop to my hands and wrap my legs around the rafter. I swing upside down and tuck into a flip. My hood flies back as I land squarely on the lower beam.

I can surprise a Bone Crier, too.

A steady *clap, clap, clap* breaks my concentration. *Gaspar is early.* My muscles tense, but the voice I hear is throaty and female.

"Bravo." *Jules.* She leans against the blacksmith's unlit forge. Her straw-blond hair glows in a dusty beam of light from the open window. She flips a coin on her thumb.

"Is that real gold?" I wipe my wet brow on my sleeve.

"Why don't you come down here and find out?"

"Why don't *you* come up here?" I walk back to my lodged knives. "Unless you're afraid of heights." I yank the blades out of the crossbeam and sheathe them.

Jules snorts. "I jumped from the butcher's roof to steal that goose last week, didn't I?"

"Was it the dead goose who squealed?"

Jules's eyes narrow to slits, but she rolls her tongue in her cheek to keep from grinning. "Fine, Bastien. I'll come up there if you want to play with me."

Not exactly what I meant.

She saunters to one of the supporting posts, grabs the hooks for Gaspar's tools, and climbs. Her snug leggings show off the lean muscles of her body. I look away and swallow.

Fool, I chide myself. If I can't keep my head around Jules, how will I manage being near a Bone Crier? They're breathtaking and irresistible. Or so the legends say. My one run-in with a woman in white is proof enough. Even though I was terrified—even though I came to hate her—I can't forget her rare, unsettling beauty.

I sit on the rafter, one knee drawn to my chest while the other leg dangles. Across the beam, Jules pulls herself to her feet. Her chest heaves above her bodice. She's been lacing it tighter for two months, ever since I put an end to kissing her. "What now?" She rests one hand on her hip, but her legs shake. "Are you going to make me walk over to you?"

When I don't answer, she bargains, "How about you meet me halfway?"

"Hmm." I drum my fingers on my chin. "Nah."

She scoffs and flashes her coin at me. "I was going to share this, but now I think I'll keep it for myself. Maybe buy a silk dress."

"Because that comes in handy for a thief." I can't imagine Jules in a gown. She's the only girl in Dovré that dresses the way she does, and if any boy gives her grief about it, she blackens his eye. If he goes a step further and calls her "Julienne," he'll walk away doubled over with his hands between his legs. "Come over here." I beckon with a lazy hand. "The ground is just fifteen feet below. If you fell, what's the worst that could happen? A cracked skull? Broken neck? A nice chat up here is worth it, don't you think?"

"I hate you."

I grin and lean back against the post. "No, you don't." Everything between us feels right again. I'm goading her, annoying her, just like old times . . . before I made the mistake of kissing her. Jules and her brother, Marcel, are like family to me. I was wrong to mess with that.

Her braid falls in front of her shoulder as she eyes the ground. "So, is this officially a dare?"

"Sure."

"What do I get if I make it across?"

"You mean if you *live?*" I shrug. "I'll let you keep your coin."

"It's mine, anyway."

"Prove it."

She takes another glance at the ground and purses her trembling lips. In a knife fight, Jules would best me any day. But everyone has a weakness. She inhales a long breath and shakes out her hands. Her hazel eyes take on the gleam of the Jules I know best. The Jules who will follow me anywhere. She and Marcel will be with me in nine days. Together, we'll find vengeance. My friends lost their father, too.

I never knew Théo Garnier. I was twelve years old and ready to pickpocket an apothecary when I first heard his name and learned of his fate. I overheard the apothecary speak of a strange illness he'd failed to cure three years earlier. He'd never come across anything so unnatural as the mysterious bone disease. It was the last tragedy Théo was destined to suffer after being abandoned by his wife and then his lover.

Suspicious that a Bone Crier might be involved, I spent the next month tracking what became of Théo's two children. According to the apothecary, there was no family to take them in. I finally found Jules and Marcel in another district of Dovré, scavenging the streets like me to survive. We pieced together the puzzle of our fathers' deaths and realized we had a common enemy. Together, we pledged to make the Bone Criers pay for what they took from us.

Jules stows the coin between her teeth and spreads her arms wide. She takes her first step.

My smile fades as I study her technique. "Look ahead, not downward. Focus on the distance in front of you. Find a target there and stay locked on it." She exhales and does as I say. "Good, now keep your pacing even."

I didn't dare Jules just for fun. I'm helping her. If she can rise above her fear of heights, she'll be unstoppable. She'll scale the rooftops of Dovré. She'll leap from one to the next with the ease of an alley cat. The perfect thief.

She's halfway across the beam, her face flushed with victory. Then her brows twitch, her confidence cracks. She's *only* halfway across.

"Steady, Jules. Don't think. Relax."

She holds her breath. Veins pop at her temples. Her eyes lower. *Merde.*

She pinwheels sideways. I lunge, but she falls too fast.

I dive for her arm, and the beam smacks my chest. Our hands scramble to connect. Her weight yanks me, but I anchor myself to the beam. She flails and releases a tight-lipped cry.

"I've got you, Jules!"

She grabs my wrist with her other hand. By some miracle, the coin is still in her mouth.

"The anvil's right below you," I warn. "I'm going to pull you back up, all right?"

She nods with a whimper.

I squeeze the beam with my thighs and lift her slowly, hand over hand. She finally makes it upright, and we straddle the beam, face-to-face and panting. Her arms fling around my neck. She's trembling all over. I hold her tighter, cursing myself for daring her in the first place. *If I lose anyone else . . .* I close my eyes.

"Well done." I fight for breath. "That was beautiful."

She bursts with manic laughter. "If you tell Marcel about this, I'll kill you." Her words slur around the coin in her mouth.

"Fair enough."

She draws back to see my face. Our noses are almost touching. She juts up her chin slightly. She's inviting me to take the coin. I peel one hand from her waist and pluck it from her teeth.

She licks her lips. "Well?"

I give it a little bite of my own. "It's real," I say with a sheepish grin.

Her lashes lower. She looks like she's about to kill me.

But then she's kissing me.

I'm so taken off guard I lose my balance. This time it's Jules who anchors me to the beam. Her mouth doesn't break from mine.

I can't help but give in to her. She's too good at this. My hand digs into her waist. Her breath falls in gasps, fanning warmth across my face. I start to deepen the kiss, but then my stomach tangles in a hangman's knot. I'll cheat and steal from anyone in Dovré, but not the two people I care about most. And that's exactly what this feels like—cheating, stealing. It took me every day of the six weeks Jules and I were together to figure out why: I'm giving what I don't have to give.

"Jules . . ." I gently push her, but she doesn't budge, a fighter to the core. It's why I love her . . . just not the way she wants me to. Not yet, anyway. Maybe not ever. "Jules, *no*." I scoot back. Her hands drop to the beam.

She searches my eyes. Her own brim with hurt. I can't go down this road again. She'll only grow to hate me. I wish I could tease her and slink away, my hands in my pockets. Instead, we're stuck in these rafters together.

I sigh and drag my hands through my hair. It needs washing and a good cut. Usually Jules handles the shears. "Keep the coin," I say, and place it between us. "Buy that silk dress. You can wear it to the spring festival."

"I'm not going to buy a dress, idiot." She snatches the coin and shoves it in her pocket. "What we need is food."

"Well, in nine days—"

"In nine days, *what*? You'll clean up your act? Find an apprenticeship? Suddenly gain a good reputation?"

I shrug. "In nine days we can leave Dovré. Start over in another city."

"That's what you say every full moon," Jules snaps, then shakes her head, trying to rein in her quick temper. "We've been doing this for over a *year*, Bastien. We've watched every bridge. It's time we own up to the fact that Bone Criers probably died out or moved on somewhere else—like *we* should."

My eyelid tics, and I tighten my jaw. "South Galle has more Bone Crier lore than anywhere. The earliest myths come from here, not somewhere else. They haven't died, Jules. Women like that don't just die."

Her gaze narrows into the glare she's mastered. "Why, because you wouldn't have a reason to wake up every morning?"

I'm done with this conversation.

I swing my legs up and stand on the beam. Jules stays stubbornly put. "Come on." I extend my hand, but she ignores me. "Fine. Good luck up here." I turn to leave.

"Wait," she groans, and I look back. "I want to avenge my

father's death, too. You know I do, but . . . what if we don't? What if we *can't?*"

My ribs squeeze against a sharp pain in my chest. I can't think about failing. How can she? Jules and Marcel didn't watch their father get murdered on a bridge like I did. Théo still died, but he died slowly.

Years after their mother passed away, he brought home a beautiful woman. She mended their clothes, sang them songs, and slept in their father's bed. They called her heaven-sent. She helped Théo in his work as a scribe, smoothing the parchment with pumice, marking out lines with a ruler and awl. When his income doubled, they ate sweetmeats and drank high-country wine. Then one morning Jules found the woman standing over her sleeping father and holding a knife carved from bone. The woman startled at Jules and ran from their cottage, never to return. Théo soon grew ill, and his bones turned as brittle as glass. Each time he fell, another bone broke. Finally, one injury was so terrible it ended his life.

I glare at my friend. "I *will* get my vengeance. Give up if you want, but I never will."

Jules bites her lower lip. The small gap between her two front teeth is her only feature that reminds me of the girl I met when we were twelve. We're eighteen now, old enough to worry about what comes next in our lives. What we'll do after we give our fathers peace. I can't think about anything else just yet.

"Who said *you* were the stubborn one?" Her smirk masks the worry on her face. "I was just testing you. Put me on solid ground come the next full moon, and I won't be running away. You'll get your kill, and Marcel and I will get ours." I've told my friends about the second woman I saw when my father died. Marcel searched through all the books he's stashed around Dovré—those he salvaged from his father's library—and he figured out Bone Criers always travel in pairs. Convenient for our one night of murder. "Now help me down from here before I shove you onto that anvil," Jules says.

A warm chuckle bursts out of me. "Fine." I guide her to the crossbeam, where she can climb down. She's nearly to the ground when the lock on the door rattles. Jules curses and jumps the rest of the way. I follow after her and roll to break my fall. The door flings open. We're caught in a bright square of sunlight.

Gaspar gapes at us in a drunken haze. One of his suspenders has fallen, and his gut bulges over the waistband of his patched trousers. We dart past him, and he bellows, grabbing one of his fire pokers. He'll never catch us. Jules and I join hands on the street, and our strides fall in perfect rhythm. I laugh at our near escape—we've had so many—and she flashes me a dazzling smile.

I could kiss her right then, but I glance away before I let myself.

Nine days. Then I can think about Jules.

4
Sabine

"I SWEAR ON MY FATHER'S bones," Ailesse growls, tripping over the hem of her dress again. I grab her arm to steady her, and she lifts her skirt off the dusty path in the forest. "Isla made my dress too long on purpose. She's determined to make tonight as difficult as possible."

Odiva asked Isla to sew Ailesse's white ceremonial dress, and I've never seen a finer one. The wide neckline clings elegantly to the edges of her shoulders, and the snug sleeves flare at her elbows. Isla took careful pains to fit the bodice, but Ailesse is right about the skirt. Its excessive train and front hem are hazardously long. Isla is too talented a seamstress for it to have been a mistake.

"Maybe she did you a favor." I shrug. "Your *amouré* might find you more alluring in an impractical gown." When Ailesse shoots me a skeptical glance, I add, "Remember the painting we saw carted into the city last autumn? The lady in the portrait was nearly drowning in her ridiculous dress, and the men guarded it like it was the most valuable treasure in Galle."

"Men must be attracted to defenseless women," Ailesse grumbles, but then her dark eyes sparkle in the moonlight. "Won't I give my *amouré* a surprise? He'll be luckier than the other dense men of Dovré."

Luckier. I grin, but my stomach sinks. Like the rest of our *famille*, Ailesse believes the man the gods choose for her tonight is fortunate. One day when Ailesse dies, her *amouré* will greet her with gratitude for taking his life, and together they'll live a better life in Elara's Paradise. I wish I could stake my faith in that. Tonight would be so much easier.

I shiver as a mist creeps into the forest and disturbs the warm air. "What do you imagine he'll be like?"

Ailesse shrugs. "I don't let myself imagine anything about him. What good would that do me in this life?"

"You've never once daydreamed about your *amouré*?"

"Never."

I level a hard stare at her, but she maintains her stubbornly impassive expression. "Well, I think you should take a moment to dream before you go through with your rite of passage. Maybe the gods will pay attention, and you'll help them make their choice."

She scoffs. "I don't think that's how it works."

"Humor me, Ailesse. Dream."

She squirms like her rite of passage dress is suddenly itchy.

"Would you like him to be handsome?" I prod, linking arms with her. "Let's start with that."

She grimaces. "I'll allow him to be handsome if he isn't in love with his appearance. Nothing's less attractive."

"Agreed. No vanity will be tolerated."

"Speaking of looks . . . I wouldn't mind if he had dimples and curls."

"Dimples and curls—do you hear that, Tyrus and Elara?"

Ailesse shushes me. "Don't be irreverent, or they will summon me a troll."

"Don't you worry. Trolls are a myth. We're the only creatures to fear on bridges."

She giggles and leans her head on my shoulder. "My *amouré* must also be passionate and powerful."

"Naturally, or else he'd be no match for you."

"But he should balance that strength with tenderness and generosity."

"Or else he couldn't handle your mood swings."

She laughs, elbowing me. "In short, he must be perfect."

I rest my head against hers. "You wouldn't be dreaming if he were any less."

We round a bend in the path and intersect a seldom-used road outside the city walls. Twenty feet away is Castelpont, the bridge Ailesse has chosen for her rite of passage. Our smiles fade. My heart thuds. We're here. Ailesse is really doing this.

The full moon hangs over the bridge like a white eye shrouded in mist. Night insects buzz and chirp, but the sounds diminish as we leave the forest, travel down the quiet road, and advance to the crown of the bridge.

Castelpont is old and made of stone, built in the days when King Godart's ancestors ruled the land. Back then, the Mirvois River transported inland goods to Château Creux, and the bridge's high arch accommodated passing vessels beneath. But now the riverbed is parched and desolate. After Godart died without providing an heir, another royal family declared their right to rule. They built another home, Beau Palais, on the highest hill in Dovré, and rerouted the river. Castelpont gained its name because, looking to the west, you could once see the towers of Château Creux. And now, looking to the east, you can see the newer castle, Beau Palais. Ailesse and I have never been inside that castle, and we never will. Odiva forbids the Leurress to enter Dovré's city walls. Discretion is essential to our survival.

"Are you sure about the bridge?" I ask. The windows of Beau Palais are like another pair of eyes staring down at us. "We're too exposed." This is nothing like our pastime of spying on travelers from the safety of careful hideouts in the forest.

She leans her folded arms on the half wall of the parapet and surveys the limestone castle. Her auburn hair flows soft and loose on the breeze. Concealed beneath it is her ritual bone knife, sheathed in a harness on her back. "No one can see us from this distance. We're perfectly safe."

I'm unconvinced. Ailesse chose Castelpont for the same reason she killed a tiger shark. Out of all the bridges in South Galle,

Castelpont presents the most challenge: it's closest to Dovré. A rite of passage here will impress the other Leurress. Once Odiva forgives Ailesse, it might impress her, too.

Ailesse twirls around and takes both of my hands. "I'm so happy you're with me, Sabine."

Though her smile is radiant, her hands betray a slight tremor. "I'm happy I'm with you, too," I lie. Whether I hate this rite of passage or not, she'll never back out of it, so I wish her to be sure and swift about her kill. If it's clumsy and her *amouré* suffers a slow death, Ailesse will regret it for the rest of her life.

She unclasps her necklace, slips it off her shoulder, and passes it over to me. "Shall we begin?" The rite of passage is the only time a Leurress can access her power without wearing her bones. But she must stay on the ritual bridge.

I inhale a deep breath and offer her a small yew chest. She opens the lid. Inside, the ancient bone flute rests on a bed of lamb's wool. Ailesse reverently withdraws the instrument, and her fingers run over the tone holes and trace the engraved symbols. The Leurress claim the flute was made from the bone of a golden jackal, but the sacred beast is mythical, at least in my mind. No one in my *famille* has ever seen one in Galle.

A sudden gust carries the sound of faint voices. Something rustles in the trees, and I glance behind us. "Ailesse"—I grab her arm—"someone is here."

As she shifts to look, a silver owl swoops from the branches and arcs overhead. A nervous laugh spills out of me, but Ailesse grows solemn. Owl sightings portend either good or bad fortune. You don't know which until the inevitable happens.

"Go, Sabine," Ailesse says, as the owl screeches and flies off. "We can't delay."

I kiss her cheek and hasten away to do my part. "Good luck." A witness does more than bear record of the ritual sacrifice. I must also bury Ailesse's grace bones beneath the bridge's foundations and retrieve them afterward. When she plays the siren song on the bridge, the gods will choose a man for her. Whether her promised lover is near or far, whether he hears the song or feels its music inside him, the two of them will be bonded, and he'll be drawn to meet her. Our *famille* has been known to attract *amourés* from all quarters of Dovré, and even miles outside the city walls.

Ailesse kneels on the bridge, closes her eyes, and lifts her cupped hands to the Night Heavens. She murmurs a prayer to Tyrus's bride, Elara, separated from him at the dawn of time by the mortal world that formed between their kingdoms.

I steal a glance at Elara's milky veil of stars and offer up a prayer of my own. *Help me endure this night.* I rush away, fumbling with Ailesse's shoulder necklace. All three of her grace bones are tied onto it with waxed cording. I feel none of their power.

I unravel the knots, remove the bones, and I climb down the steep bank of the riverbed. The soil at the bottom is cracked and dry, so I grab a jagged rock to dig the first hole. I bury Ailesse's first bone, the wing bone of a peregrine falcon, then hurry to the second foundation corner. I'm grateful I don't have to get wet. If Ailesse had chosen a bridge over water, I'd be swimming right now. I'd have to tie her bones to the foundations beneath the waterline.

Every flutter of the wind makes me flinch and scan our surroundings. If anyone other than Ailesse's *amouré* comes this way and grows suspicious, Ailesse might not be able to defend herself—not until I'm finished down here and she plays the siren song. She can't wield her graces until then.

I bury the second bone and rush to the other side of the riverbed to bury the third bone. Each hole is shallower than the last, but I don't trouble myself to dig any deeper. I leave the fourth corner undisturbed, reserving that spot for the man Ailesse will kill. It will be his grave—the last honor he'll receive in this life. Yet another reason to be grateful this isn't a bridge over water. Casting a dead man in a river, to be washed up who knows where, seems a poor form of thanks after taking his life.

"I'm finished!" I call, and throw one more handful of earth over the last grace bone. "You can begin."

"I'll wait until you're back up here." Ailesse's clear and relaxed voice echoes back to me. Her prayer must have calmed her. "Otherwise you won't be able to see me."

I stifle a groan and start climbing the riverbank. "It's not as if your *amouré* is going to materialize when you play the first note. He could live on the other side of Dovré for all we know."

She lets out a loud sigh. "I didn't think about that. I hope this doesn't take all night."

As much as I want her rite of passage to be done with, part of me wishes her *amouré* never comes. The gods demand enough of a Leurress over her lifetime. They shouldn't ask us to make a sacrifice like this, too. But Tyrus is said to be exacting. His cape is made from the smoke and ash of oath breakers and cowards, the worst sinners in the Underworld, those caught in the eternal fire of his wrath. Even murderers suffer a better fate on the Perpetual Sands, Tyrus's scorching desert where thirst is never quenched.

I finally reach the top, panting, and brace my hands on my hips. "I'm here. Go on."

Ailesse rolls back her shoulders. "Let's see if I can kill a man without getting his blood on my dress." She winks. "That will show Isla."

My stomach folds on itself. I don't smile back. This is really happening. Ailesse is going to meet her match, only to slaughter him. "Be careful," I say, even though her promised lover is the one who's in danger. Still, I can't shake my sense of foreboding.

"I'm always careful." Her daring grin betrays the very opposite and doubles my worry. A little fear is wise.

Resigned, I retreat to the nearest tree and stake my place behind it. I'm partially hidden, but I can still see my friend.

Ailesse brushes her hair over her shoulder, neck tall like a swan, and brings the bone flute to her mouth.

5

Bastien

TONIGHT I'LL HAVE MY REVENGE. I feel it deep inside, past the jittery energy that's kept me awake the last twenty-four hours. After tonight, I'll sleep in peace.

I tighten the strap of the sheath harness on my back. Both my knives are hidden there. The Bone Crier will ask me to dance— part of her twisted cat-and-mouse game—but I won't reveal *I'm* the cat until the time is right.

"I still vote we attack from the trees," Marcel says, the last to crawl out from the cellar tunnel of La Chaste Dame. The brothel is near the south wall of the city. We could have taken the path through the catacombs, but this tunnel—the one Madame Colette turns a blind eye to if I toss her a coin—leads out of Dovré on the way to the bridges we'll scout tonight. Last full moon, Jules, Marcel, and I started west and worked our way east. This time we'll travel down from the city to the royal shipyard on the coast. South Galle is webbed with water and bridges.

"No, we're going to do this properly, face-to-face." I'm clean for the first time in weeks. We snuck into the Scarlet Room of La Chaste Dame, where Baron Gerard likes to slum around. Jules scrubbed my hair with his soap and used his razor on my face. She even gave me a splash of the baron's fragranced water. Now I smell of licorice, watercress, and cloves. It's enough to make me sneeze, but Jules promises the scent is enticing. When the Bone Crier plays her song, I should pass off as the fated boy she lures. Whoever he is.

"How do I look?" I ask for the first and hopefully last time in my life. *Lunge, strike, parry.* I practice my formations in my mind as Jules fusses with the cape I "borrowed" from the brothel. It's fastened across my back and one shoulder, the same way upper-crusters from the noble district wear them. We'll return it to the Scarlet Room once we're done tonight. Madame Colette will poison us in our sleep if she learns we're thieving from her regulars.

"Almost perfect," Jules replies. "The only flaw is your breath. The sausage was a mistake."

"You're the one who pilfered it—and ate the other link."

"I'm not the one trying to impress a demigoddess." Jules turns away and rummages through the underbrush.

"Bone Criers aren't immortal." Marcel wipes his dusty hands on his trousers. "They live as long as we do. The old songs perpetuate that myth, but if you look closely to their source, specifically the epic poem *Les Dames Blanches* by Arnaud Poirier, you'll see where the confusion began," Marcel divulges in a lazy drawl. He isn't trying to impress us, and he isn't worried much about changing our opinion either. He speaks like he always does, sharing whatever pops into his head and turns the cogs of his mind. "'With divine gifts, they lure, they kill,' Poirier says, but of course he means Bone Criers derive *power* from the gods, not that they *are* gods. They just claim to descend from them."

Jules plucks a handful of leaves, half listening to her younger brother. "Mint," she announces, not a moment before she shoves it in my mouth.

I choke and spit out a couple leaves. "I don't need the whole plant!"

"Maybe you do." She fans her face and strolls past me. I don't miss the sultry sway of her hips. She's wearing all black from her leather bodice to her boots. She even sports a black hood-piece to hide her blond hair. Jules is always the shadow in our hunts, and I'm the distraction. Although she's doing a better job at that right now. As for Marcel, we try to keep him out of sight. He's good for strategy, but when it comes to stealth, he has two feet in the same boot.

He lags a step behind as we creep through the forest. The dry mulch cracks and snaps beneath his feet. The girls in Dovré don't mind his clumsiness. I've heard them whisper about Marcel's "sweet face" and "honey eyes." If they whisper about me, I don't hear it. Truth is, out of the three of us, Marcel is the only one who's approachable. *Slash, duck, roll.* My muscles tense as I think through each move. The Bone Crier will be fast, but I'm ready for her.

"The title of Poirier's poem is further responsible for the misconception that all Bone Criers are fair-skinned," Marcel continues, "when in fact '*blanches*' refers to their dress color."

"Are you still talking?" Jules skips faster down the deer trail. "This will take until dawn if you don't keep up."

She's right. I wheel back to help Marcel. We've been hunting bridges for over a year now, and my itch to finish this is festering. *Tonight, Bastien, tonight.* "How about you ditch the pack and bow?" I suggest. Marcel looks like a mule with all he's carrying. "That gear slows you down every time."

"I'd rather be slow than defenseless." His eyes stray to a leaf caught on his cloak, and he touches its jagged edges. "Vervain," he identifies, and sticks it in his pocket. "Besides, the book stays with me. You know that."

I do. The book goes everywhere Marcel does. It's the main reason for his pack. The lore of Old Galle is in those folktales. They don't hold up to Marcel's logic, but the book was on his father's bedside table when he died. I understand the need for it. My father's unwieldy knife isn't as bulky, but I also never go anywhere without it.

The breeze shifts, and I cough at the sudden scent of roses. "Did one of Madame Colette's girls corner you on the way out?"

"What? No. Why would you—?"

"The fragrance." I wink. "Pretty sure someone rubbed half a bottle off on you."

Marcel sniffs at his collar and curses under his breath. "She's not a brothel girl," he mumbles, and speeds up to move past me.

I chuckle, following right on his heels. "Let me guess—Birdine?" The frizzy-haired ginger works at a shop near La Chaste Dame. Her airy voice and warm laughter put customers at ease while her uncle swindles a high price for cheap perfume. "No one else wears that much rosewater."

Marcel groans. "You can't say anything. Jules will roast me over a pit if she smells this on me."

"What's it to her?"

"She holds a grudge against anyone who looks my way."

"Especially when you look back." I give him a knowing grin, but he doesn't laugh like I expect him to. He's too busy rubbing crushed pine needles all over his neck and shirt and scouring the path ahead for his sister. I've never seen him so flustered. Marcel's normally as unruffled as they come. "You're serious about this girl, aren't you?" I cock my head. "Want me to talk to Jules? Ask her to ease off the leash?" Marcel's only sixteen, same age as Birdine, but that's old enough to have some fun without worrying about your sister's eyes on your back.

His face brightens. "Would you?"

Jules will skin me alive for even bringing it up. She's mother, father, and more to her brother. That kind of responsibility can't be easy to shake off. Before a Bone Crier wrecked Jules's and Marcel's lives, their mother did her own fair share of damage. She abandoned Théo for a sailor when the kids were small and left port on a ship that never returned. "Of course." I step over a gnarled root and set a quick pace again. *Spin, dive, slice.*

"Birdie is tired of perfumery. The musk makes her head ache."

"Oh?" I'm not sure what he's getting at, but I smirk at his

nickname for her. "She got another way to make a living?"

"She wants to assist me in my work."

"Pickpocketing?" *Jump, stab.* I bet the Bone Crier will choose one of the bridges in the deep forest south of Dovré. Some bridges are forgotten and hard to find. Not for me. "Or did you mean the revenge business?"

"*Scribe* work," Marcel says slowly, not realizing I'm teasing. "I still have most of my father's tools. There's parchment to prepare, lines to rule—plenty for Birdie to do. A scribe does more than merely read and write," he adds, like all poor kids in Dovré can do the same.

I scratch the back of my neck. Is Marcel really so anxious to go off and commit to a profession already? I never let myself think past the next full moon. "Listen, I could have picked up a chisel and hammer over the years." If my father were alive, that might have made him happy. But he isn't alive. Now I can only give him justice. "Turns out all I needed was a knife."

Marcel pushes a reedy branch out of our path. "I don't follow your point."

"Look, have a good time with Birdie—when you can, anyway. But don't lose focus. Jules and I need you." I give him a brotherly slap on the shoulder. Without Marcel, we wouldn't know the finer details about Bone Criers, even though that knowledge is patchy. "Becoming a scribe is sure to make your father proud, but his memory needs to be put to rest first, all right?"

Marcel's chest sinks, but he musters a brave nod.

Jules whistles a birdcall, impatient for us to catch up. We hurry along faster, but Marcel's footsteps fall heavy. I nudge away a prick of guilt. Reminding him to keep his head in the present is nothing Jules won't tell him herself. At least from me it doesn't come with a shouting match. Marcel was seven when Théo died. Jules was nine. The two years she has on him give her a harder understanding of what they lost. Marcel needs revenge as much as we do. One day he'll thank us for making him stick it out until the end.

By the time we spy Jules ahead, she's nearing the first bridge on our route. She's about to step out of the forest and onto the road when she stops abruptly.

I freeze, always in tune with her, and hold up a hand to stall Marcel. Someone must be nearby. Jules will wait for him to pass. We're known thieves. If we came across the wrong person—

Jules's silhouette grows stiff. Hitched-up shoulders. Spread fingers. Not good. How many people are out there? She backtracks slowly, ducking lower with each step.

"What's happ—?"

I clamp a hand over Marcel's mouth.

Jules hits a low-lying branch. She's never that clumsy. "*Merde,*" she says, and drops flat to the ground. The wild grass rustles. She crawls through it. When I see her again, she's pointing wildly behind her.

Marcel and I crouch. The three of us gather in a tight circle of heads. "Soldier?" I ask. The king's guard doesn't patrol this far from the city wall, but I can't think of who else could have Jules in a panic.

She shakes her head. "Bone Criers."

My throat runs dry. I blink stupidly at her. Even Marcel is speechless. "What, *here?*"

She nods.

"Castelpont?" I'm still disbelieving. I never considered this bridge could be a target, just a shortcut. It's in full view of Beau Palais.

"A woman in white is on the bridge and another one is retreating from the other side. *That* woman is wearing green, though, so your all-in-white theory doesn't stand, Marcel."

"Perhaps the white is ritualistic," he muses. "In the legends, Bone Crier sightings happen during the dance on the bridge. Only one story mentions witnesses, and it doesn't note the color of their dresses, but . . ."

I scarcely hear a word as Marcel drivels on. Jules finally smacks him, which shuts him up. She looks back at me, and her smile splits wide. "Bastien, we've done it! We've found them!" She stifles a burst of crazed laughter.

I don't grin back. I can't think, can't find my breath. My pulse throbs behind my eyelids. I knew in my gut I'd have my revenge tonight. The scene I've captured in my head—the scene I've imagined for years—unfolds before me.

I step on the bridge. The Bone Crier and I clap eyes on each other. I pretend to be spellbound. We dance. I'm playing her game. Then I announce who I am. I name two of the men her people have killed. My father. Jules and Marcel's father. I slit her throat with my father's knife, and Jules kills the witness. We don't bury their bodies. We leave them where they die.

"Bastien." Jules shakes me.

I swallow, coming back to myself. I rub my hands together to get my blood pumping. "Marcel, guard the road—back where it's out of sight of the bridge. The Bone Crier's true soulmate will come at some point. With any luck, we'll be finished by then."

"I'll climb a tree and watch for him." Marcel looks upward, and his hair flops over one side of his face. The one eye I can see is already distracted by the variety of trees above us.

Jules frowns at him. "Don't mess this up. No comparing sap or bark or whatever else fascinates you."

"I'm perfectly capable of staying on task."

"Are you?" She arches a brow. "Prove it. Stick to your post until we call for you, not a moment sooner. Leave the fighting to us. I don't want to mop up your guts when this is finished."

"He'll be fine," I say, and lean close to Marcel's ear. "Think of rosewater." I nudge him. After tonight, our revenge business will be done.

He tamps down a smile and gives me a private nod.

"Are we ready, then?" I ask my friends. "This is everything we've worked for. We've got to be flawless. That Bone Crier out there"—I point, as if I can actually see her—"will be lethal in ways we can't even imagine. We have no idea what powers she'll possess."

"She won't use them," Jules says. "I'll see to that. I'll take her buried bones before you're finished dancing."

The two of us exchange a fierce glance. I trust Jules with my life, and I know she feels the same about me. "I'm counting on it."

Marcel reaches for his bow. "If I *do* see the soulmate, I'm only aiming to maim, correct?"

I cringe, imagining all the ways that could go wrong. "How about you stall him with your words? The Bone Crier can't catch a glimpse of the other man. That's the most important thing to remember."

Marcel gives me a lopsided grin, like he hopes he'll still get to see some action. He better not.

"Don't even think about—"

A mournful cry quivers on the air.

No, not a cry.

A melody.

A tremor chases up my spine and shudders across my shoulders. I'm ten years old again, alone in my father's cart. I leave the cart and follow the song, walking in the small shoes my father made me. The music warbles. The low tones sound so ancient they spark memories I don't have, shapeless echoes of a time before I was born, or my father was born, or any soul lived and died upon this land.

"Bastien." Jules grabs my leg, and I inhale sharply. I realize I'm standing and facing the bridge.

"Stick to the plan," I say gruffly, and spit out the rest of the mint leaves. I'm fine. If the Bone Crier wants a soulmate, I'll give her one. I'll give her me. Then I'll break her.

Jules lets go. I stalk forward through the wild grass and roll out a crick in my neck. When I take my first step onto the road, my breath catches. The Bone Crier's ghostly white dress stands out against the dark stones of the bridge. She's real. This is finally happening. My fists tighten. I approach like the thief I am.

Her back is to me, her hair sleek and long and deep copper. My eyes follow the loose waves down to the curved line of her hips.

I can't look away. Why should I? I tread louder, scuffing the bridge stones, bold and reckless. *I'm here for you. The trap is mine this time, not yours.*

Fifteen feet ahead, the Bone Crier pulls the flute from her mouth. Her shoulders rise as she breathes in. Like some creature from a dream, she turns to me. Her trailing dress resists the movement and clings to the ground in spiraling folds. She looks sculpted from marble, like something my father would have painstakingly crafted, one chisel strike after another. My skin flushes with heat.

The girl's hair billows around her slender shoulders. Her beauty is unfair, masking the vicious predator within. But didn't I expect that? Then why is my blood pounding?

Her large eyes glow umber in the moonlight. Her lashes are dark, not warm in color like her hair. I'm near enough to notice that now. Somehow I've moved another ten paces closer, drawn to the look she gives me. Feral, sure, astonished. I'm mirroring that look. We're both staring at our destiny. Certain death. But I won't be the one to die.

"What is your name?" the girl asks in a slightly high-pitched voice. She's young, I realize. Close to my age. Was the Bone Crier who killed my father so young? Did she only seem older because I was a child?

"Bastien," I blurt. So much for giving a false name. I meant to reveal my own in due time. I won't slip up again.

"Bastien," she repeats, her mouth carefully trying the word like she's never heard it before. It makes my own name feel new to me. "I'm Ailesse." She twists the bone flute in her hands. A sign of nervousness. Or a trick to make me *believe* she's nervous. "Bastien, you were chosen by the gods. It is a great honor to dance with a Leurress, a greater honor to dance with the heir of *Matrone* Odiva's *famille*."

"Are you asking me to dance?" I play along and steady my feet. This girl, Ailesse, is the equivalent of a princess. My perfect victim. Her people will think twice before they kill another man.

A surprising bubble of laughter spills out of her. "Forgive me, I'm getting ahead of myself." She smooths her hair back, walks to the parapet, and sets the bone flute on the ledge. When she returns, her eyes are focused like the huntress—the murderess—she is. "Bastien, will you dance with me?"

I fight the urge to glance over my shoulder. Jules should be under the bridge by now. With any luck, she's already dug up the first bone.

I bow like I've seen barons do, one arm folded in front of me. The strap of my knife harness pulls tight across my chest. "It will be my greatest pleasure to dance with you, Ailesse."

6
Ailesse

I INHALE A LONG BREATH, blow it out, and sneak a glance at Sabine. She peers at me and Bastien from between the branches of an ash tree in the forest. My peregrine falcon vision sharpens on her upper lip, caught between the tight press of her teeth. She's just as anxious as I am. Maybe she thinks I won't take the dance seriously, like the time I practiced it with her. Giselle taught us the movements together, and whenever they became too intimate, I crossed my eyes at Sabine. She finally fell into a fit of giggles, and Giselle threw her hands up and ended our lesson for the day.

I take three steps closer to Bastien and hold his gaze. We're almost touching. We soon will be. Nothing about the *danse de l'amant* seems humorous now.

A rush of warmth prickles across my skin, and I restrain a shiver. *Time to begin.*

Fog rolls onto the bridge and clings to the lower half of my dress, blending into the white of my skirt. It makes it appear even longer. I lift my leg and turn on one toe, the fog swirling with me.

Bastien's lips glisten and part as he watches. When I finish revolving, he flexes his hands and reaches for my waist. I touch his wrists and whisper, "Not yet."

"Sorry." He flinches back, his voice hoarse.

"All you have to do is watch for now. This is my part of the dance. When it's your part, I'll guide you."

He swallows. Rakes his hand through his hair. Clears his throat. "Got it."

His pensive expression draws a smile out of me, but he doesn't smile back. Are all boys this focused? One day I'll find out what it takes to rouse Bastien's laughter. I'll make a game of discovering all the ways to lighten his mood. I'll . . .

You'll do nothing, Ailesse. Not in this life. He dies at the end of this dance.

My stomach sinks, but I straighten my shoulders. I glide in circles around Bastien. My arms rise in the elegant arcs and patterns Giselle taught me. I'm representing life through the elements. The breath of the wind. The currents in the sea. The energy of the earth. The heat of flickering flame. The everlasting soul. Bastien's sea-blue eyes follow my every move.

Do you think it's cruel to tempt a man with life when you're inevitably going to kill him? Sabine asked last night, riddling me with questions about the *danse de l'amant* before we went to sleep. *Would you play with a hare all day before you ate it for supper?*

You wouldn't eat a hare, anyway, I said, and poked her stomach. *It's just a dance, Sabine. Just another part of the rite of passage. When I'm done, I become a Ferrier. That's all that matters.*

That's all that matters, I remind myself as I twist and turn and show Bastien every angle of myself. I stroke my face and brush the back of my hand down my throat, my chest, my waist, my hip. *You're offering your body,* Giselle explained. *The shape of your figure, the beauty of your face, the strength of your limbs.*

I gather my hair in front of my shoulder. I comb my fingers through it so Bastien can see its length and auburn color, its shine and waving texture.

Fire burns in his gaze, and my breath trembles.

It's just a dance, Ailesse.

I close my eyes and force my mind away from here. I see myself wearing my same rite of passage dress, but I'm standing on the soul bridge, not Castelpont. I hold a staff in my sure grip and take my post alongside my sister Ferriers. At the end of the bridge, in front of the Gates of the Underworld and Paradise, my mother plays the bone flute and lures the dead. I lead the willing souls, and I fight the resistant. I ferry with just as much strength and skill as Odiva, and when the last soul crosses the bridge and the Gates close, she turns to me. Her eyes shine, warm and loving and proud, and she smiles and says—

"Are you finished?"

My eyes fly open. My mother is gone. Bastien is staring back at me. He fidgets in his fine clothes like they itch him. "You said I had a part to play," he prompts, and darts a quick glance around us.

Is he nervous or eager? The breeze tousles his dark and glossy hair. My fingers twitch, longing to touch the wild strands that grow long and shaggy over his ears and the nape of his neck.

"Will you show me?" he asks, his voice treading between gruff and soft. "Will you . . ." He looks down and scratches his sleeve. Even under the night sky, my graced vision captures the flush rising in his cheeks. His gaze crawls back up to me. "Will you take your time?"

My blood quickens. I begin to understand why the gods chose Bastien for me. Beneath the tame sea of his eyes lies a tempest, a strength to match mine.

I sweep my hair back so it conceals my knife harness again. I take Bastien's hands and place them on the circle of my waist. I arch my brow at his tentative hold, and his fingers settle and tighten, seeping warmth through the cloth of my dress.

I lift my palms to his face and trace the bones in his cheeks, jaw, and nose. Every movement carries rhythm, every touch a part of the dance. I've shown myself to Bastien, and now it's my chance to consider what he can offer me.

My falcon vision focuses, and I see every green and gold fleck buried in the depths of his blue irises. He even has a tiny freckle in the lower rim of his right eye. My gaze drops to his lips. I'm supposed to touch them right now, study their shape and texture, as if my fingers can tell me what it would be like to kiss him.

The sixth sense from my tiger shark thrums like a second heartbeat from all this nearness to Bastien. It pounds harder as my hand floats to his mouth and my fingertips skim across it. Bastien shuts his eyes and releases a breath of quivering heat. It takes all my ibex grace to keep me balanced. I *want* to kiss him, not just imagine it. Kissing isn't a part of the *danse de l'amant*, but Bastien wouldn't know that.

Sabine would.

She'd think me cruel to cross that line of intimacy, when I mean to kill him on this bridge.

I lower my hands to Bastien's neck and chest, and his eyes open. My nerve endings stir at the hungry look he gives me. My body flashes hot then cold.

Can any part of him sense how this will end?

My bone knife. His heart. My proof to the gods that I'm ready to become a Ferrier.

Keep dancing, Ailesse. Keep dancing.

7
Sabine

Past the ash tree in the forest, I watch Castelpont and the progress of the *danse de l'amant*. My heart pounds faster. My best friend is that much closer to killing a human being, and I've sworn to witness every moment of his death.

Don't dwell on the horror of this, Sabine. Think of the good that will come from it. Ailesse will be a Ferrier. She'll help the souls of the departed find their new home in the Beyond. They'll be at peace—at least the ones destined for Paradise will be.

Ailesse extends one of her *amouré's* arms and slowly twirls outward along its length, then inward to his chest. She stops when her back is pressed against him. Her arms rise like wings and fold behind his neck. The boy eases into her movements, becoming one with her. They're beautiful together. My eyes prick, but I hold back the tears. I promised myself I wouldn't cry tonight.

I scrutinize the boy who arrived only moments after Ailesse started playing the flute. Did the gods choose him out of convenience, or is he truly her perfect companion? I frown, finding nothing wrong with him. Any flaws at first glance are only virtues in disguise. His awkwardness is charming as she spins around him. His solemn nature reflects a life of discipline.

I begrudgingly accept that the gods chose him well, but my chest aches. Ailesse has always done everything before me, and now she has something far more valuable than another grace bone. She has the promise of love. She has met her *amouré*. I fear I'll never have the courage to do what it takes to meet mine.

A flash of black winks out from the fog across the bridge—just enough that I see something creep down to the riverbed. If it's a predator, it will be drawn to the blood when Ailesse kills the boy. I worry at my lip. I'm not supposed to intervene tonight, but that rule probably means I shouldn't interfere with Ailesse's *amouré*, not whatever it is I just saw.

I hang my friend's shoulder necklace on a branch, duck under it, and tiptoe to the edge of the riverbank. Ailesse's *amouré* doesn't notice me. He's watching her walk around him and trail her hand around his torso. I have to hurry. I need to return to my post before the dance is finished. By then, the luring spell of the bone flute will dwindle away, Ailesse will withdraw her bone knife, and I must be back in time to witness her completion of the rite of passage.

The fog churns thick again. I move as fast as possible down the steep bank. At last, I reach the bottom and scan around. I can only see seven feet or so in each direction. The rest of the riverbed is a blanket of white. If I were out hunting, I'd have my bow or dagger, but as a ritual witness, I'm defenseless. The Leurress performing the rite must prove she is adept on her own.

I continue forward carefully. My salamander grace steadies my feet on the uneven ground. It also heightens my sense of smell, an ability I've often rolled my eyes at for its lack of helpfulness, but now I'm grateful. I let the scent of leather and wool and light perspiration guide me to the other side, where I hear a small grunt of exertion. It comes again, this time accompanied by faint scraping. The fog parts around a crouched figure—a girl. She jerks her head to me, and her hood falls back.

For a split second I'm baffled, unsure why she's here. Then my blood turns to ice. Her hands are covered in dirt. The earth beneath her has been dug up in one spot. I curse myself. She must have found the place easily due to the crudely overturned soil.

The girl tenses, ready to attack or flee. My heartbeats crash. I struggle to think. She doesn't have Ailesse's grace bone yet. Ailesse would have noticed and cried out to me. I still have time to stop her.

I lunge for the girl. She anticipates me and rolls to the side. I whirl around to find she's already up on her feet, holding a knife. My nerves light on fire, but I swallow my scream for help. Ailesse needs to focus on the boy.

The hooded girl jumps at me with her outstretched knife. I

have nothing to shield myself with but my arm. Pain bursts through me as she cuts through my sleeve to my skin. I gasp and stumble backward.

Control yourself, Sabine. You will heal. It's the one thing you're good at.

I pick up a rock as large as my fist.

"Do you think you can stop me?" the girl hisses. "I'm ready for you."

I throw the rock at her head. She dodges it with a mocking grin. She tosses her knife from hand to hand. "You're only wearing one bone," she says. "It won't even be a challenge to kill you."

She knows about grace bones? I fumble for another rock. "Who are you?"

"The daughter of a man a Bone Crier killed." She practically spits the words. "Ashena pretended to love him for a year, and then cursed him and left him to die. Slowly. Painfully."

Ashena? My lips part. She braided my hair once. When my mother was killed, Ashena gave me a pearly seashell. "Ashena loved your *father*?" It never occurred to me that an *amouré* could already have children of his own.

"*Pretended*," the girl clarifies. "It wasn't real."

"Maybe it was. Ashena didn't kill her *amouré*, not directly." She confessed that much to our *famille* when she returned to Château Creux. If she *had* killed him with her ritual blade, the magic of the soul-bond would have spared her life. "Ashena died for loving him," I add, my throat tightening. It happened in an instant, one year from her rite of passage.

The hooded girl's eyes shroud, conflicted and confused. "That doesn't matter. Ashena's death doesn't right the wrongs done to my father."

"What will?" I'm stalling for time as my fingers close around the rock. I already know her answer.

"Your death." She sneers. "And the death of your friend."

"You could never defeat Ailesse."

"Yes, we can."

We?

In one swift motion, she dives for the overturned earth. I throw my rock. It crashes against her shoulder. She grunts, but the pain doesn't stop her.

She pulls her hand from the dirt. In her tight fist, she holds Ailesse's falcon wing bone. I remember the day Ailesse shot her arrow and plucked the bird from the sky. She gave me its longest feather.

Anger blazes like a wildfire inside me.

I charge at the hooded girl. My heart pumps pure rage.

At the same moment, Ailesse releases a cry of terror.

"Sabine!"

8

Ailesse

My limbs grow heavy. I drop to my heels from my toes. The violet tinge of my vision fades, along with its crispness. I wrest out of Bastien's arms, and my hand flies to the base of my throat. My falcon wing bone is gone. Not from my necklace, but—

I race to the parapet and look over the ledge. I can't see the riverbed through the fog below, but I hear the sound of a struggle.

Something is terribly wrong.

"Sabine!"

I listen, but only hear muffled thuds and grunts. Then my friend cries, "Ailesse, run!"

I freeze. My knuckles clench the half wall. I *can't* run. Sabine is in danger. But I also can't leave the bridge. Not yet. The ritual magic is alive. I have to choose. About Bastien. No, there is no choice. I have to kill him. Now.

My muscles scream to help Sabine, but I force myself to turn and face Bastien. "I'm sorry." I shouldn't apologize. It's an honor to be my *amouré*. An honor to die. I reach for the bone knife at my back.

He reaches behind *his* back. "I'm not," he says.

I withdraw my knife. He withdraws two. My eyes widen. "What is this?"

"This"—every tender, conflicted expression on his face contorts into a vicious grimace—"is revenge." His blades slash out for me.

I jump back. I haven't trained for a knife fight. Killing an animal with one is entirely different than this. "Why?" I ask. Hurt nicks my pride after the dance he and I just shared. "What have I ever done to you?"

His nostrils flare. Rage beats off of him in waves. My sixth sense vibrates up my spine, alert for his next move. "Your kind killed my father," he growls, speaking of the Leurress as if we're less than human. "I was a *child*. I watched him die. A Bone Crier sliced his throat and bled the life out of him."

My stomach gives a sickening lurch. "You—you shouldn't have been there. You weren't *supposed* to be there."

"Is that your apology?" Bastien scoffs, his nose wrinkling with hatred. "My father *died*. A good, kind, unforgettable man died because he crossed the wrong bridge on the wrong night."

I wasn't there. It wasn't me! Weak words I won't say. "It wasn't a coincidence. He was chosen by the gods."

"Oh, yes?" He strides closer. "Tell me what sort of gods you worship that would tear a man from his family and allow him to be sacrificed by a woman he's never known?"

The jibe strikes my heart and the sanctity of *amourés*. Without that mandate from the gods, the Leurress might as well be murderers. Blasphemy. I refuse to believe— "You know nothing!"

"I know more about your black soul—and those of your cult—than I care to."

Bastien leaps at me, and I barely dodge his knife. I lost the edge of my speed when I lost my wing bone. He grins. His eyes say I'm easy. I'm Sabine's salamander, no sharp teeth or claws. He's wrong. I curl my lip. Raise my knife arm. I've scaled icy mountains and slaughtered a great ibex. I've plunged into the sea and conquered a tiger shark. Bastien is nothing. Only a boy with two knives. A boy who is meant to die, anyway.

I strike out. He blocks my blow with his knife. His other blade arcs for my side. I grab his wrist—my tiger shark speed is plenty fast when I focus—and kick him hard in the chest. He flies backward ten feet and rolls to the ground.

His eyes flash wide. I exhale with satisfaction. "Jules!" he calls. "She's still powerful!"

"I know!" A female voice. Winded. *She's below the bridge, fighting Sabine.*

"Did your friend steal my wing bone?" I prowl toward Bastien. He crab-walks backward. "I'll kill her after I kill you . . . and whoever else you brought with you, perched in those trees off the road." Now that I'm attuned to my sixth sense, I know a third person is out there. Energy buzzes from the direction of the forest canopy, a half mile away, and it's too strong to be a bird.

Bastien stiffens and steals a glance that way. "You'll never get the chance."

He sweeps out his arm and tries to trip me. I jump, but his arm lashes at me again. He's unnervingly fast for someone with no graces. *He's been training for this.*

He flips upright into a crouch and keeps attacking low, near the ground. I stumble backward and hop from one foot to the other. My feet tangle in the excess length of my dress and hinder my ibex agility. *Curse Isla.*

My back hits the parapet of the bridge. Bastien has me cornered, and he knows it. I fling my blade at his chest, but he twists his body, and the knife glances off his shoulder. A sheath must be hidden under his cloak. My bone knife skitters across the bridge and lands in the shadows.

I try to run for my weapon, but Bastien's boot traps the train of my dress. With a hard yank, I rip the hem away. He swipes his blade again, and I leap backward with my ibex grace and land on top of the parapet. The ledge is narrow, less than a foot wide, but I'm balanced and in my element. I'm also an easy target.

To my surprise, Bastien doesn't throw his knives. Instead, in one fast and fluid movement, he hoists himself onto the parapet and stands to face me, six feet away. I lift a brow and return his brazen smile. He's drawing out his moment of attack. Amusing. As if he could intimidate me.

"The gods chose you well," I concede, noting how dauntlessly he disregards the forty-foot drop to the riverbed below. But he can't be a true match to my skill. I've trained, too—to battle souls of the dead, no less. For that I don't need a knife. "I will enjoy your death."

He scoffs and kicks the bone flute I set on the ledge of the parapet. I stifle a gasp as it plummets into the fog of the riverbed. If it breaks— If I lose it— "Oops," Bastien smirks.

He charges at me while I'm still in shock. I quickly jump back and arch into a handspring. I tumble again and again in fast circles. He's keeping up. I sense his nearness with my shark grace. When I come upright again, his knives are at my throat and heart. I grab the hilts and hold them still. Veins strain at his temples as he struggles to drive in his blades.

"The gods didn't choose me." Bastien gasps under the iron pressure of my grip. "I hunted you here."

"You couldn't have set one foot on this bridge unless the gods sanctioned it. Your life is *mine*."

With a sharp twist, I wrench the knife from his left hand. It's the finer blade of the two. He shuffles back and guards his other knife. Interesting that he favors it. "Any time now, Jules!" he yells.

She doesn't respond. No one does. "Sabine!" I call. Nothing but the howling wind answers back.

The fog scatters just enough that I catch a glimpse of a figure below, prostrate on the riverbed.

My heart kicks. Is she alive? My sixth sense vibrates dully, but that could be the energy of the other girl down there.

"If Sabine is dead"—my gaze cuts to Bastien—"you will die

slowly. I won't bury you with your bones; I'll wear them. I'll take them from your body before you draw your last breath." No Leurress has ever touched the bones of her *amouré*, but I don't care. The rite will begin with me.

Bastien's jaw muscle tightens. "And if Jules is dead, I'll decapitate you."

"I won't give you the chance." I hold his knife the way he does, like a shield, the hilt never far from my face and constantly moving. I'm quickly learning his defenses, his attacks. I lunge for him, and we begin a new dance, this one more deadly, more passionate, more inflamed.

I deflect his strikes. He deflects mine, forearm against forearm. I never extend my elbows. I counterattack swiftly. Bastien makes for an excellent teacher. His mistake. The predators in me are cunning students.

He treads the narrow parapet with ease. His powerful desire for revenge is a grace of its own.

Once I learn the rhythm of his movements, I take greater risks. I use more force when I slash for him. I shove him back when our arms connect. He might be brave, but he's weak. I could snap his bones. Maybe I will.

Perspiration wets his brow. He grunts with each blow, each block, each counterattack. I'm tempted to push him to his limits and discover his breaking point. But I can't. If Sabine is injured, there's still a chance I can help her. *Please, Elara, let her only be injured.*

"Thank you for the dance, *mon amouré*," I say.

"You call this dancing?" Bastien strikes for my face, then my leg, deftly switching his knife hands.

"Forgive me, were you fighting?" I dodge both attacks, ibex nimble. "I'd love to see you try, but I'm afraid we're out of time."

"Why? You can't be tired already. Unless you lost all your endurance with one little bird bone."

My nostrils flare. He has no idea what he's up against. "I still have the combined stamina of a tiger shark and a great alpine ibex."

"Strength you stole."

"Strength I earned."

"Not enough to beat me."

My veins torch with blistering rage. *Now you die, Bastien.* "Watch me."

With every measure of my ibex grace, I leap ten feet into the air and raise my blade with both hands. All the ferocity and muscle from my tiger shark gathers in my body. I focus on Bastien on the parapet below. He looks small. Easy to conquer.

He steps back into a defensive stance, his eyes wide and ready.

I plunge.

He swings his fist a moment before I strike. I can't move fast enough. The tension inside me falls slack. He hits my arm and knocks my knife from my hand. It flings into the thinning mist and clatters onto the stones of the riverbed.

Shocked, I barely catch my fall on the ledge. My muscles cramp in protest. My surroundings dim. The energy shifts around me. My sixth sense is gone.

The shark tooth. Bastien's accomplice has it.

"Sabine!" I cry again. My eyes burn. She's the limp figure on the ground. She has to be.

I abandon all thoughts of my rite of passage. I won't kill Bastien here and now. I'll hunt him down later, even if it takes me a year. Then I'll have his blood. "I'm coming, Sabine!" *Be alive, be alive.*

I move to jump from the parapet and onto the bridge, but Bastien grabs my arm. I gasp at his painful grip. I can't break free. He isn't such a weakling, after all.

"Let go of me," I shout. I still have my ibex grace, which gives me strength in my legs. I kick him hard in the shin. He grimaces in pain, but doesn't release me. "I need to help my friend. She's innocent."

"So you admit you're not?" Bastien yanks me closer when I try to kick him again. He sets his knife at my throat. I swallow against its sharp edge. He can end my life at any moment.

This is all wrong. An *amouré* isn't supposed to kill a Leurress. It's never happened, not in all our long history.

I can't believe it will happen to me.

Bastien's breath is hot in my face. "None of you are innocent."

9
Bastien

Ailesse doesn't close her eyes as she anticipates death. She stares at me directly. Her body shakes as I hold her at knifepoint on the parapet, but she doesn't blink. She's afraid of this moment, but not what's beyond it. Death. The afterlife. Everything I can't imagine when I think of my father.

Don't hesitate, Bastien.

"This is for Lucien Colbert." My forearms flex. My heartbeat pounds through every space of my head. Ailesse's umber eyes glisten.

"Bastien, stop her!" Jules's shout echoes from the clearing mist of the riverbed. "It's done!" Ailesse sucks in a sharp breath and staggers in my arms.

What does Jules mean? "I am!"

"Not her, the other one!"

Behind me, I hear the crunch of toppling rocks. I glance over my shoulder. A dark-haired girl in a green dress—the witness—climbs up the riverbank near the foot of the bridge. Blood streaks down her injured head.

"Sabine!" Ailesse's voice clangs in my ears. She's struggling to free herself—and almost succeeds while I'm distracted.

Sabine sees my knife at Ailesse's neck. Her face twists with horror. "Let her go!" She bolts toward me.

I tense. She could have the strength of a bear, for all I know.

She races onto the bridge, but then her head sways to the side. She grips a post for support. Another rush of blood streams from her hairline.

"Sabine, stop!" Ailesse cries. "You can't fight like this."

"Neither can you." Sabine's stubborn voice wobbles.

"You're not supposed to intervene."

"I don't care."

"Please go!"

"I'm not leaving without you!"

"You can't save me! Go warn my mother. Tell her the flute fell in the riverbed and . . ."

I stop listening. My attention snags on the moonlight reflecting off my blade. Ailesse's neck tendons strain beneath its sharp edge. What am I waiting for—her to scream or act more afraid? This moment is supposed to be my ultimate victory. It will be. I can slit one Bone Crier's throat, and then deal with the other.

I grind my teeth in determination, but my stomach churns.

Do it, Bastien!

"Bastien, the witness! She's getting away!" Jules's voice rings closer. She's climbing up the riverbank, pursuing Sabine.

I jerk around in Sabine's direction. She's already off the bridge. She and Jules will cross paths at any moment. "You can grab her before I can!"

"Hurry!" Ailesse calls to her friend.

Thump, drag, thump. Jules clears the top of the riverbank. She's limping.

Sabine tries to get past her, but Jules whips out her knife. Sabine shrieks as it slices across the side of her waist.

"No!" Ailesse wrestles against me. "Run, Sabine!"

Sabine barely dodges another swipe from Jules. Both girls are slow from their wounds.

Jules misses again. Sabine takes her opening and kicks Jules's hurt leg. Jules cries out and clutches her knee.

Ailesse's muscles tense. "Now's your chance! Go, Sabine!"

Sabine shoots Ailesse a fierce look. "I'll come back for you!" She whirls away, hurrying as fast as she can down the road to the forest. One of her hands presses to her bleeding head. The other holds the gash at her waist.

Jules struggles to stand upright again. "Bastien, we have to do something! She'll go back and get the rest of her people. She told me they can track us with their magic."

I shift, suddenly dizzy. "Marcel would have said if that were possible."

"Marcel doesn't know everything!" She stumbles after Sabine.

Marcel. He's off the road and in the trees somewhere, on the lookout for Ailesse's soulmate. But now I need him here. He can prove Jules wrong. I shout his name, but he doesn't call back.

Ailesse's upper lip curls. "None of you fathom how deeply this night will cost you."

I draw my knife back a fraction from her throat, then check myself. What does she know? I've thought through my revenge countless times—through every possible scenario. If one of the Bone Criers happened to escape, we planned to kill the other and—"Leave her bones! The ones belonging to *her*." I rattle Ailesse, and she almost falls off the parapet. Jules must have stolen her last bone, and Ailesse's balance with it. "That's how their magic works. If we don't have them anymore, her people can't find us."

Sabine, who is ten feet from the border of the forest, freezes. Her pained eyes flash to Ailesse. Jules turns and considers me. I nod to show I'm serious. I'll kill Ailesse, then hunt down her friend. But if Sabine manages to outrun me, we don't have to worry.

Ailesse's glare holds steady. "They'll still find you."

I snort. "Your people won't stand a chance. I've lived on the streets of Dovré since I was a child. The best hideouts in the city and the places beneath it—they're *my* territory."

"It doesn't matter," she spits. "My *famille* doesn't need my grace bones to track you. You and I are soul-bound. That's enough." She draws herself taller. Blood trickles down her neck from my blade. "You're right that our magic lies in bones. I used them to summon you here. You came when you heard my song, and the gods let you because they chose you for me. Now your soul is mine in life *and* in death." The mist rises behind her, clinging to her body. "If you kill me, you'll die with me."

My palms sweat. I tighten my grip on the knife. "Nice try, but you're a terrible liar."

I start to drive in my blade, but Jules shouts, "Bastien, wait! What if she's right?"

"About what—that I can't live without her?" I scoff. "You really believe that?"

"Think about it. What if that's why my father died, because he was soul-bound to Ashena? She died soon after she left him—the witness told me so tonight. Her death might have set off his."

I breathe harder, faster. Could I really be soul-bound to a Bone Crier? Waves of hot and cold crash through me. If Ailesse is telling the truth, she wouldn't have been so scared of dying a moment ago. Then again, was she really so afraid? I caught that spark of confidence behind her terror.

Marcel doesn't know everything.

Maybe I *haven't* thought through every outcome tonight.

Now I'm the one who's shaking. *I need Ailesse's death.* The words sear inside me, and I press even closer to her. Her foot slips off the edge of the parapet. I catch her back. My blade wavers at her throat.

"Bastien, stop!" Jules cries.

"Shut up!"

I've planned for this moment for eight long years. It can't end with letting her go.

"Are you about finished?" Marcel calls. Hazily through the mist, I see him lumber toward the bridge. At the same time, Sabine reaches the forest border behind him. Marcel doesn't see her. He's found his own path here through the trees. "I haven't seen any soulmate," he confesses, taking no pains to be quiet. "The man must live on an island. Either that or he's as slow as molasses—or crystallized honey. That's thicker." He shuffles to a stop and takes in the three of us. Ailesse. Jules. Me. "Oh. Not finished, then."

"The witness, Marcel!" Jules points wildly, unable to get to Sabine fast enough on her wounded leg. "Hurry! She'll bring more of them. They'll kill Bastien!"

Marcel wheels around and stares dumbly at Sabine, a few yards away from him. She's bent over from another dizzy spell.

"Did you hear your friend?" Ailesse hisses in my ear. "He hasn't seen another soulmate." I turn to her, drawn to the gaping black of her pupils. "You are *mine*," she says.

Faster than seems possible, Marcel drops his pack and pulls an arrow from his quiver.

Ailesse gasps. "No. Sabine, run!"

Sabine painstakingly lifts her head. She looks feral with a stripe of blood smeared down her face and over one eye.

Marcel strings his bow. His shoulders bunch up like he's about to be sick.

"Run!" Ailesse shouts again.

Marcel startles and lets his arrow fly. It whizzes past Sabine, just shy of her head. She snatches something from a tree branch and rushes away. The forest swallows her from sight.

"*Merde!*" Jules buckles to the ground.

Ailesse's spine relaxes under my fingers. Her gloating eyes flick back to me, and my jaw muscle clenches. Her friend is free, and now Ailesse thinks I won't dare to slit her throat because we're soul-bound. Or so she says. I'll find out soon enough. Then I'll make her suffer. She'll beg me to end her life.

"You *will* die, Bone Crier." My scathing tone cools to a deadly simmer. "Because *you* are mine."

10
Sabine

I RACE INTO THE RUINS of Château Creux and past King Godart's carved crest of the crow and the rose. Fire and ice chase through my veins with each thunderclap of my heart.

Ailesse is gone. Her amouré *killed her. I'm too late.*

I swipe my tears with shaking hands. My fingers come away sticky with blood. It's everywhere—on my neck, in my hair, all over my dress and sleeves. It's in places I can't see. Ailesse's throat. The stones of Castelpont. Her *amouré's* knife.

I squeeze my eyes shut. *Calm down, Sabine. You don't know Ailesse is dead.*

The boy kept hesitating. She could still be alive. I'm not too late.

I bolt through the tide-carved tunnels beneath the ancient castle, then down the last tunnel toward the courtyard. The night is half spent, but Odiva should be awake and awaiting our return.

How will I explain what happened? This is all my fault.

I'm about to burst inside when a rush of dizziness seizes me. I grit my teeth and brace my hand against the tunnel wall. My salamander grace has helped me recover from the hooded girl's attack, but I've lost too much blood. On the way here, I nearly passed out and had to rest with my head between my knees. It cost me precious time. I can't let that happen again.

"I have given you everything possible these past two years." Odiva's voice is a murmur, but it resonates throughout the large cavern.

My chest tightens. For a moment I think she's speaking to me—my mother died two years ago—but when the black spots clear from my vision, I see my *matrone* standing under a pool of moonlight in the center of the courtyard. Her back is turned to me and her arms are outstretched. She's praying—fervently—or else she'd notice me. Her stingray's sixth sense and bat's echolocation would have picked up on my arrival.

"Now the time is nearing an end," she continues. "Grant me a sign, Tyrus. Let me know you honor my sacrifices."

Tyrus? I focus on Odiva's cupped hands. They're turned downward to the Underworld, not upward to the Night Heavens. I wrinkle my brows. The Leurress worship Tyrus—we offer him souls of the wicked on ferrying night—but our prayers travel to Elara, who hears the pleas of the righteous. Or so I was taught.

I push away from the wall. It doesn't matter. Ailesse is in danger. I'd pray to any god to save her. *"Matrone!"*

Odiva stiffens. I emerge into the silvery glow of Elara's Light, and she turns to face me. At the same time, her hands close around something dangling from a gold chain over her three-tiered grace bone necklace. She quickly tucks it into her dress, and I catch a glint of sparkling red.

"Sabine." Her ebony eyes narrow as they flick over the gashes on my arm, my head, and waist. She hastens to me. "What happened?" A slight tremor skims across her lower lip. "Is Ailesse hurt, as well?"

I suddenly can't meet her gaze. My throat runs dry, and tears flood my vision. "We were unprepared," I choke out, not knowing where to begin.

Odiva steps closer, and the noctule bat skull fastened to her asp vertebrae crown looms over me. "Unprepared? For what?"

"Her *amouré*. He was ready for us. So were his accomplices— two of them. They knew what we were. And they wanted us dead."

Lines of fury and confusion form between the *matrone*'s dark brows. "I don't understand. Ailesse is the most promising Leurress our *famille* has seen in a century." I agree, though it's a compliment she's never paid my friend. "How could mere commoners—?" Her voice breaks like she can't find her breath.

"A girl stole Ailesse's grace bones under the bridge." I withdraw my hand from behind my back and present Ailesse's depleted shoulder necklace. My final task as her witness would have been to tie her grace bones back onto it. Shame burns from deep inside me and scalds my cheeks. Until tonight, I believed my best friend was invincible, but I should have buried her bones deeper, guarded them better. Then Ailesse could have defended herself. "The girl claimed her father was killed by Ashena, so Ailesse's *amouré* must have been helping her seek vengeance."

Odiva grows statuesque. The funneling breeze wisps through her raven hair and sapphire dress, but her body is motionless. Finally, her lips crack apart. "Is she alive?" she whispers. "Did they kill my daughter?"

A broken sob rips out of my chest. "I don't know."

She grips my chin. "Where is the bone flute?" Ice crawls up my spine as her black eyes bore into me. I've never seen Odiva so vicious and desperate.

"It's" . . . *lost in the riverbed.* "They took it."

Her teeth grind together. "Are you sure?" she asks slowly, pointedly.

"Yes." My stomach quivers. I've never lied to the *matrone*. I'm not sure why I am now, except for an ominous feeling that warns me Odiva shouldn't have it yet. Especially when she seems more concerned about the flute than her daughter. "We should start tracking Ailesse now. If she's alive, she needs our help."

She whirls away from me. "Have you any idea of what you've done, Sabine?"

"I—?" I shrink back. Odiva's never scolded me before. She saves that for Ailesse.

"How could you let this happen? Did *you* lose your grace bones, too?"

Grace *bone*, not bones. Singular. Pitiful. "I tried to help, but I was injured."

"That's no excuse. You should have trusted your grace to heal."

I stare at her, my mouth slack, completely at a loss for words. I'm covered in dried blood and struggling to stay upright. My salamander grace may have quickened my healing, but my wounds were deep at Castelpont. "I'm sorry."

She shakes her head and paces the courtyard, her dress rippling as she changes directions every few feet. I scarcely recognize the woman before me. She's nothing like the cool and collected *matrone* who rules my *famille*. "Is this your sign?" Her furious shout echoes off the cavern walls. I wince, even though she isn't speaking to me. I don't know what sign she's talking about, but her onyx eyes stab a glare of accusation toward the ground.

Within moments, three of the elders—Dolssa, Pernelle, and Roxane—race into the courtyard from various tunnels. Their hair and clothes are bedraggled, but their eyes shine alert. They scan the cavern like they're searching for a source of danger. "Is everything all right, *Matrone*?" Dolssa asks.

Odiva clutches the lump of a red gem—or whatever it is she's hiding beneath the neckline of her dress. "No, it is not." She takes a labored breath and releases her grip.

Pernelle's gaze turns to me and latches on to my blood-smeared face. "Ailesse . . . is she?"

"She's alive." *Please let it be true, Elara.* "But she needs us." In as few words as possible, I repeat what I told Odiva.

The *matrone* wrings her hands and paces another length of the courtyard. "Wake the rest of the elders," she commands the three Leurress. "Go track my daughter. Start at . . ." She looks to me.

"Castelpont."

Odiva shuts her eyes. "Of course, Ailesse chose Castelpont."

"We'll find her, *Matrone*." Roxane motions to her companions. They quickly leave to gather the others. I hurry to join them.

"I'm not finished with you, Sabine."

I freeze and turn around. Odiva has regained her composure, but something about her pale, almost bloodless skin—gleaming even more pallidly in the moonlight—makes my scalp prickle.

She wanders toward me. "Have you been taught the difference between the Chained and the Unchained?" she asks, like I'm a child still learning the concept of ferrying—like this is an opportune time for a lesson.

"Yes," I reply warily, and steal a glance over my shoulder. The elders are already gone from the courtyard, and I don't want them to leave the castle without me. Why is Odiva bringing this up right now? "The Unchained are those who led a righteous life and deserve an eternity in Elara's Paradise," I say. "The Chained are the sinister souls, those who were wicked and merit punishment in Tyrus's Underworld."

Odiva nods and sweeps nearer.

"Can this wait, *Matrone*? Ailesse—"

"The elders will search for Ailesse."

"But—"

"You have *one* grace bone, Sabine. You can't do anything to save her right now."

Her words hit me square in the chest and echo Ailesse's at Castelpont: *You can't save me!* I believed my friend. That's why I finally ran for help.

"I will tell you what you *can* do, however," Odiva continues. "But first you must listen. I need you to understand." I shuffle back a step as she comes closer. I hate the softened edge of her voice. I don't want any tenderness from the *matrone*, especially when she gives none to her daughter—who we should be searching for right now. "When the Leuress are ready to become Ferriers, I teach them the ultimate threat of the Chained. I taught Ailesse just yesterday."

I frown. Ailesse didn't tell me. Which means the knowledge must be sacred.

"Now I will teach *you*, Sabine."

"But I'm not ready to become a Ferrier."

Odiva's stark-red lips curl, and the hair on my arms stands on end. "You may soon find out you feel differently." She draws up taller. "Do you know what happens to the souls of the recently departed when they hear the ferrying song?"

I shift on restless legs. "Their spirits rise from the grave and gain a tangible form."

"Which makes them dangerous in the first place. But do you know what becomes of souls when they cannot pass through the Gates of the Beyond?"

I try to picture the Gates I've been told about but have never seen with my own eyes. Elara's Gate is supposed to be nearly invisible, while Tyrus's Gate *is* visible and made of water. When the land bridge emerges from the sea, both Gates crop up at the summoning of the bone flute, just like the dead are also lured by its song. "They don't get punished?" I ask, speculating about the Chained, though my answer is obvious. I've never heard of any soul who successfully evaded ferrying.

Odiva shakes her head. "It is much worse than that. The Chained become even more sinister, and if the Leurress are not able to restrain them, they can flee the bridge and *retain* their tangible form. Do you understand the implications?"

A commotion rises from the tunnels. The elders. They must be gathered now and ready to leave. "The Chained return from the dead?" I ask, impatient to finish this conversation.

"If only it were that simple. The souls are neither alive nor dead in the mortal realm, where they should no longer be. In this frustrated in-between state, the Chained seek more power and feed off the souls of the living."

Feed? I forget about the elders and give the *matrone* my full attention. "How?"

"They steal their Light."

My eyes widen. Elara's Light is the life force within all mortals—strongest within the Leurress. Without it, we would weaken and ultimately die. "Then what . . . what happens if the Chained take *all* of their Light?"

Odiva grows silent, her gaze distant. The feathers of her talon epaulettes flutter on the breeze, and one catches on the largest talon, the carved pendant bone of an eagle owl. "They die an everlasting death. Their souls are no more."

Dread, deep and black, overwhelms me, like my Light is already fading. What she's speaking of is the worst form of murder—to murder a soul—something I never thought possible.

This is the reality Odiva has been laboring to drive into me: to her, the loss of the bone flute is worse than the loss of her daughter. And I'm responsible.

"I'm sorry." My voice wavers, flimsy as seagrass. After the rite of passage, it was my job to place the bone flute back on the bed of lamb's wool in the cedar chest. Now, not only is Ailesse's life at risk because of me, but countless other lives are, as well. Ferrying needs to happen in fifteen days, during the new moon. "What can I do?"

"You can grow up." Odiva grimaces like it costs her to reprimand me. "I have been too soft on you, Sabine. You are not a child anymore. If you had obtained more graces before tonight, you would have been able to overpower your assailant. Ailesse would have had a fighting chance."

Fresh tears gather in my eyes, but I deserve this chastening. "I promise to hunt for more, *Matrone*." I have to get over my qualms about killing animals. "But first . . . please, let me help my friend. Let me go with the elders."

"With the graces of a fire salamander?" Odiva's eyes fall to the tiny skull on my necklace. "Absolutely not."

All seven elders emerge into the courtyard to cross through. Their most striking grace bones gleam under the moonlight. Roxane's stag antler hair wreath. Dolssa's snake rib necklace. Milicent's vulture wing bone earrings. Pernelle's fox vertebra pendant.

Nadine's eel skull hair comb. Chantae's boar jawbone choker. Damiana's wolf fang bracelet.

I fight the urge to hide my own pitiful grace bone as they leave through another tunnel on their way out of Château Creux. "Please, *Matrone*. I'm the one who was with Ailesse tonight. I've seen what her *amouré* is capable of. He and his accomplices must have studied the Leurress. They knew what they were doing. What if they've abducted her?" As terrible as that would be, at least it would mean Ailesse isn't dead. "What if the elders can't find her?"

"If they cannot, it is no matter." Odiva's raven brows lower over her sharpened eyes. "*I* will find her. Ailesse is blood of my blood, bones of my bones. There is magic between a mother and daughter that even the gods cannot explain." A deep ache rises in my chest, a yearning to experience what Odiva is talking about. *Mon étoile*, my mother used to call me. *My star.* "I will draw on that magic to track her. I will save my child." Her voice exudes calm confidence. "Ailesse is alive. I can feel it now."

A cautious breath fills my lungs. "Truly?"

"Truly." Odiva smiles, but it doesn't reach her eyes. "Now go to sleep, Sabine. Your wounds will finish healing while you rest. Tomorrow, you will begin the hunt for your new graces. The gods may have need of you sooner than you think." Her hand drifts to the lump of her hidden necklace. "I want you to be ready."

I try not to squirm under her lingering stare. Odiva wants me to become a Ferrier—she's made that painfully clear—but I also have the uneasy feeling she wants something more from me. Something I won't like.

"Ailesse will survive," she reassures me. "I possess the strength of five grace bones. I will see to it. So do not pursue her." Her tone is clear and final. "Leave my daughter to me."

Odiva turns away, signaling the end of our conversation, and she withdraws to the place where I first saw her praying. She starts to murmur an unfamiliar chant. I can't make out all her words, but I hear Ailesse's name as Odiva lifts her hand to her bat skull crown. She cuts her finger on its teeth and drips her blood onto the limestone below, where the Leurress have etched the face of Tyrus's golden jackal in the curve of Elara's sickle moon. My stomach turns. I've never seen or heard of a ritual like the one she's doing.

The *matrone*'s pitch-dark eyes slowly rise to me while her blood keeps spilling. "Goodnight, Sabine."

My knees wobble. "Goodnight."

She turns her back to me again, a mirror reflection of before— her arms outstretched in prayer, her cupped hands tipped downward. A marrow-deep shiver runs through me, and I hasten away.

In my room, I grab my bow and a quiver of bone-tipped arrows. I have no intention of sleeping tonight. I'd only toss and turn. Instead, I sneak through a side tunnel, bypassing the courtyard, and I leave Château Creux.

Clutching my wounded side, I run as fast as possible. Once I clear the castle by a mile, I remove my salamander grace bone and tie it onto Ailesse's shoulder necklace. The act of clasping it around my own neck and shoulder seals my vow to her.

I will *save you, Ailesse.*

I can't rely on the elders or Odiva to do what I must, especially since my *matrone* is more concerned about the bone flute.

As I begin my journey to Castelpont, Elara's Light, like courage, seeps inside my soul. Even stronger is my fierce determination. I'll search for the flute in the riverbed, then I'll strike out for the hunting grounds of the forest. I'll kill to obtain my last two grace bones, if that's what it takes to save my friend. And this time I won't weep.

I *will* be like Ailesse.

11
Ailesse

CURSE BASTIEN AND EVERY BONE *in his body.* I can't see anything through this blindfold. My foot catches on a tree root— or maybe a rock—and I pitch forward. He hoists me back up before I hit the ground. I thrash against his iron grip on my arm. "Let go!" But he won't. He hasn't since we left Castelpont—since I failed to kill him.

Humiliation scalds my cheeks. My mother will never believe I'm capable again. Far worse than losing my grace bones, I lost the bone flute. Sabine will go back for it—that's my only consolation—but I can't shake the image of my mother's furious eyes when Sabine tells her what happened.

I struggle to stay on my feet as Bastien continues to drag me through the forest. His two friends hedge us in, helping to guard me as we travel, Marcel in front and Jules behind. Their footsteps fall loud and clumsy. Marcel shuffles as he walks, and Jules limps on her hurt leg. *Thank you for that, Sabine.*

"You're playing a game you'll never win," I warn them. "If you three had any wisdom between you, you'd let me go while you still have the chance. My mother will come looking for me, and you do not want to face her wrath."

Bastien's grip tightens, and my arm prickles with numbness. "If your mother wants you back, she'll have to come to us in our territory."

"You really think you can hide me?" I scoff. "There is nowhere you can dream of that my mother won't find."

"I'm counting on it."

We come to an abrupt stop in the forest. I've tried to track my steps over the past hour and a half, but we've changed directions too many times. We've even walked through streams, with the current and against it. Bastien is trying to disorient me, and without my falcon, shark, and ibex graces, it's working. Maybe he fears my mother will see through my eyes—impossible—and he thinks his tactics will help outrun her. *Fool.*

"You first, Jules," Bastien says. "Then you can guide the Bone Crier through to the other side."

"I say we let her squirm." I startle at the nearness of Jules's voice, just behind me, deep and scratchy for a girl. If I had my shark tooth, I'd have sensed her closeness. But my grace bones are in her possession now, a fact she keeps gloating about when she's not hissing about her hurt leg. I hope it falls off.

"Our first priority is to get her deep underground," Bastien replies.

Underground? My chest tightens at the suffocating thought. The courtyard beneath Château Creux is different from wherever Bastien means; it's at least open to Elara's Night Heavens and the breeze from the Nivous Sea. "Where are you taking me?"

His spicy scent hits me as he shifts nearer. "The catacombs. I'll let you guess by which entrance."

My heart hammers. The catacombs are rumored to have several entrances, and some sections don't join up with others and lead to dead ends. "No, you can't . . . *I* can't . . ." I'll be starved of moonlight and starlight, my last sources of strength. I have to get away. Now.

I shove Bastien hard in the chest. His hold breaks, and I run— only four feet. He grabs my other arm and twists it behind my back. I suck in a sharp gasp of pain.

He chuckles. "You were right, Marcel," he calls a little ahead of us.

"Was I?" Marcel replies. "I mean, I usually am, but what about this time?"

"Bone Crier magic comes from more than just bones." Smug satisfaction drips from Bastien's voice. "They're creatures of the night."

"Ah, yes . . ." Marcel drawls indifferently. "That's partly why they worship Elara." He doesn't sound like he has the venom to commit murder, like Bastien or Jules, or even help them strip me of all my magic. But his apathy could be a mask for viciousness. "They need sustenance from the goddess's moon and stars."

"And without it," Bastien adds, adjusting his hold on my arm so he's no longer twisting it, "the princess here will be nothing except a lure for her queen."

"Lure?" Jules asks, wariness creeping into her tone. "What are you talking about?"

I grind my teeth. It's clear enough to me. "Is that your big plan?" I turn my face to Bastien. "Using me as bait to kill my mother? How? You won't be able to steal her grace bones—and she has the finest in my *famille*." I throw all the cruelty I can into my tight-lipped smile. "She will utterly ruin you."

"Bastien . . ." Jules says from behind me, her voice low. "Maybe we should rethink this."

I feel him bristle. "I *have* been rethinking this. Our fathers deserve more than the death of a random Bone Crier. We need to stop ritual sacrifice once and for all. The smartest way to do that is strike for the head—take out the queen." His tone tempers with an edge of desperation. "This is our best chance, Jules."

"I just hope you know what you're doing."

"Don't I always?"

She huffs. "Hilarious."

"Keep moving," he says. "We're almost there."

She walks past me and slams her shoulder into mine. My jaw stiffens. I kick backward and bash her shin with my heel. She hisses a curse. I must have hit her wounded leg. *Good.*

My left cheek smarts with a bright burst of pain. I stumble

backward with a jolt of dizziness. "Careful, Bone Crier," Jules warns me.

I lift my chin, wishing I could rip off this blindfold so I could stare her down. I barely know her, but I already hate her. Jules hurt Sabine. I haven't forgotten that.

She limps away from me. I hear her for a few paces, then I don't hear anything at all. Has she already entered the catacombs?

A fresh wave of panic assaults me. I drag my feet and wrestle against Bastien. He yanks me forward. "You're next."

I can't go in there. I won't. I stomp on his foot. His arm wraps around my throat in a chokehold. I can't breathe. I thrash harder.

"Stop fighting!" His voice trembles with exertion. "Or I'll hurt you so badly you'll wish you were dead."

I don't doubt him. Blood pounds through my skull, but I won't back down. I pry at his hands. I claw. I kick. I clamp my lips together so I don't mouth, *Please.* I won't beg. He won't steal my self-respect, as well as my graces.

"Um, Bastien?" Marcel says with nail-biting sluggishness. "I think she understands your point now."

Bastien's grip hardens. My eyes water. I fear my neck might break. Maybe he'll end my life right now. *I dare you,* I think, even while my head prickles on the verge of unconsciousness. If he kills me, he'll die with me.

"*Merde,*" he says, as if he's had the same thought. He releases my throat.

I collapse and suck in burning mouthfuls of air. Before I've a chance to recover, he lugs me up again and hauls me forward.

We trip forward a few feet, and the ground steeply declines. My legs are knee-deep in wild grass; this isn't a catacombs entrance. We're moving down the side of some kind of cliff or ravine. Before the terrain levels out, my left foot plummets into a burrow. "Put the other foot in there." Bastien shoves me. "That's the entrance. We've arrived."

I try to scramble away, but he grabs me and holds me still. I jerk against his grip. "All right," I say, "I'm going." He slowly releases me, but the warmth from his body still hovers nearby. I square my jaw. Bastien thinks I'm nothing without my graces. I'll prove he's wrong and hasn't stripped me of my courage.

I place both feet in the hole and kneel to slip in headfirst.

"No, *feetfirst* or you'll get caught inside," he says, and I suppress a growl. If this is a trick, I'll make him suffer for it.

I take one last breath of fresh air and drink in what I can of the moonlight. I pray its cool energy will be trapped beneath my skin long enough to help me survive the darkness.

I slither into the hole.

The space is tight. I'm forced to shimmy in on my back. My head slides in last, and I swallow hard. I've wriggled through small tunnels before. The caves beneath Château Creux are riddled with them. But I never did so feetfirst and trapped between three people who want me dead.

"In thirty feet, you'll feel another hole, the opening of a side tunnel," Bastien tells me. He sounds irritated, like it chafes him to offer me assistance.

I yank my blindfold off so it hangs around my neck. My

surroundings are still dark and smothering. I squirm downward at a diagonal angle until I find the branching tunnel. I shove my legs in, but the tunnel angles upward, opposite the way I'm trying to slide through. Panic builds inside me like growing thunder. I start to whimper. I never whimper.

Laughter echoes, but I can't tell from which direction. "It's fun to hear you struggle," a husky yet feminine voice calls. *Jules.* "But now I'm bored, so here's the secret: move down *past* the second tunnel, then climb back up and go through it headfirst."

I close my eyes against the blow of my own stupidity. Why didn't I think of that? I've been held underwater by a tiger shark and confined in cramped snow caves in the north, but I've never panicked like this and lost my right mind.

I take a calming breath and follow Jules's instructions. At least I'm sliding forward on my elbows now, rather than creeping backward. About fifteen feet later, I emerge from the second tunnel into a larger place where I'm able to stand.

Unlike in the tunnels beneath Château Creux, the air is warm here with none of the coolness from the sea. I blink and try to adjust my eyes to the darkness without my keen peregrine falcon vision. Some tunnels under Château Creux are dim—even black, if you go deep enough. But they're not this black. Nothing could be darker or more unfathomable. I feel Elara's Light already leaching from my body, and my natural strength fading with it.

A terrible pang of loneliness squeezes my chest, even though I'm not alone. I miss Sabine. I could endure this if she were here with me.

A thump comes from behind. "Why haven't you lit the lamps, Jules?" Bastien says. *Swish, pat, flick.* He must be brushing dust from his clothes.

"I wanted the Bone Crier to have a proper welcome." I hear the smirk in Jules's voice, though her words sink into the dense limestone. "Meet the pitch-dark gloom of the catacombs."

"The pureness of the black is breathtaking," I reply just to vex her. The pause that follows assures me I've succeeded.

A tiny spark ignites, along with the scrape of flint and steel. My brows shoot up. Jules is only four feet ahead of me, not several feet away, like I expected. This place has an unnerving way of eating up sound. She blows on her tinder and lights the wick of a simple oil lamp. The flame isn't brilliant—it only stretches five or six feet past Jules, and beyond that, the unrelenting blackness reigns.

"You've removed your blindfold," Bastien remarks. In the darkness, his sea-blue eyes have turned the color of the midnight sky. My skin flushes with heat. For a moment his gaze turns from hateful to conflicted, like he's searching for something within me, and he's nervous about what he'll find.

"We're inside now," I reply. "Why should I wear it anymore?"

"This isn't our final destination."

A heavy thud makes me jump. An overpacked shoulder bag falls from the tunnel hole. Marcel's head of floppy hair pops out next. "I abhor this entrance," he says, though his tone isn't distressed. "Next time we should—"

"Marcel." Bastien gives him a pointed look. I glance between them and understand: there's another, easier entrance to this part of the catacombs, which means this quarry passage doesn't lead to a dead end. Useful to remember as I plot my escape.

Jules removes two more oil lamps from a natural ledge on the limestone wall, where she must have also retrieved her tinderbox. As she lights each wick, Bastien drags me close and reaches for the blindfold at my throat. I jerk away and untie it myself, then rewrap it around my eyes. He tightens the knot, even though I cinched it.

We walk deeper into the bleak tunnel. Bastien doesn't grip my arm like he did aboveground; instead, he prods me forward with little jabs on my back. I know where each of my captors is by the sounds of their footsteps. Jules is in front of me, limping, but in a focused rhythm. Bastien is right behind me, his stride a balanced blend of confidence and caution. And Marcel is behind Bastien, shuffling along in a pattern of ease and distractedness.

I spread out my arms. The tunnel is just big enough for me to support myself against the walls and occasionally the low ceiling. I keep checking the height to make sure it doesn't dip and ram into my head. I doubt Bastien would warn me.

Up ahead, a muffled splash startles me. "What was that?"

"Jules jumped in the water."

I plant my feet. "Water?" My mother never told me about any water down here.

"Groundwater," Marcel replies faintly. I cock my head to him. He's probably closer than he sounds. "At least half the catacombs are flooded."

I shudder. Up until now, I haven't touched any human bones, but the water must carry decomposed fragments like the sea carries salt. Odiva forbids our *famille* to enter the catacombs because bones are sacred to us. We only take what we need, and we honor the creatures we hunt. But no honor was given to the people whose bones fill this place. In the days of Old Galle, after a century of wars, the mass graves in Dovré started caving in on the limestone quarries beneath the city. The quarries were shored up so Dovré wouldn't collapse, and the bones in the unmarked graves were dumped inside them. Abominable.

"Move." Bastien shoves me hard. I stagger forward.

Two steps, five steps, nine. *Elara, protect me.* My foot hits an edge where the slick ground drops away. I flail to catch my balance; Bastien does nothing to help. With a small shriek, I plummet. The fall isn't far—maybe three feet. My stomach slaps the water, and my knees graze the ground. My head surfaces, and I cough up a mouthful of lukewarm water. It's gritty with limestone silt and probably the dust of human bones. I cringe and stand, shaking some of the wetness off my arms. The water reaches the level of my thighs.

Slosh. Swish. Bastien eases into the water. For the sake of preserving his lamplight, dimly glowing through my blindfold, I resist the urge to knock him on his backside. "Go on." He jabs my spine.

"I will kill you slowly," I promise. "And when you beg for mercy, I will cut out your tongue."

The water stirs as he wades closer. His hot breath is in my face. "You'll never get the chance. After I kill your mother, I'll find a way past your magic and stop your heart. Your body will rot until you're nothing but bones, just like all the men you've slaughtered."

"I've never killed a man," I snap. "Each member of my *famille* kills only one." For someone who knew enough about my strengths and weaknesses to kidnap me, Bastien has surprisingly slim knowledge about the Leurress. He probably studied how to kill me without bothering to learn why my people do what we do in the first place—and how difficult it is.

He scoffs. "How generous."

I wish my glare could burn holes through this blindfold.

The water burbles behind us. Marcel has caught up. "How far ahead is Jules?" he asks.

"Just past our ring of light," Bastien replies. He releases a tight exhale and pushes me along. "Let's go."

I take care not to slip as my flared sleeves trail through the water. Every time my feet hit an obstacle, I shudder, fearing it's a human bone.

We slowly press forward. The path forks at least fifteen times until it inclines and I'm back on dry limestone. Praise the gods. From here, we only change paths six times, then a hand grabs my shoulder to make me stop. "Are we here?" I ask. All I want to do is to lie down and dream I've completed my rite of passage and become a Ferrier of the dead.

I want to wake up from this nightmare.

"Yes." Jules's voice is strangely sweet. "You can take off your blindfold now."

I hesitate. She's up to something.

"Wait until we're inside the chamber," Bastien says.

My jaw tightens. I'm tired of submitting to him. I yank off my blindfold and cast it on the ground. No sooner have I done so than I wish it back again. Twelve feet before me, the tunnel widens and dead-ends into a massive wall of stacked skulls.

I clap my hands over my mouth and shrink backward. My eyes pool with tears. "Where—?" I choke on my words. "Where are their other bones?"

Marcel removes his pack. "There's a gallery of femurs in the west catacombs." He rolls out his shoulders. "But most of the bones—ribs and clavicles and the like—are lying in heaps behind monuments such as these." He shrugs lackadaisically. "I suppose our ancestors couldn't spare the time to arrange all of them."

"Are all their skeletons separated like this?"

"Mm-hmm."

My tears spill over. This is sinful, abhorrent, revolting. The Leurress bury men *whole*. The gods forbid us to remove human bones from their bodies. If we did, their souls would suffer a state of endless unrest in the afterlife. They wouldn't be reunited with their bodies. They wouldn't be able to touch or act upon things. They wouldn't be able to embrace their departed loved ones.

"Why are you offended?" Bastien's brows furrow. He grabs a crate tucked against the wall and passes it over to Jules. "Your kind wears all sorts of separated bones."

"That's different. Animals are ordained for us by the gods." I wipe away another rush of tears. "Their souls were granted inferior glory."

Jules snorts. "She's unbelievable."

"But humans were crafted in the image of the gods," I go on, ignoring the disgusted look she gives me as she crouches and removes several clay lamps from the crate. "We're destined for a higher place in the eternal realms."

She rolls her eyes. "Naturally."

Why am I explaining sacred things to hateful people? My gaze drifts back to the wall of skulls, and I tremble, numb with shock, sick with horror. I drop to my knees and lift cupped hands to the Night Heavens, somewhere above all this rock and death.

"What is she doing?" Jules asks. I hear the *whoosh* of flame as she lights all the lamps with hers.

"She appears to be . . . praying," Marcel says.

Grant these souls peace, Elara. Tell them I mourn for them.

After a brief spell of silence, Bastien mutters, "Watch her, Jules. Come on, Marcel. Help me carry in these lamps."

As their footsteps retreat, Jules scoots beside me. "So let me guess—you Bone Criers receive the *most* glory." Her snide laugh grates on my ears.

"My soul chose this path, just as you chose yours. Do not mock what you don't understand. To be a Leurress requires great sacrifice."

"Yes, but not for your people. You consider the men you kill to be your sacrifices—my father, Bastien's father. But *we're* the ones who have suffered, not you."

I meet her hard gaze, and guilt nicks my stomach. "Is that why the three of you banded together? Because you all lost your fathers?"

Jules roughly swipes a hand under her nose. "We were only children."

My guilt cuts deeper, but Jules doesn't understand. None of them do. "Your fathers are in Elara's Paradise, a place of great joy and beauty." I recite what I've been taught. "They're happy, and they accept their deaths."

Jules spits in my face. I recoil with wide eyes. "Do you know what *does* comfort me?" She pushes to her feet and walks to the dim edge of our circle of lamplight. She withdraws something tucked under the neckline of her bodice. I squint and barely make out that it's long, slim, and pale. "Knowing you Bone Criers won't be able to lure another man without your flute."

Adrenaline flashes through my veins. She has it. Found it. Took it from the riverbed. She *stole* it. "That belongs to my mother!"

"Does it?" She unceremoniously holds the flute over her knee.

And breaks it in two.

My heart stops. I gape at the severed pieces in her hands. "What have you done?"

"Don't worry, Princess. Your mother can surely stoop to carve herself another one."

My mind reels. *No, she can't.* Not without the bone of a rare golden jackal. A beast that isn't even native to Galle. No living Leurress knows where to travel to hunt one.

Jules tilts her head. "Unless it's irreplaceable." She grins and fury builds inside me. "Do all you Bone Criers share the same flute?" I school my features, though blood roars through my ears. My silence betrays my answer. She tosses the pieces of the broken flute into the darkness. "Excellent."

My rage peaks. I lunge for her. "You monster!" She jumps out of my path and steadies her weight on her good leg. Not good for long.

I kick her knee with my heel. She shrieks and swings her fist at my face. I duck, then ram my head into her stomach. She falls back on the ground. I tumble on top of her. "I'll kill you!" The dense air muffles my shout. She grabs my wrists to keep me from striking her. I thrash to break her hold. "The gods will bind you in chains for this!"

"Jules?" Bastien's muted but alarmed voice grows louder. He charges into our ring of lamplight.

She tosses him a smug grin, even as we wrestle harder. "I just confirmed what Marcel suspected," she says, panting. "Ailesse's bone flute is the only one that exists. We don't have to worry about another one."

Bastien yanks me off of his friend. "Good."

"I hate all of you!" I rail against him and manage to clip his jaw. *My mother is going to murder me when she finds out about the flute.* "You're pathetic, soulless excuses for human beings!"

"Feeling's mutual, Bone Crier." He wrenches my arms behind my back and pulls me with him along the wall of skulls. Jules rises, limping to follow.

A few kicking and stumbling paces later, we reach a square opening that leads into a chamber. Light from the extra lamps that Jules lit pours out from within.

Bastien hauls me forward past a panel of skulls resting beside the entrance—a false door to keep the secret room hidden. He pushes me inside, and I duck my head under the low clearance. I catch a glimpse of the door's back. It isn't made of stone, but only thatched straw and thin clay. It can't weigh more than I do; it will provide for an easy escape. And I vow to escape soon.

In fifteen days, the tides will recede to their lowest and reveal the land bridge in the sea. On that new moon—like every new moon—the Leurress need to summon the dead from their graves and ferry their souls past the Gates of the Beyond. If they don't, the souls will grow restless and leave their burial places on their own. *The dead must be ferried*, my mother told me as I prepared for my rite of passage, *or they'll wander the land of the living and wreak devastation.*

But the Leurress can't summon the dead without the bone flute and the song Odiva must play on it. I see only one solution: I have to make a new bone flute from the bone of a golden jackal. Somehow I'll find one. I need to make this right. It's the only way to prove myself to my mother.

Bastien and Jules follow me into the chamber. He lugs me to the back and shoves me down onto a limestone slab. He binds my hands with rope from Marcel's pack, then all three of my captors roll a heavy stone over the end of the rope that's tied around my ankles. "Get comfortable," Bastien says, knowing full well that's impossible. "And pray your mother comes quickly."

12
Bastien

I can't be the Bone Crier's soulmate.

A bead of sweat drips down my spine. My hand slides to my sheath. I graze the hilt of my father's knife.

I could kill Ailesse now.

She sits on the stone slab in the corner of our secret catacombs chamber. I'm standing a few feet away, leaning against a limestone wall. I haven't been able to sleep, unlike Marcel who's sprawled out and snoring, smack in the middle of the oblong room. This space has always felt large—fifteen paces wide and twenty long—but with Ailesse among us, I'm cramped. She holds her knees to her chest with her tied hands looped around them, and rests her cheek on top. Curled up like that, she looks so small. So easy to murder.

Her head turns. Her umber eyes collide with mine. In the warm glow of the oil lamps surrounding us, she holds my gaze with the same ferocity she did at Castelpont.

A wave of heat rushes through my body. I clench the muscles along my jawline to make it stop. I slowly pull my hand away from my knife, but now the blade feels lodged between my ribs.

What if we are soulmates?

Her death would be my death. My father would have no justice.

"Here." Jules limps over to me and presses a wooden cup into my hand. "The water has settled."

I unhitch my back from the wall and take a long swallow. I don't mind the mineral kick of the limestone water, especially when it's not choked with the silt we dredged up in the tunnels. "How's the leg?" I ask, putting the cup aside.

"It'll heal," Jules replies, the scratch in her voice raspier than usual. She takes my hand and turns it over, examining all my cuts and bruises, like I'm somehow hurt worse than her. I let her warm touch linger. We're going to figure out how to make it through this mess like we always do—together. Not only will we survive, we'll find a way to get our revenge.

"Take off your shirt," she murmurs.

My gaze flies up to her hazel eyes. "What?"

"I need to wash it," she explains, biting her lower lip to hold back a grin.

My ears burn. Ailesse is still watching me, one of her brows lifted. I keep my face straight, pull my shirt over my head, and pass it over to Jules. We always rinse our silt-drenched clothes after the water settles in the catacombs. She doesn't need to make a game out of it.

"Come with me." Her eyes drift over my bare chest. "It's dark where the water is. Private."

"Knock it off, Jules."

Her jaw muscle tics, but she laughs like a tavern girl, completely out of character. "Look how tense you are." She pokes my abdomen, and my muscles involuntarily flex. "The queen won't come tonight. It's almost dawn. Even if she tracked her daughter's bones, she could never get all the way down here. She'll wait until she has a whole night, when she's at her strongest." Jules unties the muddy laces at the top of her blouse, and the rough-spun cloth parts lower. "Plus, once she realizes we're in the catacombs, she'll have to rethink her strategy. So you can afford to let down your guard, Bastien." She traces a thin scar above my navel.

I push her hand away. "Hurry up with our clothes, all right? We have work to do." She shouldn't have kissed me in Gaspar's shop. I shouldn't have kissed her back. "I'm not leaving the Bone Crier alone with Marcel."

Jules scoffs and glances at Ailesse. "Why? She's a weakling now."

"Go, Jules." I push her again, this time with more force.

She catches my wrist and squeezes hard. We haven't gotten into a scuffle since we were kids, but the glint in her eyes says she's itching to break that streak. She finally lets go and forces a sultry smile. "Suit yourself. Have fun with your soulmate," she says in a singsong voice.

On her way out of the chamber, she throws a pointed look at Ailesse while flinging my dirty shirt across her shoulder. Ailesse's glare is just as hateful.

I drag a hand over my face when Jules leaves. It's laughable, really, the idea of soulmates. If the Bone Crier and I really are bound by ritual magic, it's not because we're meant for one another. That would mean my father was meant for the woman who killed him, and I refuse to believe he was meant for anyone else besides my mother. Even if I don't remember her.

"I know why you resist her." The smugness in Ailesse's voice claws under my skin.

"You know nothing about me."

She tilts her head to study my face. She's filthy from the chalky tunnel water, and there's a nick at the base of her throat, along with a smear of dried blood. My blade did that. I glance away and rub a knotted muscle in my arm. "I know you have a spark of Elara's Light," she says. "Everyone does. It's the whisper in your head, the thoughts behind your thoughts. It tells you your friend might prick your heart, but she doesn't pierce your soul."

I snort. "Your gods aren't my gods, Bone Crier. They don't speak to me. They sure as hell don't dictate my life."

Her nostrils flare. I'm still a few feet away, but she leans toward me and tucks her bent knees to the side. The movement pulls on her dress, and it falls off one of her shoulders. I try not to stare at the creamy softness of her skin. She doesn't notice. She's too busy throwing darts with her eyes. "I wouldn't have chosen you either, Bastien."

My chest jolts when she says my name. It's too personal, too familiar, coming from her. Ailesse stiffens. I realize I have a death grip on the hilt of my knife. Her hands close into fists. She's ready to fight back, despite her bonds and lack of power. A pulse of admiration trips through my veins.

Marcel lets out a loud snore and rolls over, lugging his pack onto his chest. Even in his sleep he's guarding his book—as well as Ailesse's bones. Jules stuffed them inside after we entered this chamber and threatened Marcel on pain of death—which means nothing, since Jules says it so often to him—to keep the pack out of Ailesse's reach.

The worst of my tension diffuses. I let go of my knife and walk over to Marcel. I scoot away his pack with the toe of my boot. It's the only way to wake him up. I swear he'd sleep if his bed were burning.

He jerks upright and swipes at me with his eyes still closed. I slide his pack out of reach. "Get up, Marcel. I need your help."

"Why?" He absently licks his lips. "It isn't morning. I wasn't dreaming. I start dreaming two hours before dawn."

Leave it to Marcel to determine the time, even though he can't see the moon or sun. "We need to sleep during the day from now on."

His eyes slit open and he peers back at Ailesse, who watches him like a predator. "Oh, right. We've stolen a Bone Crier." He blinks. "And I told Birdie I'd walk with her by the river today—and tomorrow, and the day after that." He releases a heavy sigh.

"Get out your book." I toss him his pack. He doesn't catch it fast enough, and it thunks against his chest. "You want to see Birdie? Start reading."

His brows wrinkle. "I fail to see the connection."

I crouch beside him, my back turned to Ailesse. "The queen will track us here as soon as tomorrow night," I whisper. "We're not getting out of these catacombs alive unless we form a proper plan to"—I slice my finger across the base of my throat—"her. That involves you doing what you do best: reading between the lines of those Old Galle folktales."

"Ah, I see." He pulls into a cross-legged position and glances at Ailesse before he winks at me. Twice.

"Listen, we'll talk more after the Bone Crier is sleeping, but for now . . ." I scoot closer and lower my voice another notch. "Do you know how strong the queen will really be down here? Will she be able to use any of her bone magic?"

"I think so . . ." Marcel unfastens his pack. "But it will cost her more energy. Eventually, she'll run out, though I have no idea how long that will take. It isn't mentioned in any stories here." He pulls out his father's book and sets it in his lap. "Unless I've forgotten something." He turns the pages, and the book falls open where the spine has cracked. I twist to look at it with him. Ailesse sits up taller and tries to peek at it, too. *Can she read?* I always imagined Bone Criers doing things like drinking blood from horns or eating the raw flesh off animals, not studying out of books. Hell, *I* can barely read.

I tip up the book so she can't see inside. The story I'm looking at is a myth about Bone Criers, complete with an illustration of a woman with unbound hair. The train of her dress is so long it spreads from the center of the bridge to the foot, where an unassuming man comes near. I see my father. I see Jules and Marcel's father.

I see me.

Acid rage hits my stomach. I abruptly push up on my feet and stride away from Ailesse. She isn't close, but she's still too close. I lean against the only brick wall in the room—a place like others in the catacombs that's been shored up to prevent the tunnels from collapsing—and fight to breathe.

"Are you all right?" Marcel asks, a vague note of concern in his voice.

I wait for my pulse to slow. "Just hungry. You?"

"I suppose."

I steady my legs. Pull away from the wall. Rummage through a few jars and tins on the jutting bricks we use as shelves. *Keep yourself together, Bastien. Focus on a plan.* Like food and supplies. We don't have much, except the little we left last time we had to hole up in here. If we have to stay much longer, one of us will need to make a run to Dovré.

Jules ducks back inside the chamber and brings a puddle of water with her. The clothes she wears are soaked, but not dirty anymore. She's fully bathed, something each of us always does in turn—part of our routine here, or else the silt-mud itches like the plague.

She wrings out her hair, lugs in a bucket of water, and shuts the door panel. "Marcel, you're actually awake." She chuckles, already in a better mood for being clean. "The way you were snoring, I thought you'd sleep another fortnight."

He grunts distractedly, his head bent over his book.

She limps closer to me and totes the bucket along with her. I arch my brow. "More drinking water?"

She nods, passing me my rinsed shirt. I hang it from a brick to dry. "Anything good in there?" She eyes my tin.

"The usual." I offer her a piece of dried meat.

She pops it in her mouth and chews it for a moment. "You know, I've been thinking." She limps toward Ailesse. "Wouldn't it be a shame, if when the queen comes, she doesn't even recognize her own daughter?"

Ailesse tenses and slides back on the slab. But she can't escape. Jules tosses all the contents of her bucket at her. Ailesse breaks into a coughing fit and shudders.

Jules grabs a fistful of her dripping hair and studies Ailesse's face. "There, much better. Now the muck is gone, and we can see the monster."

Ailesse's mouth forms a vicious line. She thrusts out her ankle-bound legs and kicks Jules hard in the stomach.

Jules flies backward and hits the ground. As soon as the shock fades from her face, she's back on her feet, her eyes livid.

Merde.

"Jules," I warn. She doesn't listen.

She draws the knife sheathed at her thigh.

Ailesse lifts up on her knees, agile even tied up. "You want my blood?" she sneers. "Come and take it. Watch Bastien die with me."

Jules's grip on her knife turns white-knuckled. Marcel shuts his book. I take a tentative step forward. "Jules," I say again. *I'm not going to die. I can't be the Bone Crier's soulmate.* "The queen will know if she's dead." My pulse pounds harder as I look at Ailesse. "Won't she?"

Ailesse's feverish eyes drift from me to the sharp point of Jules's blade. She presses her lips together and nods.

Jules cries out in frustration and throws the knife. Ailesse jerks aside, but the blade flies wide and clatters against the stone wall.

A flood of cool relief washes over me.

Scratch, scratch.

I glance behind us. Something chirps faintly. I frown and move near the small door of our chamber. The scratching comes again. Another chirp. An animal? I've never seen so much as a rat down here.

"What is that?" Jules asks.

"No idea." The scratching intensifies, the chirping grows louder. There's more than one creature out there in the tunnel. And they really want in. What if Ailesse's mother is with them?

Impossible. She couldn't have tracked us that fast.

I crouch and tentatively push at the false door. I've spent enough time in the gutters and alleys of Dovré not to flinch at rodents, but that doesn't mean I want my finger bitten.

The door cracks open. The muffled chirps amplify to a chorus of screeching. A fuzzy brown head with a squat face pops in through the gap. The lamplight reflects off its beady black eyes. Another head burrows in.

"Bats." I grimace.

"Bats don't roost in the catacombs," Marcel says.

With a sinking feeling in my stomach, I turn to Ailesse. She's staring at the creatures fighting to get in, her eyes bright with hope. This is Bone Crier magic, though I don't understand it.

I reach to yank the door shut, but the first bat squirms inside. It unfurls the velvety membranes of its wings. Huge for a bat. Twice the normal wingspan.

"A giant noctule." Marcel gasps in awe. "But they're tree-dwellers, so they shouldn't be . . ." His words trail off. His face pales as the bat bares its fangs at me. "I don't think it likes you."

Jules draws a sharp breath. "Bastien, watch out!"

The creature shrieks and flies at my face. I scramble back and try to beat it away. More flapping wings swarm around me. Other bats have pushed inside.

"What do we do?" Marcel shouts. He's on his feet, using his book as a weapon, but there are too many. At least ten. No, fifteen.

"Shut the door!" Jules cries. She fights a bat tangled in her hair.

I swat at the creatures clawing my arms and push at the door. But the force is too strong on the other side. How many are out there?

A terrible image flashes to mind. Jules's knife. On the ground near Ailesse. Jules never got a chance to get it back.

I let go of the door and spin around. Through the storm of black wings, I see Ailesse. The ropes at her wrists are already cut away. Now she's sawing the ones at her ankles.

I plow forward with my arms up to protect my face. The swarm thickens. "Jules!" My voice sounds faint under the deafening screeches.

The lamps in our chamber start to extinguish from the rushing wings. I'm halfway across the room. Ailesse sees me coming. The bats aren't harassing her. She works harder, frantically trying to cut herself free.

More lamps snuff out. I shove against the tide of wings, shrieks, and claws.

Ailesse has almost severed the rope, but she can't finish. I'm within reach. She swipes out with the knife, but the bats throw off her aim. I scramble to grip her forearm before she can attack again. I bash her hand on the slab—once, twice, and she loses the knife. I give it a hard kick, and it skids across the ground into the chaos.

She thrashes and pounds me with her fists. I crawl on top of her and wrestle to pin her down. I can't find another length of rope to tie her wrists back together again.

"Bastien!" I crane my neck at Jules's muffled shout. Through the choking black, I see dim flashes of her. She has an arm around her brother. They're pressing toward the door. "Hurry!" she calls. "We have to get out of here!"

"You can't escape this." Ailesse's soft but savage laughter heats my ear. Her words are only loud enough for me. "My mother has found you."

I break into a cold sweat. I'm not ready for the queen. I haven't made a plan.

Only one lamp burns now, the one nearest to us. In the last snatches of light, Ailesse's pupils are large and fathomless pits. Hell is inside them, the dark Underworld she worships, the endless night where Tyrus reigns.

No. My breath catches. We're not in Hell yet. This night isn't endless.

"Don't go!" I shout to Jules and Marcel. "The bats will follow you. This is the queen's magic. It will fade when dawn comes. We just have to ride it out."

It's only a hunch, but it's the best hope we have. Jules is right—the queen won't come here tonight. And if her strength is truly weaker in the catacombs, then her magic will be weaker, too. By morning, the bats will leave. At the very least, they'll be defeatable.

Jules and Marcel do as I say. I catch a glimpse of them crouching against the far wall by the door. Jules bends over Marcel, shielding him from the worst of the onslaught. "Don't let Ailesse escape, Bastien!" she cries.

I'd die first.

The bats scratch my back and screech in my ears. The last lamp extinguishes. Ailesse's body flinches beneath me as we're thrown into complete darkness. I have a strong grip on her arms now, and her hips are wedged between my knees. I can't hold her in this awkward position until dawn. Painstakingly, I wrestle her onto her stomach. She's strong, but thankfully not as strong as she was on the bridge.

I sprawl on top of her to anchor her to the slab. Her ankles are still bound together, so I press most of my weight onto her upper body. I fold my arms around her waist to lock her arms at her sides. She wriggles and elbows and bucks beneath me. I press my head into the crook of her neck and struggle to keep her down. I hate being this close to her, my bare chest against her back, and the wet fabric of her dress the only barrier between us. "If you were wise, you'd stop fighting and save what little strength you have left," I say, using all my willpower not to strangle her in the dark. "You know you can't outmatch me."

She pants for air. "You're wrong. We *are* perfectly matched. That's why the gods paired us together. So if *you* were wise, you'd stop resisting me and accept your fate." Her nose brushes my cheek as she turns her head toward mine. "You *will* die. You answered the call of my siren song. The ritual has been set in motion, and now it can't be broken. If I fail to kill you, the gods will complete the task."

My chest tightens. I wet my dry lips. "You're a liar and a child of murderers—a murderess yourself."

"I speak the truth, Bastien."

Unearthly screeches pierce the air. Bat wings rail against me. I barely notice. Ailesse's words echo through my head. Her poison warmth heats my body.

"Your death is mine," she tells me. "The gods will make sure of it."

13
Ailesse

I'M SLEEPING IN MY MOTHER'S bedchamber in Château Creux, wrapped in the fur from the albino bear she hunted to claim his graces. I'm warm. I'm comforted. I believe she might love me.

I open my eyes to the purest black. I'm not swathed in bear fur, but pressed beneath the weight of my *amouré*. My greatest enemy.

The bats must be gone. I don't hear their shrieks or flutters, only Bastien's deep and even breathing. His body has shifted in the night. He's sleeping at my side, no longer lying on top of me. One of his legs and an arm are draped over my back.

This is my chance to escape. My chance to kill him first.

I test the strength of the ropes around my ankles. They loosened during our struggle, unraveling in the spot where I tried to cut them.

With the careful quietness I've learned from hunting, I ease out from under Bastien and slip off the stone slab. I can't move far—the rope around my feet is still lodged beneath the large stone—so I sit and start prying the rest of the rope apart. The last fibers are tough. I need something sharp. I feel along the ground and find a limestone shard. As I saw at my bonds, I form the rest of my plan. I'll creep over to where Jules and Marcel should be sleeping. I'll follow the sound of his light snoring. Then I'll sneak into his pack. My grace bones must be inside, based on how adamantly he was guarding it.

Two rope fibers break. Only one strand remains. I saw with more urgency.

A scrape sounds, followed by a burst of orange light. My chest deflates.

"A valiant attempt to escape," Bastien commends me. He's no longer lying on the slab; he's standing over me, and he's managed to light an oil lamp. The flickering glow catches on every sculpted muscle of his chest. More proof he's stronger than me without the graces I've worked so hard to obtain. I bless the bats for every scratch they gave him.

"I wasn't trying to escape." I return his smirk with a spiteful glare. "I was trying to kill you."

He snorts and sets his lamp on a stool-sized stone. Enduring the bats has strengthened his confidence. He crouches and opens his hand, nodding at my shard of limestone.

My fist closes around it. It's a pitiful weapon, but it's the only one I have.

"Jules," Bastien calls. My gaze darts to her. She's huddled against the far wall beside Marcel, both of them freshly awakened.

She rises to her feet. Her light golden hair is a mess of tangles, and claw marks cover her skin, but the steady glimmer in her eyes says she hasn't been defeated. She limps to the knife I lost last night—resting near the open door—and kicks it to Bastien. He snatches it up and points the blade at my shard, a silent command to relinquish it.

I hate him.

I throw the shard at his face. He dodges it with ease.

Tyrus and Elara, why did you give me this boy?

Marcel pulls something from his pack, and Bastien groans. "It would have been useful to know you had more rope in there all this time."

"Spare rope wasn't foremost on my mind." Marcel tosses it to Bastien. He tends to his bleeding lip while Bastien and Jules drag me onto the stone slab to bind me up again. I don't resist them; Elara's Light is already dwindling inside me. Curse Bastien for being right about me needing to reserve my strength.

"Aren't you going to join me?" I ask with a smile I hope is sultrier than Jules's. If I can't fight my *amouré*, I'll goad him. "There's room for two on here." I pat the slab. "You certainly took advantage of that last night."

Jules freezes. "What is she talking about?"

Bastien shrugs. "I had to hold her still, didn't I?"

"Is that what you call that full-body embrace?" I arch my brow. Even by the light of one lamp, I see his ears flush red. He scoffs and looks between me and Jules, then abruptly strides away. "Help me with these lamps, Marcel," he grumbles. He grabs his dry shirt, yanks it back on, and steals an uncomfortable glance at me. I grin and wink at him.

Jules's teeth set on edge. "I'm going to make a run for food."

"Not on your bad leg," Bastien tells her.

"I'm fine," she snaps. "I need the fresh air."

"A supply run? Excellent." Marcel slowly nods, which I've come to understand is a sign of excitement. "Get the rest of my books, will you?"

Jules pulls a face. "I'm not carting a library down here."

"I only need my Bone Crier collection."

He has more than one book about the Leurress? I didn't realize any existed. We have a few books in Château Creux, thanks to Rosalinde, who learned to read from her *amouré* and taught all the novices. But none of the books are about us.

Marcel rights a tipped-over lamp and pours more oil into it. "I came across a passage once about ritual soulmates, but I can't remember the exact phrasing. If I can find a way to break the bond between Bastien and her"—he waves an idle hand at me—"then we can kill her. Problem solved."

Jules smiles. "In that case, I'll happily be your pack mule."

I bite my tongue. Their efforts will be pointless. The gods forged the bond I share with Bastien; no mortal can break it. But the longer these three are preoccupied by trying, the better my chances will be to outsmart them.

"One book is in the loft above Troupe de Lions," Marcel says, stifling a yawn like he's had the most uneventful night of his life.

"Two are in the threadmaker's cellar, and the fourth is in the abandoned stables behind Maison de Chalon."

Why are Marcel's books scattered throughout the city instead of in one place? Doesn't he have a home? Do any of them? Or are they always on the run?

"Got it." Jules heads for the door. I fidget on the slab. I hope I won't have to relieve myself while she's gone. I'm not asking one of the boys to take me to wherever it is that passes as a privy chamber down here.

Bastien lights another wick. "Pinch some more lamp oil if you can." *Pinch?* As in *steal?* Why am I not surprised? "And be back before nightfall. The queen will come tonight, and we need to be ready."

Jules nods. "Be careful while I'm gone. That Bone Crier is shiftier than the three of us combined."

"I won't take my eyes off her."

Jules frowns like that's exactly what she's afraid of. She ducks out through the low door and pushes it closed. The air is a little lighter now. Until Bastien spins around to face me with folded arms. His biceps flex beneath his sleeves. I sit up straighter and square my shoulders, showing him I have plenty of my own strength left. "Do you intend to stare at me until my mother comes?" I ask, offering him a honeyed smile. "What a brilliant strategy."

His eyes narrow. He rolls his tongue in his cheek. "Marcel, open your book again." He turns away and scrubs a hand over his face. "We have work to do."

"Good luck." I settle back against the slab wall. "You're going to need that and a miracle."

14
Sabine

I TREMBLE AS I REACH the bend in the forest path, intersecting the road to Castelpont.

Please, Elara, let Ailesse be alive.

I take a steeling breath and step onto the road. Twenty feet ahead, the ancient stone bridge and dry riverbed beneath it look stark and desolate in the morning sun, no longer mysterious under the full moon or foreboding in surrounding fog. Now they're only a painful reminder of Ailesse's overconfidence and my own inadequacy.

My feet pad the ground as I force my quaking legs closer. No sign of Ailesse yet, but her *amouré* could have stashed her body in the shadow of a parapet.

I set foot on the bridge. I don't see Ailesse lying on the stones. I glance at the riverbed below. She's not dashed to pieces down there either. Swallowing, I tentatively press forward to the high arch of the bridge, craning my neck so I can see down its other side. No sign of her. My legs give way with relief, and I lean against a parapet.

Ailesse is alive.

She has to be. Her *amouré* wouldn't have taken the pains to drag her anywhere else, only to kill her when he could do it here. He abducted her, like I suspected. Which is terrible, but at least her heart is still beating.

A glimpse of white snags the corner of my vision—five feet to my right, tucked up against the parapet.

Ailesse's bone knife.

I move to pick it up. This isn't the ritual weapon she used to kill the tiger shark; it's the knife she crafted for her rite of passage. Every Ferrier before her has done the same. I've never been taught if that's because of custom or necessity. Will Ailesse need this knife to make her sacrifice acceptable to the gods? I slip it under my belt, just in case.

I hurry off the bridge and climb down the riverbank, praying I'll see another flash of white. Odiva's warnings flood my mind.

The Chained need to be ferried. If they aren't, they'll feed off the souls of the living. Innocent people will die an everlasting death.

I walk the width of the riverbed, then back again several times, scanning any area where the bone flute could have fallen. I turn over rocks and kick the loose earth where I buried Ailesse's grace bones. It's no use. The bone flute isn't anywhere. The lie I told Odiva must be true—Ailesse's captors took it. I have to find them.

I race up the riverbank, but stop short when I see an elder Leurress peek out from the forest, using a different trail than mine. "Sabine," Damiana calls quietly. Her wolf fang bracelet glints in the sunlight as she motions me closer with a rapid wave of her hand.

I rush over to her. "Where are the others?" I glance around for the six elders she set off with last night. "Have you found Ailesse?" Desperate hope fills my chest.

She steals a look at Beau Palais over the wall of Dovré and pulls me off the road, under the cover of the trees. "We're still searching for her. We followed her captors' trail for six miles, but they kept changing paths." Her deep-set brown eyes lower. "We eventually lost their tracks where they merged into a stream."

I give her hand a comforting squeeze. Damiana tried her best, but I hope the other elders didn't give up so easily. "Didn't anyone pursue them down the stream?"

She nods and rubs her wrinkled olive brow. Damiana is almost sixty years old. I can't imagine she'll ferry much longer—or spend many more nights joining search parties for the *matrone*'s missing daughter. "The stream soon met a wide river, you see. Pernelle, Chantae, and Nadine are still there, doing what they can, but when I left, Nadine still hadn't picked up Ailesse's scent." Damiana shakes her head. "Her sense of smell is powerful, too."

I nod, picturing Nadine's eel skull hair comb. "What about Milicent, Roxane, and Dolssa?"

"They set off in separate directions in a blind search for Ailesse. Meanwhile, I traced the captors' trail back here to make sure we didn't miss any clues as to where they could have gone."

"I've already searched Castelpont and the riverbed." I say. "All I found was Ailesse's ritual knife."

Damiana releases a heavy exhale. "None of us want to return to Château Creux until we've exhausted the search, but we finally agreed to meet there by nightfall to report to the *matrone*. You should go there now, Sabine. You can tell her what I've told you."

"No." I shrug a step back. "I can't. Not without Ailesse. Not without more graces." My brows pull together. "I should have had them to begin with."

Damiana tilts her head and pats my cheek. "It's best not to fight your life's design for you, Sabine."

"And what is that?" I force a shaky smile. "To be a killer?" Every Leurress who survives has the same destiny.

"No, my dear." Damiana leans closer. Her silver-streaked braid slips in front of her shoulder. "An instrument of the gods. Neither Tyrus nor Elara can walk this earth, so they trust *us* to guide departed souls into their realms. We must do what it takes to rise to the occasion."

I meet her fervent eyes, and a measure of courage steals into me, as strong as a heady breath of Elara's Light.

I need to do what she says—rise to the occasion and be the person I'm meant to be. Someone capable of rescuing Ailesse. My friend won't be saved without me. It isn't just stubbornness that tells me so, but a deep sense—an innate grace all its own—that warns me her life is in my hands. The elders haven't found Ailesse yet, and who knows if the strange ritual Odiva performed last night resulted in anything? I don't trust it. Or her.

I need more graces. It's as simple as that.

I give Damiana a parting embrace and hurry away into the forest. My focus for now must be hunting.

The hours pass swiftly as I search for the right animal—maybe a pit viper for heat vision or a wild boar for muscle—but I only come across small birds, martens, and rabbits. I shoot two arrows at what I hope is a fox, but it's only the wind howling through the tall grass.

Twilight descends, and I've still found nothing satisfactory. I'm somewhere in the forest, maybe two miles outside Dovré. I weave through the trees, my senses alert. I don't have Ailesse beside me to warn when the breeze shifts and I should move downwind of my prey. I've never had a gift for hunting. I traveled with her and mimicked her stealthy movements, but I put off learning the art of killing for myself. Now I must learn. And quickly.

Sweat collects on the back of my neck. I wipe it away and readjust my grip on my bow. Despite my resolve, every tense muscle in my body whispers what I'm doing is wrong. Why should an innocent creature pay for my mistakes? But Odiva's voice rings louder in my mind: *You are not a child anymore. If you had obtained more graces before tonight, you would have been able to overpower your assailant. Ailesse would have had a fighting chance.*

The branches close in around me, and I tread deeper into the woods. A dull ache throbs through my head; my wounds have almost healed. If only my fire salamander grace could give me endless energy. I haven't slept in thirty-six hours, but I can't stop now.

I blow out a shaky breath. *You can do this, Sabine.* If I'm killing creatures to save Ailesse, I can forgive myself. I *will* forgive myself.

Something rustles above me. I flinch and glance up. My eyes grow wide.

A silver owl.

I fumble for an arrow in my quiver. Elara is finally smiling down on me. An owl will give me heightened hearing, as well as talon-grip strength.

I nock my bow. Swallow. Fire my arrow. The silver owl is too quick. She swoops from the branches and dodges my clumsy aim.

A few feet ahead, she lands on another branch. I grab a second arrow, but when I move closer, the bird screeches and flies another two trees away.

I stare at the owl. She stares back with her striking black eyes. A prickle of familiarity runs through me. Is this the same owl that flew over Castelpont before Ailesse's rite of passage?

No. What a ridiculous thought. Many silver owls must live near Dovré. Still, I can't take another owl sighting lightly. Ailesse and I didn't heed the owl's warning at Castelpont. We should have left when we saw the bird.

What if this *is* that same owl?

The owl doesn't blink or move. If she were telling me to abandon the hunt, wouldn't she leave here and not come back?

I take one step. Then another. On the third step, the silver owl spreads her wings. She flutters away until she reaches the edge of my vision in the darkening haze. She lands again, but this time on the ground. Uncharacteristic for an owl. It's almost like the gods are giving her to me.

I tentatively press forward, my fingers tingling with the urge to string my bow again, but I resist. This isn't the way a hunt works. An animal shouldn't make herself an easy target.

Conscientious of each swish of my dress and snag of my hem on the brambles, I reach the owl, stopping when I'm six feet away. My pulse thrums. The bird and I are standing in a small clearing. Twilight has passed, and the waning moon showers a soft glow over us. Elara's Light funnels into me and straightens my spine.

The silver owl tilts her head, as if she's waiting for me. I finally withdraw another arrow. Like all ritual weapons, each one in my quiver has an arrowhead carved from the bones of a stag. Death at its strike will mark the owl's soul and give her greater glory in Paradise.

That doesn't ease my conscience.

Gather your courage, Sabine. Smother your reservations.

Tears sting the back of my throat as I nock the arrow. The moment I do, the owl flies in my face. Her claws tear into my shoulder. I hiss and bat her away. She circles me and swoops off in the same direction as before. When she's almost out of view, she lands and peeks back at me. My rushing heartbeat slows.

She doesn't want me to kill her. She wants me to follow her.

I do, although none of this makes sense. Animals can't communicate with people. Not like this.

The owl moves deeper into the forest. Sometimes she flies short distances. Sometimes she skips from one spot to the next. The moon rises higher in the sky. The warm air grows a little cooler. At length, the owl brings me to the top of a grassy ravine. I wait for her to lead me onward, but she screeches three times and launches off her tree branch. She zooms away, straighter than the shaft of my arrow, and darts deep into the distance. She doesn't come back. Strange.

I glance around me and wrap my arms around myself. Why did the silver owl lead me here? The warm humidity drapes over me like a damp cloak. My skin itches from my dried blood. I'll bathe tomorrow while I boil the flesh off the animal I kill. Somehow, I'll endure it.

I hear a scuffling noise and freeze. I duck to the ground and grab another arrow. Maybe the owl brought me here to hunt the *best* prey.

I creep to the edge of the ravine. Halfway down to the bottom, a shadowy figure crawls out of a burrow. That's all I can make out from my twenty feet away.

The creature turns and starts climbing the steep hill. I backtrack a little. I don't want to spook it.

I nock my bow and flex my hand on the grip. I have to aim true. A smart creature will run or attack before it gives me time to shoot twice.

My heart pounds faster. Perspiration drips down my temples. Ailesse is the better archer, the better huntress, the better Leurress.

Enough, Sabine! You were born into this famille, *just like her. Your mother was a fierce Ferrier. Be the person she'd want you to be.*

The creature rises above the crest of the ravine like a black moon. I hold my breath.

I let the arrow fly.

Too late. It's seen me. It quickly flattens to the ground. My arrow whizzes into the empty air.

"You're going to have to do better than that," a deep and throaty voice calls. Feminine. *Human.*

A shock of cold hits me. I know that voice, that girl. She mocked me beneath Castelpont.

I suddenly understand. The owl didn't bring me to kill a creature. She brought me to the girl I fought under the bridge.

She brought me to Ailesse.

Her captors must be holding her in some kind of cave.

I nock another arrow and aim low at the grass. "Watch me."

My arrow flies wide. I hoped to hit her arm or leg—injure her, not kill her—but she's hidden too deep in the grass.

"Do you want your daughter?" she shouts.

I instinctively duck lower. She thinks I'm Odiva.

"Good luck. You'll have to walk past thousands of scattered bones. If you aren't brave enough to do that, then we'll kill your daughter slowly. We'll cut her into pieces, limb by limb, until she begs to die."

My heart rises in my throat. I can't find my breath. Ailesse isn't in a cave. Her captors took her to the catacombs.

I cast aside my bow and yank the bone knife from my belt. My hands shake with adrenaline. Ailesse can't be in that place. She's brave, but it's unholy. It will strip her of her Light. Kill her.

Elara, help me.

I launch at the girl. A furious but terrified cry peals from my lungs. The girl's face comes into focus as I race nearer.

Her smile slips.

I swipe my blade out at her. Her blond braid whips as she whirls aside to dodge it. Her wounded leg hasn't slowed down her reflexes.

"Your queen sent *you?*" she asks incredulously. "Well, tell her Bastien won't bargain with a servant. The queen must come herself."

"Bastien?" I slash out again, driving her backward to the edge of the ravine. "Is that the name of Ailesse's *amouré?*"

The girl's eyes tighten with hatred. "It's the name of the boy who will kill her."

Blood roars through my ears. I try to stab her, but she takes another backward step and drops out of sight.

My breath catches. I dart to the edge of the ravine. The girl is tumbling, but her fall is strategic. Halfway down, she straightens her body and pulls to a stop near the burrow hole. Without another glance at me, she slips feetfirst inside.

No! I can't follow her there. Not because of the Leurress' rules, but common sense—the one gift I have that surpasses Ailesse's. If I crawl inside that burrow, I'll face three opponents instead of one. I'll enter darkness devoid of Elara's Light, and with only one grace to aid me. It will mean my sure death. I'll have no hope of rescuing Ailesse.

"Sabine?"

The distant sound of my name stops my heart. *Ailesse?*

I jerk around and scan the moonlit forest. A silhouette comes into view. I make out the clear-cut outline of a crown, and I stiffen. It's not Ailesse. It's my *matrone*.

15
Ailesse

JULES STILL HASN'T RETURNED TO our catacombs chamber, even though it must be nearing nightfall, maybe later. Bastien takes a break from rechecking his supplies and pacing. He sits with one knee bent to his chest and draws serpentine patterns on the dusty ground, then grumbles at his pictures. I know what he's doing—plotting a strategy to kill my mother with his knowledge of the mazelike catacombs—though he doesn't look like much of a killer at the moment. He's chewing on the end of his tongue, the way a little child does, and it softens every harsh edge of his expression.

He sits back and runs his hands through his dark hair. His sea-blue eyes trail over to where I'm bound up on the limestone slab, ten feet away. His brows furrow. Too late I realize my gaze is soft on him and my lips are curved upward. I immediately stiffen and school my features.

Bastien picks at his fingernails, then scoots over to Marcel and whispers something in his ear. The younger boy peers up at me. "All right," he says, and shuts his book. He stands and stretches, then picks up a tumbler of settled water and brings it over to me. My throat parches at the sight of it. This was Bastien's idea? I glance at him, but he's studiously avoiding my gaze.

"It isn't poisoned," Marcel says, when I don't touch it. Of course it isn't poisoned. My captors wouldn't risk killing Bastien by killing me. "Although you do have to grow accustomed to the taste," he adds.

I accept the tumbler, sniff the water, and take a tentative sip. The mineral taste of limestone is heavy, but at least no grit coats my mouth. I drink the rest in one long gulp and release a small sigh. "Thank you." The words spill out before I think better of them, and Bastien's brows lift and wrinkle again. I pass the tumbler back to Marcel.

"So . . . how many of you are there?" Marcel asks.

"What are you doing?" Bastien frowns at him.

"Until I get my other books, I've no better resource than her. I might as well try to learn something. Jules will be back any time now, which means the queen will be, too."

Bastien snorts. "Good luck getting her to talk."

Unruffled by the challenge, Marcel crosses his arms and stares me down. He doesn't look as though he's trying to intimidate me. Maybe that's why I answer him.

"Forty-seven." Or maybe I answered because Bastien said I wouldn't.

Marcel's eyes fly wide. It's the most animated I've seen him. "So many?"

Bastien huffs. "She's lying. Everyone would know if that many Bone Criers lived around here. *We* certainly would."

My gaze flits between the boys. I wasn't lying. "Would you like to know more?" I ask Marcel, making a point to speak to him and not Bastien. I can test Marcel's knowledge of the Leurress while he tests mine—and make sure he doesn't know anything more that can endanger my *famille*. Better yet, I'll distract him from plotting a way to kill my mother.

He gives an unabashed laugh. "I *always* like to know more. About everything."

I smile. I shouldn't like him, but I do. Marcel's candidness reminds me of Sabine. He's a year or two younger, like her, maybe fifteen or sixteen. "Then why don't we strike a bargain? For every question I answer, I'll do so truthfully, but you must answer one of mine in return."

"This is ridiculous," Bastien says, but Marcel waves him off like he would a gnat.

"Agreed."

I scoot into a more comfortable position and prop myself against the wall of the slab. "Do you know why the Leurress exist?" I begin.

Marcel cocks his head. "*Leurress?*"

"You call us Bone Criers."

"None of my books mention that name."

"I doubt any were written by my *famille*."

He gives a conceding nod. "Well, you exist to—"

"Torment men," Bastien interjects. "Murder them. Sacrifice them to your gods."

"She wasn't asking you," Marcel says. Bastien rolls his eyes. "You Bone Criers—*Leurress*, that is—are parasitic in nature. You can't thrive on your own. You need the moon and stars and animal bones . . . and, well, what Bastien said—human sacrifice."

"What if I told you that you were wrong?"

Lines pinch between Marcel's brows. "Isn't it my turn to ask a question?"

"Yes."

He shuffles another step forward and sits on the stone anchoring the rope I'm tied up with. "So"—he scratches his head—"*why* am I wrong?"

"We aren't parasites. We exist to ferry the dead." I wait, hook baited, for Marcel to bite, to tell me if he knows *where* we ferry the dead. But his expression is blank.

"Pardon?"

"We labor to obtain the sacred gifts that give us strength and skill to guide souls into the eternal realms." *Doesn't he know about the soul bridge?* "The rite of passage is our test of loyalty to become a Ferrier. That's the whole point."

Marcel's mouth slowly parts. "Oh." He nods a few times. "Well, that's illuminating."

Bastien's vivid eyes narrow on me. He looks . . . conflicted.

"You really weren't aware that the Leurress are Ferriers?" I ask Marcel. He shrugs. Once more, I'm amazed at the holes in my captors' knowledge. If they don't know something this fundamental, maybe I shouldn't worry about them knowing my biggest secret—that no one but me can kill Bastien or *I* will die; the curse goes both ways. For that reason, my mother won't kill him when she comes for me. If she did, she'd sacrifice her only heir. I'd lose all my leverage if Bastien knew that.

"One of the folktales *does* mention the dead being ferried," Marcel says. "But I thought that part was mythical—something that happened when you killed your victims. I didn't realize you *were* the Ferriers, or that Ferriers were real at all."

"Believe every story you hear," Bastien murmurs, his gaze distant. Marcel and I pause to look at him. He blinks and rolls a crick from his neck. "How kind of you to lead souls to Hell *after* you slaughter them."

I take a steeling breath. He'll never understand the Leurress aren't evil. I turn back to Marcel and pose my next question. "Was your father chosen by the gods, too?"

Bastien scoffs. "Meaning did he have the good fortune to be murdered by your family?"

My fingers curl, but I ignore him and wait for Marcel to answer. Marcel's still acting a little dumbfounded, hunched over and resting his elbows on his knees. "My father? Um, yes . . . I was seven when he . . ." He clears his throat. "Jules was nine."

Marcel and Jules are siblings? Except for rare twins, siblings are unheard of among the Leurress. We don't live with *amourés* long enough to bear more than one child.

"He fell ill after the Bone Crier left us." Marcel's gaze drops, and he rubs a stubborn stain of limestone sludge on his trousers. He isn't bitter like Jules or vindictive like Bastien. Marcel must have stayed with them all this time to survive—and because they're family.

Bastien's jaw muscle flexes. "He didn't deserve his fate."

"No one would, but . . . well, he was a great father." Marcel's mouth quirks in a half smile. "He used to make up songs while he was working. He was a scribe, you see, and some of the texts he copied were tragedies. So he'd change up the words and set them to a silly tune. Jules and I would roll on the ground laughing." He chuckles, but doesn't stop picking at the stain.

A surprising wave of sadness wells within me, and I forget about our game of questions. "I never knew my father," I say quietly. "He died before I was born, like every father of every daughter in my *famille*. I'll meet him in Elara's Paradise one day, but . . ." My voice quavers. "The ache of not knowing him in *this* life is very real." I press my lips together and inwardly shake my head at myself. I sound so much like Sabine. She's the one who laments the cost of being a Leurress. I spent so much time striving to ease her conscience that I never allowed myself to mourn and wonder *what if*.

My eyes lift and fall on Bastien. The expression on his face treads some middle ground between confusion and anger and, perhaps, ever so fleetingly, his own sorrow.

I tense and look away. My bruises remind me he can't be pitied. I offer Marcel a gentle smile. "At least you were blessed to know your father for a few years."

Bastien stands. "You're outright appalling, do you know that? You think Marcel's luckier than you?"

I recoil and meet his glare head-on. "I'm only saying I lost my father the same as you did."

"Oh, yes?" He stalks closer. "Tell me, did *you* love your father before you lost him? And when he died, were *you* left with nothing?" I swallow, resenting the heat flushing my cheeks. "Did you have to beg from strangers and learn to steal when their charity ran dry? Do you know what it's like to spend cold nights in the alleys of Dovré, huddled in garbage just to get warm?"

I shift uncomfortably. "I'm not the woman who killed your father, Bastien."

"No." His voice sharpens to a deadly point. "You're just the girl who's sworn to kill his son."

"I'm trying to spare you from a more painful death! Do you want to end up like Marcel's father?"

Marcel winces, and I immediately regret my words. "I'm sorry. I didn't mean to—" Why am I apologizing to one of my captors? *Because Sabine would.* She'd extend thoughtfulness to someone mourning a loved one. "I'm only trying to say I'd never want anyone to suffer like he did."

Bastien scrubs his hands over his face, so frustrated he can't even speak for a moment. "Do you hear yourself? *You* cause the suffering!"

My hackles rise. I'm not like Sabine. "I can't help the fact that the gods chose you for me, or that you're destined to die the way you will. Why can't you understand that?" I blow out an exasperated breath. The sooner I kill Bastien, the better I'll feel. We can work out our differences in the afterlife.

The door to the chamber slides open. Jules ducks in. She eyes all of us suspiciously. The tension is so thick it sticks to my lungs. She limps over to Marcel and breaks the awkward silence, saying, "We better eat this bread before it turns to mold." She presses a round loaf into his hands and drops a heavy bag of books at his feet. "I carried all that weight on my head through the water. You're welcome."

He inhales deeply and smiles. "You're a goddess."

"I'm better than a goddess. Those books weren't the only things I kept dry." She hefts another pack off her shoulder and hands it to Bastien. "Keep that away from the oil lamps," she warns.

He gives her a quizzical look and pulls out a small barrel from the pack, no longer than the length of my forearm. "I'm guessing this isn't ale."

She grins and leans on her good leg. "It's black powder."

Black powder? What is that?

Bastien's eyes widen. "You're joking. How did you break into Beau Palais?"

"I didn't get it from the castle."

"But Beau Palais has the only cannons in Dovré."

"Not for long. At least fifty powder casks were carted from the king's alchemists to the royal shipyard today, and let's just say His Majesty should have sent more than four guards on the journey."

Bastien stares at Jules, and then bursts into warm laughter. "You really are a goddess."

A pretty flush dusts her cheeks, and she rocks back on her

heels. Black powder must be a weapon of some kind.

"Anyway, we need to hurry." Jules crosses her arms. "Night has fallen, and one of the Bone Criers—that witness from Castelpont—is already lurking outside."

My stomach tenses. Sabine. She shouldn't come in here. She only has one grace bone.

"Found it," Marcel says around a mouthful of bread. He's already sprawled on his stomach with three of his four books open. "It's from *Ballads of Old Galle*."

Bastien carefully sets the cask of black powder on the ground. "Go on."

Pushing his floppy hair out of his eyes, Marcel reads:

The fair maiden on the bridge, the doomed man she must slay,
Their souls sewn together, ne'er a stitch that will fray,
His death hers and none other 'cross vale, sea, and shore,
Lest her breath catch his shadow evermore, evermore.

Marcel rolls into a sitting position and sets the book on his crossed legs. "There, Bastien. That should comfort you."

He frowns. "It should?"

"'His death hers and none other.'" Marcel taps the words on the brittle page. "Because Ailesse summoned the magic on the bridge, only she can kill you, or she'll die with you."

My muscles go rigid. Jules steps forward. "Where did it say that?" She steals the words from my mouth.

"Her 'breath' is her life, and his 'shadow' is his death," Marcel explains. "I never read it like that before, but now it's obvious.

Ailesse will 'catch death,' like you'd catch a cold, if someone other than herself kills Bastien."

Bastien rubs his jaw. "But . . . I still die?"

"Yes, but that isn't the point," Marcel says. Bastien doesn't look so sure. "This is one less thing you have to worry about when the queen comes tonight. She won't dare to kill you. She isn't going to risk her daughter's life."

A sudden coldness grips me. My leverage is gone.

Bastien cocks a brow, finally understanding, and swivels to face me with a crooked grin. "Thanks for making me invincible."

My stomach rolls, and I close my eyes. Bastien is going to be bolder now. As if he needed any more confidence. My mother will have to exercise caution around him, but he won't have to hold back any vengefulness. I only pray she doesn't bring Sabine. I won't let Bastien near her.

I raise my chin and meet his poisonous stare with more venom. "You forget you cannot shield yourself from your greatest danger, *mon amouré*. I am the instrument of your death, not my mother. And I swear I will kill you before you even attempt to kill her." *Or Sabine.*

Conviction burns inside me, like a sudden burst of Elara's Light. Behind Bastien and the others, the air ripples with silvery heat. I've never seen anything like it.

A flickering image appears. I gasp. Bastien whips out his knife and looks over his shoulder, but the image is gone. In an instant, what I saw sputtered out and disappeared.

A silver owl with outspread wings.

16
Sabine

ODIVA SWEEPS NEARER TO THE edge of the ravine, where I stand, still quaking from seeing one of Ailesse's captors. Four of the elder Leurress fan out behind her: Milicent, Pernelle, Dolssa, and Roxane. Next to Odiva, they are our *famille*'s strongest Ferriers.

"Why are you here, Sabine?" Odiva asks, her curious gaze traveling over my necklace—Ailesse's necklace—to see if it bears a new grace bone. I know why *she's* here. And how. Odiva told me last night she'd be able to track her daughter with familial magic, blood of her blood, bones of her bones. Magic I don't possess.

I open my mouth to explain about the silver owl, but then I hesitate. I can't tell Odiva that an owl of all creatures—a bird my *famille* finds superstitious—guided me here of its own volition. She'll think I've gone mad. "I was hunting for more graces and found one of Bastien's accomplices in the forest. I chased her here."

"Bastien?" Odiva arches a sleek brow.

"Ailesse's *amouré*. The girl spoke his name."

The *matrone* nods slowly, her black eyes drifting past me to the ravine.

"She slid into some kind of tunnel opening down there. It looked small."

"Nothing we don't have the strength to claw through."

I bite my lip, delaying the last thing I must tell her: "It leads to the catacombs."

A small furrow mars Odiva's smooth forehead. The other Leurress exchange tense glances and step to the edge of the ravine. Odiva waited until nightfall to confront Ailesse's captors, which means she must have been counting on the full strength of Elara's Light. And in the catacombs, she and the elders will be cut off from it. They'll have to rely on the reservoir inside them, in addition to their graces.

"Are you sure?" Dolssa holds her snake rib necklace to her chest as she leans forward to take a closer look down the ravine.

"Unless the girl was lying," I reply. "She said the bones of several thousand skeletons were scattered around in there." Pernelle winces.

Odiva is unmoving for a moment, her bloodred lips pursed in thought. "The catacombs beneath the city *could* reach this far. The quarries are extensive, and the victims of the great plague were countless in number." Her eyes narrow. "Ailesse's captors must know we receive strength from the Night Heavens. That is why they have taken her here—and why they want us to follow."

My stomach tightens. "So it's a trap?"

A faint smile touches her mouth. "Ailesse's *amouré* is a clever boy, isn't he? I will enjoy watching her kill him."

I swallow the bitter tang in my mouth. I understand that Bastien has to die so Ailesse can live, but it doesn't mean I take pleasure in it.

"Come," Odiva commands the other Leurress. "We will show these commoners our graces are still treacherous when weakened by the dark."

The elders raise their chins. Some lift their eyes to the starry sky above, soaking in one last measure of Elara's Light. They descend into the ravine, one after another—Roxane, Milicent, and Dolssa.

Pernelle hesitates. A slight tremor runs through her ivory hands. At thirty-nine years old, she's the youngest elder, and the only one to betray any fear. It's a comfort to know I'm not alone. She watches the others as they claw the burrow hole wider with powerful strength. "Isn't there another catacombs entrance we can use?" she asks Odiva, her honey-blond hair rippling across her face in the breeze. "One that doesn't lead to a trap, and gives us the advantage?"

Odiva's perfect posture doesn't budge. "We are Ferriers, experienced in fighting the vicious dead. We have seventeen grace bones between us. What more advantage do we need? Summon your courage." The *matrone* sets her finger on the fox vertebra pendant hanging around Pernelle's neck. "This should give you fortitude, if you do not resist."

Pernelle presses her lips together and musters a small nod. She climbs down the ravine to join the others. I follow her, but Odiva clutches my arm.

"No, Sabine. If you do not have the tenacity to kill another animal, how can you help us tonight?" Her voice isn't cold, only concerned, but her words hurt all the same. "What you *do* need to do is earn another grace bone." She sighs and gently squeezes my arm before releasing it. "Do not return to Château Creux until you do."

My eyes burn hot. "But—"

She turns away and plunges into the ravine.

My legs tense. I walk three steps after her. Then stop myself. Shift back and shake my head. Grip my salamander skull. Panic builds inside me. "Please, please, please . . ." I need to be with the elders. I should be rescuing Ailesse. But my grace bone isn't enough. *I'm* not enough.

I spin away and run. Tears stream from my eyes. I furiously swipe them away.

Stop crying, Sabine!

I'm not weak. I'm not a coward.

I'm tired of everyone believing I am. I'm tired of believing it myself.

I run faster. I claw past branches and kick away underbrush. I nock an arrow on my bow and scour the ground, search the trees. I burst into a copse of pine.

A fluttering noise rustles above me. A shard of moonlight shines on the bird I've startled. White stripes blaze across the bend of its dark wings. A nighthawk. Common. No bigger than a crow.

I don't care.

My arrow flies. The bird falls. I thank the gods, and I curse them. I'm crying again. I can't help it.

I've killed my second creature.

And now I'll claim his every last grace.

17
Bastien

ALL I SMELL IS AILESSE. Earth, fields, flowers. Everything green and alive. A twisted trick of her magic. I have to remember what she really is. Darkness. Decay. Death.

My nose brushes her hair. I fight a shudder of prickling heat. I have to hold her this close, or she'll make a run for it. She's only tied up by her hands right now. I cut her ankles free so she could walk here with me tonight. We're standing in a dangerous tunnel of the catacombs—a place I'll use to my advantage—if I can get my mind off the warm girl in my arms.

"Is it safe?" I ask Marcel, eyeing the wooden plank in front of us. He and I spent the last hour dragging it here from a scaffold in the crumbling limestone mines beneath us. Now it's stretched across a chasm, fifteen feet wide, where the floor has caved in.

This tunnel would look like any other catacombs tunnel without that gaping hole near its dead end.

Marcel steps on the end of the plank and bounces a little, testing it one last time. "I wager yes." But it's the floor under the weight of the plank that worries me. I pull Ailesse back a little, steering her clear of the fissures at our feet. Jules hangs back, too, her face pale. As long as only one of us stands on the fragile area at a time, the tunnel should hold.

Marcel strolls back to us. Once he's past the cracks in the floor, I let go of Ailesse and nudge her toward the plank to cross it. On the other side of the chasm is a six-by-six-foot ledge, all that remains of the tunnel floor before it hits the dead end. "Go on," I prod her again. She finally moves away, and I inhale a steadying breath of Ailesse-free air.

She walks, light on her toes, to the edge of the chasm, then looks below and goes rigid. I know what she sees—nothing. When Jules and I first found this spot a few months ago, I dared her to come close to the edge. We threw bits of limestone rubble in the pit and tried to hear it hit the bottom. No sound carried up to us, even when we rolled in a large stone.

Ailesse squares her shoulders, exhales slowly, and walks onto the plank. Because her hands are tied, she can't hold out her arms to stay balanced. She reaches the middle of the plank and wobbles. I tense, fighting the urge to run and help her. She's lost the agility she had at Castelpont.

When she arrives on the far ledge, her head falls back in relief. My shoulders relax. Why am I so worried about her?

Because if she dies, you die, too, Bastien.

Right. I flex my hands and pull Marcel aside. He smells faintly of black powder. "Is everything ready?" I ask, aware that Ailesse is straining to hear us. We've kept the most important part of our plan a secret from her so she can't warn her mother.

"Yes." Marcel side-eyes her. "The, um, *black trail* is set, and the *thunder* will *clap* when you're ready." I wince with each word he emphasizes. That was about as subtle as a flying brick.

"Go take your post, then." I give him a bolstering slap on the shoulder. He doesn't show a scrap of uncertainty, but I know him better than that.

As he swaggers away with an oil lamp, Jules shakes off some of the dried mud from her sleeves. She never had a chance to rinse the limestone silt from her clothes after the supply run earlier. She glances from me to Ailesse and fidgets with the end of her braid.

"Are you going to be all right, being alone with her? Who knows how long we're going to have to wait for the queen to come."

I snort. "Of course I will be. Is the pulley rigged?" Marcel and I nabbed one from the scaffolds, along with the plank.

She nods. "And I found a safe hiding spot for myself."

"Good." I grab a flaming torch from one of the crude sconces along the tunnel wall, more relics of the quarrymen who once worked down here. Over the last couple years, Jules and I made a ready supply of torches for catacombs exploring. They don't burn as long as oil lamps, but they're much brighter. Six more torches are lit on this side of the chasm. They'll help me see any move the queen makes.

Jules adjusts the quiver of arrows she's slung across her back. "Bastien?" she says in a timid rasp. For a flicker of a moment, she's the girl I met six years ago. Desperate, starving, eager to make an ally. She starts to reach for me. "In case this goes wrong tonight, I want you to know—"

"Nothing bad is going to happen, Jules."

She nods again and glances down at my hand. I realize I'm holding hers, though I didn't mean anything by it. I swiftly let go. "See you soon." I make quick work of crossing the plank.

When I join Ailesse on the ledge, she looks at me with thoughtful eyes. Almost sympathetic. I slide my torch in a sconce and glare at her. My best mask is anger. I don't need her telling me Jules doesn't pierce my soul again.

"You're cunning, Bastien." Ailesse's voice is smooth and sure. "I acknowledge that. But whatever trap you've laid for my mother is certain to fail. She won't be coming alone either. She'll bring the most skilled among my *famille*. Remember, I warned you."

I smirk. She's been saying much of the same all day. Empty threats. Vain attempts to intimidate me. It doesn't rock my confidence. Within the hour, I'll take the queen's life and have my vengeance. As for any others she brings, I've planned for them, too. I'll take all their bones so they can never hurt another man again. Then I'll deal with Ailesse and our soul-bond. The thought makes my stomach wrench.

Don't think about the bond now. Focus on the task at hand.

Across the chasm from one another, Jules and I shove the plank into the pit. It falls silently into the darkness, and I swallow hard. Now the queen won't be able to get to our side, and Ailesse can't escape the ledge. But I can't either. I'm stuck here with her perfect smell and warm body until Jules brings both of us back across the chasm when this is over. She's already devised a way involving rope.

Jules picks up her gear and forces an encouraging smile. I try and fail to give her one back. She's risking her neck, same as me, but I don't want to lead her on. Instead, I nod and look away—from both girls, my soulmate and my best friend. *Merde*, my head is a mess.

Jules's ring of lamplight fades. Then she's gone. My heart kicks faster. I'm hyperaware of being stranded with Ailesse. If I moved a little closer, I could fill my lungs with her scent. I could touch her hair and . . .

I blow out a sharp breath. *Pull yourself together, Bastien.* Ailesse's allure is still affecting me from her dark spell at Castelpont. It should have worn off after Jules dug up her last bone under the bridge.

What if it *did* wear off and my attraction is real?

I pace the narrow length of our six-foot ledge. I rub the back of my neck and roll out my shoulders. I try not to meet Ailesse's eyes. Or wonder. But as the wait drags out for the queen to come, my curiosity builds. There's so much I still don't know about Ailesse. The conversation she had with Marcel keeps needling my mind. "Why do you need physical strength to ferry the dead?" I blurt, unable to resist talking to her. "If that's the point of your bone magic, I don't understand. The dead don't have bodies, right? They're just ghosts."

Ailesse's brows lift at my sudden interest. "Not exactly. The dead are kind of in between. They become tangible after they rise from their graves." She brushes a few strands of tangled hair from her eyes with her tied hands. My fingers twitch, wanting to help her. "Some souls are destined for the Underworld, and they rebel."

I chew on that for a moment. "What happens if they don't go to the Underworld?"

"They escape back to the mortal realm and hurt innocent people."

"So your goal is to *protect* people?"

"Yes."

I can barely comprehend that. My chest grows heavy, and I shift on my feet. I can't shake the realization sinking inside me. I have no idea who Ailesse really is. "If you're trying to protect the innocent, then why do you kill them—the ones you meet on bridges?"

Lines crease between her auburn brows. "Because . . ." Her mouth parts as she searches for what to say. Has she ever even thought about this before? "Tyrus and Elara won't let us help anyone if we don't."

And just like that, my blood runs hot again. "You know, there's a reason people stopped worshipping your gods."

She stiffens. "Slaying our *amourés* proves our commitment to the gods and *their* path for our lives, not our own. It's about loyalty, obedience."

"That absolves everything, doesn't it?"

Her nostrils flare. She takes a step toward me. I take a step toward her.

She's facing the chasm. My back is to it. One sharp kick, and she could send me to my death. I quickly step aside. Ailesse's breath catches as she stares across the pit. I jerk around to follow her gaze. In the distance, just past the last of the six torches, a dim figure appears.

The queen.

I react on instinct. Withdraw my knife. Grab Ailesse. Hold her against me on the ledge, her back to my chest, my blade to her throat.

The queen sweeps into the amber glow of the torchlight and stalks forward. Four attendants flank her. I only spare them a brief glance. I can't tear my focus from Ailesse's mother, the most formidable woman I've ever seen.

More torchlight shines on her as she draws closer. Her dress is waterlogged with the catacombs' silt, but it only makes her look more threateningly beautiful. Light-headedness rushes through me. She's almost lovelier than her daughter—except in a severe and opposing way. Stark-white skin and raven hair. Black eyes and bloodred lips. Smooth cheeks and a sharp jawline. I make a quick study of her bones of power: a jagged crown, a necklace of claws, and talons on each shoulder. One claw and one talon are bigger, whiter. They're the carved bones.

She takes another step, five feet from the drop-off of the pit, and another fifteen feet from where we're standing on the opposite ledge. "That's far enough." I nod, pointing out the fragile ground at her feet. "Unless you want the princess to die where she stands."

She stops without tensing and lifts a hand. The other Bone

Criers halt. I look at each woman closer. A wave of hot then cold rolls through me. They're all stunning and unique, with different shades of skin and impressive bones, especially the wreath of antlers on one woman and the rib cage necklace on another—though none are as striking as the queen's. "You won't kill Ailesse," she says calmly, but her rich voice cuts the dense air and booms across the divide. "She must have told you that you would die, too."

I give her a stony glare, though my stomach drops. She just confirmed my life really is tied to her daughter's. "You'd be surprised how far I'm willing to go for revenge." I bear down on my blade, and Ailesse sucks in a pinched breath.

The queen's eyes linger on her. If there's any love in her expression, I can't read it. Maybe she won't make this exchange. "What is it you want, Bastien?" she asks me.

I flinch at my name, startled she knows it. "The bones," I reply. "All of them."

"We are in the catacombs. You will have to be more specific."

She knows very well which bones I mean. "The bones that give you magic."

"Ah, our grace bones." She folds her hands together. "The power you call 'magic' is a gift from the gods. It is not to be trifled with, lest the gods smite you. But if you insist—"

"I do. A small price for your daughter's life."

"My daughter *and* the bone flute," the queen stipulates.

Ailesse opens her mouth to speak, but I hold the knife tighter against her throat, a silent warning not to reveal that Jules broke the flute. "Agreed," I say, though I have no intention of keeping my promise.

The queen gestures to her attendants. They share troubled glances.

"One person at a time," I order. "I want to see three bones from each of you."

The queen lifts her chin, a challenge in her gaze, and nods at each Bone Crier. A basket lowers from a gap in the tunnel ceiling. The hidden pulley wheel screeches. Jules is up there doing her part.

The Bone Criers place their bones in the basket, and I count them. Some are set in bracelets, anklets, necklaces, earrings, and even hair combs. One woman blinks back tears, as if she's passing over a child. Good. I want this to be painful for them.

I've lost track of the queen. She's somewhere at the back of the group. She murmurs something to her attendants, and they part to let her pass. She glides forward to the basket, locks eyes with Ailesse, and removes her talon epaulettes, her claw necklace, and, last of all, her crown. It's made from a twisting vertebra. Probably a deadly snake.

As soon as the queen sets her last bone in the basket, she grips the rope so it can't be hoisted up. "We will make the exchange at the same time," she tells me. "Lower another rope for Ailesse."

"The terms are mine, not yours," I counter. "Let go of the basket and come to the edge of the pit."

Her black eyes narrow. She releases the rope and glances at the fractures on the floor. "I'll do this alone," she says to the other

Bone Criers. They shift backward.

I hope Marcel is ready. There's a second tunnel beneath us, a near copy of this one. At its end, the floor has also crumbled away into the chasm.

The queen slowly approaches the pit, her posture flawless. She's four feet from the edge. Three feet. A hairline fissure cracks beneath her. She hesitates.

My chest tightens. The queen needs to come a little closer, where the ground is most fragile. We only have one cask of black powder.

Two feet.

"A clap of thunder," Ailesse murmurs to herself. Her body goes rigid with understanding. "Run!" she screams at her mother. "The tunnel is going to rupture!"

The queen's eyes fly wide. "Fall back!" she commands the other Leurress. "Roxane, the bones!"

"Now, Marcel!" I shout.

Roxane whips out a knife from a hidden sheath at her thigh. She cuts the basket free and races away with it.

I yank Ailesse back to the far wall of our small ledge and brace for the blow. My heart pounds three times. Nothing happens. How long is Marcel's powder trail?

The queen grins. She hasn't retreated like her attendants. She tenses to jump. I eye the fifteen feet between us. "She'll never make it."

"You've forgotten something," Ailesse says to me. "A *matrone* wears five bones, not three."

Five?

I never forgot—I never knew.

The queen leaps. Her arc is tremendous.

I release Ailesse and take a defensive stance. Ailesse rushes to the drop-off of the ledge toward her mother.

The queen is halfway across the chasm.

BOOM.

Chunks of stone burst in the air. I'm thrown on my back. Dust clouds choke my lungs. I push up to my feet, coughing. I wave away the smoke.

I can't find the queen.

And Ailesse is gone.

18
Ailesse

I CLING TO THE CHASM wall, my hands tied. I'm barely able to keep purchase on the thin outcropping of rock. Rubble rains down on me. My muscles tense. Fingers cramp. If I fall, how long will it take before I hit the bottom and shatter every bone in my body? *Don't think like that, Ailesse.* I'm not ready to die.

"Mother!" My ragged cry doesn't echo. It's swallowed by the settling debris and thick air.

All I see above me is a veil of dust, dimly lit by torchlight. How far down the wall did I slide? I glance across the chasm to the opposite wall to find my bearings. When I was standing with Bastien on the ledge, I saw another tunnel below ours. That's where Marcel must have placed the black powder. But no sign of that tunnel exists anymore. It's either fully collapsed or I've plunged far below it. I whimper at the thought.

My feet dig at the wall, groping for a foothold. Each time my toes catch a ridge, it crumbles away. I heave a panicked breath. If only I had my ibex bone.

Stop, Ailesse. Pining for what I've lost isn't going to help me. I briefly close my eyes, trying to feel the strength and balance of my ibex grace. My muscles must remember.

I steadily drag one leg up until my toe finally grips a foothold. I carefully set my weight on it, my calf cramping. I slide my other leg up, but my foot can't find purchase. The other foot slips, and my knee slams the wall.

"Mother!" I hate the sob that rips from my lungs. How weak she'll think me. My legs dangle uselessly, my hands tremble. I can't hold on much longer.

"Ailesse!"

My head snaps up. My mother's voice is faint. I can't tell if she's near or far due to the way the catacombs eat sound. "I'm down here!" I instinctively shout. But she doesn't need to hear me or see me to gain a sense of direction. She still has her tooth band from a whiptail stingray and the skull of a giant noctule bat. She pried the latter from her crown when Bastien wasn't looking. Between the two bones, my mother has a sixth sense and echolocation. Even if she can't see me, she'll find me. As long as I can hang on.

My hands grow clammy. My grip is sliding. I squeeze with all my might. *Elara, help me.*

My vision blurs, shimmering with silver. A hazy form appears.

Ghostlike, transparent. Its wings take shape and unfurl.

The silver owl. The same one I glimpsed for a moment in the secret chamber.

The owl screeches, and a surge of strength flows into me.

"I'm here!" my mother says. I startle. The owl vanishes. So does my newfound strength. I gasp, my mind reeling. What just happened?

"Ailesse!"

I look behind me at the opposite wall of the chasm. The dust thins. My mother's lithe figure descends. She must have been blasted back to that side of the tunnel from the force of the explosion.

She eases down a rope—the severed pulley rope. She's extended it to its full length. "I'm going to swing out for you."

I nod with a steadying breath. This torture is almost over.

She kicks away from the wall and propels across the fifteen feet between us. She grazes my wall, but her rope hangs askew, throwing off her aim. Her momentum pulls her back to her starting point before she's able to reach me. She tries again, but her body suddenly twists when she's halfway across. An arrow whizzes by her.

"Careful!" I cry. Jules must be above with her bow.

My mother doesn't look worried. She hovers against her wall of the chasm, waiting for a gap between the arrows. Jules is firing blindly, so my mother has the advantage. She'll sense the arrows as they fly.

"Hurry," I beg, my body trembling with exertion. My fingers feel like they might break if I have to hold on much longer.

More chunks of limestone fall from above. Another section of the tunnel is caving in. My mother scrambles sideways and scales the wall with impressive ability—another grace from her bat skull. She doesn't wait for the rubble to clear. She launches for me again, taking advantage of the distraction. My chest swells. She must love me, or she wouldn't endanger herself like this.

She lands closer to me this time and grasps a protruding stone to anchor herself. She's two feet away, her waist level to my head as she hangs by the end of her rope. I could reach her leg if not for my bound hands.

She scans the nearly smooth wall around me. She can't find anything else to grab on to. "We need to cut your hands free."

"How?" The rock I'm clinging to isn't sharp enough to saw through my rope.

"I have a small knife. I'm going to toss it to you."

"But I can't let go to catch it."

"Find a foothold to distribute your weight, then open one hand."

My heartbeat thrashes. Blood pounds behind my eyes as I try not to panic. I grapple with my feet once more, struggling to find purchase. Nothing. With one last burst of adrenaline, I pull up a little higher and my right knee knocks against a jutting stone. I wrench my leg up and balance my knee on it. I'm not fully secure, but some of the pressure eases off my hands. "I'm ready," I say, sweat dripping down my face.

My mother holds her rope by one hand and pulls a thin knife from a concealed slit in her dress. "On the count of three."

I nod, praying I can grab it.

She exhales in concentration. "One. Two. Three."

She drops the blade. I lean into the wall. Release one hand from the rock outcropping. Grasp for the hilt.

My mother's aim is exact, but my hands are bound too tight. The knife glances off me, nicking my skin as it tumbles into the darkness.

Three more arrows zoom by. I clutch the rock outcropping again. One arrow almost strikes my head before it pings off the wall.

My fingers slip off my handhold. They're down to their last knuckle grip. "Mother!" I cry.

Her eyes fill with pain. She shakes her head. She doesn't know how to help me. Her rope jerks down a foot before it catches still again. She glances up. "They're cutting the rope."

I feel blood drain from my face. My mother can leap a chasm with her bat grace, but she can't spread wings to fly out of one. How will she save herself? Or me?

We stare at each other. The brief moment suspends. I can't breathe, can't think. We're both going to fall and die. Then my mother's expression changes. It's subtle, only a twitch of her jaw. A flicker of remorse in her eyes. If I wasn't her daughter, I might not notice.

"The bone flute," she says urgently. "Did he give it to you?"

"Pardon?"

Her rope drops another fraction. "Bastien said he would give me you *and* the flute. *Do—you—have—it?*"

My heart sinks to my stomach. No, it crashes to the depths of the pit. I've been a fool. She doesn't love me. She came for the flute. "No," I whisper. "They destroyed it." I almost told her when she first bargained for the flute, despite Bastien's knife at my throat, but I feared she wouldn't make the trade just for me. I was right.

Odiva growls in sheer frustration, nothing like herself. "I won't let you take her, do you hear me?" she yells into the pit.

The rope dips a third time. Our eyes meet. Hers are shining. With anger or sadness, I can't tell. "I have tried, Ailesse. This is the only way."

"What do you mean?" Tears scald my cheeks.

She pushes off the wall toward the other side of the chasm. The rope breaks, but she doesn't fall. She lets go and grips the jagged stones of the opposite wall. With perfect dexterity and remarkable speed, she climbs out of the pit. And leaves me to my death.

I choke out a sob. This can't be happening. This is cruelty, pure and cold and heartless.

This is the end.

My grip is about to give way when hands close over my hands. Warm. Strong.

I look up. Bastien's face swims into focus. It isn't flushed with anger, but pale with fear.

He leans down, precariously dangling from a ledge I've been unable to reach. He grasps one of my wrists and holds it fiercely. Chalky dust falls from his hair as he saws my bonds apart with his knife.

I don't understand, can't comprehend. He can't be rescuing me. It's unfathomable.

He sheaths his knife and opens his hand to me. I hesitate to take it. My mind is black, already sucked into the depths below. How can I return to a world where I mean so little? It would be so easy right now to let go and give my soul to Elara.

"Reach for me!" Bastien says. His eyes are wide and desperate. He'll die if I die. Now I understand why he's come for me.

"I can't." I curse every tear streaking down my face, every quaking muscle in my body. "My mother abandoned me."

"But *I* won't." The panic leaves his voice. It's steady now, sure. It paves a solid foundation beneath me.

I gaze into his eyes. The sea blue is deep, enveloping, beautiful. Is it possible Bastien isn't saving me just to save himself?

I can save him, too.

All I have to do is find the strength to reach.

"Ailesse," he says. "Pull yourself up. Take my hand."

I imagine myself a warrior, the Ferrier I always wanted to be. I imagine Elara's Light coursing through my veins. I picture the silver owl, her wings outspread and championing me.

I set my jaw. And I reach.

19
Sabine

I RUSH INTO THE COURTYARD of Château Creux. Sweat slicks my palms as I glance around the moonlit cavern. Odiva and the elders aren't back yet. The ravine entrance to the catacombs is a little over seven miles away from here, but even in the dark, they should have run that distance in an hour with their graces. It's been three hours since I left them. Traveling through the catacombs might have slowed them down. Injuries could, too.

So could failing to save Ailesse.

My shoulders fall. *Did you really believe anyone else could save her, Sabine?* I drop my head and tuck the nighthawk under my arm. He's unnaturally stiff, and he's lost his warmth. My stomach squirms.

I did this to him.

"Sabine?" Maurille, a middle-aged Leurress, steps out from another tunnel. Lines of worry cut across the bronze skin of her brow.

I startle and angle away. My bow and quiver thump against my back, and I poke the nighthawk's feathers out of view.

"Are you all right?" The beads woven through Maurille's rows of ebony braids clack against each other as she tilts her head. She gave me two of her best beads after my mother died, ones made of red jasper. I later threaded them onto my necklace beside my fire salamander skull. I don't know why I'm acting so guarded around her. Maurille was my mother's closest friend. "I haven't seen you since Ailesse . . ." she starts to say, then shakes her head and sighs. "I hope you know that wasn't your fault."

People only say such things when it probably is. "The *matrone* is rescuing her," I reply. "She'll be back with her soon."

"You must be eager to see your friend again."

I give a small nod. I am, but I should have been part of the rescue. I should have already obtained all my graces. The nighthawk grows heavy, and I immediately regret the thought.

Maurille comes closer. I shuffle back a step. "What is it you have there?" she asks me.

My muscles tense to run, but I root my legs. I returned home because if Odiva *does* rescue Ailesse, she won't be of any comfort to her. Ailesse needs me. "A bird," I confess.

"Sabine, you're shaking." Maurille frowns. "When is the last time you ate?" She reaches for the nighthawk. "Let me help you cook that."

"No!" I whisper-shout, and pull away. "Please, I don't want anyone to eat it." The elders say we must honor our kills by not wasting any part of them, but I can't bear the thought of the nighthawk becoming a meal. "I *chose* this bird." *Because he was unfortunate enough to cross my path.*

Maurille's eyes widen. "Oh." She peers around me to take a better look. "You killed him for his graces?" Her brows crinkle. Sacrificial animals are rarely this small, though my fire salamander was much smaller.

"He's a nighthawk. He'll give me better vision in the dark," I say, compelled to justify myself. His other abilities—increased speed, jumping farther, and having the sight to see the dead—are obvious. All birds see with more color than humans, and one of those colors is the color of departed souls.

"Well . . . that's wonderful." Maurille's smile is too wide and tight. "Would you like any help preparing the grace bone?"

A flush of nausea grips me. "No. I'd like to do it myself." It's the only way to salvage my dignity.

Maurille sucks in a breath. At first I think I've offended her, but then she turns to the tunnel leading outside. She's sensing something. Her bracelet of dolphin teeth gives her keen hearing.

"Are they back?" I ask.

She nods.

My heart leaps, and I race for the tunnel—then through the tide-carved corridors, up the ruins of the castle, and under the collapsed archway to the crumbling stone staircase. I stop halfway up the flight. Odiva stands above me. Waning moonlight shines down on her. The ends of her raven hair are coated in chalky mud.

I forgo the usual courtesy I pay the *matrone* and call out, "Ailesse?" I crane my neck to look around Odiva. I wish I already had my night vision.

"Is that for supper?" she asks flatly, eyeing my nighthawk.

I don't answer. There's no point. "Where is she?"

The four elders step into view. Their faces are drawn. Pernelle's eyes are wet. I don't see Ailesse. She should have been the first in their party; she would have run down to see me. Unless she were badly hurt or— "She didn't escape?" I sag back a step. No one denies it. "What happened?"

Odiva raises her chin, but slightly averts her gaze. "We need to focus on what *will* happen—ferrying night is in thirteen days. We must find a way to fulfill our duties." She looks at each of us in turn. "We are going to craft a new bone flute."

Milicent exchanges a pensive glance with Dolssa. "Forgive me, *Matrone*, but how will we make a flute without the bone of a golden jackal? They're all but extinct."

"They aren't even native to Galle," Dolssa adds. "We would have to leave these shores. How could we do so and return within thirteen days?"

"Where is your faith?" Odiva lashes out in a sudden burst of anger. "Tyrus will provide for us. He *demands* his souls, and this is the last time I can . . ." She briefly lowers her head. The prayer I overheard her whisper last night surfaces to mind. *The time is nearing an end. Grant me a sign, Tyrus. Let me know you honor my sacrifices.* The feverish gleam in her eyes cools as she smooths out her sleeves. "The golden jackal is sacred to Tyrus. We must appeal to him."

Pernelle openly stares at Odiva. Roxane and Dolssa hold themselves statuesque and tense. Milicent gives a curt nod. "Of course, *Matrone*."

Odiva's chest broadens with regained composure. "We must make haste. We cannot neglect the next ferrying night. A war has broken out in the north of Dovré. Rumors of many dead are running rampant. Every Leurress of able age will hunt until we find the jackal and make the new flute." She descends another step and levels her black eyes on me. "That means you, Sabine."

"But . . . what about Ailesse?" What's the matter with all of them? Why are we even talking about wars, golden jackals, and bone flutes?

Roxane presses her quivering lips in a tight line. Pernelle wipes at her eyes. Odiva looks up at the Night Heavens like she's searching for the right words. "Ailesse is dead."

"What?" Every muscle in my body turns to ice. "No . . . you're wrong. That can't be." A gust of wind whips through the skirts of the elders' dresses. My heart squeezes, struggling to beat.

"I am sorry, Sabine." Odiva places a hand on my shoulder. "It might have been better for you if Ailesse had never been . . ." She shakes her head.

"Born?" My eyes narrow. "Is that what you were going to say?"

Her raven brows pinch together. Milicent hastily steps forward to prevent another outburst. "You forget yourself, Sabine. You mustn't talk to the *matrone* that way. Of course she doesn't regret

Ailesse's birth. Ailesse was her *heir*, the child of her *amouré*."

"That does not mean I loved him," Odiva murmurs, so quietly I wonder if any of the elders' graced ears can hear. She brushes past me to the castle, but not before I catch her pulling out her hidden necklace. I glimpse it clearly for the first time—a bird skull with a ruby caught in its beak.

If this were any other moment, I'd question why she has another bone—she should only have five—but all I can do is gape in amazement as she walks under the archway of Château Creux. How can she be so heartless about her own daughter? How can any of this be happening?

Ailesse can't be gone.

"Oh, Sabine." Pernelle comes down and embraces me. My arms hang stiffly by my sides. "We did our best, but Ailesse's *amouré* made the tunnel collapse, and it was Ailesse who fell. The *matrone* tried to save her, but it was too late. The pit was deep, you see, and . . ." Her voice hitches as her tears spill over. My eyes sting, but I hold back my own tears. None of this makes sense. Ailesse isn't dead. I would know it. I would feel it.

"Did the boy die, too?"

Pernelle nods, her face darkening. "We can thank the gods for that. Odiva said his life ended the moment Ailesse's did."

I frown. "You didn't see it happen?"

"We were already gone." Roxane joins us. Milicent and Dolssa hover nearby. Their grief is almost palpable, pressing a great weight on my chest. "The tunnel was unstable, so Odiva commanded us to leave."

I shake my head slightly. Everything they're saying hinges on Odiva's word alone. It isn't enough for me.

"Go inside and rest." Pernelle rubs my arm. "You can join the hunt tomorrow."

She means the hunt for the golden jackal. Ridiculous. "No, I'll go today. I'll go now." I shrug away from them, but I still feel their worried eyes bore into the back of my skull.

"What about your bird?" Dolssa asks.

Dazed, I glance down to see my nighthawk limply dangling from my hand. Oh.

On wooden legs, I walk to the ruins of the garden wall. Flop the bird onto a stone. Withdraw Ailesse's bone knife.

Thwack.

I take the severed leg. Cut my palm with the sharp bone so it meets my blood. There. The ceremony is finished. I close my fist around the leg, its claw still attached. The elders watch in strained silence.

I cast the nighthawk aside on the stone. I leave the elders, the overgrown garden, the rocky grounds of the Château Creux. I run. Away from the sea cliffs, across the plateau, into the forestland, past webbing streams and rivers, across bridge after bridge after bridge. I keep going, pushing myself past my limits, until I'm numb to the burning in my lungs and the cramping in my side. Until the cut in my palm stops stinging and my eyes run dry.

I'm almost to the catacombs entrance. I have every intention of blazing inside, but when I near the edge of the ravine, I come to an abrupt stop.

All my breath leaves my lungs. My heart shoots up my throat. I waver on my feet.

The beautiful and knowing eyes of the silver owl are staring back at me.

She's here. Under the stark moonlight. On the ground, not in a tree. She's perched on the cusp of the ravine.

She's a sign I was right.

Ailesse is alive.

I move another step closer, and the silver owl spreads her wings and points them downward in a defensive stance. She doesn't want me to pass.

My racing heartbeat slows. I register the ache in my muscles and trembling limbs. Blood drips from my fisted hand. The leg and blunt claw are still curled inside and digging at my wound.

I never received the nighthawk's graces, I realize.

Did I offend the gods? It was a kill made in rage and a grace bone taken thoughtlessly.

"I'm sorry," I say to Tyrus and Elara, but I'm looking at the silver owl. "I did it to save Ailesse."

The owl folds her wings.

Warmth rushes over my skin, and I startle. The world around me changes like another sun has risen, only it casts a faint violet glow. I know what I'm seeing—Ailesse described this after she killed her peregrine falcon. This is vision with an additional color. I haven't seen the color yet. But I will whenever I first see the dead. Every Ferrier needs this grace.

The gods have forgiven me.

"I will save her," I tell the silver owl, like we speak the same language. "I know I'm the only one who can."

She screeches softly, almost a purring sound.

"And I'll be wise when I choose my next kill." The nighthawk's graces aren't worthless, but they don't give me strength, which is what I need most. "I'll also be clever and strategic." If Odiva and four elder Leurress couldn't rescue Ailesse, I'll need to plot as carefully as Bastien and his friends have done.

The owl bobs her heart-shaped face, forward and back, side to side.

My resolve forges bone-deep. I'm going to have to exercise patience in order to succeed. I can afford a little time. Ailesse must have told Bastien by now that their soul-bond ties them in life and death, and he must believe her or he'd have killed her already, especially after losing his chance to kill her mother.

"I won't fail."

The owl opens her wings. My vision changes again. This time it isn't cast in violet, but shimmers with silver, like the ring around a full moon. Whatever I'm seeing, it can't be from my nighthawk grace.

An image appears in my mind. Or maybe I'm actually seeing it. It's translucent and struggling to take shape before me.

I gasp. It's Ailesse. She's sitting on a stone bench, tied up by her wrists and ankles. Her head droops to the side as she listlessly leans against a wall. Her auburn hair is matted. She's scraped up and filthy, and her eyes look hollow. All her fire is gone. "Oh, Ailesse," I whisper, my chest aching.

As soon as I speak, her gaze lifts. Our eyes meet. My heart quickens. "Sabine?" Her voice cracks with shock and hope.

I smile with desperate relief. I believed she was still alive, but it's another thing to *see* her. "Stay strong," I tell her. "I'm coming for you."

A tear streaks down her face.

I reach out to touch her arm. She's that close. But as soon as I try, the vision ripples like disturbed water. Ailesse disappears.

My heart gives a hard pound. "What just happened?"

The only one listening is the silver owl.

She beats her wings. Lifts off the ground. And flies away.

20
Bastien

Marcel hisses as I pick another bit of gravel out of his wound. "Almost done," I tell him. We're back in our chamber, and he's sitting on an overturned mining cart we use as a table. His right sleeve is rolled back, exposing a gouge mark that runs the length of his forearm. A rock struck him during the explosion; he misjudged how far away he needed to be from the cask of black powder. "Jules will be back soon with the water. We'll wash this up and help it heal into a proper scar. Birdie will find it irresistible." I wink at him.

Marcel forces a grin past clenched teeth. "You think so?"

"'Course." I pluck out another piece of debris. "She already knows you're brilliant. This will make you look tough, too. She'll be smitten."

Ailesse gasps in amazement, and I bristle. But as soon as I turn to where she's propped up on the limestone slab, I see her expression, and it isn't mocking. She's sitting up, body rigid. Eyes wide. Face pale. My stomach tenses. Is she in pain?

I rush over to her. She croaks out, "Sabine!" A tear rolls down her cheek. She isn't looking at me. She's staring straight ahead. She gasps again and blinks a few times. "Sabine?" She shakes her head a little. "Where did she . . . ?" Her eyes take focus on her surroundings. Then me. Tears cling to her lashes. "Bastien?" she asks, like my name is a desperate question.

That's when I realize I'm on my knees beside her, my fingers woven through hers. Her grip is as tight as mine. Just as tight as when I dragged her out of the pit.

"Is everything all right?" Jules asks.

I startle. Ailesse and I release each other's hands.

"Just checking her ropes," I answer quickly. I give the knot at Ailesse's wrists an obligatory tug. "She was thrashing." My face burns at the lie. "She's a bit delirious." That much is true. "I think she hit her head when she fell into the pit."

Ailesse sags against the slab wall, like she's considering my words. She *does* have a nasty bruise on the side of her forehead.

Jules says nothing. I can't meet her eyes when I get back up to my feet. The chamber is unnervingly silent as I walk over to where she stands by the door. I reach for the bucket of water she just brought in, and she takes a step away from me. "I've got it," she says, her voice clipped. She shrugs past me to move to her brother.

I sigh. I hate this tension between us. Jules was far from happy when I dragged Ailesse out of the pit, but what choice did I have except to save her? I run both hands through my hair and stroll over to a stack of Marcel's books. I grab one at random and hunch down on a stool, trying to make myself useful. Though I don't even know what my end goal is anymore.

"What now?" Jules asks, as usual in tune with my thoughts, even when we're at odds. She dips a handkerchief in a bowl of settled water and gently dabs Marcel's wound. "The queen isn't going to be fooled next time, and the catacombs didn't cut off her power as much as we thought."

Marcel nods, watching Jules work. "I've been thinking it must take a little time—perhaps a few days—for a Bone Crier's strength to sufficiently weaken down here. Take Ailesse, for example. She didn't lose her vigor all at once."

"Makes sense," I reply, and sneak a glance at Ailesse. If she's listening, she makes no sign of it. She just stares at her limp hands.

"At least the queen knows she isn't dealing with simpletons," Jules says. "We're as dangerous as she is."

I don't know about that, but I'll let Jules have her show of confidence. She couldn't cut through the pulley rope before the queen climbed out of the pit. She's lucky the queen didn't have time to find her hiding place. When another section of the tunnel broke away, the queen ran off with the other Bone Criers.

"How soon do you think she'll return?" Jules wets the handkerchief again.

"She's not coming back," Ailesse murmurs. We all look at her. A tremor runs through her chin.

Jules's gaze hardens. "Are you Bone Criers mind readers, too?"

"I'm not what my mother came for," Ailesse replies on a weak breath. Even her tone has no fight in it.

Jules scoffs. "Then what *did* she come for?"

Ailesse's eyes shimmer. She turns her head away.

"Are you going to answer me?"

"Leave her alone," I mutter.

The look Jules shoots at me is the same look she gives Dovré boys when they leer at her. A split second later, they're on the ground with broken noses. "Why are you defending her?"

"I'm not defending anyone. I just want a moment's peace while I figure out how to get the three of us out of this mess." I jab a page of my book for emphasis, even though I've found nothing helpful. Reading isn't my best talent.

"This is *your* mess, Bastien," Jules snaps, "not ours."

"What are you talking about?"

"We're not the ones caught up in a magic spell with a siren. We could leave you to deal with it any time."

I stare incredulously at her, completely blindsided. From the first moment I met Jules and Marcel, we've been in this together, no matter the complications. Don't they still want revenge for their father? "Go on, then." My voice shakes with hurt I try to pass off as anger. I make a shooing motion for the door. "I never said you two had to do anything for me." I just trusted they would, like I would for them.

Marcel raises a finger. "If I may, I'd like to say two things: one, my sister doesn't speak for me; and, two, for the sake of common decency, Julienne, will you please go easy on my arm? I do have a nervous system."

She winces and pulls back from punch-cleaning him. She drops her handkerchief in the bowl and sighs. "We're not going to leave you, Bastien. That's not what I'm trying to say. It's just that"— she nibbles on her lip—"we never bargained for *you* to be the soulmate. That's knocked everything off balance. I mean, are you two *really* even soulmates? That was never proven."

"She has a fair point," Marcel adds. "We based that conclusion on the fact that no one else showed up at the bridge. Ailesse's true soulmate could have been too ill to come, or maybe he was farther away and hadn't made it there yet."

I gape at them, amazed we're even having this discussion. "What do you suggest, that we test that theory by killing Ailesse to see if I die, too?"

Marcel lowers his eyes. Jules bites her lip again.

"Bastien is my *amouré*," Ailesse says quietly. "If you could feel what he does, you would have no doubt."

I frown. "You can't know what I feel."

"No, but I can see it." She finally lifts her umber eyes to me, and I swallow hard. I picture those same eyes staring up at me from the pit. She looked terrified and alone, the same way I felt after losing my father.

I slam my book shut. Ailesse isn't the victim here. "I don't have any affection for—"

"Affection has nothing to do with it." Her voice betrays no hint of emotion. She's listless, almost indifferent. "You were designed for me, and I was designed for you. You feel it as well as I do, Bastien."

Heat rises in my cheeks.

Jules shakes her head in disbelief. "She's insufferable."

Ailesse shrugs and turns away.

I rub my hand over my face. "Can we get back on topic, please?"

"What topic is that?" Marcel leans back.

"What we do now. We need to rethink our strategy." I don't mention another plot to bait the queen. I agree with Ailesse that her mother won't return. "We'll continue to stay down here—that's a given—and we'll make runs for food and supplies. As for breaking the soul-bond, we already have Marcel's books handy. We'll comb over every passage a hundred times until we find the answer. Even if it takes weeks."

"And *then* we kill her?" Jules crosses her arms.

My pulse jumps. I want to look at Ailesse, but I don't. Instead, I stare at Jules. For years we've been hell-bent on revenge, but the Jules I know isn't this bloodthirsty. She's only callous when she's hurting inside. I have to prove I won't forget the pact that sealed our friendship.

"Yes," I reply, though my stomach twists. "Then we kill her."

21
Ailesse

SABINE LIES BESIDE ME ON her back. We're in a meadow near Château Creux, gazing up at the Night Heavens. The stars are brilliant, the Huntress and Jackal constellations shining down on us in perfect clarity. "It's the new moon," Sabine tells me, one arm tucked behind her head. "This should have been your first ferrying night."

"Yes." A deep ache rises from the back of my throat. "But no one can ferry now, and there's nothing I can do about it."

"Are you sure? Don't give up, Ailesse. There's always something you can do."

"But the bone flute is broken." I turn to her, but my best friend is gone.

I'm staring into the eyes of the silver owl.

"Ailesse."

Someone nudges my arm. My eyes crack open. Jules leans over me. "I'm heading out on another supply run. You want me to take you to the privy first?"

The thought of that reeking corner of the catacombs isn't what startles me wide awake; it's the tone of Jules's voice. Calm and straightforward. No temper. It reminds me she and I have come to a gradual acceptance of each other over the last few days. It reminds me I've been a prisoner down here for more than two long weeks. And my mother never came back for me.

"No, I'm fine." I slowly pull up into a sitting position on the limestone slab while Jules watches, unconvinced. Even that simple movement takes muscle-cramping effort. My captors have been feeding me and giving me water, but I'm almost completely starved of Elara's Light. "Marcel?" I call over to him. My weak voice is barely loud enough to grab his attention. He looks up from the wreckage of books he and Bastien are poring over on the overturned cart table. "When is the new moon? Have you been keeping track?"

"Yes, in fact, I have." His grin is lazy with delight as he digs underneath his books and pulls out a sheet of parchment, marked up with his scribbles. "I've been charting the days by the hour down here. Whenever one of us comes back from our trips to Dovré, I compare what time it is outside to my calendar, and so far it's been accurate." He taps twice on the parchment. "The new moon is tonight."

Bastien looks from Marcel to me. "Is that significant?" His gaze roams over my face, and I try to smooth away any trace of anxiety. "What happens on the new moon?"

I shake my head. "Nothing . . . I just . . ." I glance away from him. His concern confuses me when I know he plans to kill me. "I had a bad dream, that's all." I can't hold myself upright anymore, so I scoot back to the corner wall of the slab and lean against it.

Now Jules stares at me with worried eyes, too—which is even more disconcerting. "How much strength do you have left?" she asks, and lowers her voice. "Does it run out on the new moon?"

I have no idea. "I'm fine," I reply, though I know it's really Bastien that Jules is distressed about. Who knows how much longer I can stay alive once my last spark of Elara's Light is gone?

She shifts her weight onto her left leg. Her knee has finally healed. "You should rest while I'm gone, all right?"

I give her a halfhearted nod. That's all I do, anyway.

She grabs her empty pack and heads for the door, stopping when she reaches Marcel. "We're running out of time," she murmurs to him. "You need to figure out how to break the soul-bond *now*."

"What do you think I've been trying to do every day?" He gestures at his piles of notes and books all over the table.

"Well, try harder," she snaps. He frowns, and she drops her head with a sigh. "Sorry, just please . . . try harder." She kisses his cheek, then turns pained eyes on Bastien before she ducks out of the chamber.

Try harder. Her words remind me what Sabine said—or what the silver owl said—in my dream: *Don't give up, Ailesse. There's always something you can do.*

What does it all mean? Am I having visions? I brushed off the flickering image I saw of Sabine two weeks ago as a hallucination brought on from my head injury. I haven't seen another one since. But now I wonder . . . has she found a way to communicate with me? Hope sparks in my chest.

Bastien walks over with a tumbler of settled water. His footsteps are cautious, his gaze averted, his expression blank. It's how he usually handles being this near me. He passes me the tumbler, and our fingers graze. My skin prickles with warmth, and I release a shaky breath. Being this close to him is no small task for me either. I balance the tumbler between my hands—a tricky endeavor because they're still tied—and drink until the water runs dry. "Thank you."

Our eyes collide. He looks startled, questioning. I've never thanked him for anything, not directly.

I give him back the tumbler, and this time when our hands touch, it's Bastien who shivers. "Do you want more?" he asks. Before I have a chance to answer, he adds, "I can get you some more." He walks over to the water bucket and peeks inside. "Oh. Empty, too." He shoots me a nervous look. "That's all right." He wags his thumb at the door and walks backward toward it. "I'll just— I won't be long." I suppress a smile as he trips out of the chamber. He's never this awkward.

It's almost adorable . . . for someone who wants me dead.

Marcel lifts another piece of parchment from the table and mumbles something about moons, earth, and water.

I tilt my head at him. "It's strange . . . I didn't think anyone knew about the Leurress, until I met you three."

He turns around and blinks twice, still half lost in his thoughts. "Some people do. There are legends, superstitions, the occasional folk song . . . but not really much to go by."

"Yet *you* know so much."

He gives a modest shrug. "It's a bit of a hobby, really. I'm restless unless my mind has something big to chew on."

Marcel, restless? My shoulders tremble with stifled laughter. He grins, unsure why I'm amused. I can't help warming up to him. Unlike Bastien and Jules, Marcel doesn't seem to have a natural prejudice against me. "What if I told you that you didn't know enough?"

"I'd admit that's no surprise. Can anyone really know enough— about anything?"

I bite my lip. "What if I also told you I'm willing to add to your knowledge?"

His brows crinkle, and he darts a glance at the door. "Is this a trick?"

"It's an offer. Believe it or not, I don't wish to die. And since I can't kill my *amouré* at the moment, I want to help you break my soul-bond with him." I shut out the ingrained voice in me that says that's an impossible task. Instead, I listen to Sabine's voice: *Don't give up, Ailesse.*

Marcel slides a hand in his pocket. A sign he's getting more comfortable. "All right." He drifts nearer, mulling over his sheet of parchment. "Can you tell me what an upside-down crescent moon means?"

"What does that have to do with the soul-bond?"

"I don't know. That's the problem—but maybe it's the answer, too. I often find solving one mystery unlocks the next."

That makes sense, and I suppose we need to start somewhere. "An upside-down crescent is a setting moon. But it can also represent a bridge."

"A bridge . . ." Marcel scratches his jaw. "I hadn't thought of that. And what if it's touching another symbol?" He shows me his sheet of parchment, and my brows rise. It's a drawing of the bone flute. I didn't realize Marcel had a chance to study it before Jules broke it. "See here?" He points below the lowest tone hole on the flute to an inverted triangle that's balanced on an upside-down crescent moon—right in the spot where the engraving was on the real instrument. "That triangle means water, right?"

I nod. "When the symbols are placed together like that it means the soul bridge."

"Soul bridge?"

"The bridge the dead must cross to enter the Beyond."

"Ah, where you Bone Criers do your ferrying."

"Yes." Bastien must have told Marcel what I told him.

"Not on Castelpont, obviously. No water in that riverbed." He sits beside me and taps on the inverted triangle of his picture.

"The soul bridge is beneath the Nivous Sea."

"*Beneath* the sea?"

My mother would disown me if she heard me now, revealing the mysteries of the Leurress. But then I remember she already gave me up. *I have tried, Ailesse. This is the only way.* My chest pangs, and I swallow against the tightness in my throat. "The soul bridge is a land bridge." I pause, concentrating on the effort it takes to slide my legs off the slab to make more room for Marcel. He scoots closer. "It only emerges from the sea during the lowest tides."

"So during the full moon and new moon?" he asks, once again impressing me with what he's stored in his mind.

"Yes, but the Leurress can only ferry on a new moon."

"Tonight?"

I nod. "That's when the dead are lured to the soul bridge. The bone flute . . . it was used for more than luring *amourés* to bridges. It also lured the dead to cross the soul bridge." I sigh. My mother must be beside herself with worry. If the dead aren't summoned tonight, they'll rise from their graves on their own and feed off the Light of the living. They'll kill souls. Eternally.

"A soul bridge that's a land bridge . . ." Marcel shakes his head. "Fascinating. Do you think that's what this means?" He reaches into his pocket, and my heart nearly leaps out of my chest.

He's holding the bone flute.

It's whole. Intact.

He turns it over to show me a symbol, but my vision rocks with dizziness. "How did you . . . ?" A flush of adrenaline seizes me. "That was broken. I *watched* Jules break it."

Marcel chuckles. "Oh, she told me about that." He bats a dismissing hand. "She was just trying to rattle you. What you saw her break was a random bone from the catacombs. The flute was in my pack the whole time."

"What?" My mind reels as I think back on my first terrible

day down here. I never really saw what Jules was holding—not in detail. She said it was the flute, and I believed her, but in the dim light of her oil lamp, I only made out that she was holding a slender bone.

I've been such a fool.

"So is this a symbol of the soul bridge, too?" Marcel points at the side of the flute without the tone holes. My mind finally clears enough to register it. This symbol has a horizontal line carved through the middle of the inverted triangle—the symbol of earth, not water.

"Um . . . yes," I mumble, just to say something. I've never thought much about the small difference between the symbols, and it still seems unimportant. All I can picture is my mother's amazed and grateful face when I set the flute in her hands. She'll welcome me back. She'll smile one of her rare smiles. She'll touch my cheek and say, "Well done."

A riptide of clarity flashes through me. I have to escape. Tonight. At midnight, the Leurress must ferry the dead, and my mother will need the bone flute.

"I had no idea there was a land bridge around here," Marcel says, still caught up on that fact.

My gaze strays to his cloak, but it's not parted wide enough for me to see if any knife glints within. "No one knows but my *famille*. It's off a shore that's hard to access." I'm blurting now, telling him anything I can to keep him captivated. "The cliffs above the land bridge are impossible to descend unless you know where the hidden stairway is." I shift to directly face him.

"Oh?" He mirrors my movement, and his cloak opens farther. My pulse races. I see a knife on his belt. It's small, but that doesn't matter.

"And that place can't be used as a harbor; the water is ridden with sea stacks and jagged rocks." I'm going to have to be quick. Grab the knife—which will be difficult with my wrists tied; threaten Marcel so he stays silent; cut my own bonds; grab the flute, and then my grace bones. Bastien hid them in a chipped pitcher when he thought I was sleeping. "The most hallowed part of the land bridge is what's at its end," I say, casting my final lure. "Maybe I shouldn't tell you. This knowledge is sacred."

Marcel leans closer. "You can trust me, Ailesse."

"Can I?" My body thrums with nervous, almost frenzied energy. I grasp his cloak and pull him nearer, as if to search his eyes. He gulps, but I don't let go. The hilt of his knife is a fingerbreadth away from my hand. "You must swear an oath never to share what I'm about to tell you," I say, though this secret isn't any more significant than what I've already revealed.

"All right. I—I swear."

I bring my mouth to his ear. I curl my fingers around the fabric of his cloak. "A pair of Gates divides the mortal realm from the eternal." I close my hand around the hilt of his knife. "They aren't made of wood, earth, or iron." I carefully withdraw his weapon. "Tyrus's Gate is made of water, and Elara's Gate is made of . . ." I really don't know, except it's unearthly and almost invisible.

"What are you two whispering about?"

My heart jumps.

Bastien is back. He's standing just inside the chamber by the door, his eyes suspicious. The water bucket in his hands drips on the ground.

I jerk back from Marcel. I slide his knife under my thigh. The pooled fabric of his cloak conceals the move.

Marcel offers Bastien a casual smile. "Ailesse was just telling me about the symbols on the bone flute," he replies, keeping his promise not to mention the Gates.

Bastien's frown deepens. "Why would she do that?"

Marcel lifts his hands, baffled. "To help us figure out how to break the soul-bond."

I steady my gaze on Bastien and add, "You're not the only one who wants to end this relationship."

His grimace lingers a moment, and then he lowers his eyes. I stifle a prick of guilt. "Relationship?" he mutters, setting down his bucket. "That implies I had a choice to enter into it." He strides to the shelves and peeks into a few random pots and jars. "Next time you have something important to say, say it to me, too."

"Fine." My chest tightens. The blade of Marcel's knife is cold beneath my leg. I could fling it at Bastien now. Maybe I don't need a ritual weapon to kill him and end our soul-bond.

He looks back at me and crosses his arms. "Well?"

I shrug. "I'm out of important things to say for the day. I need to rest now."

Marcel sighs, a little disappointed. "Well, this has all been most helpful, Ailesse. Thank you." He eases off the slab, and my stomach tenses as he pockets the bone flute again.

I shift, little by little, struggling to keep the knife out of sight as I lie down. I close my eyes, conscious that Bastien's skeptical gaze is still upon me.

I feign sleep for the rest of the day. By what must be nightfall, Jules returns, and my three captors discuss all that I told Marcel. At length, they fall asleep, one by one. Even Bastien drifts off, though it was his turn to keep watch. He must trust me a little by now.

I tamp down the guilt that gives me. I cut apart my ropes and tiptoe over to Marcel. I slide the flute from his pocket and sneak to the shelves. When I pull down the chipped pitcher, my pulse races. My bones are within.

I grab a small leather pouch that Jules uses for coins and replace the coins with my bones. Energy tickles me as I touch each one. The pendant of an alpine ibex. The wing bone of a peregrine falcon. The tooth of a tiger shark. When I pull the necklace cord over my head and the pouch settles against my chest, I breathe in deeply and close my eyes. I feel my power steel inside me.

I'm whole again. Balanced.

I'm Ailesse.

My graces are weaker than before—I've been in the darkness too long—but I can remedy that.

I fetch an oil lamp and quietly push the small door of our chamber open. I tighten my grip around the hilt of Marcel's knife and look back at Bastien. His dark hair has tumbled across his closed eyes, and it flutters with his heavy breathing.

A flood of sensations rushes into me. The coolness of the water he gave me. The strong press of his hand when he pulled me out of the pit. The echo of his words: *Pull yourself up. Take my hand.*

I find myself softly smiling at him.

I tuck the knife into the sash of my dress. I won't kill Bastien. For now. I'll return to my mother, give her the flute, and ferry the dead at her side. And before the year ends, I'll track Bastien down and do what I must.

I sneak outside the chamber and take one heart-pounding glance at the wall of skulls, then face the looming tunnel ahead.

Elara, help me find a way out of this prison.

22
Sabine

My full quiver bobs against my back as I race across the cliffs above the Nivous Sea. I haven't shot one arrow since I killed the nighthawk. I don't know what I'm hunting for, but my heart pounds with a deep sense of urgency. I need to decide and make my final kill.

Ailesse has been underground for fifteen days. I can't wait any longer for the silver owl to come back and give me a sign that I made the right choice of grace bone. So far I've pursued a wild boar, a feral horse, and even a rare black wolf, but I hesitated when I had an opportunity to seize them. Would that animal give me enough ability to rescue Ailesse? Why won't the silver owl tell me? I haven't seen her since she showed me the vision of my friend.

The smell of salt and brine fills my lungs as I run faster, scanning the plains that sprawl out before me. Each blade of swaying wild grass comes into clear focus. I'm still amazed by my nighthawk grace to see well in the dark. It looks as bright outside as it does during a full moon. But this is a new moon. Ferrying night. None of the Leurress were able to hunt a golden jackal in time, so as a last resort, Odiva carved a new flute from the bone of a ritual stag, giving it all the same markings as the original flute. Whether or not it has the same power remains to be seen. My *famille* has been on edge about it for days.

When I race another half mile, my path inclines on a rolling hill. I near the top, and a group of women holding staffs approaches from the other side. Ferriers, led by Odiva. My brows lift. They've left Château Creux already. Is it that close to midnight? I tense to run the other way—I shouldn't be out tonight—but it's too late. They've already seen me.

We crown the hill at the same moment. I stop and come face-to-face with my *matrone*. She's wearing her five grace bones in their epaulettes, rows of necklaces, and her striking crown, but she's not wearing her customary sapphire-blue dress beneath. Tonight, she's clothed in a white dress, like the other Ferriers, though the color looks unearthly on Odiva, not holy.

"Sabine." She looks me up and down, and thin lines crease across her forehead. "What are you doing here? You're needed at home." On ferrying night, I'm supposed to remain with the younger girls and those too old to ferry, while the majority of the Leurress attend to their duty on the soul bridge.

"I'm on my way there, *Matrone*." I don't know why I'm lying; Odiva wants me to earn my third grace bone as much as I do. She might approve of why I'm out here. "I lost track of the time." One disadvantage of night vision is that I can't judge the light of the sky very well to determine the hour, even though I've had this grace for two weeks. I hope I'll acclimate.

"Hurry along. Your new grace bone should help with your speed."

"Yes, *Matrone*."

She passes by me, and the other Ferriers trail behind her. I know without counting there are thirty-four of them, including Odiva. As they walk, they assert a strong elegance, their staffs in hand and posture exact. Each of them maintains a rigorous training schedule to prepare for monthly ferrying nights. They don't look prepared now. Their lips move quietly, and their pleading eyes glance to the Night Heavens—and even below to the Underworld. They're offering desperate prayers, more anxious than ever about the new bone flute.

When Odiva reaches the bottom of the hill, she turns to consider me again. "On second thought, Sabine, I would like you to come with us."

"Come *ferrying?*" My voice pitches higher.

"No, to observe ferrying."

My breath bottles in my chest. I can't summon a response. Novices aren't allowed to come anywhere close to the soul bridge. It's too dangerous to be near the Chained.

Odiva beckons me with a subtle wave of her hand. I reluctantly go to her, my gaze dropping from her black eyes to the lump of her hidden necklace beneath her dress: the bird skull with a ruby in its beak. I bite the inside of my lip. What else is the *matrone* hiding from me—and all our *famille*? "You will be able to see the dead now, thanks to this." She lifts the nighthawk leg bone I wear on Ailesse's shoulder necklace.

"Yes, but . . . I don't have my third grace bone. What about my rite of passage?" A sick flush of nausea cramps my stomach. "I'm not ready."

I don't dare move. Odiva still hasn't let go of my nighthawk leg. She traces its claw with her pointed fingernail, and my pulse throbs in my throat. "Some members of our *famille* have confided in me their concerns about you," she says, shaking her head with false sorrow. "They say you are unsure if you want to become a Ferrier at all."

"I'm only sixteen." My voice cracks. "I still have time to decide."

"No, Sabine. I am afraid *time* is the last thing you have." She releases my necklace and tips up my chin. Her touch is gentle, but her fingers feel like ice. "Time is at an end for all of us." My brow wrinkles. What does she mean? Her eyes glitter with anticipation, but it's feverish and forced. "Come, we mustn't delay." She walks on, confident I'll follow. "You will watch from a safe distance on the shore. Perhaps if you witness ferrying for yourself, you will understand the importance of your duty."

I consider sneaking away and facing punishment later, but then I think of Ailesse. This night would have been her first time on the soul bridge. Every long hunt she endured, every grace she won, she did to achieve her dream of becoming a masterful Ferrier.

I draw a sustaining breath, fist my clammy hands, and join the sisters of my *famille*.

I'll go to honor Ailesse.

We soon arrive at another set of high cliffs that drop into a sheltered inlet of the Nivous Sea. The Leurress lead me through a narrow gap between two boulders, and the space inside widens just enough so we can walk single file. A steep, carved stairway descends at our feet. I support my hands against the limestone walls and tread carefully, wishing for the balance of Ailesse's ibex grace.

I count 167 steps before I walk onto the fine sand of the shore. I'm standing in a cave. Grayish light glows beyond its mouth. I advance toward it with the Ferriers, and we trail out onto a starlit beach. The water laps gently, and a shower of awe prickles across my shoulders. A faint shimmer of rocks dot an increasingly visible pathway in the sea.

The tide is lowering. The land bridge begins to emerge.

23
Bastien

AILESSE ISN'T GONE. SHE CAN'T *be*. But no matter how hard I try to convince myself, I can't peel my groggy eyes off the evidence. The limestone slab. It's vacant. Except for a pile of rope.

My pounding heart is a physical pain in my chest.

This is impossible.

No. I catch myself. No, this was very possible. I knew all along Ailesse was capable of outmaneuvering me—even bound, even weak, even without her grace bones.

Her grace bones.

I jump to my feet and run, tripping over Marcel and Jules asleep on the floor. "Ouch!" Jules growls. Marcel's snoring catches.

I scramble for the shelves. The chipped pitcher isn't there. I spin around and see it on the table. A few coins from Jules's pouch are scattered around it. I rush over and peer inside the pitcher. Empty. "*Merde!*" I shove it back. It slides off the table and shatters on the ground.

Jules bolts upright. Half her hair has come undone from her braid. "Bastien, what are—?" Her gaze lands on the slab, and her jaw drops. She grabs her brother's shoulder and rattles it. His eyes crack open. She points to the slab.

He pushes up onto his elbows. Blinks slowly at where Ailesse should be. "Oh."

"Oh?" I pace and try not to bite off his head. I know exactly how this happened. "Show me that small knife you carry."

He reaches under his cloak, and his face blanches. "It's gone. The bone flute, too."

I kick a shard of the pitcher.

Jules turns incredulous eyes on her brother. "How did you let Ailesse get that close?"

He lies back down and shakes his head. "*I'm* the one who got close to her. Ailesse told me about the symbols on the flute and . . . she said she was trying to help." He presses the heels of his hands to his eyes. "Tonight is the new moon, too." He groans. "Her ferrying night. She practically spelled it out to me. I'm a fool."

I sigh. Marcel isn't entirely to blame. I saw him sitting right beside her. I didn't ask him to move away. "We've all been fools."

Jules looks affronted. "Excuse me? I wasn't here. Don't blame me for—" She frowns. "What are you doing?"

I cinch the strap of my sheath harness on my back. My father's knife presses against my spine. *I'll make this right,* I promise him.

I grab an oil lamp. Kick the door open. Duck outside and charge into the dark of the catacombs. Ailesse is still here. She has to be. I couldn't have been sleeping for more than a half hour, and this place is a labyrinth.

Jules bursts out of the chamber. "Wait!" Her hazel eyes glitter in the light of the lamp she's just snatched up. "You have to think. Ailesse has *all her bones* now. We need a proper plan. We're not prepared for—"

"I'm not letting her get away." My throat tightens. I saved her from the pit. Didn't that mean anything to her?

You also tied her up again, Bastien.

"I'm coming, too!" Marcel rushes to join us.

I stiffen when I see the bow and quiver slung over his shoulder. "No one kills Ailesse, is that clear?"

Jules narrows her eyes. "Are you worried about *your* life or hers?"

"What difference is there?" I snap. She flinches and takes a step back from me. My shoulders fall when I see her eyes are watering. I've only seen Jules cry twice before—six years ago, when I caught her weeping at her father's grave, and a little over two months ago, when I told her we just needed to be friends. I reach out and touch her arm. "You know what I mean, Jules."

Her nostrils flare, and she shoves my hand away. "Nothing is clearer. We may have to guard your precious soulmate's life, but that doesn't mean I can't make her suffer." She yanks her knife from her belt. "I, for one, haven't forgotten my mission." She marches past me to take the lead, furiously wiping at her eyes.

I blow out a heavy breath and follow.

Marcel sidles up to me once Jules has outdistanced us by several feet. We rush along, trying to keep up with her. "Sometimes I think she really could kill Ailesse," he murmurs.

"Come on, Marcel. She wouldn't do that." We duck our heads to dodge a low section of the ceiling.

"But would *you*?" His voice takes on a nervous edge. "I mean, now that you know Ailesse? Assuming the soul-bond wasn't a component, of course."

I rub an uncomfortable stitch in my side. Ailesse could have killed me tonight, but she didn't—even though she had Marcel's knife and her grace bones. "What about you?" I throw his question back at him, and he frowns. It's a stupid thing to say. Marcel never trained to be the tool of our revenge. Jules and I never wanted him to get blood on his hands.

A dull splash sounds ahead where the tunnel is flooded. Jules has jumped into the water.

I clap Marcel on the back. "We need to hurry. At the rate Jules is going, she'll cross half of Galle before we even get out of these tunnels."

We trudge onward, moving as fast as we can. We slip through the cracks of hidden paths and comb at least a dozen routes Ailesse could have taken.

She's nowhere.

A horrible thought takes hold of me.

Her grace bones are helping her escape.

I don't know which animals give Ailesse her power, but I do

know that most have an uncanny sense of direction—birds, dogs, cats. She was blindfolded when we came here, but she has to have a buried memory of the path we took to our chamber. Her grace bones could have helped her remember.

I come to a sudden stop. "Jules!" I shout. Marcel bumps into me from behind.

Her faint ring of lamplight stills ahead, then slowly bobs back to me. She's sheathed her knife again. A good sign?

"Ailesse isn't here," I say.

Jules arches a brow. "How can you be sure?"

I hesitate. She'll hate my answer. I give it anyway. "I feel it." Maybe it's the soul-bond. Maybe it's just a gut instinct. Whatever it is, it feels urgent and pulse-pounding.

Jules presses her lips together. She nods with bitter acceptance that borders on ridicule. "So what do we do now?" She tosses her braided hair behind her shoulder. "Ailesse could be anywhere."

"I don't think so. Her family is ferrying souls tonight on that land bridge she told Marcel about. She must have gone back to help them."

Jules rolls her eyes. "Bone magic and eternal soulmates are one thing. But ghosts?" She shakes her head. "I'll believe it when I see it."

I don't argue her point. "We need to head for the ravine exit."

"Whoa, hold on." She grabs my arm as I rush past her. "How exactly are we going to find this mysterious land bridge? There are over a hundred miles of coastline off the Nivous Sea."

"I have no idea, but if we don't find Ailesse tonight, we lose her forever." My neck flushes with a cold sweat.

"You mean we lose our chance for *revenge*." Jules scrutinizes me.

I shift away. "Same thing."

"Actually, the land bridge might not be so hard to find." Marcel pushes his floppy hair off of his face. "Ailesse mentioned sea stacks and great rocks that prevent ships from sailing nearby. That narrows the location to seventeen miles along the west coast where the rocky water is. That's also where you'll find the steepest cliffs: Ailesse said you have to take a hidden stairway to get down to the shore."

"Seventeen miles?" I turn to consider him. "But it's over six miles to even get from the ravine to the west coast. That's too much ground for us to search in one night."

"Not if you think a little harder."

"Think *for* me, Marcel."

"Well, it stands to reason that Bone Criers ferry somewhere secluded, for instance a small bay or a lagoon. Then you must factor in the complexities of the land bridge itself, which doesn't emerge at a normal low tide; it emerges twice a month at an *extremely* low tide—spring tides, they're called, though that term has nothing to do with the season—and likely due to the shape of the bay. So the most probable place would be a narrow arm-shaped inlet, and I've only seen one such inlet on maps of the west coast."

I'm a little dizzy trying to follow him. "So can you lead us there?" I try my best to have faith in Marcel's brilliance. He would have had to memorize an ink trail of tiny squiggles to find the place he just described.

He gives me a lopsided grin. "I know I can."

24
Sabine

As the land bridge continues to surface, I have to force myself to breathe. I gaze at the serene beauty before me, the silvery sea in the embrace of the limestone cliffs, the silhouetted sea stacks and large rocks guarding the mouth of the inlet. At the dawn of time, this was the place where the first Leurress was born. Elara gave birth to her in a beam of silver moonlight, but when Tyrus tried to catch his daughter's fall, he couldn't reach the Night Heavens from his Underworld kingdom. To save her, he formed a bridge between worlds out of the earth that later became South Galle. The child lived and thrived, and the gods taught her how to open the Gates to their realms and ferry the dead.

The dead. A chill skitters up my spine. I'm about to see their souls for the first time. I glance left, right, and behind me, past the Ferriers pinning me in. I'm not skilled enough for this. I don't even have a staff to herd souls onto the bridge. My bow and arrows will do me little good if I'm attacked.

Odiva has a word with Élodie, and the ash-blond Leurress guides me away from the others to a spot thirty feet from the head of the land bridge. I squirm and wrap my arms around myself. I'm in plain sight on the open beach. "Can't I watch from the cave?"

"Don't fret," Élodie tells me. "No soul will bother you here. The siren song will lure the dead onto the bridge; that much they can't resist. If they put up a fight, they will do it there."

"What if they *aren't* lured?" The hair on the back of my neck rises. "Do you really think the new flute will work?"

"Have faith, Sabine." Élodie squeezes my hand, but her trembling fingers reveal she's not as certain as she'd like me to believe.

She joins the other Ferriers, and they wade out ankle-deep in the water as the tide slowly recedes from the rocks of the land bridge.

My Leurress sisters look beautiful, all clothed in ceremonial white. Most of them wear the dresses from their rites of passage. I've mended holes and torn seams after their ferrying nights. I've also watched new Ferriers dry their own tears. These are the same dresses they wore when they ferried their own *amourés* after killing them. I feel sacrilegious and starkly different in my rough-spun hunting dress, and with two grace bones instead of three. I pray the souls of the dead won't notice.

I look back to the sea, and an amazed breath escapes me. The land bridge has almost fully emerged. Only a few webs of water spin around the rocks. From where I stand, the path looks like a cobblestone road on a rainy day, cutting through the current. Odiva is the first to set foot on it, and the others follow without beckoning.

The Ferriers spread along the length of the bridge in even intervals and hold their staffs ready. The elders choose the more precarious places—areas where the rocks are more uneven or the twelve-foot width of the path narrows to six feet. Odiva assumes her post at the end of the bridge, at least forty yards away, half the expanse of the inlet. Thanks to my nighthawk grace, which not only gives me better vision in the dark, but also far-reaching sight, I can see her in detail.

The *matrone* sweeps her raven hair behind her shoulder and lifts the new bone flute to her mouth. An eerie but lovely song rises above the sound of the lapping water. I've never heard this melody. It's different from the one Ailesse learned for her rite of passage. No one practices the song for the soul bridge, I suppose, since Odiva is the only one who plays it.

I brace myself against being lured to the bridge myself—each initiated Ferrier has labored for the strength to resist it—but the temptation only feels like a weak itch. The song, however, is enough to bring the dead.

I gasp as the first soul appears at the threshold of the cave I came out of. A little boy. His transparent body is the new color I've been told about, neither warm nor cool. The Leurress call it *chazoure*.

He walks onto the shore, wearing the nightclothes he must have been buried in. His eyes are round, like he's been startled awake from a deep slumber. He trips forward toward the bridge, though he looks afraid.

Vivienne is the first to greet him. Her chestnut hair fans around her shoulders as she crouches eye level to him. "It's all right." She offers him a kind smile. "We will help you."

The boy shyly takes her hand, and Vivienne guides him to Maurille, the next Ferrier in line.

I blow out an exhale. That wasn't so bad. Hopefully most of the dead are like this boy, earnest and sweet.

I've had the thought too soon.

I flinch when I see the next soul, a grown man. He scales down a cliff headfirst like a spider. *Chazoure* glows from the forged links wrapped around his neck and torso. He's Chained, marked for eternal punishment in Tyrus's Underworld. He's committed an unforgivable sin.

Vivienne's smile vanishes. She touches her wildcat jawbone necklace and holds her staff with both hands in a defensive stance. The man approaches the bridge, but stops at its head. Vivienne's frown mirrors my own. Élodie told me that all souls would at least ascend the bridge.

The man paces back and forth, muttering under his breath and tugging at his chains. At the end of the bridge, the siren song warbles on an off-note. Vivienne glances back at Maurille, who shrugs, as baffled by the man as she is. Vivienne cautiously steps off the soul bridge and approaches the Chained. As she reaches for his arm, he shoves her back. I've been taught how souls grow tangible, but I'm still shocked to see someone transparent make physical contact with a living person.

Vivienne's eyes flash, and she flexes her grip on her staff. She's a Ferrier. She's ready.

Almost faster than I can see, she feints with her staff and sweeps out her leg. The man is thrown on his backside. Before he can react, she hauls him up and swings her staff, driving him onto the bridge. His boots slide on the slippery rocks. He doesn't have Vivienne's graced balance. He finally escapes her hold, but Maurille is prepared. In one great leap spanning twenty feet, she lands in front of him and strikes her staff hard on his jaw. He staggers back, but she grabs his chains and drags him farther down the bridge. I don't see what happens next. A streak of *chazoure* draws my eye out to the sea.

The soul of a young woman is in the water. She swims toward the middle of the bridge. I can't see the rest of her body to know if she's Chained.

"Excuse me, mademoiselle."

I yelp and spin around. A *chazoure* man I haven't seen yet is three feet away. Unchained, thank the gods.

He takes off his hat and holds it to his chest. "Can you tell me about that path running through the water? I wonder if I should cross it, but, well, I don't know if it leads anywhere." His chin twitches beneath his beard. "You see, there's nothing at the end."

What is he talking about? I look at the bridge and focus where Odiva is guarding the Gates of the Beyond. Except there are no

Gates. The bridge ends with nothing but the sea.

My mouth falls slack. I don't understand. I thought the Gates were supposed to appear when the siren song summoned them. I'm not surprised that I can't see Elara's Gate to Paradise—it's said to be nearly invisible—but I should be able to see the Gate to Tyrus's Underworld. According to the Ferriers, it's made of water and hangs on nothing but air. Some describe it as a waterfall; others say it's more like a flowing veil. But the man beside me is right—it's not there. Which means Elara's Gate is missing, too. The song of the stag-carved bone flute wasn't powerful enough to raise the Gates.

My pulse quickens. "You should try to cross," I say to the man, though my tone is far from reassuring.

The Ferriers will know what do, I tell myself, but I worry at my lip as I watch Odiva. Her frown deepens as she glances back and forth at the oncoming souls and the space where the Gates should be. She pulls out her bird skull and ruby necklace, clutches it fiercely, and mouths, *Please, please, please.* If our Gates don't open tonight, no other ferrying Gates in the world will. The bone flute is supposed to unlock them all.

The man puts on his hat again and pastes on a *chazoure*-glowing smile. "*Merci.*" He tentatively walks toward the bridge.

Seven more souls pour out from the cave. Five descend from the surrounding cliffs. I gasp and backtrack in the sand. The dead are no longer trickling here; they're flooding. How many people in South Galle have died this past month?

Warily, the souls gather toward the land bridge. I'm amazed by the number of Chained—more than half of the gathering souls. Many of them wear soldiers' uniforms. I remember Odiva said a war had broken out north of Dovré.

The Ferriers' staffs whirl, strike, and jab. All of them are fighting now. When the Chained don't step on the bridge, some Ferriers run onto the shore and confront them. Dolssa battles two at once. Roxane dives into the water in pursuit of a man who swims farther out to sea.

My heart pounds against my rib cage. Élodie told me the dead can't resist being lured to the bridge, but the ones on it are trying to get off. They have no destination. They're going mad. Even the Unchained are starting to fight back. What I'm seeing is a twisted version of every story I've been told about ferrying night. I pictured a system of order, the necessary attacks on the Chained quick and graceful. Only a rare soul would prove too lethal.

Like the one who killed my mother.

The only way to truly defeat the Chained is to send them through the Gates. Which is now impossible. Ferriers can fight the dead, but the dead can't be killed again.

One of the Chained catches Maurille off guard and throws her off the bridge into shallow water. I backtrack another five steps in the sand. This is chaos. I have to leave. I'm not skilled enough to help anyone or to defend myself. I clutch Ailesse's shoulder necklace. I only have two grace bones and . . .

My breath hitches. Maurille is bleeding from the head. She must have struck it on a rock. She rises to her feet in the water, coughing and flinging rows of braids off her face. She tries to walk, but she staggers.

The Chained man who attacked her jumps off the bridge and lunges for her in the water. Maurille is a seasoned Ferrier, but her graces won't help her if she can't even stand up straight.

The Chained throws his fist. It connects with her jaw. "Maurille!" I cry as she careens down again.

I'm running. Faster than I've ever tested my grace. Maurille was my mother's closest friend. I can't let her die ferrying, too.

The Chained grabs Maurille's neck and holds her head underwater.

"Stop!" I frantically pull my bow off my back and grab an arrow from my quiver. I shoot and strike the Chained man's arm. He winces with a growl, but doesn't bleed like Maurille. And he doesn't let go of her.

Chazoure flares in the corner of my eye. More souls flock the beach. They're attacking each other now, as well as the Ferriers.

A brawling pair crashes in front of me and blocks my path. I don't stop running. I jump. I've seen other Leurress do better, but I've never cleared this much air. Another grace from my nighthawk.

I land without tumbling over and don't pause. I sprint for Maurille.

She's twenty feet back from the shoreline. Her legs thrash in the water. Bubbles spray above her head, then slow down. She's expelling her last breath. The Chained man won't release his vicious hold.

I kick through the water. I'm not moving fast enough. My adrenaline doesn't give me the strength I need. I should have killed the boar, the horse, the wolf.

Ten feet from Maurille, I unsheathe Ailesse's ritual knife from my belt. It won't kill the Chained man. I pray it will at least ward him away.

I charge the remaining five feet.

With a sharp cry of exertion, I strike for his chest.

25
Ailesse

THE NARROW TUNNEL I SQUIRMED through when I entered the catacombs has been dug out—probably by the Leurress when they tried to rescue me. Now my path is wide and easy to climb.

My graces guided me back here, like being pulled by an invisible string.

A silvery beacon shines at the end of the tunnel. I shudder with a feral pang of longing.

The Night Heavens.

Elara's Light.

I crouch and break into a run, lunging at it, charging for it. I'm a tiger shark, thrashing through the water. A peregrine falcon, diving through the sky. I'm desperate to breathe the open air and feel Elara's energy.

The tunnel opens, and I burst outside. Elara's stars shatter the darkness. I gasp as strength floods into my limbs and lifts me light on my toes like wings. I laugh, tipping my head back. How I've missed this vitality. It steels my bones and rushes like blood through my veins.

I sprint up the steep ravine with ease and race through the trees. I'm beaming, laughing harder, running faster and faster. The ground is soft at my feet. The air in my lungs is fresh and clean. I've risen from the graves of Dovré and the blinding dark of the catacombs. I'm alive. I'm *me* again.

A tall boulder looms ahead. In one jump, I bound onto it and land with perfect ibex balance. I pivot and take in my surroundings. My falcon grace stretches my vision two miles in every direction. My tiger shark's sixth sense helps me feel even farther. It doesn't take long before I orient myself in the vast forest outside Dovré.

I look up at the constellations and draw an imaginary line from the lodestar on the Huntress's brow to the two stars on the claw of the Jackal. I make adjustments for the day of the month and general position of the lodestar, and then determine the time. It's already midnight.

My pulse spikes. I need to hurry.

I spring down from the boulder and launch toward the west coast, praying I can find the land bridge quickly.

Trees rush past me as I pick up speed. I leap over streams and rivers and scarcely use a bridge. The pines give way to a grassy plateau, and I breathe in salty air. Along the horizon, the cliffs of the Nivous Sea appear. I race to the edge of one and gaze below.

Waves crash onto the shore, but I don't see the Ferriers. I didn't expect to on my first try. The location of the soul bridge is a secret that the Leurress only learn after completing their rites of passage.

I follow the curving cliffs to the south. Why haven't I found the bridge yet? It should be within a reasonable distance from Château Creux. I backtrack to my starting point and set off northward, searching in the other direction.

All I see with my far-reaching vision are lapping waves. All I feel from my sixth sense are buzzing vibrations of sea creatures.

Then a prickle of energy rises above them. It heightens to a thump, then a beat, then a distinct and forceful pound.

My heart stops as I hear a new noise, like a rushing waterfall. When I listen closer, I realize it's a chorus of shouts and battle cries.

The Leurress have started ferrying. Somehow *without* the bone flute.

I dash to the edge of a high cliff where the sound thrashes loudest. I glance over the steep drop-off and suck in a sharp inhale.

The soul bridge.

A flurry of white dresses dances within a storm of *chazoure*. I've never seen the color before, but this must be it. The dead are wearing it. They're made of it.

It's more breathtaking than I thought possible.

Tears prick my eyes. I'm really here. For as long as I can remember, joining the Ferriers has been my dream—standing alongside the elite of my *famille*, wrestling the Chained and gently leading the Unchained.

But then I blink. And I see. My stomach hardens like a rock. None of what's happening below is gentle. The souls are waging war on the Ferriers, and the Ferriers are ferociously fighting back.

My mother's face comes into focus. The calm strength she always exudes is gone. She's frantic and distraught, battling five Chained souls at the end of the bridge. I look just beyond her, and my eyes fly wide. The Gates haven't appeared. That's the reason for all this madness. Odiva can't send any souls to the Beyond.

Perspiration flashes across my skin. I have to help her.

I sprint along the cliff in search of the elusive hidden stairs, but I don't see any sign of them. I can't jump from here. The beach must be at least a hundred feet below. I have to find another way to get down there. My mother needs to play the flute while on the land bridge. That much she taught me.

I clutch the pouch of grace bones around my neck, remembering my crescent pendant. The ibex grace can help me scale down the cliffs.

I hitch up my skirt and run toward the rougher cliffs on the other side. When I pass the inner bend of the inlet, my nerves tingle on the right side of my body. A mile across the plateau, in that direction, I see three people. My vision pulls to Bastien, and my heart trips faster. I grind my teeth and turn away. He's no threat to me now that I have my graces.

I keep running, but then I glance out to the sea and my knees lock. I stumble to a stop. The land bridge has started to submerge. The Ferriers are now standing in an inch of water. The Chained tug at them, trying to drag them into the depths. I don't have time to descend the cliffs. I need to act now.

I draw the bone flute from the sash at my waist. The unique siren song that opens the Gates is imprinted in my mind. My mother often played it on a wooden flute in a secluded meadow near Château Creux. I'd hide in the wild grass and watch her. She had the deepest look of longing in her eyes.

I blow in the mouth hole. The song comes clumsily at first, but then I steady my trembling fingers. Coming from the bone of a golden jackal, the siren song sounds so much richer and more harrowing.

Will anyone hear me? The chaos below is cacophonous.

Maurille looks up from the beach. She has a hand pressed to her bleeding head. Soon Giselle, Maïa, Rosalinde, and Dolssa turn and lift their eyes. They're on the shore, closer to me, and have the sharpest hearing. A moment later, another Leurress follows their gaze.

Sabine.

My chest swells with a rush of happiness, despite the horror below. Her face mirrors my shock and my joy. The fifteen days I've spent without her have felt like a thousand.

She's holding a bone knife—my ritual knife—in a defensive stance. I don't understand. Is Sabine a Ferrier? A lump forms in my throat. The two of us have never hunted for grace bones without each other.

Chazoure streaks off the sinking land bridge. The color floods the water and swarms onto the shore. The dead are coming closer to me.

The Leurress aren't the only ones who heard my song.

I trip back a step. I can't think about Sabine right now. I've failed to open the Gates. The dead are flocking to *me* now, like I'm a living Gate—a door that some want to embrace and others want to destroy.

I curse the names of the gods.

I desperately pray to them.

Tyrus, Elara, what do I do, what do I do?

Past the oncoming flood of *chazoure*, I meet my mother's dark and determined eyes. She's not looking at me directly. Her gaze is latched on the bone flute in my hand. She holds another flute, but its color isn't aged. And it clearly didn't open the Gates.

My mother's nostrils flare. She strides toward me through the rising water above the bridge, another half inch deeper. She must think I lied about the flute. But I didn't. I thought it was gone.

A Chained man retreats off the bridge. He's slower than the others—and he's in Odiva's way. Her lips curl back, and she springs for him. She delivers a powerful kick on his back. He slaps the water face-first. She drags him up, spins for momentum, and hurls him into the sea. He crashes against a protruding rock. She turns back to me, her eyes narrowed.

I ball my hands into fists. Bastien and the others are a half mile behind me and getting closer. I can't worry about them yet. Several Chained are scaling the cliffs. Any moment now they'll reach me.

I inhale and set my jaw. Slide the flute into my sash. Focus on my graces.

I'm my mother's daughter, and she's just dared me to prove it to her.

26
Sabine

I GASP AS THE DEAD flood to Ailesse. The Ferriers look as shocked as I feel. Odiva doesn't pause. She charges through the water of the sinking land bridge and attacks every Chained in her path. Her eyes are livid and desperate. She thought Ailesse was dead. Or she lied, saying she was. Either way, she must be frantic about retrieving the bone flute. It's the only way to get rid of the dead—if it's not too late to raise the Gates.

"We have to stop the Chained!" I call to the Ferriers. "Ailesse can't fight them all at once!"

Élodie squares her shoulders. Roxane lifts her chin. They chase after the souls, their staffs lifted. The other Ferriers shout a battle cry and follow after them.

Maurille is sitting on the stone I eased her onto after saving her from the Chained man. Blood drips down her brow, but she seems more alert now. "Take my staff," she says.

I look to where it's floating in the water near the shore. I've trained to fight with a staff like every novice Leurress, but only halfheartedly. I never wanted to harm my sparring partners. And I never wanted to be a Ferrier. "Will you be all right?"

She nods and squeezes my hand. "Go. Ailesse needs you."

I suck in a steadying breath and race for the staff. I feel like I'm diving into the lagoon all over again, but this time it's a horde of Chained that can't be killed, not a tiger shark, that threatens my best friend.

I kick through the shallow water, grab the staff, and dash back to the beach, grateful for my graced speed. Almost every Chained who's on the shore is engaged by a Ferrier. Another flare of *chazoure* draws my focus to a Chained man. He's climbing the cliff wall to get to Ailesse. He's too high for me to reach, so I draw an arrow from my quiver. I shoot and miss. It takes a second try for me to hit him. His body lurches, but he doesn't fall; he keeps climbing.

I cast off my bow and quiver and bolt for him, praying my nighthawk grace will help me clear enough air. I plunge the end of my staff in the sand and vault as high as I can. I fly even higher than the Chained man and kick him as I arc down.

He's knocked from the wall. Before I drop any farther, I push off the wall and flip backward. My landing isn't elegant, but the sand absorbs most of the shock as I crash and tumble on the ground. I'm up again in a moment. The Chained is just pulling himself to his feet. His *chazoure* face turns a shade darker as he growls with rage.

I pluck up my staff, amazed at what I just did. Ailesse will laugh with pride when I tell her.

Ailesse.

My pulse quickens. She can't defeat all these Chained on her own. I glance up. Some souls have already climbed over the cliff, and two more are nearing the top. I can't vault that high.

The Chained I attacked lunges for me. I swing my staff and bring it down on his head. It strikes with a sickening crack, but there's no gash, no blood. He cries out in pain and stumbles to his knees. I cast aside my quiver and bow—the staff is a better weapon—and rush for the opening of the cave and toward the base of the hidden stairs. I'll get up to Ailesse this way.

The cave isn't empty. Three of the dead are also racing for the stairs at the back. Dolssa is in here, fighting to drive them away. Her staff whips one direction then the next as she attacks from all angles. I jump in to assist her.

I strike one of the Chained from behind. He's thrown into the air. Dolssa skewers him. I swallow against the brutality and turn to confront the next soul. A man. Unchained. The one with that hat who asked me why the land bridge led to nothing. He tries to scurry past me to the stairs, but I block him. "You shouldn't go up there."

His lip trembles. "But the song . . . it's calling me home. My wife is already there."

My chest sinks. "That isn't the way home. You need to stay near the land bridge until you hear the song again." Odiva might get the bone flute back tonight, but it can't make the tides recede. That won't happen again for another month. *What will the Ferriers do about the dead until then?*

"I've waited long enough!" he says, and shoves me back with surprising strength.

Just as I fall to the ground, Dolssa swings her staff. The man's head jerks to the side, and he crumples. I blink at her in shock. "He was Unchained!"

Her face is severe and unrelenting. "All the dead are dangerous now."

Another Unchained soul barrels into the cave. Dolssa runs to stave her off. More Chained are darting from the beach toward us—toward the hidden staircase in the cave. They're after Ailesse.

I push to my feet and begin my chase up the flight.

I'll battle every soul on the 167 steps, if I have to.

I'll get to Ailesse first.

27
Ailesse

My mother is calf-deep in the water above the sinking land bridge. Our eyes briefly meet as she charges forward, fighting three souls at once. She's still struggling to get to me—to the flute—but she's only made it halfway down the flooding bridge.

On my left, a flare of *chazoure* rises over the cliff—a man with a shaved head and a thick neck wrapped in chains. I bolt for him in one leap and strike his head with my heel. He loses his grip on the limestone and plummets off the cliff. I wish I had wings to fly with him. I need to get down to the shore and give my mother the flute so she can rein in this crisis. But dozens more souls riot between us and continue to flood toward me.

Another person climbs up the cliff on my right. She hefts

herself up onto the grass and stands. I tense to attack, but I don't see any chains.

"Help!" She clutches the loose-fitting gown over her stomach and runs to me. "They won't let me see my baby." Translucent tears spill down her cheek. "I need to go back. I didn't even get to hold him."

My heart squeezes. She must have died in childbirth. "I'm sorry, I can't give you back your life."

"Please." She falls to her knees.

A broad-shouldered man races toward me from behind. I've no idea where he came from. He's wearing a chain-clad uniform. A soldier, trained to fight.

"I killed in the name of my king!" he shouts. "You can't drag me to Hell!"

"If the gods marked you with those chains, you must have lusted for your kills."

He lunges for me with a savage growl. I pull back from the woman, but she catches my skirt. I'm knocked off balance, and the man cuffs my jaw. I gasp with a bright shock of pain. He grabs my arms and slings me across the ground. I roll to the edge of the cliff.

"Ailesse!"

My heart kicks. *Bastien.* He sounds concerned. I want none of it.

I jump back up and duck another punch from the Chained. I barrel into his chest and push him to the brink of the cliff. His feet dig into the chalky dirt. Pebbles skid off the edge. He seizes my shoulders and shoves against me. He's strong, but not as strong as my tiger shark. I can drive him over the edge. But if I do, he might pull me with him.

I wrest one of my arms away. I yank Marcel's knife from my sash. With a cry of exertion, I stab the soldier in the chest. His eyes bulge in pain. If he were alive, this would be a killing blow.

It's how I would have killed Bastien on the ritual bridge.

I swallow the bile scalding my throat. This isn't murder.

Like my rite of passage would have been.

Another cry escapes me, this one mangled with rage. I stab the Chained again, but he only grips me harder. I keep stabbing, keep screaming. I fight to control my betraying thoughts—the image of Bastien if I'd done this to him.

No blood spills from the Chained, although my blade plunges deep. I'm hurting him, but not disabling him.

"Let her go!" the Unchained woman shouts, and rushes at him. "I need her to—"

I gasp as the soldier flings her over the edge, but I can't pause to feel pity. While he's distracted, I jerk away and swivel out of his hold. I whip my leg out and swing back for him. My kick strikes like a hammer, and he's thrust off the cliff.

I've barely turned around when the next person confronts me. She doesn't glow with *chazoure*. She's alive.

I slash my knife through the air between us, a warning. I'm all too aware she can bleed. "Don't interfere, Jules."

"With what?" she demands, but her wide eyes dart around us. "What are those voices? What are you fighting against?"

She knows—I told all my captors in the catacombs—but she's still unbelieving. "The dead."

She swallows and looks over the cliff, keeping as far back from the edge as she can. Jules doesn't have the vision to perceive the *chazoure* of the souls, but she can hear their raging screams and see thirty-four women below battling an invisible army.

I scan past her while she's stunned. A faint and deadly glow shines fifty yards away, limning two boulders. The entrance to the hidden staircase? More dead will emerge from there any moment and join those scaling the cliffs. I need my former captors out of the way. I need to get to my mother.

I whirl to my other side, feeling Bastien close in. Under the starlight, his rough-cut beauty is stark and raw, a siren song of its own. A rush of warmth prickles through me, but I stare him down. "You shouldn't have come here." He's going to get himself killed.

"You shouldn't have left." He glances around us. "You were safer in the catacombs."

Is he mocking me? He starved me of Light. Stripped me of my grace bones. He might as well have cut out a vital organ. "Is that why you came back, to keep me safe?" I chance another peek at the boulders. If I make a run for the stairs, maybe I'll have fewer Chained to fight there. "Are you going to protect me or kill me?" I throw a pointed look at the crude knife in the white-knuckled grip of his hand.

"Excellent question." Jules briefly tears her gaze from the growing roar of the dead.

Bastien's jaw muscle flinches. "Wouldn't you kill me if you were able to?"

"Gladly," I snap, but my conviction dies in the truth blazing between us. My heart skips faster. He knows I spared his life tonight when I ran away. And he spared mine when I fell into the pit. Still, how does that change our fates? "I've trained all my life for this. I don't need your protection."

He doesn't look so sure. "Why are the shouts coming louder now? The land bridge is gone."

My chest tightens. I spin around. The soul bridge has submerged so deeply that no one is standing on it anymore. My mother is in the shallow water near the beach, wrestling two Chained. Maybe I can throw the flute down to her. Maybe it's not too late. If she can't raise the Gates tonight, we'll have to wait another month for the next new moon.

A glowing hand slams over the edge of the cliff. A woman's hand, close to Bastien. Her *chazoure* wrist bears chains.

"Move away!" I reach for him. Jules dives at me. I twist to dodge her, but not in time. She grabs the bone flute from my sash.

I gasp. "Give that back!"

The Chained woman drags herself up. Her hair glitters with jewels. I don't have time for this.

"Please, Jules, you don't know what that really is."

"It snared Bastien to you, and now it's summoned the dead. It's evil and needs to be destroyed." She arcs her arm back to throw it into the sea.

"Stop! My mother needs that," I rush to explain. "When a different song is played on the flute, it opens the Gates of the Beyond—the afterlife, Heaven, Hell, whatever you want to call it."

"It's a key?" Marcel lopes toward us. "Then it may help break the soul-bond."

That's the last of my worries right now. "If the dead can't cross the soul bridge, they can't leave this world."

"I will *never* leave this world." The Chained woman stalks forward and unties a velvet ribbon from around her neck. "My riches are mine."

The color drains from Jules's face. She looks to Bastien. "Did you hear that?" she rasps.

He nods soberly. "Don't throw that away."

The Chained woman doesn't bat an eye at them. She stretches her ribbon tight between her hands.

Jules shoves the flute in her pocket. "Fine. Then let's get what we *really* came for." She twirls her knife. "Come on, Bastien."

His face hardens, but I note the tremor in his knife hand. He and Jules draw in closer toward me. They don't know it, but they're flanking the Chained woman.

I backtrack for more room to fight. I can handle four people.

Marcel retreats in a different direction. "Ailesse has my knife," he points out.

Jules turns worried eyes on him. "Stay near, do you hear me? We don't know what . . ." He hurries away. "Marcel, wait!"

Three people, then. Even better.

Jules looks back at me with gritted teeth. She's the first to attack. No surprise. When her blade slices for me, I leap into the air and cartwheel over her head. The move is so quick she doesn't have time to react before I land and nick her arm. She hisses and whirls to face me. She tries to stab me three times, in places she won't kill me, but her strikes are easy to block. She fights in an identical style as Bastien did at Castelpont.

He hovers at the edge of our struggle, his brows pulled tight. Is he hesitating or just trying to find a way to cut in?

Flares of *chazoure* burst above the cliff like twin suns. Two more Chained climb over the top. They're not stealthy like the jeweled woman. Once they're on their feet, they race toward me, but Jules stands in the way.

"Watch out!"

She doesn't. One of the Chained—a man—grabs her by the waist and heaves her aside. She screams and flies several feet before tumbling to the ground. The Chained man comes at me next. I prepare to strike, but I'm snagged back. I can't breathe. The Chained woman has her velvet ribbon wrapped around my neck. I choke and struggle, and the Chained man punches me in the stomach. My eyes squeeze shut against a shock of hot pain. I sense the third Chained circling like a vulture.

My vision pulses as I open my eyes. I see Bastien in flashes. He's trying to get to me, aimlessly slashing his knife through the air. He can't abduct me if I'm dead.

He can't *live* if I'm dead.

And I can't get the flute to my mother if I'm dead.

Think, Ailesse. My brain is foggy, starved for air.

I lean back against the woman to support myself. When the second Chained rushes at me again, I swing my legs up and kick him hard. He's thrown onto his back and skids across the ground.

I remember my knife. By some miracle, I haven't lost my grip on the hilt. I plant my feet and reach past my shoulder. I slice the woman's left wrist, then her right one. With a raging scream, she lets go of me. I suck in a burning gasp of air and shove her into the third Chained, stealing his opportunity to lunge at me. Before the two souls regain their balance, I spring in the air, turn my blade down, and fall on each of them. I wound them deeply, then dart away toward the entrance to the stairs.

I don't make it far. Three new Chained pour out from between the two boulders. A moment later, two more follow. I halt and scramble in the other direction.

Bastien catches up to me. He makes no move to attack when I freeze as more souls flood over the cliff. He takes a defensive stance, positioning himself with his back against mine. "Where are they?" he asks, his knife drawn.

I shake my head. "Everywhere."

Five more Chained pull up to their feet after they finish climbing. Two of them I've already fought—the soldier and the man with the shaved head. Their *chazoure*-glowing eyes lock on mine. They're not after Jules and the flute; they're after me. I played the siren song.

There's magic at work here I don't understand. But if a song from the flute bound me to Bastien, what does that mean for me and the dead?

The Chained converge on us, picking up speed. "Mother!" My desperate cry shudders through the air. The Chained can't be killed, only ferried. All this fighting is in vain. If I can't get the flute to Odiva quickly, she'll have to come and take it from Jules. I glance around for her, but can't find her past the oncoming swarm. "We're surrounded, Bastien. There are too many!"

The muscles in his back tense against mine. "How do we break through them?"

I rake my gaze over the tightening circle. "I don't think we can. Stay close to me."

"I'm not leaving you."

"I'll tell you when to attack."

"I'll be ready."

The Chained man with the shaved head is the first to charge at me. The woman with the velvet ribbon leaps for Bastien. "To your left!" I cry, and swipe my knife at the man. Bastien blindly stabs the woman with his blade, and Jules's throaty voice cuts the air.

"Stay away from them! It's me you want." I see Jules now, standing on a lone boulder several yards away. Wisps of her golden hair have sprung loose from her braid. She holds the bone flute high in her right hand. "I'm the one with the flute, and I can send every one of you to Hell with it!"

A bluff, but the Chained man and woman stop attacking. *Chazoure* flashes as the other souls turn conflicted gazes on Jules. Bastien's brows hitch up. "Jules, what are you—?"

"Run!" she shouts, and jumps off the boulder. She sprints across the plateau and away from the cliff.

Half of the Chained follow.

Bastien expels a sharp breath. "*Merde.*" He bolts after her.

I race alongside him. My heart beats a frantic rhythm. "Come back!" I yell at Jules. She just saved us, but she can't take the flute away from here. It's the only thing that can stop the Chained.

If Jules hears me, she makes no indication. She only runs faster, keeping her distance from the Chained. Marcel jogs a little ahead of her. His floppy hair whips in the breeze. Eventually they'll both tire, but the Chained won't.

The souls that don't follow Jules pursue me and Bastien. "Careful!" I say, as one draws near him. I reach for his hand and tug him out of the way. We keep our fingers locked as we race onward. He veers when I pull him. "On your right!" I warn. He whips out his knife and cuts another Chained man across the chest.

"Is he dead?" Bastien looks back as we race faster.

"He was already dead."

"Right." He tightens his grip on my hand.

Two Chained come at us from both sides. "Duck!" I shout.

Bastien drops to the ground and dodges a brutal punch. I roll over his back and stab one of the Chained men in his side. I turn to fight the second one, but Bastien's already sliced his legs. He kicks him down, then jumps back up.

Our hands come together again, and we keep running. I glance back and scan the now-distant cliff for my mother. Or Sabine. Or any Ferrier. But all I see is the grassy plateau glowing with the *chazoure* of the dead.

I have to stop them before they reach Jules and Marcel—and then all of South Galle.

I have to get the flute.

28
Sabine

MY LEGS BURN AS I near the top of the long flight of stairs. I've fought and outrun two Chained already, but at least five more are ahead of me. Finally, I'm close enough to one to attack.

I raise my staff to slam it down on him, when someone grabs my dress from behind. I swing my staff around, but the staircase is too narrow. My staff hits the limestone wall with a loud *crack*. Instinctively, I kick and shove the Chained off me. But then I see she wears no chains. She's only a young girl, at the most twelve years old, with *chazoure*-glowing ringlets.

Her eyes round as she tumbles backward, falling down the steep stairs. My chest pangs. "I'm sorry!" I run down three steps after her, but then I force myself to stop. I've hurt her, but she won't die. Ailesse might.

I turn around, but the other Chained are already gone. I race up the last steps and squeeze through the narrow gap between the boulders. Once I'm through, my mouth falls open. The bluff is lit up with *chazoure*. Twenty or more of the dead are up here. Mostly Chained. Some are fighting among each other, as well as a few Unchained. The rest retreat from the cliff.

Hope surges through me until I see Ailesse in the distance. Her auburn hair billows as she runs directly away from me, across the plateau. The souls aren't leaving her—half are following her, and she's chasing the rest.

I start to call her name, but my throat runs dry. My sharp vision focuses. The Chained around her separate just enough for me to see that she's with someone—Bastien. And they're holding hands.

My feet trip. A rush of dizziness seizes me. I don't understand. Ailesse escaped Bastien to come here and bring back the bone flute.

Didn't she?

She's running with him, not being dragged behind. It almost looks like she's leading him.

Of course she is. She's the only one who can see the dead. And if the dead kill Bastien, she'll die, too. She's only fleeing with him because it's her better chance to survive the Chained. Though that doesn't explain why she's pursuing some of them.

It doesn't matter. She still needs help.

She still needs me.

I race after her, then shriek as another soul lashes my arm. He's using his dangling chain as a whip. The blow knocks my staff away.

I clutch my arm and stagger backward. The man comes for me again. He swings his chains above his head. I have no weapon to block him.

His chains slash downward. I drop, wrapping my hands over my head to protect myself. Nothing hits me. I look up and gasp. Odiva is here. The skirt of her dress drips with seawater. Her raven hair ripples like black fire. The man's chains are caught around the end of her staff. With incredible strength, she throws him far off the cliff.

I'm awestruck as she pulls me to my feet. "Are you all right?" she asks.

I nod, dazed, and release a shuddering breath. "But Ailesse . . . Bastien has her again."

Odiva winces, just a slight flare of her nostrils, and looks across the plateau. The moment she notices them, she stiffens and curls her hands. Her darkening glare makes my blood run cold.

Pernelle dashes over to us. "Did you see her, *Matrone*? Ailesse is alive!"

Finally, I'm vindicated for never doubting.

Odiva averts her eyes. "Yes, she must have survived her fall in the pit."

"Her *amouré* survived, too." Pernelle steps forward. "I thought you said he died with her."

Odiva lifts a single black brow. "I am as shocked as you are."

Pernelle shoots another frantic look at Ailesse. "We need to go after her at once, or the boy might take her back to the catacombs."

"Or before the Chained reach her first," I say, flinching as another rush of souls streaks by.

Odiva's mouth forms a determined line. "Call the others, Pernelle. Some are fast enough to outrun the dead. Tell them to stop fighting and to race after my daughter. Retrieving the bone flute is our priority now."

"And saving Ailesse," I add.

Odiva takes a tense breath and briefly meets my gaze. "Of course."

"What about the boy?" Pernelle asks.

"Capture him, but do not kill him. Ailesse must be the one to do that."

My fingers wrap around the hilt of Ailesse's ritual knife at my belt. Pernelle bows to Odiva and runs off to do her bidding.

I lunge to chase after Ailesse, but Odiva grasps my arm. Her hand is alarmingly rigid. "Wait."

"But she's getting away." I struggle against her hold.

"I am commanding you to stay back, Sabine."

My cheeks burn. "Why?" Why isn't *she* running after Ailesse straightaway? Odiva is faster and stronger than any of us.

When the *matrone* doesn't answer, I turn to her. Her unblinking gaze is riveted on something to the north. On the far horizon, at the very last stretch of my graced vision, I spy a silhouetted animal. Maybe a wolf.

"It is a sign, Sabine," Odiva says in a hush of great reverence.

What is she talking about? Why are we stalling when Ailesse needs us? "A sign from whom?"

"A god." Odiva clutches her bird skull and ruby necklace, and the hair on my arms rises. "He's accepted my sacrifices," she murmurs, like she's forgotten I'm even here with her. "He's giving me one more chance to bring back . . ." Her voice goes hoarse with emotion, and she shakes her head. "But I must do this his way."

"Do what?" I ask. My stomach folds as my *matrone*'s face hardens into a mask of cool resolve. The last time I saw this same expression was when she claimed Ailesse was dead.

I frown and take a closer look at the animal on the horizon. Its tail and legs are a little shorter than a common wolf's. It also has a longer torso and a narrower, more pointed muzzle. "Is that—?"

"Tyrus's gift to us." A slow smile spreads on Odiva's gravely beautiful face. "That's his golden jackal."

29
Bastien

AILESSE'S WARM HAND PRESSES TIGHTER against mine as we race into the forest, past the edge of the plateau. "How many of the dead are still behind us?" I ask. I hear their pounding feet, growls, and vicious cries coming closer.

A strand of her auburn hair whips across her face as she glances backward. "At least twenty. All of them are Chained. I don't know what happened to the others."

"Chained?" I pant for breath as we keep running. Ailesse isn't winded at all.

She shakes her head. "I'll explain later." We weave around a large tree.

"Psst!" Marcel waves both arms at us. He's behind a rocky knoll to our right.

I look at Ailesse. She casts another quick glance around us and nods. "Hurry, before they see us."

We bolt for the knoll. On its other side is an overhang with a shallow cavity of earth beneath. Marcel ducks into it, and we tumble in next. Jules is down here, too. I end up wedged between her and Ailesse.

The horde of the dead grows louder. Ailesse holds a finger to her lips. We wait in tense silence as they rush past us. Female voices soon follow, shouting as they chase after them. Another long moment passes, and then Ailesse gives a reassuring nod.

Marcel heaves a sigh. "Well, that was exciting."

"Too exciting," Jules says.

"You saved us back there," I tell Jules, jostling her with my shoulder. "Don't get me wrong; I hated it. Promise me you'll never do something like that again. I thought those dead were going to run both of you through. But it took a lot of spine. It was very Jules."

It's dim under the knoll, but I catch the corners of her mouth lift. "You'd do the same for me . . . wouldn't you?" Her voice wavers with uncertainty.

I snort. "Do you even have to ask?"

It takes her a moment to reply. "You can let go of Ailesse's hand now."

Ailesse and I glance at each other. Our hands break apart at the same time. Mine is suddenly cold.

"Where's the flute, Jules?" Ailesse asks.

"It's . . . safe," she replies.

My gut twists. Something is wrong. I see it in the desperate but determined look on Jules's face. "What are you doing?"

She swallows. "What you can't do, Bastien."

"Jules . . ." Ailesse's voice trembles dangerously. "That flute is the only real weapon my mother has against the dead. *Give—it—to—me.*"

"I will." Jules takes a steeling breath. "Once you give me all your grace bones."

"What?" Ailesse's leg muscles tense up against mine. "You can't be serious. The dead will attack Dovré next if they're not stopped. Give me the flute. Now."

"No."

In a flash, Ailesse pulls into a crouch and lunges for Jules.

Jules anticipates her and jumps out of the hollow. Ailesse bounds after her. Marcel and I share a wide-eyed glance and scramble to intervene.

Ailesse is already on top of Jules, pinning her down. "Where did you hide it?" She shakes her, but Jules stubbornly mashes her lips together. Ailesse turns furious eyes on Marcel. "Tell me where it is!"

He freezes, halfway out of the hollow. "I . . . promised not to."

Ailesse's lip curls. She springs off Jules and pounces for Marcel. I jump between them, and Ailesse knocks into me instead. We both topple to the ground. She jerks up to her knees, and I pull up and grab her shoulders. "Wait!" I'm well aware she has the strength to break free anytime she wishes. "We can talk this through."

"We don't have time!"

"Then give me your bones." Jules sits up, forest mulch in her braid.

Ailesse's eyes narrow. "That's like asking me to cut out my heart."

"I understand." Jules spares me a pained glance. "But it's the only way to protect Bastien from you."

I stare incredulously at my friend. "Ailesse could have left me in the middle of those invisible monsters back there. She just rescued me!"

"So she can kill you on her own terms—on a bridge or with a special knife or whatever ritual she requires."

"She *does* need a special knife," Marcel concedes, brushing dirt off his clothes.

Ailesse flinches and glances westward. "One of the dead is nearby." She shifts protectively in front of me.

I can't see or hear anything unusual, but I believe her. "Jules, give her back the damn flute."

"And then what?" Jules hisses. "Do you really think Ailesse will willingly surrender?"

"I don't know!" I whisper. "Everything is different now. We can't be rash about a new plan."

"Our plan has always been *revenge*."

A fierce cry of rage splits the air, maybe fifty yards away. Ailesse freezes. "He's seen us."

Merde.

Ailesse rushes to Jules. "Please. I'll take the flute and run far away from here. The soul will follow *me*, and Bastien will be safe." Her brow twitches. "All of you will be."

"For now, anyway." Jules holds out an open hand. "The flute for your bones," she tells Ailesse. "I'll give them back after we figure out how to break the soul-bond."

Ailesse ignores her. She darts back to the knoll and scours the hollow beneath it.

The dead man shouts again. Thirty yards now. I pull out my knife. "We have to go! We'll come back for the flute later."

"No!" Ailesse keeps searching for it. She digs through the wild grass beside the knoll.

Two more shouts. From the east this time. My pulse races. "They're surrounding us!"

"I can't leave it!"

The dead roar closer. Jules moves defensively toward Marcel.

Ailesse kicks at the grass and releases a cry of frustration.

Jules points to a spot between her and Ailesse, twelve feet away. "Throw your bones on the ground there, then I'll fetch your flute."

Ailesse purses her lips. She glances east and west. The dead will be here any second. "No one touches my bones until I have the flute in my hands. Agreed?" I can almost see her thinking, *I'll get them right back.* She might have a chance. She's still fast without her graces.

"Agreed," Jules says quickly. "Now, throw them!"

Ailesse squeezes her eyes shut. Whispers something about Elara. Yanks the small pouch off her neck and tosses it on the ground. At once, she's noticeably weaker. Drooped shoulders. Strained brows. But she still holds her jaw stiffly. "The flute. Hurry!"

Jules whips it out of her boot. My eyes widen. Ailesse blows out an enraged breath. Jules had it on her the whole time.

A ragged shout blasts into my ears. The dead man. He's right here. I leap in front of Ailesse and slash out with my knife. I strike nothing. She wildly swings her fisted hands at the air. They connect with an invisible force, but it doesn't stop the dead man I can't see. Ailesse is hurled on the ground like a cloth doll.

I rush over to her. She's flat on her back. She blinks at me, eyes dazed. "I can't see them anymore."

"The dead?"

She nods.

She needs her bones, as well as the flute. I spring for the pouch, but it's already gone. Jules slips it over her own neck. Her chin quivers. "I'm doing this for you, Bastien."

"Doing what?" I frown.

Ailesse cries out. She's thrashing on the ground. The dead man is on top of her. My chest tightens. I race over and grab blindly at the man. I manage to shove him off, but a moment later he jabs me roughly in the gut. I double over, coughing.

Jules backs away, her hand on her brother's arm. "Marcel and I will figure out how to break the soul-bond." She bites her lip and glances at the flute in her hand. "I'm sorry, but he said we might need this."

I gape at her. "Jules . . ."

"This is the only way to save you. You're too smitten with her, Bastien." Her brow furrows. "We'll find you when it's done."

I throw a desperate look at Marcel, but he only lowers his eyes. They both run away.

I struggle to my feet. "Wait!"

Someone barrels into me from the other direction. Invisible. Another of the dead. I grapple with it—him, her, I can't tell—and slice my knife across its arms. It shrieks and lets go.

"Leave both of them alone!" Jules shouts at our attackers. Several yards away, she waves the flute as she races off with Marcel. "It's me you want!" Footsteps pound after her. A spike of adrenaline hits my veins. Not again. She shouts over her shoulder, "Go, Bastien! Take her and run for the catacombs!"

Ailesse stops moving. Her eyelids flutter and close. She lies lifeless on the ground.

Merde.

I bolt over and fall to my knees, gathering her up in my arms. Her head flops against my neck, and her breath warms my skin. I release a shaky exhale. She's alive, but she has a large lump on the back of her head. The dead man must have bashed it on the ground.

I stand and heft her up with me. Cradling her close, I run as fast as possible—painstakingly slow—but at least no more eerie cries come from the forest. For the moment, the dead are gone.

I rush after Jules and Marcel, but quickly lose their trail. I don't stop. And I don't run for the ravine catacombs entrance. My friends won't be there, and I won't take Ailesse where Jules can find her. If Jules *does* find a way to break the soul-bond, she'll come after Ailesse.

I square my jaw, inhale deeply, and take the path that forks to Dovré.

What are you doing, Bastien? This is the girl you wanted to kill.

I don't know what I want anymore, but it's not harming Ailesse—not in any way.

The city is still dark by the time I stumble in past the walls. My muscles burn, but I'm driven onward with almost manic energy. Ailesse is still limp in my arms, but she's becoming coherent. She mumbles, "*Chazoure* . . . can't see it." The word has something to do with the ghosts we fought tonight. I still haven't processed all the surreal events.

I race through alley after alley. Every rustle and whisper makes me jump. I keep tensing for an invisible enemy to attack. I have to get Ailesse well out of sight.

In one of the poorer districts, the crumbling spires of Chapelle du Pauvre struggle to reach the sky. The church for the poor is in a state of near ruin and hardly used anymore. I adjust my grip on Ailesse and hurry inside. In one of the alcoves behind the altar, I yank a moth-eaten rug off the floor. Beneath it is a hatch. I flop it open on its hinges. I set Ailesse on her feet, my hand on her waist to support her, and guide her down a rickety ladder.

"What's going on?" Her legs wobble. It's like her body didn't feel the toll of all her fighting tonight until she lost her graces. "Is Jules down here? I need the flute. My mother . . ." She clutches her head and staggers to stay standing.

We reach the cellar, and I help her sit on a crate. "Jules ran off with the flute and your bones," I reply, and my jaw muscle hardens. "Marcel is with her."

Ailesse gasps. "But the dead—"

"We'll figure out what to do about them later."

"I can't hide down here while innocent people are in danger." She makes a break for the ladder. I grab her and pull her back. She tries to fight me, but her strength is spent. I push her down on the crate again.

"You're hurt, Ailesse—and you don't have your graces anymore. For tonight, we rest. I promise to look for Jules tomorrow. In the meantime, I'm sure the other Bone Criers are doing something about the dead. It doesn't all fall on you. Can't they pen the dead in somewhere?"

She sits back. "I don't know. Maybe." She buries her head in her hands. "This has never happened before. At least not in my lifetime."

I try to think of something comforting to say, but my mind runs blank. Nothing like this has ever happened to me before either.

I feel around in the dark for the tinderbox I've stashed down here. I finally find it at the back of a dusty shelf and light a lantern. The candle inside has already melted to a stub. I'll have to get more soon, along with other supplies. I can't remember how much I've stored in my hideout. I spent so much time here as a child, back before I met Jules and Marcel. This is the one place I never told them about, and here I am, about to show a girl I've only known for a couple weeks. A girl I'm desperate to keep alive.

I open a door leading off the cellar. Ailesse stiffens as I reach for her. Her pupils flicker and reflect the candle's flame. "Does that lead to the catacombs?" she asks.

I nod. This entrance beneath Chapelle du Pauvre was built long ago for families who couldn't afford burial plots above. Here, they were able to carry down their departed loved ones and place them in unmarked graves below. "Can you think of any safer place from the dead?"

She shakes her head slowly. "The dead don't want to believe they're dead. The catacombs are a reminder."

I lean against the doorjamb. "They won't stop chasing you, you know. You're like a beacon to them."

She twists her hands in her lap and gives me such a long look that my ears prickle with heat. "I won't go in there as your prisoner," she says, her voice iron.

I could make her. She's lost her strength. It would be easy to bind her up again. "And I won't show you the hidden place in there if you try to kill me," I counter.

"I've proven I'm not going to kill you."

I sigh. "I'm not going to take you prisoner again, Ailesse. We're just going to have to trust one another."

She shifts on the crate. Her dress and the ends of her hair are still caked with gray silt mud. I'm coated in a good layer myself. We've brought the old catacombs with us. "Why are you helping me?" she asks.

I give a little shrug, averting my gaze. "If you die, I die, right? So I figure we need to stick together."

"And you promise to search for Jules?"

"I promise. I know everywhere she'd think to hide."

Ailesse exhales. "Everything you saw tonight—all the chaos and danger—happened because my mother played the siren song on the wrong flute. I have to get the right one back to her by the next new moon, or else—"

"I know." I want the ghosts of the dead ferried, too.

Ailesse bites her lower lip. It's cracked and parched. Did I give her enough water to drink in our old chamber? I glance at her wrists, raw and bruised from the ropes I tied her up with.

She has every reason to hate me.

"Fine," she says. "I'll go with you."

A rush of coolness washes through my chest. Relief? I don't understand myself. "Can you walk now?"

"I think so."

I flex my hand and reach for hers. As our palms slide together, my heart gives a hard pound. I briefly meet her umber eyes. They're uneasy, but also warm.

They're also damn gorgeous.

I swallow a lump in my throat and guide her past the door, then into the tunnel toward my secret hideout in the catacombs.

30
Sabine

AILESSE, WHERE ARE YOU? I'VE recovered my bow and quiver from the shore and have an arrow drawn as I pretend to hunt the golden jackal. I follow Ailesse's and Bastien's tracks as far as a knoll in the forest, where they meet up with other tracks—no doubt, her other captors—but then the tracks diverge and Ailesse's are lost.

"Stay where I can see you, Sabine," Milicent says, her voice firm though not unkind. "I may have vulture vision, but I can't see through a thick copse of trees."

I weave out of the copse, where I've found no sign of Ailesse, and mask my resentful glare. Odiva assigned Milicent to accompany me, while the other Ferriers were allowed to set off on their own, in order to gain more ground on the hunt for the jackal. The *matrone* is having me watched. She wants to ensure I don't risk my life by trying to rescue her daughter. Isn't Odiva worried about risking *Ailesse's* life?

"It's almost dawn." Milicent sighs and looks up at the sky. "We need to turn back. Hopefully the others had better luck."

Yes. Vain hope fills my chest. Maybe one of them found Ailesse.

We return empty-handed to the meeting spot Odiva designated—the cliffs over the submerged land bridge. Several Ferriers are already here. But no Ailesse. A painful lump rises in my throat. She was so close after all these days we've been apart. How did I let her get taken again?

Milicent and I near the other Ferriers, and their whispers reach my ears.

"Where have the dead gone?"

"Toward the city, of course, where the most people are."

"They want Light."

"What are we going to do about them?"

"Yes, Ailesse is alive."

"Why hasn't the *matrone* sent us to find her?"

Because the matrone *has secrets.* I don't know what they are, but they have to be the reason she's failing her daughter again and again.

The sun rises, casting a blade of light across the plateau, and Odiva finally rejoins us. Without the golden jackal. Claw marks scrape along the right side of her face and neck.

"*Matrone.*" Giselle gasps. "Are you all right?"

Odiva holds her head high and wears a reassuring smile. "I came *this close* to the jackal," she tells all of us, gesturing to her wounds like they're tokens of honor. "Tyrus is almost ready to give him to me."

I frown, examining her scrapes closer. The lines are grouped three scratches wide, not four like the front claws of a canine. Plus, there's a white feather with an amber edge caught among the eagle feathers of Odiva's epaulettes. I know which animal it belongs to—the same animal whose talons match the marks on Odiva.

The silver owl.

"We will retire to Château Creux and offer prayers to Tyrus," Odiva says. "Tomorrow, we shall begin the hunt anew."

"What about Ailesse?" I blurt.

Pernelle looks at me like she's wondering the same thing. She fidgets with her fox vertebra pendant and steps closer to Odiva. "I can lead another search party, *Matrone*. We might have better luck this time."

Odiva takes a moment to respond. Her eyes are on Pernelle, but the noctule bat skull on her crown seems to stare down at me. "No one is more concerned than I about my daughter," she says carefully. "But we must place our trust in the gods. If Tyrus has shown us the sign of his sacred jackal, we can rest assured he will protect Ailesse until the beast is ours."

My teeth set on edge. Maybe my faith is weak, but I don't trust the god of the Underworld to safeguard my friend. Odiva has been praying to him in secret, murmuring of the sacrifices she's given him and something she wants brought back in return. Whatever it is, it means more to her than Ailesse.

She gives Pernelle a curt nod. "We hunt the jackal first. We are sacred Ferriers, and this is how Tyrus has chosen to help us take care of the dead. We must honor his wishes. Sometimes our loyalty must be tested again, even after our rites of passage."

"Yes, *Matrone*." Pernelle bows her head, but I can't. My neck is stiff, and my head won't bend. I can't help thinking of Ailesse's failed rite of passage. Odiva promised me the gods would protect her daughter. Now I wonder if she chose me to be Ailesse's witness because she knew the gods *wouldn't*—at least Tyrus wouldn't—and I wouldn't be strong enough to intervene.

Tyrus's sign may be the golden jackal, but I'm starting to suspect the silver owl is Elara's. If the goddess sent her owl to attack Odiva, then she doesn't want Odiva to take the jackal's life.

"Our plan remains the same," Odiva tells the Ferriers. "Should any of you find the jackal before I do, capture it but do not kill it. As *Matrone*, I must be the one to make the sacrifice."

Maurille squints at Odiva with her good eye. The other one has swollen shut from the blow she took tonight. "Forgive me, *Matrone*, but Ailesse already has a working bone flute." Exactly. None of this is necessary. "Perhaps a few of us *should* search for her, as Pernelle suggested, while the others pursue the golden jackal. Surely Tyrus would understand our wish to work toward all options."

Odiva remains perfectly still, except for a thin smile, while her gaze narrows on Maurille. "Then you do not understand Tyrus at all. Fortunately for our *famille*, I do. The god of the Underworld is a jealous and exacting god. If we do not demonstrate our full allegiance, do you really believe he will lead us to his jackal?"

Maurille slowly shakes her head and casts me an apologetic glance.

Odiva looks around at the others. "Does anyone else care to speak a contrary word, or can we agree to submit to the path Tyrus has shown us?"

More heads lower in obedience. I only lower my eyes.

Odiva exhales. "Good. Let us go home, then, and recover our strength for tomorrow."

Go home? When Ailesse is known to be alive and missing? When the dead are loose and set upon Dovré?

Odiva never knew how to be a mother, and now she's forgotten her priorities as our *matrone*.

She walks close beside me as we head back for Château Creux. My heart won't stop pounding. I feel like I'm already in a cage, unable to run from her presence. By now, Ailesse could be anywhere in South Galle. I'm frantic to give her back her ritual knife. The more desperate I become to save her, the easier it is to stomach the thought of her killing Bastien.

"I feel your disappointment," Odiva says. My skin crawls when I meet her probing black eyes. "I had such high hopes for your first experience at the soul bridge. It should have brought you joy, not grief."

I don't know how to respond. "Joy" is the last word I'd have used to describe ferrying.

"I would like to think that even Ailesse would have been happy for you when . . ." A faint blush sweeps across her pale skin. She looks radiant for a moment, warm and full of feeling.

"When what?" I ask.

Her raven brows pull inward as she searches my eyes. Her mouth opens, struggling to form words, then shuts tight again. She exhales through her nostrils and walks onward, looking away from me. Her ceremonial dress trails through the wild grass. "When you would have seen the great Gates of the Beyond," she finally answers, a forced lightness in her voice.

Another lie. Another cover-up for secrets. My throat burns, but I'm tired of swallowing down the bitterness. I'm done shrinking from my *matrone* and accepting every excuse that falls from her lips. "Does that necklace you wear help you ferry the dead when the Gates *do* open?" I ask, my pulse racing from my boldness.

Odiva touches the three rows of her grace bone necklace and frowns. "Which bones do you mean, the bear's or the stingray's? They both help me ferry."

"I mean your *other* grace bone—that bird skull you keep hidden under the neckline of your dress."

Odiva freezes. Any color that remained in her cheeks drains away. "Go," she tells the Ferriers following us. Her voice is strained, though she affects a calm smile. "We will meet you at home shortly."

As they walk past, Odiva moves off the path and wraps her arms around herself. Pernelle shoots me an inquisitive look. Maurille squeezes my hand. I shrug at them like I don't know why Odiva wants to talk privately with me. Like I didn't just confront her with the crime of owning another grace bone. She already has five. A sixth is an offense to the gods and the sanctity of an animal's life. Still, my limbs shake when Odiva returns to me after the Ferriers are gone. Her expression is eerily calm and resigned.

"This is not a grace bone." Odiva withdraws the hidden necklace, and the ruby in the mouth of the bird skull glints in the sunlight. "It was a gift from my beloved."

My lips part. I take a closer look at the skull. The bill is black and a little smaller than a raven's but stouter than a rook's. "Why would your *amouré* give you a crow skull?"

She grins at me, and my scalp prickles with uneasiness. "I see nothing escapes your notice, Sabine." Her feather epaulettes rustle as she lifts a shoulder. "I suppose my love knew I had an affinity for bones."

"You didn't hide them from him?" A Leurress is supposed to put away her grace bones when she spends a year with her *amouré*.

"He was exceptional. He accepted me for what I was. He loved me without fear."

I eye the ruby again. He was also wealthy and clearly powerful if he could be that kind of match to Odiva. "Then why do you keep his gift a secret? Ailesse would want to know that her father—"

"Enough about Ailesse," Odiva snaps. I stagger back a step at her burst of frustration. She shoves the crow skull back under the neckline of her dress. "Not everything must be divulged, Sabine. Love is sacred. Private."

I stare incredulously at her. She was the first to mention Ailesse a moment ago. But all Odiva's warmth is gone now. I suddenly recall what she confessed after I killed the nighthawk. I was too distraught to give her words much weight, but now they tear through my mind: *That does not mean I loved him.* She was speaking of her *amouré*.

But then who gave her the necklace?

A small movement draws my keen eye to where the forest meets the plateau. There, perched on a low-lying branch of an ash tree, almost as if she's heard my thoughts, is the silver owl.

A breath of hope fills my chest. The owl is a reminder of Ailesse. Odiva may have turned her back on her daughter, but Elara hasn't forgotten.

The owl will lead me to her, just like she led me to the catacombs.

Odiva turns to follow my gaze. Once she sees the owl, she stifles a gasp.

I dash away toward the forest.

"Sabine," Odiva calls after me. "Where are you going? I have told all the Ferriers to return to Château Creux."

"I'm not a Ferrier," I shout back. "But if you want me to be, you'll let me hunt."

"You need your rest."

"I need a third grace bone. I'll come home once I have it." *And once I've saved Ailesse.*

I cast a fleeting glance over my shoulder, but my *matrone* isn't racing after me. She stands frozen on the path, one pale hand on the claw marks the owl gave her.

When I reach the tree line, the owl flutters away. I pursue her deeper into the forest. Just like before, she lands within sight, and once I catch up, she flies off again. I grin, running faster.

We play this game, mile after mile. I pay little attention to my surroundings; I focus all my attention on keeping the owl's gilded feathers in sight. But once I cross a thoroughfare to Dovré and spy a bridge twenty feet ahead, I stumble to a sudden stop. This bridge is made of stone and has a high arch and a dry riverbed beneath. It's within view of Beau Palais, which looks down on the bridge from the highest hill in Dovré.

I'm at Castelpont.

And the silver owl is gone.

My breath scatters on a swirl of morning mist. Why did the owl bring me here? Would Bastien really take Ailesse back to the place where she tried to kill him?

Tentatively, I walk toward the bridge. Maybe the owl knows something I don't. Maybe there's another entrance to the catacombs nearby. But a dark sense of foreboding tells me something more dangerous is at play.

I slip my bow off my shoulder. I draw an arrow from my quiver. My muscles string taut as I step onto the bridge. I glance to my left, to my right, and to the riverbed below. I see nothing.

I take another step and freeze. My graced sense of smell catches a musty and sharp scent, like damp leaves and wet fur. I've almost placed what it belongs to, when a creature comes bounding for me. Fangs bared. Hackles raised. Incredibly fast.

Time slows my pounding pulse to a sluggish beat as I meet the jackal's golden eyes. The silver owl swoops in behind him. She shrieks and goads him forward with her claws.

She brought him to me.

The jackal is halfway over the bridge. A fleeting thought

crosses my mind. I'm meant to injure the jackal. Capture him, not kill him. Odiva's command.

The jackal pounces at me. Leaps into the air. Opens his jaws.

The owl didn't want Odiva to kill him. The owl wants the jackal's graces to be mine.

I nock an arrow.

Blow out a shuddering breath.

And shoot straight for the golden jackal's heart.

31
Bastien

AILESSE'S GRIP TIGHTENS ON MY hand as we walk by the arranged bones and skulls along the tunnel walls. "We'll be past them soon," I tell her. After a few branching corridors, the catacombs open into one of the old limestone quarries under Dovré. My lantern only shines a little way into the wide pit before us.

"Please tell me that has a bottom," Ailesse says.

"It's a forty-foot drop to the ground," I reply. Still enough to kill a person if they took a fall, but the lines of worry smooth from Ailesse's forehead.

We climb down scaffolding on the near side of the pit. She's still weak. Her legs are shaking, and she has a strained expression like she can barely keep herself upright. I want to carry her again, but that's impossible at the moment. When we're twenty feet down, we step off the scaffolding and into a quarry room, half the size of our last chamber and open to the pit on one side.

I set my lantern in the middle of the floor. It barely casts enough light to fill the space. Ailesse looks around at what will be her home for the next who-knows-how-many days, and heat creeps up my cheeks. I shove a few crates aside and shake the dust from a moth-eaten blanket. "We'll make this place comfortable, I promise."

"Who made this?" Ailesse asks reverently.

"Made what?" I turn around and find her staring at the far wall of the room. It's a relief of Château Creux. My chest twinges with pain. I've only seen the castle ruins from a distance. The old fortress looks nothing like it does here—majestic, with tall towers. On one side are the sun god and earth goddess, Belin and Gaëlle, and on the other side are Elara and Tyrus, the goddess of the Night Heavens and the god of the Underworld. I fold my arms and unfold them. "My father carved that."

"Your father?" Ailesse turns to me. For a moment, I stop breathing. I can't look away from her large and beautiful eyes, her wavy hair, the fullness of her upper lip . . . If I had my father's talent, I'd carve a statue of her.

I finally nod and dig my hands into my pockets. "He was a sculptor, a struggling one." I tip my chin at eleven figurines I salvaged after he died. "He sold these at the market to make ends meet. He couldn't afford blocks of limestone, so he snuck down here and quarried them out for himself."

Ailesse's gaze travels over the figurines I've arranged on the ledge of the right wall. Eight are sculptures of the gods, two are miniature carvings of Beau Palais, and five are forest animals and sea creatures.

A soft smile lifts the corners of Ailesse's mouth. "Your father was a master, Bastien."

Warmth stirs deep inside my chest. Then I remember that a Bone Crier—someone like Ailesse—killed my father and a rush of coldness chases it away. The hunger for revenge I've harbored for so long hasn't stopped gnawing at my gut, but I don't know what to do about it anymore. I sit down and lean against the wall, opposite from her, putting as much distance as I can between us. "My father's name was Lucien Colbert," I say, my voice suddenly hoarse. "Did anyone in your *famille* ever mention it?"

Ailesse's auburn brows draw inward. She shakes her head slowly and eases down on the ground to sit across from me. "I'm sorry. Not everyone in my *famille* speaks about their *amourés*. Some never take the opportunity to know them before they . . ." She lowers her eyes.

I shrug a shoulder like it doesn't matter, when of course it matters. "If the gods truly singled out my father to die, then no one should worship them." The edge in my voice is back. Good.

Ailesse winces. "You can't speak like that."

I shoot her a dark look. "Are you joking?"

She presses her lips together and rubs the lump on the back of her head. It's probably bigger now. "Maybe there's another way to complete a rite of passage . . . I don't know." Her words come haltingly and with great effort. She pulls her hand away and folds it in her lap. "Maybe no one prayed hard enough to find out."

My brows twitch. I'm openly staring at her. Did she just admit a pivotal event of her life could be wrong? "If *you* pray hard enough, do you think you can break our bond?"

She cracks the smallest smile. "So you believe the gods should be worshipped, after all?"

"Depends." I suppress a grin.

Her shoulders shake with silent laughter, but then her expression falls. "Our bond is already set in motion, Bastien. Praying can't break the inevitable outcome."

"Is it really inevitable?" I scoot closer. "I mean, if we protect each other—and promise not to kill each other—then we'll both come out of this alive and kicking, whether we're soul-bound or not."

She tugs on a thread of her ruined dress. "Actually, the outcome is more complicated than that."

"How?"

"Once an *amouré* is claimed, his life is forfeit."

"Claimed . . . as in killed?"

"No, claimed from the moment the siren song calls him to the bridge."

My throat closes on a forced laugh. "Well, I'm still living, right?"

She swallows. "For now."

"What do you mean?"

Ailesse tips her head back, like she's staring at a sky I can't see. "You have one year, Bastien." Her chest sinks in. "If I don't complete the ritual before then, you'll die regardless. The gods always find a way."

I grow silent for a moment, thinking about how Jules and Marcel's father died. "And how are you punished if you fail?"

She draws a long breath and holds my gaze. "The gods find a way to kill me, too."

My heart struggles to beat. "What kind of raw deal is that?"

Ailesse looks down at her hands. "No worse than the fate of Tyrus and Elara, I suppose."

"What, eternal glory?" I scoff.

"They have suffered, too. They married in secret when the world was formed. Belin and Gaëlle forbade their kingdoms to join, but Tyrus and Elara wanted to be together. When Belin found out, he cast Heaven into the night sky, and Gaëlle opened the earth to swallow Hell. Tyrus and Elara have never been able to be together since."

"So let me get this straight. They want you to feel their pain?"

"Or they want us to learn how to overcome it. Maybe it would show them how."

I rub a hand over my face and push up to my feet. I have to get out of here. I can't listen to stories of gods that punish mortals because they can't figure out their own problems. "Stay here and rest, all right? I'm going to find Jules and Marcel and get back your bones."

"And the flute?"

I nod. "See you soon."

She fists her hands. "I can't stay down here for long, Bastien. I won't. I'm a Leurress. It's my job to protect people from the dead."

"I know."

But I have a job, too. And right now it's to protect her. She'll be able to defend herself best if she has her graces back. "Stay, Ailesse. I won't be long."

32
Ailesse

I PACE AT THE EDGE of the pit. I imagine I still have my tiger shark vision to see in the dark and the eyesight of my peregrine falcon to perceive what's far ahead of me. Maybe then the weak light of my lantern would be enough to illuminate the limestone quarry at the open end of this room that I share with Bastien. But then again, if I had my graces, I wouldn't be hiding down here, waiting for him with all my nerves strung taut. I don't know how long he's been gone—I can't tell how long I slept—but I've been awake for at least ten hours.

What if one of the Chained attacked Bastien and that's why he hasn't come back? My stomach twists into a tight knot. I can't stay here any longer.

I grab the lantern and hurry over to the scaffolding. My legs shake like brittle autumn leaves as I climb. I grit my teeth and push past my weakness. If the moon was full last night, it would have filled me with a greater well of Elara's Light, but the strength I felt under the stars is gone, as well as the strength from my grace bones. No matter. If I killed the tiger shark after almost drowning in the lagoon, I'll find the stamina to fight the dead.

There are only a few branching tunnels down here, nothing like the catacombs maze that led off the ravine. I hold my breath when I pass a section lined with bones. Soon enough, I find the door to the chapel cellar. I climb the ladder, open up the hatch, and shove the tattered rug aside.

Once I'm out, I lean against the altar for a moment. I'm already out of breath. Not a good sign. I glance around the chapel's interior, and my gaze rivets to several boarded-up arched windows. The muted light from the heavens funnels inside through the slats. It's nighttime. My heart pounds. I need that energy.

I push away from the altar and rush for the tall double doors at the front of the chapel. The bruise on the back of my head throbs, and my vision starts to spin like it did last night.

I reach the doors and fumble with the latches. They're stiff and won't budge. I ram my shoulder against the splintering wood. Once, twice. Perspiration wets my brow, but the effort is worth it. The door budges open.

I stagger out into the street just as the air shudders with a crack of thunder. A few drops of rain splash on my face. I release a heavy sigh and curse my bad luck. The thickening storm clouds dilute

Elara's starlight even more, and only a feeble measure of strength steals into me.

I turn in a circle, trying to decide which way to go. My eyes widen at the looming structures all around me. Nothing is green or leafy. Everything has hard edges and stinks of refuse. This area isn't pristine like the buildings towering above the city wall near Beau Palais. It's decrepit and filthy. My chest pangs for Bastien. He spent his life on these streets.

On a whim, I run left. More windows are lit from within in this direction. It makes it easier to see where I'm going. I wouldn't need the help if I had my tiger shark vision. The sky flashes with lightning, and rain pelts the cobblestones. The few people still outside run indoors for cover.

"There she is!" a woman's voice hisses from an alley to my right.

"Finally," a man grumbles behind me.

I whirl around and shove my wet hair off my face, but I don't see either of them.

"We've been looking for you." Another voice. Male and bodiless and right in front of me.

I jolt and whip out the small knife I stole from Marcel. I don't know if these souls are Chained or Unchained, but they definitely shouldn't be here. "You need to go back to the inlet with the land bridge," I tell them.

"Why?" I startle at yet another voice. Robust and female and crowding in on my left. "So you women in white can herd us like dumb sheep?" A cold finger slides up my cheek. I gasp and jump back. "The land bridge is gone."

"We like it *here*." Icy breath prickles in my right ear. "So much to feast on."

My nostrils flare. I swing my knife out. The soul shrieks as I slice into it. I quickly jab to my left, then slash in front and behind me, anticipating a group attack. But my blade only grazes one of them. Two others slam into me and knock me to the ground. Pain erupts from the back of my head. I've hit my bruise again.

I kick and thrash, blindly fighting with my knife, but too many souls converge on me. More are coming. Their growing roars rise above the thundering sky.

"Ailesse!"

Bastien.

A jolt of adrenaline rushes through my body. I'm not alone.

I wrest my right arm free and drive my blade into what feels like ribs. With a shrill scream, one of the souls slumps off of me. Rain pummels my face. I sputter and gasp, but keep attacking the others. Out of the corner of my eye, I see Bastien seize an abandoned cart and run it toward me like a battering ram.

"Get off her!" he shouts.

Most of the souls let me go. I roll out of the way just as the cart barrels through the rest of them.

Bastien is immediately at my side. He hauls me up and grabs my hand. We race down the street and away from the chapel.

Invisible hands claw at us. Bastien veers for the sun-symbol flag of Dovré. Its pole extends from a bracket on a building. He yanks it out and swings it behind us, using its pointed iron tip like a spearhead. It thuds as it strikes a few unseen opponents. "I told you that you were a beacon to them," he says to me.

I pick up a loose cobblestone and lob it through the air. It stops halfway in its arc and strikes one of the souls. "Did you find Jules?" I ask. There's no point in wasting more breath by telling Bastien he was right.

"No." Rain streaks off his flexed jaw muscles. He swings the pole again. "I'll try again tomorrow."

My stomach rolls. "What do we do now?" The dead are swarming us, backing us up against the wall of the building.

Bastien rapidly assesses our surroundings. "Follow me." He races into a slit between buildings, an alley so narrow I didn't notice it before.

I chase after him, my knees shaking as my weakness threatens to overwhelm me. My shoulders bang and scrape against the alley walls. The dead rage behind me, but at least here they can only pursue us single file.

The rain falls in angry sheets as we emerge into a courtyard and dash through it to a stable. Bastien kicks open the gate, breaking the lock, and passes me the flagpole. I whirl around and stab at the air. I hit a soul. The heavy rain bounces off of the contours of an invisible body.

A moment later, Bastien bursts out of the stable on a large gray horse and reaches for me. Anxiety and anticipation trip through my veins. I've never ridden a horse before. I spear another oncoming soul, then grab Bastien's hand.

He hoists me up behind him on the saddle and straightaway gallops out of the courtyard and onto a wider road.

"Come back, thief!" someone yells from an open window.

I find myself laughing. I can't help it. Despite my fatigue and the vicious cries of the dead, the thrill of actually riding an animal and feeling its strength pound beneath me is exhilarating.

Dovré rushes past me in flashes of lightning as the storm rages on. Bastien weaves aimlessly through street after street, trying to outrun the dead. I glimpse arched façades and domed towers and humbler dwellings with thatched roofs. The rebelliousness of being in this forbidden city sends another shiver of elation through me. I don't even care how furious this would make my mother. I wrap my arms tighter around Bastien's chest.

He steers the horse into another alley and slows the stallion to a walk before he stealthily slips around another corner. The rickety spires of the chapel that we started from rise above the cluster of rooftops in front of us. Bastien swiftly dismounts the horse, and then pulls me down with him. "From here we go on foot," he says. "Quietly." He yanks off his dripping cloak, wraps it around my shoulders, and draws up the hood. "Do your best to stay out of sight."

I stare into his sea-blue eyes and the raindrops collecting in his lashes. Maybe it's my bruised head, but my knees go a little wobbly. "Where are we going?"

"Back to my hideout under Chapelle du Pauvre."

"The catacombs? Again?" All my euphoria vanishes, and my chest caves inward.

"I'm sorry, Ailesse." His brows pull together. "I don't know anywhere else that you'll be safe."

I look away from him and slowly run my hand over the stallion's neck. I could leap up on this strong horse and ride away from here, back to Château Creux. But the horde of the dead would only follow me and endanger my *famille*. The Leurress can't attempt to ferry them for another month, not until the next new moon. Can I last that much longer in the darkness?

"We're not giving up, all right?" Bastien tentatively touches my shoulder. "I'll keep searching for Jules. She and Marcel are off somewhere working to break our soul-bond. You and I can do the same thing. I bet we'll even have better luck. Marcel might be brilliant, but I have *you*." He blinks, catching what he just said. He lowers his eyes and bites the corner of his lip. "You have me, too, Ailesse."

My heartbeat steadies. A flood of warmth calms the tension in my body. Maybe I *can* bear the darkness. I take Bastien's hand and hold it tight. He meets my eyes, and his mouth gently curves upward.

We set off for the chapel.

33
Sabine

I STAND IN A MUDDY four-foot hole and scoop up another handful of sodden earth. I push a dripping curl off my forehead with filthy hands. The rain is relentless. I should have buried the golden jackal right after I killed him, but when I dragged him into this hollow, I couldn't bear to look at him, let alone touch his limp body. I covered him with fir branches and did my best not to cry while I set off on another vain search for Ailesse.

That was yesterday. By evening today the jackal's body has started to stink. Someone without a graced sense of smell might not notice, but I do, and that means others in my *famille* will, too. They'll track his scent here. They must be hunting for him again, and I've gone directly against the *matrone*'s wishes by killing the jackal myself.

I slop out one last handful of mud. The pouring rain masks the odor of decay for now, so I have to hurry and finish this. I climb out of the hole and rush over to where I stowed the jackal's body. I pull the fir branches off him and swallow the bile in my throat. The jackal is rigid now, and a milky substance is filming over his eyes. "Forgive me," I whisper, kneeling beside him. I pull Ailesse's bone knife from the belt of my hunting dress and start to hack at his hind leg.

I shut my eyes as much as possible. I'm grateful that the loud rainfall covers most of the noise. The tendons are tough and require me to twist and yank the bone. *Elara, give me strength.*

Finally, the bone breaks away. I've severed the jackal's whole leg, from his femur to paw. I have to bury what I can't use—and I just need the femur. I'll carve a pendant from it for my necklace. I wrinkle my nose and start hacking again. I whimper. This is torture.

My hands are trembling by the time I'm done. I drop the knife and press the heels of my palms to my eyes. Thank the gods this is my last grace bone.

As soon as I've had the thought, my stomach twists with guilt. Should I really claim this bone for myself? I could still give it to Odiva so she can carve a new flute.

The sky crackles with thunder. A shrill cry rises above it. At first I think it's a red fox, but then the rain at the edge of the hollow glows with *chazoure*.

An icy chill grips me. I duck low, praying the soul will pass by without seeing me, but then he speaks in a rumbling voice, like another clap of thunder. "Don't bother hiding. I sense the Light inside you."

The hair on my arms lifts. He has to be Chained. And I have no time to cover up the jackal again.

I look up, and the Chained man bounds into the hollow. I drop the femur. Grab my knife. Jump to my feet just in time to stab him in his chest. He growls and shoves me down. I tumble backward once, then spring up, but I don't attack again. I can't kill him. I need to evade him. "You want my Light? You'll have to catch me first."

I race out of the hollow, more grateful than ever for my nighthawk grace. My legs are light, and my speed is powerful.

The dead man bolts after me and stays within reach, surprisingly fast himself. He's tall and lean-muscled, and his chest is wrapped in five rows of chains. Most Chained I saw at the land bridge had half that many. I'm going to have to be clever, as well as quick.

I weave through trees and change directions often, trying to lose him, but I steadily make my way toward the Mirvois River, the prominent river in South Galle.

The rain doesn't let up. I barely keep my footing on the downward slope of a grassy hill. The Chained man isn't so lucky. He slides and tumbles down the wet grass. For a moment, that puts him ahead of me, and I narrowly dodge him as I race onward.

Another hill looms ahead. At its top is the bluff above the river. I know this spot well. I hunted a stag here while I deliberated about my second grace bone. The current of the river runs wild with white water. If it weren't for the pounding rain, I'd hear the sound of it raging.

I dig in my feet as I race up the muddy hill. The Chained man swipes for my leg and grazes my ankle. I shake him off. My muscles burn, even with my graces. I need the jackal's strength.

You're almost there, Sabine. Keep going.

I pant, reaching the top of the hill. The edge of the bluff is masked by a row of trees, the torrent of rain, and the dark of night.

I pray my graces will be enough. I need agility on the slick ground from my fire salamander, the power to vault through the air from my nighthawk.

I sprint for the tree line and eye a sturdy branch that overhangs the bluff by twenty feet.

I slow my speed just enough that I'm barely beyond the Chained man's reach.

Fifteen feet to the tree line.

Ten.

Five.

One.

I plunge off the edge of the bluff. The Chained man's arms reach for me. His fingers claw the skirt of my dress, but then slip off the wet fabric. He plummets off the bluff with a guttural scream.

I fly through the air, drawing my legs up to stick my landing. My feet skid onto the thick branch. I'm balanced, but the branch is too short. I'm going to slide off it.

I crouch forward and grab the branch with my arms. It's too wet for me to gain any traction. I squeeze harder and cry out with exertion. My legs topple off. I slide onto my stomach, desperately clinging on to the branch. It's getting thinner, flimsier, as I near its end. I fumble for a forking tree branch. I grip it, and my shoulder yanks hard as I finally come to a stop.

I slump with relief, hanging on to the bending end of the branch, and look below.

The Chained man has fallen into the river. The rapids are sucking him downstream at a helpless rate.

A weighted breath purges from my lungs. *Thank you, Elara.*

I take a moment to recover my strength, then crawl off the branch and onto blessedly solid ground. I waste no time. I run back for the hollow, soaked and shivering but resolved.

I have to give the jackal bone to Odiva. The dead can't be ferried yet, but maybe she can lure them with the song and herd them into a cave. We can seal it up with large rocks. The Leurress can guard them there until the next new moon.

My lungs are on fire by the time I reach the hollow. I don't stop to rest. I pull out the bone knife and skin the flesh off the jackal femur. I'm going to present a clean and ready bone to my *matronne*. It might help her forgive me for slaughtering the beast.

My hand slips, and the blade of the knife nicks my palm.

Something gives a rasping screech six feet in front of me. I suck in a sharp breath, expecting to see another Chained. But it doesn't glow with *chazoure*. It isn't human in form either.

It's the silver owl. Here of all places. Feathers drenched as the rain pelts her.

My stomach hardens. I pull the bone onto my lap with my uninjured hand. "We *need* a bone flute," I say defensively, assuming that's why the owl has come. She helped me kill the jackal, after all, when she prevented Odiva from doing the same.

She hops nearer, tilting her head at me. She blinks her beautiful eyes. Somehow I know what she's trying to communicate. That I need to trust her. That she's well aware that the dead are swarming South Galle. And Ailesse already has a bone flute—the true flute. She played it on the cliff above the land bridge.

Claim this grace, Sabine, and use it to save your friend.

The thought comes like another voice in my mind. It showers me with calm understanding.

I stare at the owl. The rain doesn't let up, but I don't shiver. "Will you help me find her?"

The owl bobs her head, and my heart thumps faster.

I inhale a deep breath and open my palm. The rain washes away most of the blood from my nick, but it's still bleeding at a steady rate. It will be enough.

I grit my teeth and press the jackal bone against my blood.

34
Ailesse

I SIT CURLED UP NEXT to the relief of Château Creux in Bastien's hideout, my finger idly tracing the towers that no longer exist there. My *famille* didn't always live beneath the castle; we used to dwell in secluded glens of the forest and caves off the shore, but I don't remember those places. I was a baby when King Godart died from an unnatural death. That was the same year a fierce storm swept the land and battered Château Creux, adding to the rumors that the castle was cursed. But Odiva held a fondness for the place. She moved our *famille* there when it was abandoned.

I look around me at the room off the quarry where I've lived these last ten days. I've grown comfortable here—as comfortable as I can be with all my strength leaching away and my desire to help my *famille* eating at my nerves.

The scaffolding at the edge of the quarry pit creaks, and my limbs tingle with warmth. Bastien is back.

He steps off the scaffolding and into the room with a satchel slung over his shoulder and something tucked beneath his arm. The lantern light catches the angles of his strong jawline and the fresh gleam of his hair. He had time to shave his stubble and bathe while he was above. A sign that the search for Jules and Marcel was uneventful. Again.

"Any luck?" I ask, still clinging to vain hope. Maybe my grace bones and the bone flute are in Bastien's satchel, and he cleaned up to celebrate.

"Jules wasn't in the attic over the brewery," he says, and my shoulders fall. He's already checked all the places he and his friends ever took refuge in, and now he's combing through random spots in Dovré. It's all starting to feel pointless. "Don't worry, I'll find her."

I study the forced grin on Bastien's face and the lines beneath his tired eyes. He'll never give up searching—he's just as stubborn as I am once he sets his mind to something—but that doesn't mean his hope isn't failing, too.

"And the dead?" I ask. "What's happening with them?"

He sighs and walks closer to me. "More of the same. Rumors of people hearing bodiless voices. Some of them plead or apologize. Some threaten. But none of them are as violent as they were around you and the other Bone Criers." He lowers his satchel on the ground, as well as a cloth-wrapped bundle. "Seems like the dead are more cunning around ordinary people."

"But not any less dangerous."

He nods, sitting down to remove one of his boots. "I overheard a couple men in the tavern mention friends who have fallen sick." He shakes out the dust and pebbles. "But those friends don't have fevers or rashes or any obvious symptoms."

"The dead are drawing out their Light." My skin prickles as I think back on what my mother taught me before I attempted my rite of passage. If the Chained aren't ferried, they'll seek vitality from the living. And if they steal enough Light from a person, they'll kill them, body and soul. "I wish I could be out there with you, helping you find the flute."

"You need your grace bones first," Bastien replies in a soothing voice. "I can manage to avoid the dead, but you . . ." He rubs the back of his neck.

I nod listlessly and look into the black space where the quarry is. It isn't fair that I'm able to hide to protect myself when innocent people can't do the same. "What did you bring this time?" I ask, struggling to lighten my tone. I'm tired of talking in circles about an impossible situation.

He shifts into a cross-legged position and pushes his satchel toward me. I pull away from the relief of Château Creux, flushing from the effort that even that small movement takes me, and peek inside. I can't refrain from smiling as I withdraw another lantern and several candles. I look up at Bastien and find he's watching me carefully. "It's not the Night Heavens," he says, "but two lanterns are better than one."

Warmth streams inside my chest. He's doing everything he can to make this place welcoming. "Thank you."

He holds my gaze a long moment, and my warmth spreads,

radiating to my fingertips and the ends of my toes. "There's some food in there, too." He points at the satchel.

Food, I expected. I'm more curious about the cloth-wrapped bundle. "What about that?"

His brows rise when he sees where I'm looking. "Oh . . . that's, um . . . well . . ." He clears his throat. Scratches his arm. Pops a knuckle. "Really, how much longer can you go around wearing that ragged thing"—he waves a hand at the general direction of my body—"before it falls off you completely?" He winces. "Before it tears to shreds, I mean." Is he blushing? I can't be sure in the light of our one glowing lantern.

"You got me a dress?" My own cheeks warm.

He swallows and nods.

We're both quiet for a moment. "Can I see it?"

"Um, sure." He slowly passes over the bundle.

A whirlwind of butterflies dance inside me as I unwrap the cloth and see the fabric of the dress within, fine and woolen and fern green. My fingers run over its smooth weave, and I softly smile. "This is Sabine's favorite color."

"Your friend from the bridge?" Bastien asks. I lift surprised eyes at him. "Sometimes you call out her name while you're sleeping," he explains.

"Do I?" My throat constricts. I wish I remembered those dreams. I haven't had a vision of Sabine since before I saw her at the land bridge. It makes her absence all the more difficult. "She's one of my sister Leurress," I say. "Not my *real* sister—each Leurress only has enough time to conceive one child before . . ." *Before the child's father must die.* I bite my lip and chance another glance at Bastien. He doesn't look angry or resigned or even accepting. Maybe he's still trying to process the fact that a year after meeting me he'll die, whether or not my knife is in his heart. "Sabine is my best friend."

"You must miss her," he murmurs.

The deep ache in my chest rises. It feels like a lifetime ago since Sabine and I walked the forest path to Castelpont, our arms linked as she asked me to dream of who I wished my *amouré* to be. I never imagined someone like Bastien—not fully—but now I can't imagine anyone else. "You must miss Jules and Marcel," I counter.

He looks down and rubs a scuff on his boot. I pick at my fingernails, watching him. How much *does* he miss Jules? She's like family to him, that I know, but do his feelings for her run any deeper? He rolls out the muscles in his back and shoulders and stands. "Want to have a bath?"

My brows shoot up.

"*Alone*, I mean." He cringes at himself, and I suppress a smile. "I'll walk you down to the pool, if you want. You can change into your new dress afterward."

"All right."

He lights the second lantern, and I pick up the other. I move slowly, careful to pace out my waning strength. He guides me down the scaffolding and onto the floor of the quarry. One of its tunnels leads to a pool of clean groundwater. I've bathed here twice already, but when I have to put on my tattered rite of passage dress afterward, I feel dirty again.

"Do you need help coming back?" Bastien asks. "I can wait outside here."

I clutch the fern-green dress close to my chest. "I'll be fine."

Bastien nods. Twice. He runs his fingers through his hair and tries to pull an indifferent expression, the same one he mastered in our old catacombs chamber. It doesn't look so masterful now. He keeps taking deep breaths and avoiding my eyes. "See you soon," he finally says, and strides away. I stifle a laugh.

The water is warm and divine. I languidly scrub my hair and body until every speck of limestone dust vanishes, then I comb my fingers through my hair while I sit at the edge of the pool. When all the tangles are gone, I slip on the fern-green dress and leave my ruined rite of passage dress behind. A deep calmness settles over me as I make my way back to Bastien's room. I feel lighter than I have in days. My skin doesn't itch, finally able to breathe. I'll never take clean clothes for granted again.

My leg and arm muscles shake as I climb the scaffolding. At the moment, I don't mind the effort. Bastien's back is turned when I step into the room. He's lighting a candle he's placed on a shelf ledge. My lips part as I glance around me. At least ten more candles are lit within and perched on various places along the floor and walls. The flickering amber glow against the limestone is beautiful. I could grow accustomed to this place, if it always looked this way. "I thought you'd ration those candles for the lanterns," I chide him gently.

He turns his head partway and smiles. "For one night we can afford more light."

This is another gift for me, I realize, and I find myself gazing softly at him. The smallest tremble runs through his hand as he closes the lid of his tinderbox. He's still acting nervous, which is adorable because it's so unlike his usual confidence. "There's food if you want it." He angles around, but only far enough to tip his chin at the food he's laid out on a blanket for us. He hasn't looked at me directly since I came back from bathing.

"Thank you." I linger a moment longer until I feel a splash of water hit my feet. My dripping hair is forming a puddle around me. I move to the edge of the pit and lean over to wring my hair out. It's then I catch Bastien finally looking at me. I freeze and hold my breath. His eyes are timid, almost fearful, as they sweep over my dress and gradually lift to my face. My chest flutters, and I straighten, smoothing out the folds of my skirt. "The dress fits perfectly," I say.

He swallows. "I noticed." The tinderbox rattles in his hand as he places it on the ledge. He releases a steadying exhale and goes to sit on the blanket. He plucks a small red fruit from a clay bowl.

"Wild strawberries?" I grin and come to sit across from him. So far we've subsisted on a diet of bread, cheese, and dry strips of salted meat.

"I found them growing along the road. I thought maybe you'd like them."

I take a few from the bowl and bite into one. A moan of pleasure escapes me at the burst of flavor after such bland food. "That's probably the best thing I've ever eaten."

A smile teases the corner of Bastien's mouth.

I chew and swallow two more strawberries. "I've been thinking about the engravings on the bone flute. They might help us break our bond."

"How?" He sits up taller. We've been doing our best to find a way, but we don't have Marcel's books or his brilliance, and nothing I've shared about my *famille* has gotten us any closer.

I tuck a lock of wet hair behind my ear. "Well, each side of the flute has slightly different symbols. Look." I reach for a stick of charcoal in a little tin against the wall, then scoot beside Bastien. I pull back a corner of the wool blanket. On the limestone floor beneath, I sketch an arch that looks like an upside-down crescent moon, and then draw an inverted triangle on top of it.

"That represents water." I point to the triangle. "All together, this is the symbol of the soul bridge—the land bridge that emerges from the sea. I told Marcel that much, but he didn't notice the corresponding symbol of the new moon—a solid circle. It's above the tone holes, not below them." I draw the circle and space the symbols apart. "I think the new moon is engraved on the flute to show what time the soul bridge can be used, which makes sense, because that's when the Leurress ferry."

Bastien chews on his lip. "And that's connected to our soul-bond?"

"Not exactly. But the symbols on the *back* of the flute might be." I sketch the symbol of the soul bridge again, except this one has a horizontal line running across the middle of the inverted triangle. Above that, I draw a circle that's not shaded in and set my finger on it. "That's the symbol of the full moon."

He nods. "When a Bone Crier can summon her soulmate with the flute, right?"

"Yes, but what's strange is that this segmented triangle means *earth*." I point to it. "How many bridges can you think of that have earth beneath them and not water?"

Bastien's brow furrows. "Only Castelpont."

"Exactly. And I chose that bridge, out of all the bridges in South Galle, for my rite of passage. I didn't realize it had any special significance, but it must have if it's engraved on the bone flute."

Bastien scratches his head. "I'm still not sure how any of this is connected to our soul-bond."

"Why? Castelpont is where our soul-bond was formed."

"But does that mean the *bridge* is what formed it?" He studies my confused expression. "Think about the land bridge, for starters. From what you've told me, the dead are lured there because that's where the siren song is played. You also said the reason the dead are lured to *you* is because *you* were the one to play the song—at least with the more powerful bone flute."

I nod, wondering what all of this has to do with what I've been talking about.

"Have you considered that what really forged our bond was also the song and not the bridge?" He spreads his hands open. "Maybe the bridge wasn't essential to the magic."

I sit back and drop my stick of charcoal. "I don't know. Bridges are deeply sown into everything it is to be a Leurress. They symbolize the connection between the world of the living and the world of the dead, and Ferriers are a part of that link. They're just as important as the bridge itself in taking souls to the Beyond. Bridges even represent our bodies during rites of passage. That's why a Leurress must bury her grace bones at the foundations of a bridge so the gods can channel her energy to match her to her *amouré*—and that's why her *amouré* comes to that same bridge to look for her."

"But it's still not the bridge that ultimately cements the bond, right?" Bastien gestures at my drawings. "You're saying the bone flute has these symbols on it to show what times it can be used— either to ferry souls or to call a soulmate. But if a Leurress can use *any* bridge for her rite of passage, why would the flute depict a bridge over earth? That would mean she couldn't use the flute anywhere else except Castelpont. But the Leurress *do* use the flute at other bridges—bridges over water. At least the bridge my father was on was over water when I saw him . . ." Bastien's voice cracks, and he masks it by coughing.

I start to reach for him, then draw back. I want to offer him comfort, but how can I? It was a Leurress, like me, who killed his father. I tighten my hand into a fist. For the first time, I'm bitterly angry with whoever it was in my *famille* that hurt Bastien so badly.

He rubs his fingers across his lips and takes another moment to compose himself. "What I'm saying is Castelpont can't be significant to *all* the Leurress."

"But could it be significant to *us*?" I lean closer, my pulse surging faster with hope. "Maybe if you and I return there on the next full moon, we can break our bond."

"How?"

I shake my head, trying to find a reason. "Different songs make different things happen. The song I played near the soul bridge isn't the same song I played to lure you to Castelpont. Maybe there's another song that can help us."

"Do you know any different songs?"

I sigh. "No."

A nearby candle flame quivers as we grow quiet. The wick needs trimming. On the floor between us, Bastien's fingers subtly bend and straighten. He takes a tremulous breath and slides his hand over mine. He gives it a gentle squeeze. "We'll figure it out, Ailesse."

Warmth shivers through me. I shouldn't allow his touch to affect me like this. Not when our fates are so bleak. But I can't help it. I tentatively turn my hand over. Our palms meet, our eyes connect, and I curl my fingers around his. My heart gives a hard pound, reminding me to draw breath. "Bastien," I whisper. There's so much I want to say, but I can't find the words to express how much I'm coming to care for him. "I . . . I don't want you to die."

He doesn't look away from me. Any trace of his earlier shyness is gone. "I don't want you to die either." The candles shimmer in his eyes, and he brushes his thumb over mine. "There's an Old Gallish phrase my father used to say whenever he'd have to leave for a little while. He'd hold my hand just like this and whisper, '*Tu ne me manques pas. Je ne te manque pas.*' It means 'You're not missing from me. I'm not missing from you.'"

I smile softly, committing those words to memory. "I like that."

"I'm not going anywhere, Ailesse." Bastien's gaze is earnest and tender and deeply affectionate. It's like Elara's Light shining down on me. "We're going to stick together, all right? No one's going to die."

I nod, trying my best to believe it. I lay my head on his shoulder. *No one's going to die.*

35
Sabine

I RUN OUT FROM THE catacombs tunnel and roughly extinguish my torch on the grass. With a furious cry, I hurl the torch across the ravine floor and dig my fingers in my hair. I still haven't found Ailesse.

I've lost track of how many times I've ventured here, finally daring to enter the catacombs with the help of my three grace bones. Now I resent them. If my muscles ached or I was short of breath or my fatigue felt unendurable, I might feel like I was working hard enough to save my best friend. Instead, I'm growing so agitated and angry that I want to claw anything in sight. I don't know if it's an effect of my new golden jackal grace or my own frustration with myself.

Eleven days have passed since ferrying night—twenty-six since Ailesse's failed rite of passage. She must think I haven't even tried to help her. I won't return home until I do, although I'm avoiding home, anyway. No one knows I killed the jackal.

I shake the silt mud from my hunting dress and hear the swoop of the silver owl before she lands on the ravine floor. I glare at her heart-shaped face and lovely eyes, glinting in the afternoon sunlight. She tilts her head, rasp-screeches, and flies to the top of the ravine, waiting for me to follow. I place a hand on my hip. "Are you going to lead me to Ailesse this time?"

She flaps away, and I lock my jaw, racing after her. I'm careful to run light on my toes and keep under the tree cover, but the miles pass without any cries from the dead. Lately, I've spied Ferriers trying to herd them into an abandoned prison near Château Creux, but they have to guard them constantly. Some souls have inexplicably escaped the iron bars, and the last time I checked, only twelve or so are still there—nowhere near the number that came to the land bridge.

I chase the silver owl another mile until I'm standing at the foot of Castelpont. Again. A low growl rumbles in my chest. The last few days have been a maddening circle of running in and out of the catacombs and back and forth to Castelpont. And I have nothing to show for it.

The silver owl blinks from her perch on the center of the bridge's parapet. She might as well roost here for how often she brings me to this place. "If Elara sent you, she's going to have to teach you how to speak," I snap, although Ailesse would call that blasphemy.

The silver owl scratches her claws on the mortared stones, emphasizing our location.

"That doesn't help."

She spreads her wings, flies in a circle, and lands on the opposite parapet.

I throw my arms in the air. "What do you want? I already killed the golden jackal, which isn't the fiercest predator, by the way." The best graces he gave me are more strength, greater endurance, and excellent hearing. Good, but not remarkable. A common wolf has more. So much for my last grace bone.

The owl screeches and hops along the parapet.

I shake my head. "Don't come back for me again unless you're not going to waste my time."

I steal a glance at the walls of Dovré as I leave the silver owl behind. The glow of *chazoure* hangs over the city like an eerie mist. Souls are continuing to gather here. Since ferrying night, I haven't overheard any travelers on the road mention obvious attacks from the dead, but maybe leaching Light from the living is quiet work. I pray it's long work, too, and no one dies before I find Ailesse and the bone flute. The constant gnaw of guilt inside me sharpens to a bite.

I hurry back to the hollow where I buried the golden jackal and take even more care to be covert. So far no one in my *famille* has tracked me here, and I want to keep it that way. I've been retreating to this place when I force myself to rest and eat.

I kneel beside a trickling stream. The water weaves down moss and rocks and forms a small waterfall. I check my trap, and a silver flash of scales greets me. My stomach pangs with ravenous hunger. Since I claimed the jackal's graces, I've developed an intense craving for meat, which I'm trying to satiate by eating fish. The old Sabine would shudder at that, but now my mouth waters instead.

I sit down and pull out a knife to gut the fish, but not the one I meant to. I quickly sheathe it. Ailesse's bone knife was made for one purpose only—to kill her *amouré*. I selfishly used it when I killed the nighthawk and stabbed the Chained man, but I won't do so again.

I withdraw another knife. Just as I make a slice across the fish's belly, I hear, "Hello, Sabine."

I drop the fish. Whip out my knife. Point it across the stream. Spikes of adrenaline shoot through me. Odiva is standing there. My graced ears didn't even hear her approach.

"You've cut yourself." Her black eyes lower to my hand.

My stinging pain finally registers. A red gash on my palm is pooling blood.

"I will help you clean the wound," Odiva says with a calmness I don't trust. My heart drums as she slowly advances across a shallow part of the stream, and the hem of her sapphire-blue dress drags against the rocks in the water.

She joins me on the pebbled ground. I set down my knife with trembling fingers. I pray she won't notice the new addition on my shoulder necklace among its shells, beads, and graceless shark teeth. But Odiva misses nothing.

"What is that pendant you are wearing?" She affects an indifferent tone, but a ragged edge of suspicion cuts through it.

"My new grace bone," I confess. She must realize that much.

"It looks like Ailesse's pendant," she muses, wetting her bloodred lips as she traces the crescent moon I've carved from the golden jackal femur.

"I wanted it to match hers." *And I carved it into a pendant so the bone would be unrecognizable.*

"I presume it's not also from an alpine ibex." Odiva arches a humored brow, but her eyes bore into me like the eyes of the Chained.

I force a thin smile. Why has she come here? Why isn't she reprimanding me for running away? "No, I haven't managed a journey to the northern mountains and back again in the last few days."

"Of course you haven't." She takes my hand and dips it in the water. Her touch is gentle, but her sharp nails scrape against my wrist. "You've been wandering through the catacombs instead."

My eyes fly up to meet her gaze. Cold sweat flashes across my skin.

"Your dress is covered in silt." She answers my unspoken question.

My muscles tense with the urge to run, but there's no use in denying where I've been. "I had to. I can't bear to think of Ailesse down there. I've looked through so many tunnels and walked past so many bones—human bones." I swallow and shake my head. "Maybe she isn't down there. Bastien could have taken her into Dovré or sailed away on a ship with her and left Galle completely."

Odiva holds my hand under the water. Blood swirls from my

wound. "Three grace bones do not make you invincible, Sabine. You need to be careful."

My defenses flare. Did she hear a word I said? Ailesse is the one she should be worried about.

"You've proven to be a good huntress over the past few weeks. The other Leurress should take note. The golden jackal still evades us."

"No one's found him?" My voice cracks, but I try my best to sound surprised.

"Not even his shadow." Odiva's eyes drift to the bubbling waterfall. "I was so certain Tyrus was ready for me to have him back."

Back? I open my mouth to ask what she means, but then her eyes refocus and examine mine. Can she see through me to my deceitful heart? Can she smell the jackal's carcass where I buried him in this very hollow?

"Let us hope we find him before the new moon. I have told you what the Chained will do if they are loose for too long."

I shiver under her heavy stare. The full moon is in three days, which means the *new* moon is a little over two weeks away. I have that long to decide if I should ignore the silver owl's warnings and dig up the jackal to take another femur bone. Odiva would still have time to carve a new flute.

She pulls a slim hunting pack off her shoulder and removes a rolled strip of cloth, an item any good huntress carries in case of wounds. "I have tracked you here for a solemn purpose, Sabine."

Misgiving spools inside me. "Oh?"

She takes my hand again, dips it once more in the water, and begins to wrap it. "It is about Ailesse."

All my nerves stand at attention. "Did you find her?"

Odiva's eyes fill with sorrow—too late for me to believe. "You need to prepare yourself. I know how much you care for my daughter."

But how much do you?

She sighs and looks down. "Ailesse is dead. I am sure of it this time."

My hand tenses, but she doesn't let it go.

"Tyrus gave me a sign."

The god who won't tell you where his jackal is?

"I trust him. The bond between a mother and a daughter carries a grace of its own. I've searched myself deeply, and my attachment to Ailesse is gone."

Was there ever one to begin with?

Odiva finishes binding my hand. "I am sorry I had to be the one to tell you. I can see how shocking it is."

"Yes." My voice scratches on a whisper. Ailesse isn't dead. I know it just like the first time Odiva spun this lie. If I look shocked, it's because her heartlessness knows no end. Why is she so determined to abandon her daughter and the bone flute?

"I have grieved more than you know for Ailesse. Every Leurress in our *famille* has. But we must not fall into despair. The gods expect us to perform our duty, no matter our hardships. That is why they have intervened."

What is she talking about? Perspiration trickles down the back of my neck as her grip subtly tightens.

She inhales a long breath through her nostrils and lifts her chin. "Tyrus has also given me another sign. He has chosen *you* to be my heir."

I stare incredulously at her. "What?" I yank my hand away and scoot back. "No. *Ailesse* is your heir. She's *alive, Matrone.* You can't really believe—"

"You have to stop living in denial. You need to embrace your destiny."

"My destiny?" A humorless laugh escapes me. "I never wanted to be a Ferrier. I didn't even want these." I tug at my grace bones.

"You are modest to a fault, Sabine. I see what you can become." Her voice fills with urgency. "You need to see it, too. Once you complete your rite of passage—"

"*No.*" I stand and cover my ears. She can't say things like this to me. It isn't just a betrayal to Ailesse; it's preposterous. "Heirs are always daughters."

"Unless there are none." She swiftly rises.

I stumble backward from her. "No one in our *famille* will accept me."

"I'll tell them what I told you: Tyrus gave me a sign."

"Then he's mistaken!" I fight to breathe. "I'm not qualified. Every Leurress is more talented. Everyone has better graces." I was right—Odiva *did* want Ailesse to fail her rite of passage. She knew she'd be reckless, and she hoped she'd die without having to kill her directly. I just don't understand why. Why does she want *me* instead?

"You have the bone of a black wolf, Sabine. That is nothing to be ashamed about. And when you become *matrone*, you can claim two more grace bones."

My heart pounds out of my chest. I can't listen to this. I have to get away from her. But she's blocking my path out of the hollow. I turn and rush toward the other path. My feet splash through the stream. She catches my arm when I'm halfway across. I yank against her. "Let go!"

"Don't be rash." She draws taller with poised confidence. "This is a great honor. Why are you so resistant?"

"Because I can't be Ailesse!" I shout. Angry tears scald my face. "Because you have a daughter you don't love!"

"You are wrong." Her tone rises, just as furious and passionate as mine. "I do love Ailesse."

"Then why are you doing this?"

"I've told you." Her voice breaks. "Tyrus says it must be so."

"Tyrus can rot in the darkest pit of his Hell."

"Sabine." Odiva pulls me around, but I keep my head turned. "Look at me." She grabs my chin, but I squeeze my eyes shut like a stubborn child. "Do you not believe I love you, too?"

"You shouldn't. You should love Ailesse more."

"Sabine . . ." The fight drains from her voice. "You are my daughter, too."

My shock is so deep that all the breath leaves my lungs. I open my eyes and stare into hers. They're shining with tears. "You are my daughter," she says again, a sacred whisper this time. She lifts her hand to my cheek and cradles it. "I have wanted to tell you for so long." Her brows lift inward. "I promised myself I never would."

The stream rushes over my feet and splashes at my ankles. I don't feel the cold. "What—what are you talking about?" My voice barely rises past my throat.

"Your father . . . he wasn't my *amouré*. He wasn't Ailesse's father either."

Every word she speaks falls like a hammer. "But"—I shake my head—"Ailesse and I are too close in age." I have to concentrate on facts, logic. They'll prove Odiva is wrong. "You can't be mother to both of us."

"You are barely sixteen. Ailesse is almost eighteen. There was time."

Dizziness racks my head. What she's talking about is scandal. Sacrilege. I don't want to be a part of it. "You betrayed your *amouré*!" I exclaim. The gods gave her a perfect match to spend eternity with, and she flouted it. "Didn't you ever love him at all?"

"I loved *your* father, Sabine." Odiva looks younger, reduced from the esteemed ruler of our *famille* to a girl with different dreams.

My legs threaten to buckle beneath me. I break away from her softened hold and sit down at the edge of the stream.

She drifts over and kneels before me. The skirt of her dress blooms wider in the water. "You look so much like him. The same olive complexion. The same beautiful eyes with that ring of gold in your irises." She reaches to touch my face again, and I shrink back.

"I *have* a mother," I say. "She's *my* mother." I'm not making any sense, but neither is Odiva.

She sighs heavily. "Ciana wasn't your mother, but she *was*

devout and ambitious. I told her the gods blessed me with two *amourés*, and that my gift was so sacred the rest of our *famille* couldn't know. I said the gods trusted Ciana to uphold my secret, and in return I promised they would grant her greater glory in Paradise. She readily agreed to my plan. After her rite of passage, she left Château Creux to live with her own *amouré*. I also left to conceal my pregnancy and told our *famille* I was embarking on a great hunt. While I was away, I bore you and gave you to Ciana to bring back as *her* child."

My head falls into my quivering hands. Odiva's words rip at my heart. I mourn more than ever the loss of the mother who loved me, who cared for me, even if she didn't share my blood. Even if I also feel betrayed by her.

"Two years ago, after Ciana died ferrying, I felt more responsible for you," Odiva explains. "And the more you matured, the more you reminded me of your father. I felt an even deeper connection to him through you, and I realized more than ever how much I desperately miss him." She pulls out her crow skull necklace and tenderly strokes the ruby. "He was a great man, Sabine."

"What happened to . . . him?" My throat closes on *my father*. If I say it—if I even think it—I might accept what Odiva is telling me. This is all lies, the silver owl's warning.

Her expression dims. "I never played the siren song for your father. He was never meant to be my sacrifice. But the gods took his life, anyway . . . shortly after I became pregnant with you. They punished me for loving him by wrapping him in chains." Her eyes darken to a deeper black. "When his spirit met me on the land bridge, I tried to ferry him to Elara, but the waves crashed and the winds came, and he fell through Tyrus's Gate instead."

Her tears spill over. All of this is wrong. An innocent man shouldn't have paid the price for Odiva's sin. I shouldn't pay it either. I don't want to be their child.

But I am.

The thought is a sliver under my skin. I can't pull it out—because I start to find proof. Odiva could have tracked me here because she shares a mother-daughter bond with me, too.

She shifts closer. "Do you not see you are special? The gods let *you* live."

My muscles fall limp. I'm so tired. I didn't think that was possible with my jackal grace. "They can't want me to be your heir." My breath hitches on a sob.

"They do, Sabine. I do."

I look at the woman kneeling before me. Her dress is waterlogged. All her pride is gone. Even her majestic grace bones can't draw focus from the pent-up misery written across her face.

"I need you," she says. "I've come to realize Tyrus will not lead me to the golden jackal if I do not have an heir."

Why do I feel so much pressure to say yes? The golden jackal is already dead. If Tyrus really *did* give Odiva a sign about me, it's because I'm the one person who knows where the jackal is. "How is this going to work?" I ask. "Will you tell our *famille* you're my mother?" They'll think it's just as ridiculous as I do.

"I cannot do that. You must understand, Sabine. What Ferriers are tasked with demands great faith. I would destroy that faith if they knew what I had done."

"So you're asking me to keep this a secret, too?"

"I am. You must. The Leurress will not question my choice. How can they when I tell them Tyrus is honoring Ailesse by choosing her dearest friend to rule after me?"

Ailesse.

Warmth creeps back into my limbs and wends its way toward my heart. All the Leurress call each other sisters, but now Ailesse really is my sister. That's the one truth I can embrace without flinching. It's the only part of this revelation that feels right.

Odiva takes both of my hands. Her firm hold makes my sliced palm throb harder. "The plain truth is you are, by all rights, my next successor, Sabine—blood of my blood. You must accept your fate."

I'm shaking from head to toe. How can she ask this of me? Ailesse is alive. Odiva must feel it as well as I do. She's disowning her firstborn by doing this. That can't only be because she loved my father more. She's still hiding something. I need to find out what it is.

"Very well." I can retract my words once I rescue Ailesse and return her to our *famille.* Then the game will be up. The proper heir will be home. "I accept it."

Odiva beams and presses her cold lips to my cheek. "Now come home soon. You have obtained all your grace bones. There is nothing more for you out here."

I give her a stiff nod, and she rises to her feet and leaves the hollow.

A few moments after she's gone, a silent flash of wings catches the edge of my vision. The silver owl descends on the ground a few yards away, and my eyes fly wide.

She's perched on the spot where I buried the golden jackal.

I rush over. "Move away!" I hiss, and glance over my shoulder. Luckily, Odiva hasn't come back.

The silver owl pecks at the ground and stares up at me.

My stomach turns. "I'm not digging up the jackal."

She releases the quietest rasp-screech. She's aware of the *matrone's* graced hearing, too.

This is ridiculous. The only reason to dig up the jackal would be . . . "Wait, so now you *want* me to take a bone for a new flute?"

She bobs her head.

I frown at her angled eyes. Why has the silver owl changed her mind?

Because now you're the matrone's *heir, Sabine. And heirs can open the Gates of the Beyond.*

All my nerves catch fire. "You want me to make a flute for *myself?*"

The owl hops close and combs her beak through my hair. I'm so startled she's touching me—that she's asking this of me—that all my muscles turn to ice. Even my heart seizes up. I'm not sure how many more revelations I can handle today.

The moment blood pumps into my limbs again, I reach for the owl. "How can I—?"

She launches into the air. Her wings flutter against my face.

I gasp. "Wait!"

She soars out of the hollow, and my dazed eyes lower back to the earth over the jackal's body.

Elara, I hope you know what you're doing.

I inhale a deep breath.

And I start to dig.

36
Bastien

I DUCK INTO THE PERFUMERY by La Chaste Dame, and my head immediately aches. Too many fragrances fight for space in the air. How does Birdine stand it?

I spy the top of her head behind one of the counters. The afternoon sun slants in through a leaded window and catches the dust motes above her frizzy ginger hair. She hums a familiar love song as she kneels by a shelf and organizes a row of dark bottles.

I creep up and lean my folded arms against the counter. "How's business?"

Birdine yelps and whirls around. Her hand flies to her chest, and she exhales roughly. "*Merde*, Bastien. You nearly stopped my heart." She stands and smooths her apron. "Business is business.

And, no, I haven't seen Marcel." She narrows her green eyes. "So stop pestering me."

I'm not done yet. "Is that ink?" I nod at a stain on her left hand.

She hastily tucks it behind her back. "No. I just spilled some musk oil on myself."

"What about that callus on your middle finger?"

She darts a glance at her other hand. "What about it?"

"It's new. And curious thing, Marcel has one just like it."

Birdine's cheeks mottle red. "I have a right to practice scribe work on my own, thank you very much. It doesn't mean anything shady."

I level a hard gaze on her. "Give up the game, Birdie." I deliberately use Marcel's nickname for her. "You know where he is. Marcel wouldn't have gone this long without figuring out a way to see you."

She juts up her chin. A waft of rosewater hits me square in the face. "What are you going to do, torture me for the truth? I'm not going to snitch on Marcel."

I tap my foot, trying to figure out how to crack her. I've trailed Birdine three times after the perfumery has closed up for the day, and all she does is hurry home to a room she rents above a nearby tavern. Marcel's never there.

"Look, I know you're trying to protect him, but you're putting Marcel in more danger by not telling me where he is. You're putting *all* of Dovré in danger." I lean closer over the counter. "You ever hear a bone-chilling whisper when you're walking home at night? Does it ever make you think you're going mad?"

Birdine shrinks back and bites her lower lip.

"How about your customers or your friends in the tavern? Notice any of them growing sick with a strange weakness they can't explain?"

She folds her arms around herself. "Marcel says there are bad humors in the air."

"Marcel's lying so you can sleep at night."

She suppresses a shiver.

I sigh. I don't want to scare Birdine. I just need her help. "Will you at least tell him something for me? Say people are going to die if he and Jules don't bring back what they stole." Ailesse might die, too, if she has to stay underground any longer. I can't allow that to happen.

"What did they steal?" she asks.

"I'll let Marcel explain that part. Tell him he and Jules can find me round about the place we ran to when we first got into this mess." I don't spell out the location, in case any of the dead are listening, but Marcel should know I mean our old chamber in the catacombs. If Ailesse is strong enough, I'll take her there tonight.

I step away from the counter and adjust the pack on my shoulder. "Will you do that for me?" I shrug off my needling doubts about Jules. I have to trust she won't harm Ailesse when we're all back together again. She shouldn't as long as the soul-bond holds. Jules and Marcel clearly haven't found a way to break it yet, or they would have come out of hiding already. "You'd be doing Marcel a favor. All of Dovré, too."

Birdine looks down and rubs the callus on her finger. She gives me a slow nod. "Will you do me a favor, too, whenever you *do* see Jules again?"

"Name it."

She tucks a frizzy curl behind her ear. "Ask her to give me a chance with her brother." Birdine's brows lift shyly before she lowers them in a firm line. "I'm not another flighty Dovré girl from the brothel district. I *love* Marcel. I would do anything for him."

The earnestness in her voice makes me pause. Birdine's only sixteen, but she knows her heart. More than that, she's willing to fight for her chance at happiness.

I can't help thinking of Ailesse. I hate being away from her when I'm searching for my friends every day, and once I am back with her, it takes all my energy to resist touching her—and everything else I'd like to do when I find myself staring at her lips. I hold back because . . . I don't know why. It seems selfish, I guess. Our fates are stacked against us. There's also the part of me that wonders what my father would think.

But maybe . . . just maybe my father would want me to be happy.

At least for as long as I can be.

"Marcel's lucky to have a girl like you," I tell Birdine. "I promise to say so to Jules."

Her face lights up. "Thank you, Bastien."

I give her a parting nod and stride outside. I set a quick pace for the castle district. I'm going to comb the cellars, sheds, and stables there one more time in search of my friends, in case Birdine doesn't get a chance to talk to Marcel today. Then I'll hurry back to Ailesse. Tonight is the full moon. Being stuck in the dark will be miserable for her—maybe even deadly.

I'm going to find a way to help her, whether or not I get her bones back.

37
Sabine

THE SILVER OWL STARES AT me from the stone parapet of Castelpont, but I refuse to set foot on the bridge. I understand now what I didn't when the owl first asked me to dig up the golden jackal. And tonight it will be possible.

The sun is setting, and the full moon above me grows sharper and brighter. I have my three grace bones ready. I even have Ailesse's ritual knife and a new bone flute. I spent most of the last three days hollowing it out and carving the tone holes. I've left the instrument simple, no engraved embellishments like the original flute. It should be enough that the flute is made from a true golden jackal bone.

Everything has fallen into place for my rite of passage.

Everything except my courage.

"I can't," I tell the silver owl. I can't kill a human being, even though the Chained are on a rampage in Dovré. Even though the Leurress need all the Ferriers they can get, and the savage graces of the jackal are diminishing my reservations to shed blood.

The owl drags her claws across the stones, and screeches.

"Why me?" I ask, even though some of the answer is obvious. As the heir to the *matrone*—as blood of her blood—I can open the Gates to the Underworld and Paradise. But to open the Gates, I need to be on the land bridge. And to be on the land bridge and survive the dead *and* the lure of the Beyond, I have to be a committed Ferrier. I have to complete my rite of passage.

The owl doesn't move while the thoughts chase through me. It's like she can read my mind and is waiting for her turn to speak. She stands taller on the parapet and spreads her wings open. A translucent and silver-tinged image shimmers before me. My pulse quickens.

Ailesse.

She's lying on her side on quarried limestone, which means she's underground. That's all I can make out of her surroundings. She's clean and wearing a new green dress, but her drawn expression says she's suffering greatly.

My heart rises up my throat. "Ailesse."

She doesn't look up or even bat an eye. I don't understand. Last time I had a vision of her, she saw me, but now her gaze is fixated on the ground. Maybe she's too starved of Light to sense me. I've never seen her so terribly weak before.

She holds a piece of chalk in her shaking hand and sketches a shaded-in circle. "New moon . . ." she murmurs on a hoarse breath. "Bone flute . . . bridge over water . . . land bridge . . . ferrying night." She draws another circle, but doesn't shade it in. "Full moon . . . bridge over earth . . . Castelpont . . . rite of passage . . ."

My mouth slowly falls slack. Ailesse can't know I'd consider my own rite of passage tonight. Unless the owl has somehow been communicating with her, too.

"Ferrying night?" she whispers, and traces the second circle again. She drops the chalk and painstakingly rolls from her side to her back. Pinched lines form between her brows as she stares up at a ceiling I can't see.

Then her image starts to ripple and fade.

My breath hitches. "No, wait!" I haven't had a fair chance to catch her attention. I haven't even assured her I'm doing everything I can to save her. "Ailesse!"

She flickers out. The silver owl closes her wings.

I stumble backward and steeple my fingers over my nose and mouth.

The owl rasps at me, but I shake my head. Ailesse knows I'm not ready to do what it takes to become a Ferrier. She wouldn't ask me to complete my rite of passage. She'd know I'd never go through with it unless I had no other choice.

My body quakes with guttural rage. I turn on the owl. "I know what you're trying to tell me, but I won't hear it. Ailesse isn't going to die!" I may be Odiva's daughter, but I can't really be her heir unless my sister is dead. Furious tears sting my eyes and smear my vision. All these weeks can't have been leading up to Ailesse's death and my ascension. I never agreed to be a part of that.

The owl hops off the parapet and screeches at me.

"No!" I cry. I'm not playing this game any longer. I'm not completing my rite of passage or ferrying souls or even opening the Gates of the Beyond. I'm going to focus on saving Ailesse before it's too late. There has to be another way to save Dovré from the Chained.

And suddenly I know what it is.

I'll give Odiva the bone flute—the one I spent the last three days carving.

I race away from Castelpont. I run full speed for Château Creux.

I don't care what the silver owl or even Ailesse wants me to do.

I'm not giving up on my sister.

38
Bastien

I QUIETLY STEP FROM THE scaffolding and enter the room off the quarry, careful not to wake Ailesse. She needs her sleep. Every day she needs more.

She rests on her side with her back to me. I set down my pack and drift closer to her. My body shivers with heat. Ailesse's auburn hair lies in swirls like dark flames and shining water. That's how my father would have described it. He'd study her from every angle before trying to capture her with his chisel and hammer. He'd save his money so he could afford to sculpt her from marble instead of limestone.

"Your father carved this one for you, didn't he?" Ailesse asks on a weak breath.

I stiffen. Because she's awake. And she's thinking of my father, too. Her hand is on my most prized possession. I see it on the ground over the curved line of her waist. My dolphin sculpture. I'm not sure how I feel about her touching it. It's the only sculpture my father never tried to sell. It was his gift to me. He often took me to the coast to see dolphins, my favorite animals. We'd watch them jump from the water in pairs. "What makes you think that?"

"Because it's the best one." Her slim fingers glide along its tail. "That's proof of how much he loved you."

I shift my weight from leg to leg. I don't know how to reply. I've learned to live with the pain of losing my father, but I never shared the sorrow. Jules and I shared the anger instead.

Jules. I sigh. She and Marcel weren't anywhere in the castle district. Hopefully, Birdine has better luck finding them tonight.

I set down my lantern and pack. It's filled with more food and supplies. Ailesse never asks if I steal what I bring her. Does she even understand the concept of money—what it's like to need it and never have it?

It doesn't matter. If I had a thousand francs, I'd give them away for anything that might make her smile. "How are you feeling?" I move closer, wishing I could see her face.

Except for her fingers tracing the dolphin's back, she holds perfectly still. "Did you know I once hunted a tiger shark? I killed her with a knife, and I didn't even have graced strength—not until she gave it to me."

"I have no trouble believing you took down a shark."

She rolls over and finally meets my gaze. My pulse races.

Her skin is pale and her umber eyes are weary, but she's still breathtaking. She doesn't know it, but every day when I'm gone, all I think about is her.

"I know you're strong, Ailesse."

"Not enough." Her chest falls. She glances at the lanterns and candles around the room. They're fine candles, ones that don't smoke or sputter. I never rationed them like I said I would. I keep bringing her more. "It's not enough light," she confesses.

I can't stand seeing her in pain any longer. I have to get her out of here. "Are you well enough to walk?" I offer my hand. I know somewhere that might be safe. I haven't risked taking her there yet, but now I'm desperate. "I want to show you something."

After a tense, stretched, and nerve-racking moment, she reaches up and sets her hand in mine. The warmth of her skin instantly settles me. I pull her to her feet, and her earthy, flowery smell fills my lungs, better than any perfume.

I help her down the scaffolding and onto the floor of the quarry, then lead her into a tunnel she's never been through before. My lantern faintly lights the path ahead—a mining tunnel, free from any skulls and bones. I don't want anything to upset her.

We step over rubble and duck under places where wooden beams hold up the fissuring limestone ceiling. We slide through narrow spaces and crawl over piles of bricks. Every time our hands come apart, my fingers ache to touch her again. As soon as possible, I take her hand once more, and she weaves her fingers tightly through mine.

"There used to be a great house in Dovré," I say as we come near our destination. "The baron who lived there turned the courtyard into an aviary, and he covered it with a dome of leaded glass. The house is abandoned now; half of it collapsed into a quarry. The dome fell, too, but the glass didn't shatter. It was so strong that most of the panes stayed intact."

We step out of the tunnel, and Ailesse gasps. I set down my lantern. We don't need it anymore. I let go of her hand to give her a moment alone. She walks under the wide beam of moonlight and tips her head back. Vines hang from broken sections of the dome above us, and ivy creeps all around it. Despite that, light finds its way through. A silver glow shines down in a dust-flecked shaft.

Ailesse's eyes close. She inhales a deep breath. I smile, watching her smile. She looks like herself again. "The moon is full," she whispers. "I wish you could feel it."

"Describe it for me."

She keeps her eyes closed and basks in the light. "Imagine it's the hottest day and you're parched for thirst. You finally find a spring of water and take a long drink. You know that feeling when the coolness trickles down through your chest? This is like that."

I wander closer. She lures me without any flute or song.

If my father knew Ailesse, would he like her?

"Or imagine a night that's bitter cold," she continues, "and your bones have turned to ice. At last, you find shelter and tuck close to a crackling fire. This is the moment when you feel that first burn of heat."

Can my father see Ailesse now? Is there a window looking down onto me from where he is?

Would he forgive me for wanting to see her happy?

"Ailesse?" I whisper.

She opens her eyes. Would my father forgive me for feeling peace and not hatred when I'm with her?

"Do you remember how you danced with me at Castelpont?"

She gives a small nod. Her hair gleams in the moonlight and falls past her shoulders to the middle of her back. Would my father forgive me for wanting to hold her?

"Will you dance with me like you did then?"

She takes in a breath, but doesn't say anything. Maybe that dance is sacred to the Leurress, and I shouldn't have asked her to—

I swallow; she's moving closer. The light ripples across her face. When she's almost touching me, she rises on her toes, extends her leg, and pivots in a slow circle. Her arms float above her head, wind and water and earth and fire, as she glides around me. Her hand lifts to her face, and she runs the back of her fingers in a line down her cheek and throat and chest and waist and hip. I'm barely breathing. The look on her face is giving, not vain. She shows me her hair next, a shimmer of auburn that slips through her palm.

Her hands take mine, and she pulls them to rest on her waist. My thumbs graze her lower rib cage. Drawing close, she touches my face . . . the bone of my jaw, the slope of my nose. There's a rhythm to her movements, like each motion is timed to music only she hears.

Her fingers tremble as they move over my lips and trace the length of my neck. They lower even farther, to my chest. Her breath shudders as her fingers spread over my heart. I feel it pound faster. This part of the dance I don't remember.

Her eyes close. She leans her forehead against me and turns her cheek so it lies across my shoulder. I hold her tighter, wanting to keep her like this, but the dance isn't finished.

She takes my hand and twirls away from me, slowly and gracefully, then spins back again until her back is pressed to my chest. She lifts her arms and folds them around the nape of my neck. I raise my hands and slide them around the circle of her waist. This is peace. This is right. I was meant to be here with her.

She stays in my arms much longer than she did at Castelpont. When she slowly unfolds herself and turns around, she gazes up at me, searching my eyes. "That's all I can do," she whispers. "We're coming close to the moment where . . ." *She meant to kill me. I meant to kill her.*

"Then this can be the new end." My fingers weave through her hair.

She draws a breath and releases it. "What if you and I didn't meet on a bridge? What if I was a normal girl who didn't wear bones or see the dead? Would you feel anything for me if I never lured you with a song?"

My mouth curves. "Would you feel anything for me if I wasn't your soulmate?"

She shakes her head, which worries me for a moment, but then she answers, "I can't imagine anyone else for me but you."

I sweep a lock of her hair off her face and brush my thumb across her cheek. "You never needed to play a song for me, Ailesse."

Our heads drift together, mine lowering, hers rising.

Adrenaline pumps through my veins. I can almost taste her lips. I've been wanting to kiss her for days, and those days have stretched on for ages.

She gasps and jerks back. Her eyes dart wildly around the room.

"What's wrong?" I ask, a little off balance.

"A Chained is here."

"Chained?"

"A dead person—a bad one."

"You can see him without your grace bones? I thought—"

She shakes her head, breathing fast. "I feel him. Once he snuck inside, the energy from the moon dimmed."

My muscles tense. I curse myself, realizing my terrible mistake. I shouldn't have risked bringing her here, where the dead can find her. "We have to run."

The Chained's bodiless voice snarls, "Do you think you can hide from us?" The hair on my arm stands on end. He barely sounds human.

And he's right beside us.

In a flash, Ailesse pulls my father's knife from my belt.

"Wait!" I reach for her.

She springs away and strikes the air, swiping the knife with a cry of exertion. The Chained man hisses. Ailesse's head whips to the side. She's thrown back several feet, and her body crashes against a wall of the quarry. She crumples to the ground.

I shout her name, rushing toward her. I fall to my knees and draw her into my arms. She sucks in great gasps of air. Her breath has been knocked out of her lungs. "He's too powerful," she pants. "He stole Light before he came here."

Feet pound, coming close behind us. I swing around, my hand in a tight fist of rage. I punch hard, and my knuckles connect with something—hopefully the bastard's face.

He grunts, but then I can't feel him. I jump up and swipe out again. He's gone. I remember how fast he came back at Ailesse, and grab the knife she dropped. I blindly attack the air.

I still can't find him, but I don't give up. I keep slashing, stabbing, striking. I've never felt more murderous. If he touches her again—

She staggers to her feet. "Give me back the knife."

"No."

"Bastien, I've trained to be a Ferrier. I'm—"

A frantic scream splits the air.

It's not the Chained man.

Ailesse and I exchange a quick glance and race toward the sound. She takes the lead.

The far end of the quarry is mostly caved in, smashed by the bricks of the great house above it. We climb around the first massive chunk of broken limestone.

My heart stops.

Jules.

She clutches her throat and hovers like she's dangling from an invisible noose.

"Bastien, the knife!" Ailesse shouts. "He's choking her!"

I pass it. She throws it.

She has remarkable aim, because the knife suddenly stills in the air—a handsbreadth from Jules's face.

Jules crashes to her knees and sucks in a ragged breath.

I hop off the limestone and run for her.

The knife that's lodged in the air pulls back. Lowers. Turns and points at Jules.

"No!" I barrel toward the Chained. But I'm too far away.

The knife arcs down and tears across Jules's arm. She throws her head back and screams.

I'll kill him. I don't care if he's already dead. I'll kill him harder.

I grab below the hilt of the knife and find his wrist. I wrench his arm. He howls in pain, and the knife falls.

Ailesse races to my side and catches it up off the ground. She holds it with both hands, raises her arms, and stabs the blade downward. Another howl. Ailesse jumps to the right, anticipating a counterattack.

My fist flies and hits the Chained. But when I strike again, I miss.

Ailesse's shoulder flinches back. Then her leg. He's prodding her backward. She slashes with her knife, but can't find him.

I pick up a stone. "How do we defeat him?"

She cuts the air and hits nothing. "We can't." Her other shoulder jerks back, harder this time. The Chained is driving her into a corner. "We just need to stun him long enough to get away."

I run toward the empty space she's fighting. "How are we supposed to do that?"

"I have no idea."

I throw the stone. It hits something solid and bounces off.

Ailesse's knife doesn't stop thrashing. I've done nothing to slow down the Chained man. *Merde.* I don't want us to die down here.

"Ailesse!" Jules says. She pulls something off from around her neck—the coin pouch with Ailesse's grace bones. "Catch!" She tosses it.

Ailesse's eyes follow the flying pouch. She jumps and grabs its leather strings. She quickly drops my father's knife and kicks it across the floor to me. By the time I pick it up, the pouch is around her neck. Her jaw muscle flexes, her shoulders square, and her gaze focuses just to her left.

She sees the Chained man.

With a great burst of speed, she turns around and charges straight for the corner of the quarry the Chained man has been backing her into. She leaps and springs off one corner wall and pushes off the next. She zigzags upward, catching handholds and footholds. When she reaches the high ceiling, she shoves off the wall and slingshots the other way. Her body twists to face the quarry. Toward the space where the Chained man must be.

She throws a vicious punch with all her momentum. The Chained must be hurtling backward from the strike.

Ailesse lands on her feet and bolts for a target several feet in front of her. She jumps and pounces on something in midair. Her legs grip it like a vise. Her elbow wraps around what should be the Chained man's neck. She squeezes so hard her body trembles.

I launch toward her. "Will he pass out?"

"No." She grunts. "But he can feel the suffering."

"Good." I plunge my knife into his invisible chest and twist the blade. I feel him spasm and buckle to the ground. Ailesse drops with him, and her hold breaks. He yanks out the knife and casts it a few yards away. He shoves me to the ground. I roll back a couple feet.

"Don't let him go!" Ailesse fumbles to right herself.

"Where is he?" I swing around.

"He's right—" Ailesse points. Frowns. Turns in every direction. A strand of hair catches at the edge of her mouth. She scales the chunk of limestone and stands on top for a better view. She glances around for the chains or whatever it is she sees.

Someone taps the back of my shoulder. I startle and turn, but it's only Jules.

"Bastien . . ." she says on a faint breath.

Her face is alarmingly pale. Her sleeve is drenched in blood.

My pulse trips. I reach for her.

Her head droops, and she doubles over.

No, no, no.

39
Ailesse

I hop down from the limestone and hurry over to Bastien and Jules. "We need to leave. We'll be safer once we're deeper in the catacombs."

Bastien has Jules's head in his lap. He rattles her. She won't open her eyes, but at least she's breathing.

"Bastien, please." I grab his arm.

He takes in my pensive expression. "Is the Chained man still here?"

"He disappeared." I shiver. "We have to go before he comes back."

He swallows and nods. "Right."

He starts to heft up Jules. I try to help him, but he angles away. "I've got her," he says, and leads the way as we rush out of the quarry. He doesn't take the tunnel toward his hideout under Chapelle du Pauvre.

"Where are we going?" I ask, holding the lantern near him so he can see into the darkness.

"Our old catacombs chamber." He climbs over some fallen debris. "I'm betting that's where Marcel is."

Our journey lengthens through the branching tunnels, and Bastien starts panting.

"I can carry Jules," I offer again. "I have my graces back."

"No." He lowers his brows. "Please, Ailesse, let me do this. It's my fault . . ." He shakes his head, and his eyes fill with pain as he looks at her.

We finally arrive at our old chamber. Bastien kicks open the door by the wall of skulls.

Marcel's sitting at the overturned cart table with a pile of open books. He glances up, and his face brightens. "Bastien! Ailesse!" Then he sees his sister and blanches. "What happened?"

"A Chained man attacked her." Bastien barges inside. "Sliced her arm and nearly choked her to death."

I grab a blanket and spread it on the ground. Bastien lays Jules on it and applies pressure to her bleeding arm.

Marcel stares at us, aghast. "He choked her with chains?"

"No. He was a dead man," Bastien says. He looks at me, and I quickly explain how the gods mark evil souls.

"Is Jules going to be all right?" Marcel asks.

"Yes." The edge to Bastien's voice is so sharp it dares either one of us to disagree. "Bring me some water."

I'm immediately on my feet. I step toward the bucket by the shelves, but Marcel is closer. I move out of his way as he rushes it back to Bastien. Both boys are hovering over Jules now. Bastien splashes a little water on her face. "Come on, Jules." He slaps her cheeks twice, and I wince. "Come on!" His voice breaks. "You're tougher than this. You're not allowed to die on me."

My eyes blur with threatening tears as he desperately tries to wake her. This is what it would feel like if I lost Sabine.

Jules's chest rises and falls more shallowly. Then it stills.

Marcel covers his mouth. Bastien's shoulders hitch up. He buries his head in her stomach. I step closer, my throat aching. I want to fold my arms around him.

Just as I reach out to touch him, Jules's eyes fly open. She inhales a ragged breath.

I flinch back. Bastien jolts upright. Marcel's head sags forward in relief.

"What are you all staring at?" Jules asks, her voice frail.

Bastien bursts into warm laughter. He kisses her three times on her forehead.

I grin, though a stitch of pain forms in my chest. Their deep affection makes me miss Sabine even more. I place a hand on Bastien's shoulder. "I'll find something to dress her arm with."

He tosses me a grateful smile.

I walk to the wall of shelves and look through the supplies. A roll of clean fabric is tucked behind a small pot of crushed herbs.

"I'm sorry I left you," Jules murmurs to Bastien.

I smell the herbs. Yarrow. Good for wounds.

"*Tu ne me manques pas. Je ne te manque pas.*"

I freeze.

My heart thuds slowly as I turn around.

He's holding Jules's hand the same way he held mine when he spoke those same words to me. The words his father said to him. I thought they were sacred, a gift Bastien only shared with me.

He brings Jules's knuckles to his lips and kisses them. "You were never missing from me, Jules."

A rush of weakness trembles through my knees. I have to sit down.

I stumble to a corner of the room. Then I realize it's the corner with the limestone slab. My chest tightens, and I move to sit at the table instead. I set down the fabric and yarrow and take steadying breaths.

Bastien and Jules fall deep in conversation. He laughs at something she says and smooths her hair off her face. A hollow ache carves through me.

You've been deceiving yourself, Ailesse. He could never love you as much as he loves her.

I should be used to feeling second best; my mother always favored Sabine.

Marcel wanders over and sits across from me with a lazy smile on his face. "Can you believe we're all back together again?" he asks, like I'm a tight-knit part of their family, and the three of them never abducted me. "Too bad Jules and I haven't found a way to break the soul-bond yet, but we've had a real adventure all these days without you."

"Oh, yes?" I absently flip through one of his books, trying to keep my eyes off Bastien. Now Jules is laughing with him.

"We found all sorts of new and interesting hideouts in Dovré. Bastien almost found us one time, so Jules and I decided to move back down here. We've been in this chamber all this last week."

"Clever," I reply. Bastien told me he checked here once, and when he found it empty of their belongings, he never came back.

Marcel nods, his lackadaisical enthusiasm on point. "We've got it all stockpiled with food and black powder again. I've been making some of the runs myself."

I spare a glance at a dozen or so small powder casks stacked against the wall. "Eager to blast my mother into a pit again?" *Or me?*

He snorts. "Something like that."

I force a grin and pass him the rolled fabric and yarrow. "Could you give these to Bastien?"

"Sure." He gets up and swaggers over to his friend. Bastien covers Jules with another blanket, taking extra care to tuck it tightly around her.

My eyes sting. I look back down at Marcel's book. A corner of a sheet of parchment sticks out from beneath it. My gaze lands on a small scribbled drawing labeled "bridge."

I frown, scooting the book aside so I can see the whole sheet of parchment. It's covered in a labyrinth of more scribbles. "What is this?" I ask Marcel when he returns.

He sits down again. "Oh, I updated my map of the catacombs."

"There's a bridge here?"

He nods. "Remember that tunnel I exploded? The bridge is nearby it, beneath the mines. Turns out there's a vast network of caves down there." He leans back and laces his hands behind his head. "I discovered a shaft leading to the bridge. It was a bit tricky to navigate, especially on the way back up. I thought a different path would be easier, but the hatch at the top was impossible to pry open, even with my knife."

My brow furrows as I try to follow him.

"*Merde!*" Bastien says. He stands and grips the empty sheath at his belt.

It takes me a moment to understand what's upset him. I gasp. "Your father's knife." We left it behind in the quarry. The Chained man threw it out of reach just before Jules fell unconscious. "I'll go back for it, Bastien."

He blows out a tense breath and rakes his hands through his hair. "No, you can't be exposed under the dome again."

"I have my falcon grace." I rise from the table. "I'll be quick."

"And if you're attacked?"

"I have my tiger shark grace."

"That's not going to cut it if a horde comes after you."

Marcel waves a sluggish hand. "I'll go."

The look Bastien gives him says that's the worst idea yet. "*I'm* going," he says adamantly.

My stomach clenches. "But what if the Chained man comes back there?"

"I'll be fine. Until tonight, the dead have left me alone. It's you they're drawn to, Ailesse," he says, and then looks down at

Jules. "Will you be all right while I'm gone?"

She rolls her eyes at him and smiles. But as soon as Bastien turns away, a small convulsion runs through her.

"Marcel and I will take care of her." I cross to where she's now propped up against the wall. She stares at the coin purse around my neck, and her eyes grow narrow and cold.

Bastien gives a curt nod and grabs his lantern, then he bites his lip and veers over to me. "We'll talk soon, all right?" His fingers feather across mine, and I flush with heat. His eyes are apologetic, maybe even regretful. I know the conversation he means to have when he returns. He's going to explain his feelings about Jules.

I muster a smile. I don't want him to think I'm upset. He and I were star-crossed to begin with. "All right," I whisper.

He searches my eyes, and I lower them so they don't reveal anything. "I'll hurry as fast as I can," he says.

His hand slips away from mine, and my fingers curl. He ducks under the low doorway.

And then he's gone.

A fierce ache rises at the back of my throat.

Jules shoots me a look of contempt. "You're cruel to tempt him when all you want to do is to kill him." Her body convulses with another tremor. "I saw you two in the quarry. You were about to kiss."

I stare at her, surprised by her sudden mood swing and rock-hard expression. I try to see past it to the Jules that Bastien has always known. I try to see even deeper to the girl she might have been if her father had lived. "No matter how much you hate me,

Jules, you need to believe I'll never kill Bastien. I give you my promise." I wish I could save him from his fate, but he and I have been deluding ourselves. There's no way to break our soul-bond. I knew that from the start.

She scoffs. "Your promises mean nothing."

I draw a calming breath. I know what I need to do now, and it's for the best. "What if I promise to leave your lives forever? Would you believe me then?"

Some of the malice leaves Jules's face. "You'd leave Bastien? Why?"

Because you're the one meant for him. "Wouldn't you leave the person who'd held you captive?"

She shivers with another tremor. Her body is in shock, and I'm only upsetting her more.

I look at Marcel. "Can I talk to you for a moment outside?"

His brows rise. "All right."

He follows me out of the chamber, and I shift back from the looming wall of skulls. "You've always been kind to me," I say, keeping my voice low. "That's why I hope you'll help. I have my grace bones now, but I still need the bone flute."

A shaky laugh escapes him. "You're going to have to ask Jules. If I give it to you without her knowing, she'll murder me in my sleep."

"But aren't *you* angry she was almost murdered? This is how you can get your revenge on the Chained man who hurt her."

"By giving you the flute?"

"The dead can't be killed; they can only be ferried." I lean closer. "You must know where Jules is hiding it."

His grin quivers as he rubs his earlobe. "Can we talk about this when Bastien comes back? I don't think he's forgiven me for letting you steal my knife."

"Bastien will be glad I have the flute." Tears form as soon as I say his name. I blink them back. "I might be able to break our soul-bond if I play a different song on it."

Marcel stiffens. "Could it really be that simple?"

"I hope." I don't waste another breath explaining my theory or the fact that I don't know any soul-bond-breaking songs. "Please, Marcel. Tonight is a full moon, and midnight is just over three hours away. That's when I need to start ferrying. I don't have any more time to lose."

"Full moon?" he repeats with a frown. "You said the Leurress ferry on the *new* moon."

"Yes, but the bone flute has both symbols—the new moon *and* the full moon. At first I thought the full moon was only on there to show when a Leurress could perform her rite of passage, but all day long I've been thinking . . . what if the full moon on the flute means more than that? What if the dead can be ferried on a full moon, too?"

Marcel drums his fingers on his lips. "The lowest tides *do* occur during full moons as well as new moons," he concedes.

"I have to try," I say. "The bone flute is finally within my reach again." I set my jaw and steel my nerves, grateful I have a monumental task to distract me tonight. I only pray my mother will be willing to attempt ferrying with me. If nothing else, she'll be relieved to have the bone flute back in her possession.

"Will you have enough time to find the other Ferriers and make it to the land bridge by midnight?" Marcel asks.

"Maybe—if I run fast enough." It will mean traveling out of these catacombs and to Château Creux first. My grace bones should help. "That's why I need you to hurry." I touch his arm. "Please, Marcel. Do you know what's really happening to the sick people in Dovré?"

"The dead are harassing them."

"It's more than that. The dead are growing stronger by stealing their Light—the vitality that feeds their souls. Innocent people will die if we don't act quickly."

His brows draw together. "Do you think Jules is sick like that? She's been wounded this badly before, but now she's starting to act strange."

"It's possible." Though I don't really know how a Chained goes about stealing Light. "If that dead man comes back for her, there's a very good chance he'll kill her. And when he does, he'll kill her soul, too."

Marcel's eyes widen. Now he understands.

"I need that flute."

He swallows hard. "Right. I'll be quick about it."

He shakes out nervous hands and ambles back into the chamber, assuming his usual nonchalance. I watch him and stand back from the open door to keep out of Jules's sight.

He makes his way to the wall of shelves.

"What are you doing?" Jules growls.

"Getting some food, unless I need your permission." Marcel

brings down a sack of rough-spun cloth. With his back to his sister, he rummages through it while he walks past the shelves. He suddenly stops, seized by a coughing fit. He leans his shoulder against the wall, and his fingers creep toward a protruding limestone brick. It must be a little hollow on top, because when he reaches inside, he knocks something slim and white into his sack. He straightens and pounds his fist on his chest. "You hungry?" He pulls a chunk of bread out of the sack.

"Not hungry enough to eat that mold-ridden rock." Jules's voice shakes like she's convulsing again, even though it's warm and she's wrapped in blankets.

"Fair enough." Marcel drops the bread back into the sack and strolls out of the chamber with it.

We hurry several feet away from the door. He withdraws the bone flute, and my blood quickens. I reach for it, but he pulls it close to his chest.

"You have to keep your promise and never return for Bastien," Marcel whispers. "He's Jules's best friend and also mine. We don't want him hurt." *Or killed*, he might add for the grave look in his eyes.

"I will," I reply. Then my stomach knots. "Will you tell him I know he loves Jules and that I"—my voice cracks—"that I wish him the very best?"

Marcel looks at me blankly. "Huh?"

"You saw them tonight."

"Well, yes . . . I mean, Bastien's always cared for Jules, but you're his *soulmate*."

My chin trembles. "That doesn't mean he never had a stronger attachment to begin with."

"But—"

"Bastien will be safer with Jules, Marcel. You know that. Promise me you'll keep working to break the soul-bond."

His shoulders fall. "Of course." He gives my arm an affectionate squeeze. "I wish you the best, too, Ailesse." With a heavy sigh, he looks down at the flute. I know he'll miss its mysteries. "Oh." His expression brightens. "I forgot to tell you. You know that bridge I mentioned—the one in the caves beneath the mines?"

I nod, curious.

He turns the bone flute over and points to the symbol of a bridge over earth. "This was engraved on it."

40
Sabine

THE FULL MOON SHINES DOWN into the courtyard under Château Creux. Ten or so women are still awake and conversing in the corners of the open cavern. They whisper about the Chained stealing Light and growing stronger. They debate about what can be done before the next new moon.

Maurille smiles as I rush by her. "Good evening, Sabine." Other women notice me, too. I've come home twice to satisfy Odiva after she spoke with me in the hollow. Most of the Leurress bow their heads, acknowledging me as the *matrone*'s heir. Some frown and cross their arms. Isla, Ailesse's rival since childhood, gives me a look that could freeze the entire Nivous Sea.

I give her a cold stare of my own. *Do you think I want this? I* want to say. If Isla is jealous, she should have tried harder to be kind. I was chosen because I'm Ailesse's best friend, the closest link to her. At least that's what Odiva told everyone.

I hurry into the tunnel that leads to the ruins of the castle's west tower. Odiva's bedchamber is the only room within it. I race up the winding stairs, pull the bone flute from my pocket, and rehearse what I'm going to say.

I'm sorry, Matrone. I thought you'd be pleased I made the flute. I wanted it to be a special gift for you. You're my mother.

I hope my words will calm her anger. Odiva was supposed to be the one to kill the golden jackal, and I directly lied to her about my newest grace bone. She'll piece together soon enough that it never came from a black wolf.

My footsteps slow as I near her room at the top of the crumbling tower. Murmurs rise on the air and resonate from within, like Odiva is praying. I shouldn't disturb her. I'm being bold even coming to her room. I barely know my mother. She distances herself from our *famille*, and she isn't involved in our everyday tasks. She only speaks to us out of necessity. Truthfully, I'm not sure how much I *want* to know her. My whole life is a lie, thanks to the choices she's made. Despite that, I can't help creeping closer to the door. What is Odiva like when she's alone? Maybe the unguarded version of herself is one I can learn to love.

The door isn't shut all the way. I can see about a foot-wide space around the center of the room, and a little more to the left and right if I angle my position.

The *matrone* is kneeling in the middle of the floor. She looks so small and vulnerable—she's removed all her grace bones.

They're laid around her in a circle: the claw-shaped pendant of an albino bear, as well as the talon-shaped pendant of an eagle owl; the tooth band of a whiptail stingray; the vertebrae of an asp viper; and the skull of a giant noctule bat. She spoke truthfully about her crow skull not being a grace bone, because it isn't set out with the others; it's still hanging around her neck.

Odiva's eyes are closed, her arms outstretched, and her cupped palms turned downward—the strange way I saw her praying on the night of Ailesse's failed rite of passage.

I study her straight and silky raven hair, her chalk-white skin, and vivid red lips. I look nothing like her. How can she be my mother?

But then, with my keen vision, I take a harder look. The slope between her neck and shoulders has the same curve as mine. Her eyes are black, not brown, but the shape is similar. Above all, her smooth hands are my hands, her long fingers my fingers. Even the way her smallest finger angles away from the others is a mirror of mine.

She opens her eyes. I startle and pull away from the door. Once my heart stops pounding, I tiptoe forward and peer inside again. There's a bowl within the circle now. And a bone knife. This isn't a prayer. It's a ritual. And bone weapons are only used for sacrifices.

What does Odiva mean to sacrifice?

She picks up the knife, and I wince, watching her cut a line across her palm. I shouldn't cringe. This is a standard part of sacrificial rituals. I had to cut myself with the bones of the animals

I killed, as well. If Ailesse had completed her rite of passage, she would have cut her own palm with her bone knife, wet with Bastien's blood.

Odiva reaches into the bowl. She doesn't retrieve an animal bone or any blood; instead, she pulls out a lock of auburn hair, tied together with a white string. I cover my mouth to hold back a gasp. Ailesse is the only Leurress in our *famille* with hair that color.

Odiva drips her blood over Ailesse's hair.

A sick rush of dread fills my stomach. What is she doing? This could be a ceremony to honor my sister's life—maybe Odiva regrets not saving her—but that doesn't make any sense. Odiva's grace bones are placed around her, just like Ailesse's were placed at the foundations of Castelpont so the bridge could represent her body.

I break into a cold sweat. What I fear can't be happening.

My mother can't be capable of murdering her own child.

My legs shake. I've lost all feeling in my arms. I can't raise my hand to push open the door. But I have to. I have to stop this. I can't let—

"This is my hair, Tyrus. This is blood I share with my mother."

I flinch back slightly. That isn't how a sacrificial prayer begins. That isn't how *any* prayer begins.

"Hear my voice, Tyrus, my soul's siren song. I am Ailesse, daughter of Odiva."

My heartbeat slows. Odiva isn't trying to kill Ailesse. She's trying to *represent* her before the god of the Underworld. It doesn't matter that she didn't raise the timbre of her voice to sound like

Ailesse. The blood and hair must be enough to appease Tyrus.

"I revoke my birthright, my claim as my mother's heir."

My eyes widen.

"My word is my bond. Let it be so." She releases a heavy sigh, and her posture wilts. Tears stream down her face, and she runs her fingers along the lock of Ailesse's hair. "There, Tyrus. The ritual is done." She places the hair back in the bowl and clutches her bleeding hand to her chest. "Let that satisfy you. I am speaking now as your servant Odiva. Accept my many sacrifices these past two years. Let them make amends for the two years I shared with my love."

Heat burns through my face. I hate that I'm the offspring of her betrayal to the gods.

She opens her eyes, but keeps her head bowed. "I have given you the Light of thousands of Unchained souls, Tyrus, instead of ferrying them to Elara."

A wave of dizziness slams into me. *What did she just say?*

"Now I ask you to honor your end of our bargain." She swallows. "Release my love from the Underworld. Let him hear my siren song and become my true *amouré*."

I blink, trying to scatter the black spots in my vision. Am I really understanding her? Did my mother really make thousands of souls wrongfully suffer—for eternity—in order to resurrect my father and bind their lives together?

She strokes Ailesse's hair again with trembling fingers. "As for the child of the man you and Elara chose for me, I have all but done away with her." Her breath shudders. "I beg of you, Tyrus . . .

please alter the requirement you first gave me. Do not make me kill my firstborn daughter."

My ears start to ring. Bile scalds my throat. Just when I thought Ailesse might be safe from our mother—just when I had the tiniest measure of relief, knowing even though she lost her birthright, she hadn't lost the power of her graces—I finally understand the depths of what Odiva has done, why she's committed such terrible crimes against the Unchained.

She gave Tyrus everything she could think of, if it meant Ailesse might live—everything except retracting her bargain. And that's the worst crime of all. Because I believe she'd kill my sister in the end, if it was the only way to bring my father back.

"Grant me a sign that I may spare Ailesse's life." Odiva spreads her arms and cups her hands downward toward the Underworld once more. "Grant me your golden jackal."

But I've already killed the golden jackal.

Which means Odiva will never receive the sign she needs. She'll grow desperate and resort to the final task necessary to appease Tyrus—what he asked of her when she first struck this bargain.

Killing Ailesse.

I trip backward from the door. I can't draw air. Light-headedness seizes me all over again. I brace my hand against the stone wall so I don't buckle over. I shouldn't have come here. I'm not learning to love my mother; I'm growing to hate her. I'll never give her the bone flute. If she uses it to ferry my father back from the dead, Tyrus might claim Ailesse's life, anyway. The silver owl showed me my friend is already close to dying as it is.

The silver owl.

My stomach tenses. If she leads me to Castelpont again, I'm going to . . . I'm going to . . .

The answer shoots through me like a thunderbolt.

My hands ball into fists. My muscles tighten in readiness.

I'm going to become Ailesse's proxy.

Odiva has shown me how—though I have a different ritual in mind.

I inhale and set my jaw, just like Ailesse would. I leave my mother to her vain pleadings and creep down the winding stairs until I reach the caves. I race through branching tunnels to the room Ailesse and I used to share. Her tortoiseshell hairbrush rests on a small table with her belongings. Only a few auburn strands are left on the bristles. Odiva must have taken the rest.

I stuff the brush in my hunting pack, along with my simple bone flute. Ailesse's ritual knife is already sheathed on my belt. I throw on a cloak, draw up the hood, and leave for Castelpont.

I finally know how to save my sister's life.

41
Bastien

I HURRY BACK THROUGH THE catacombs as fast as I can. My father's knife jostles at my hip, secure in its sheath again, but I'm still a mess of nerves. I hate being separated from my friends, especially after Jules got attacked under the quarry dome. And I hate being apart from Ailesse, especially after I almost kissed her.

I wasn't supposed to fall for her, but I did. Hard. Deep. I don't know how I'll ever explain it to Jules.

When I reach the wall of skulls, a guttural scream pulls me to a stop. That was Marcel. Who never screams.

I burst into the room with my knife drawn. "The Chained man—where is he?"

Jules presses her back against a wall. Marcel holds a clay pot defensively.

"What's happening? Where's Ailesse?"

Marcel hurls the pot at Jules. She ducks, and the pot shatters above her head.

"What are you doing?" I exclaim.

"He's in her!" Marcel points and grabs another dish from the shelves.

"Who's in her?"

"The dead man! He's taken over her body."

My eyes flash to Jules. She glares at her brother with a look of pure hatred. She's holding a knife in each hand—hers and Marcel's. "Jules, wait!"

She lunges for him. Marcel throws the dish. He hits her this time, but it glances off her shoulder. I race over as she slashes out for him. I wrench her backward just in time. She drops one of the knives and screams, but it's guttural and unnaturally low. I've accidentally seized her injured arm.

"Don't let go of her!" Marcel says, but I do on instinct.

"I'm hurting her!" My hand is wet with her blood.

"We *have* to hurt her to stop her. Just try not to kill her."

Try?

Jules reaches for the knife she dropped. I kick it away and scramble backward, unsure how to fight her. "When did this happen?" I ask Marcel.

"Back in the quarry, I think." He gropes the upper shelves for another makeshift weapon, but they're empty. "She's been acting strange ever since she returned. Little signs at first—convulsing, becoming more and more irritable. I blamed it on her injury, but once we were alone together, she got worse, like she was struggling to suppress him. She became weaker and he became stronger and"—Marcel's voice catches—"what if she's not even inside herself anymore? What if he's killed her soul?"

My stomach flinches. "She's still in there. She has to be." I pace a half circle around Jules, tensing up for her next attack.

She snarls. "Your Jules is weak and delusional. She's still fighting against me, but her attempts are pathetic."

I grind my teeth. I need to get the Chained man out of her. Now. "We'll see how strong she really is, if you dare to put it to a test."

Jules mirrors my pacing. Her posture doesn't belong to her, with her shoulders bunched up and her head jutting forward on her neck. "What kind of test?"

"Jules is the best knife fighter I know, but she wouldn't want you to kill me." I steal a glance at Marcel. He's sneaking up on her from behind. "Throw that knife at me, and if you miss your target, I'll know you're still the weaker one."

Jules's eyes narrow. "And if I'm the stronger one?"

I shrug. "Then I'm dead." In the corner of my vision, Marcel's gaze widens. Hopefully he's catching on.

Jules's mouth curves into a vicious sneer. "I like this game."

"Good." I covertly slip my knife up my sleeve, plant my feet, and spread my arms open. "I'm ready."

She spits on the ground. Lifts her knife. Bends her knees and takes aim.

My heart beats erratically.

She pulls her arm back.

My knife slides to my hand.

She throws hard, and I swing my knife with practiced speed. Her blade hits mine. Metal clashes against metal as I knock her knife away.

"You're stronger," I admit. "But Jules's throw is more deadly. I could have never blocked it."

She growls and springs for me. Marcel jumps on her back and wraps his arm around her neck. She thrashes violently. He grapples to hang on.

I rush over to brace him. Jules jerks and flails with both of us on her, like she's kicked a hornet's nest.

"Squeeze tighter!" I shout. Marcel shakes with exertion.

Jules rams us against the nearest wall. A bright burst of pain hits my back. Most of the air leaves my lungs. I manage to croak out, "Don't let go!"

She wheels around to ram us against the other wall. But just as she comes near it, she staggers to a stop and suddenly goes limp. Marcel releases his hold at once. I catch Jules so she doesn't crash on the ground. Together, we gently lower her on her back.

Her eyes are shut, and her face is blotched red. Marcel winces. "Please tell me I didn't just murder my sister."

"She's breathing," I reply. "Do you have any rope?" He finds me some, and I drag Jules onto the limestone slab. We tie her up and anchor the end of the rope under the large stone, like we did with Ailesse when we— "*Ailesse.*" My pulse races. "Where is she? Did another Chained attack her?"

"No." Marcel pops three knuckles and takes a step back from

me. "But she might have taken the opportunity to leave while you were gone."

I can't move for a moment. I'm a child again, abandoned in my father's cart. "Did she . . ." I try to swallow, but my throat is too dry. "Did she really think I'd hold her captive again?" I thought we'd learned to trust one another.

Marcel releases a heavy exhale and motions me several feet away from Jules. "Look," he says in a low voice, even though she's still unconscious, "I'm not an expert on romance—that is to say, I *am* madly in love with Birdie, but I can't quite put a finger on the logic of it—but Ailesse did display some classic symptoms of unrequited love: weepy eyes, angst-ridden sighs, dramatic statements of farewell."

Unrequited love? I'm not sure I'm following. "What did she say?"

"That she wishes you the very best and knows you have a stronger attachment to Jules and basically she doesn't want to come between you two." He waves a hand in the air like all of this is obvious.

"What?" I exclaim. "Didn't you tell her I'm *not* in love with Jules?"

He blinks. "Well, not exactly. I *did* point out you'd always cared for her."

I drag my hands over my face. "I'm sure Ailesse took that all wrong."

Marcel gives me a pained smile. "Maybe I'm not an expert on girls either."

A miserable laugh escapes me. If Marcel wasn't like a brother, I'd throttle him by the neck.

"Wait." He freezes. "Does this mean you're in love with Ailesse—like *love* love, not just 'she's disarmingly attractive because she's my soulmate' love?"

I stare at him and shift from foot to foot. My mouth has forgotten how to form words. "I . . . she's . . ." I swallow and pace away. My hands wrap around the nape of my neck. Ailesse is incredible. She's fierce and passionate and never backs down from a challenge. There's no one like her. It's impossible to describe how she makes me feel. "I don't even know how to find her, Marcel."

"I think I do."

I immediately turn around.

"She asked for the bone flute," he explains. "See, tonight's a full moon—lowest tides and all that. Ailesse was set on trying to ferry. The dead are getting out of hand, she said, and if one of them attacked Jules again, she might die."

I take another glance at Jules. She's twitching and grimacing in her sleep. The Chained man is still inside her, feeding off of her Light. How much longer until all her Light is gone? I hastily grab my pack. "So Ailesse went to the land bridge?" *What is she thinking? The dead will swarm her once she's outside.*

"No, to the bridge beneath the mines."

I stop. And turn. And stare. "There's a bridge beneath the mines?"

He beams and rocks back on his heels. "Recently discovered by yours truly and charted on a bona fide map."

"And why would she go there to ferry?"

"Well, a symbol on the bridge matches one on the bone flute."

My eyes narrow. "The bridge over earth?" I ask, remembering the symbol Ailesse sketched for me. "It's a soul bridge like the land bridge, right?"

"She thinks so. It's a fascinating possibility."

I slowly stalk toward Marcel, and his grin falters. "So you gave Ailesse the bone flute, knowing she'd go down there—alone?" Blood pounds through my skull. "Do you remember the scene at the land bridge, Marcel? If all those Ferriers couldn't control the dead, how do you think Ailesse will?"

He gulps. "It might not even work," he says optimistically.

Every muscle in my body tightens. Every nerve stretches and frays. Ailesse wouldn't attempt something this reckless unless she'd given up hope that we could break our soul-bond.

I grab my pack, dump it out, and hurry to the wall where Jules and Marcel have been stockpiling black powder. I stuff two small casks inside. That won't be enough. I grab Jules's pack and shove two more in there, as well.

Marcel fidgets, watching me. "Do you plan to blow up something?"

"How many dead people would *you* like to fight at once?" I ask.

He frowns at his sister. "None."

I grab my lantern and heft the packs over my shoulders.

"Keep your lantern away from those," he warns.

I nod. "Will you be okay in here with Jules?"

"Unless she learns how to breathe fire, which is highly improbable."

"All right." I walk over and open my hand. "Let's see that map you made."

"Map?" Marcel shrinks back. "Oh, that . . . well . . . I gave it to Ailesse."

I squeeze my eyes shut and groan. "*Marcel*."

"I thought of it as a going-away present," he says sheepishly.

I run my hands through my hair and take a deep breath. There's no time to argue. "Tell me how to get to that bridge."

42
Sabine

THE SILVER OWL IS WAITING for me when I arrive at Castelpont, her wings iridescent in the light of the full moon. She doesn't interfere when I remove my three grace bones from Ailesse's shoulder necklace and bury them beneath the foundations of the bridge. It's a sign that what I'm doing is right. Ailesse would do the same herself if she had her graces back.

At the center of the bridge, I clasp the necklace back on and kneel, spreading out my skirt. I didn't think to change into a white dress, but I can't see why it should matter. I remove Ailesse's hairbrush from my hunting pack and pull out the last strands. Next, I withdraw her bone knife from my sheath. With a deep breath, I slice the blade across my palm. I welcome the pain. It's been twenty-nine days since my friend was abducted, and now I'm finally doing something that will really help her.

I drip my blood over her auburn strands. "This is my hair, Tyrus. This is blood I share with my sister." I pause, wondering why Odiva didn't pray to Elara, too. I glance at the silver owl. She's perched very still on the stone parapet, her head slightly bowed to her chest, her knowing eyes fast upon me. "Hear my voice, Tyrus, my soul's siren song," I continue, deciding I must pray to Tyrus alone. I can't chance compromising the ritual. "I am Ailesse, sister of Sabine. Tonight, I finish my rite of passage." But this isn't *my* rite of passage; it's the end of Ailesse's.

Tonight, I'll lure Bastien, instead of my own soulmate, and kill him to save my sister.

I wrap my bleeding hand with a cloth from my hunting pack and push my belongings into the shadows of the bridge. Except for the bone knife. That I sheathe under my cloak. I remove the new flute, hoping the simple instrument I carved will be enough to play a true siren call. I already know the song. Ailesse and I practiced it together on wooden flutes before the last full moon. She'll never get the chance to finish this ritual for herself, but at least she'll be a Ferrier. That was always her dream, not what it took to achieve it.

I pull the flute to my mouth and tap the pattern of the melody over the tone holes before I lend my breath.

The song of love and loss cries above the night breeze. Bastien should feel its call right away. I'll fight him one-on-one, hopefully without his friends' interference this time.

The silver owl watches as I keep playing. She might as well be carved of marble. She doesn't rasp or screech or even flutter her wings. A quarter hour passes, and Bastien still hasn't come.

Don't worry, Sabine. This will work. He only came so fast last time because he was already waiting for us. Tonight he has to leave wherever he's been hiding with Ailesse, and who knows how far away that is?

My chest strains as I play on and on, not for lack of air, but my growing anxiety. At least another half hour goes by. I've been here too long. I keep glancing behind me at Beau Palais over the walls of Dovré. Someone must have seen me by now through the windows of the white stone castle.

The song trips faster now. My hands grow wet with perspiration. My fingers slip off the tone holes more than once. If the siren song needs to be played flawlessly, Bastien will never come tonight.

Just when I'm ready to give up and toss the flute into the dry riverbed, my jackal grace picks up the sound of scuffing boots on the road. My heart pounds. The footsteps are coming from the road leading from Dovré. Is that where Bastien has been holding Ailesse captive?

I keep fumbling through the melody, waiting for him to emerge around the curving city wall. Now that he's close, my insides roil. What if I'm wrong and this ritual only works for mothers, not sisters? If Tyrus doesn't allow me to act in place of Ailesse, then when I kill Bastien, I'll be killing my best friend, too.

I look at the silver owl. *You would warn me if this could kill Ailesse, wouldn't you?*

As if she's heard my thoughts, she lifts off the bridge, circles once overhead, and flits away to a discreet location at the far end of the bridge. I really wish Elara would teach her bird to speak.

The footsteps grow louder. A silhouetted figure steps around the wall, twenty yards away. He's also wearing a cloak. His hood droops over his eyes. All I can see, even with my night vision and far-reaching sight, are the vague shadows of his mouth and chin.

He steadily approaches. As soon as he sets foot on the bridge, I pocket my flute, blow out a shaky breath, and withdraw Ailesse's bone knife. I keep it hidden beneath my cloak. I'm not going to dance with Bastien; Ailesse has already performed the *danse de l'amant*. I'm going to make this quick. The jackal in me thrills at the thought. I don't suppress its thirst for blood this time. Tonight I'll need it.

Bastien's ten yards away now. I smooth down the folds of my cloak and keep my hood drawn up.

His jaw is clean-shaven. His cloak is fine, and his boots are polished. Is this a new disguise? I breathe in his scent with my salamander and jackal graces. He's not wearing the same spiced fragrance as before. Now he smells clean and minty.

He pauses fifteen feet away and tilts his head. I tuck my knife closer against my body. Can he see the shape of the hilt?

His hood flutters back a little, and the pupils of his eyes glitter. He walks forward tentatively. My pulse throbs with each step. My conscience starts to fight the jackal's desire to kill. Bastien isn't an animal, and I cried over all those deaths. How will I survive killing another human?

I glance over my shoulder to make sure the silver owl hasn't abandoned me. She remains perched on the far post of the bridge.

Calm down, Sabine. This is what Elara wants you to do. This is what Ailesse needs you to do.

Bastien's footsteps tread closer. I can't look at him. Can I stab his heart without meeting his eyes?

He stops five feet away. "Is it you?"

I feel the blood drain from my face. His voice is spun of silk and missing an undercurrent of bitterness.

This isn't Bastien.

My gaze flies up to him. His hood is cast back, and he's thrown his cloak behind his shoulders. He looks like he might be Bastien's age, but his hair isn't dark and tousled; it's strawberry blond with loose curls. His eyes *are* blue, but a stony shade of blue, and they're wide with wonder, not anger.

I can't catch my breath.

I've lured my own *amouré*, not Ailesse's.

This is *my* rite of passage.

I take two steps backward and clutch my stomach. This is the boy the gods chose for me, and I've killed him already, just by playing a song.

I set out to sacrifice Bastien tonight, but now because of me, another boy will die. The ritual is already set in motion.

"Won't you let me see your face?" he asks. His tone is gentle, but edged with desperation. He's caught deep in the web of my spell.

I flex my grip on my hidden knife and pull back my hood with my other hand. A few black curls spring around my cheeks. My *amouré*'s brows draw together. His mouth parts, but no words form. My cheeks flush. Ailesse has told me I'm beautiful, but maybe I only am in her eyes.

I'm supposed to begin the dance, I realize. I'm supposed to show why I'm perfect for him and he's perfect for me. But all I want to do is bury myself underground.

I shoot a scathing look at the silver owl. Has everything she's guided me to do over the past weeks been a trick to turn me into a Ferrier—and after that, the new *matrone* of my *famille*?

"Forgive me." The boy combs nervous fingers through his hair. "I thought I heard a familiar song."

I frown. "This isn't the first time you've heard it?"

He lifts a shoulder. "I suppose I thought . . . you would be her."

"And who is that?"

His heavy gaze drifts to the other side of the bridge. "I don't know. I never learned her name."

My pulse skips. "But you saw her?"

"She was only a specter in white from Beau Palais."

Beau Palais? I rapidly assess his clothes. He's in uniform, with medals pinned to his chest. He must be a decorated soldier.

"I left the castle as soon as I clapped eyes on her," he confesses, "but by the time I arrived, she was already gone. I caught a glimpse of her auburn hair as she ran into the forest with her friends."

I stare at him, my disbelief raw and biting. My ritual tonight worked. It brought me Ailesse's *amouré*. But it isn't Bastien. "They weren't her friends," I say coldly.

His eyes widen, and he steps closer. "You know her?"

"Ailesse is my best friend," I reply, bringing the knife from around my back to my side. I grip it tightly beneath my cloak. *And now I can save her.*

Acting as Ailesse, I lured this boy here. And as Ailesse, I will kill him here.

"Ailesse," he repeats sacredly. "I have to meet her. Now." He grasps my arm, and I stiffen. I've never been touched by a boy. "I've barely slept this past month," he says. "The people in Dovré are ill and becoming desperate. They're starting to fight among themselves. Yet, I must confess, what troubles me most is this . . ." He shakes his head and splays a hand over his heart. "I don't know how to explain, but it's why I walk the ramparts of Beau Palais at night to keep watch on this bridge. I foolishly hope she'll return." He laughs self-deprecatingly. "I don't understand why I'm drawn to her. You must think me ridiculous."

"No, I know the power of that feeling . . . it can't be ignored." No *amouré* has ever resisted it.

He studies me a moment, and his mouth curves into a warm and grateful smile. A dimple even caves in his right cheek, which isn't fair. I can't deny he's beautiful. More than that, he's also kind and sincere. Is it wrong to be jealous of Ailesse after everything she's suffered?

"I was beginning to fear I'd lost my right mind," he says. "Thank you for understanding."

"Of course." My grip slackens on my knife. Killing him won't free Ailesse from captivity.

His teeth catch the corner of his lip. "Do you think . . . ? Would you be willing to introduce me to your friend?"

I lower my eyes. "I wish I could." *Do I really?* "But I don't know where she is. Those people you saw her run away with . . . they abducted her. I haven't seen her since the night you saw her," I lie. "I've been searching for her, too."

Ailesse's *amouré*'s smile fades. His dimple vanishes, and his stone-blue eyes harden. "She's been abducted?" he says. I nod. He paces away from me, his fingers steepled on the bridge of his nose. "I should have known. I should have done something!" My brows lift at his surprising burst of emotion. Are all *amourés* so passionate? He leans his hands on the stone parapet with his head downcast. "If I'd arrived sooner that night, I could have saved her."

I move to stand beside him, strangely wanting to comfort him. At least one other person is as concerned about Ailesse as I am. "If anyone is to blame, it's me," I murmur. "I was there that night, too, and I also failed to save her. The attack . . . it was masterfully planned."

His eyes reflect my distress. "What can we do? Where have you searched for her?"

"She was in the catacombs at first. Maybe she still is, I don't know. Those tunnels are a labyrinth. It would take ages to navigate every passageway."

His fingers drum on the stones, and his jeweled ring sparkles in the moonlight. "What if I help you? I have an extensive map of the catacombs."

The silver owl screeches, and I spin around. She pushes off

the post and launches straight for us. I gasp and spread my arms protectively in front of Ailesse's *amouré*. The owl zooms close, then suddenly veers right and swoops around us. She screeches again and returns to her post.

I gape at her, stunned by whatever just happened. Ailesse's *amouré* gives an amused laugh. "What an odd creature."

I force a grin. Is the silver owl warning me *not* to hunt Ailesse with this boy? Or is she encouraging me?

His eyes drop to my hand, and he suppresses a smile. "I think we're safe now." He winks.

I realize I'm holding my bone knife in plain sight. "Oh." I blush and sheathe it. "Sorry. This bridge makes me uneasy."

He's still staring at the knife; he can see the protruding hilt. "I've never come across anything like that." His brow wrinkles. "Or your necklace, for that matter."

"They're heirlooms." The lie comes quick to my tongue, and I hope it satisfies his curiosity. I have no wish to talk about the knife, because now I understand what the silver owl wants me to do— lead this boy to Ailesse and offer him to her, along with her bone knife. This is *her* sacrifice, not mine. That means the choice is hers.

I gaze at the boy before me. He has fallen in love with a girl just by a glimpse of her dress and a beautiful song, and now all he wants to do is to meet her. I hate that I've come to know anything about him. His death will be that much harder to bear. But I have to bear it. The silver owl has led me to this moment, step by step. She's given me everything I need to find Ailesse and save her. I can't turn back now.

"How is it you have a map of the catacombs?" I ask.

Ailesse's *amouré* smiles again, but now it's a mysterious smirk. "You don't know who I am, do you?"

I glance at his uniform once more and shake my head. I can't guess his rank.

He leans in close and tells me.

I feel my eyes grow wide.

43
Ailesse

I RUSH THROUGH THE MINES beneath the catacombs. I can't find the shaft that drops to the level of the bridge. Marcel might be brilliant, but his artistic skills are wanting. His scribbles have already led me down three wrong paths, and I wasted too much time backtracking.

A branching tunnel appears at the edge of my lamplight, and I quickly check Marcel's map. I have no idea where I am. I glance back the way I came, then through the new tunnel. I hate stopping. Every time I pause, my eyes sting and I hear Bastien's voice. *Will you dance with me like you did then?* I feel his hand cradling my cheek as he whispers, *You never needed to play a song for me, Ailesse.*

I ignore the hollow ache in my chest. I sprint down the new

tunnel and bury any stray thoughts of Bastien. I focus on the bridge over earth instead. Did the Leurress ferry on it long ago? Why did they stop? Because the tunnels evolved into a desecrated mass grave?

I keep my eyes peeled for the hatch Marcel spoke about. If I can't find the main entrance he marked on the map, maybe I can spot the other entrance to the soul bridge. But the hatch isn't on the map, and I don't see any sign of it.

The tunnel curves. I run past two boarded-up branching tunnels. Am I circling the same abyss I was blasted into when my mother tried to rescue me? Is the soul bridge down there?

I pick up speed. Midnight is less than an hour away. It's too late now to race home and get my mother. No matter. She'll praise me for discovering this place. I'll prove that the Leurress can ferry on the full moon, too.

I hear Sabine's voice now. *You need to think, Ailesse. You can't ferry the dead by yourself.* Her concerned tone is familiar. She used it when she asked, *Do you really have to hunt a tiger shark?* and *Is it wise to have your rite of passage at Castelpont?* My jaw muscle hardens, and I push out her voice like I pushed out Bastien's. Sabine forgets I always achieve what I set out to do, no matter how difficult. Except breaking my soul-bond to Bastien.

I bolt around another corner and slide to a sudden halt. My oil lamp flickers, almost burning out. I advance several feet, and my pulse races. A wheel and axle is built over a hole in the ground near the tunnel's dead end. I check Marcel's clumsy drawing on the map. This is it—the entrance to the caves below.

I break into a triumphant smile. *Thank you, Elara.*

I hurry to the edge of the hole. It's really a circular shaft about five feet wide. Above it, spooled around the axle, is a rope. I remove a bucket from its hooked end, set my oil lamp aside, and crank the wheel, extending all the rope into the shaft.

I grab my lamp and pray I don't drop it while I descend. My tiger shark vision can't penetrate the dense black of the mines; I need at least a small source of light to work with.

I step to the very edge of the shaft. Needles of anxiety prick my skin. Then they heighten and pummel my spine. This isn't nerves. It's my sixth sense. Someone is coming.

I whirl around. At the same time, the shaft edge crumbles.

I slide into the shaft and scream. The rope is slipping through my fingers.

I secure my grip and hit against the shaft wall. My clay lamp shatters. Everything goes black.

Someone shouts, but the sound is muffled. A Chained soul? I'm suspended by the rope, my pulse thrashing in my ears.

Faint illumination shines above me. I see the circled opening of the shaft. I'm three feet away from the top. The light builds. It isn't *chazoure*; it's golden.

"Ailesse!" Someone reaches down. My breath catches. *Bastien.*

I grab his hand. He pulls me over the edge. I clamber to my feet and throw myself at him. Shock courses through my body. His arms wrap around me, and he holds me just as fiercely. I can't stop shaking. I clutch fistfuls of his shirt and press my nose into the crook of his neck and shoulder. I never thought I'd see him again.

He kisses the top of my head over and over. My pulse thrums through my limbs and into my palms and the soles of my feet. I close my eyes and let his musky warm scent fill my lungs.

Bastien strokes my hair. "Why did you leave?" His voice betrays a little hurt.

My lashes fan against his neck as I remember what upset me. "You have feelings for Jules. Stronger than I realized."

"She's my best friend, Ailesse. Of course I have feelings for her. But that doesn't mean—"

"You told her your father's phrase, Bastien." I pull away from him. "'I'm not missing from you. You're not missing from me.'" My throat tightens. "I thought that meant you held someone in your heart . . . and I guess—I hoped—that girl was me."

His eyes fill with deep tenderness. "I'm sorry." He smooths a stray hair from my brow. "That phrase, it's something I say to family. Jules and Marcel—they're family. But you . . ." He swallows and takes my face in his hands. "It means something different when I say it to you."

My heart beats faster. "Truly?"

His sea-blue eyes reflect the gold of his flickering lantern. "You're the girl I'm in love with, Ailesse."

A rush of heat washes over my skin. I'm suddenly weightless, breathless. "Can you repeat that again?" I cock my head closer. "I'm not sure I heard you right."

He grins. "I'm in love with you, Ailesse."

"A little louder."

"I'M IN L—"

I bring his mouth to mine. I kiss him with all the strength of my graces. He laughs against my lips and spins me back toward the wall, kissing me with equal passion. I pull him even closer. I've wanted this since he fought beside me at the land bridge and filled our room with candles and brought me to the moon under the dome.

He stumbles back a step as I push off the wall and kiss him more urgently. He lifts me so our faces are level. My toes skim the ground as he kisses deeper, harder. I want more. My back arches. I weave and tug my fingers through his hair. Heat flowers from my belly and spreads throughout my chest and limbs. He's as warm and flushed as I am.

We pull back and gasp for air, our heads leaning together. "Bastien . . ." I say, waiting for my racing pulse to slow and my breath to steady. I draw my head back so I can see him. "Look at me." He slowly opens his eyes like he's waking from a spell. I sweep my thumbs across his cheekbones. "I love you, Bastien." I need him to know I feel just the same. "I love you," I say again, in a reverent whisper.

He still has me lifted in his arms. "Ailesse," he whispers with the softest smile. He doesn't say more. He doesn't need to. He gently lowers me to the ground, and our lips touch again, tender and patient and adoring. This is a new dance between us, one that doesn't lead to death but clings to the fragile hope of life.

His mouth floats along my jaw and treads a soft path down to my collarbone. When his lips trail up again, they brush a sensitive spot on my neck. I laugh quietly and turn my head to control myself. Then my eyes land on two packs resting against the wall. They're crammed full, straining at their seams. I grin at them, though I'm confused. "What is all that?"

He glances past me. "Oh, um, a precaution against the dead. Turns out I'm not the best at fighting invisible people." He winces, and his expression darkens. "It was much easier fighting Jules."

"Jules?" My heart plummets. "What happened?"

Bastien rubs his forehead like he's angry with himself for forgetting. "The Chained man didn't leave the quarry. He went inside Jules's body."

I stiffen. I didn't realize a Chained soul could do that. I look down the mining shaft and bite my lip. I don't know how deep it goes, but the soul bridge should be at the bottom. "I think I can do something to help. When I play the siren song, it should lure him out of her."

His brows draw together. "Is that the only way?"

"I don't see any other. If the Chained man stays trapped inside Jules, he'll steal all her Light. He can't be defeated until he's ferried to the Underworld." I squeeze Bastien's hand. "I have to try."

His mouth sets in a firm line. "Then I'll help you."

"No!" My eyes widen. "You can't even see the dead."

"We've worked through that difficulty before."

"I can't let . . ." My stomach twists. "What if you die because of me?"

He shrugs. "It wouldn't be the first time I was up against that worry."

"I'm serious, Bastien. This isn't a good idea."

"Ailesse." He takes me by the shoulders and kisses me softly. "I'm not leaving you. You're worth the risk, do you hear me? You're *always* going to be worth the risk."

I exhale slowly and fold myself against him.

"Besides," he whispers, pressing his lips against my neck, "I have four casks of black powder."

44
Sabine

I PACE THE STONES OF Castelpont and wring out my hands. I've already dug up my grace bones and tied them back onto my shoulder necklace. Ailesse's *amouré* should return any moment. I'm waiting for the right time to take him captive. I need his map first.

I rub my golden jackal pendant as I search the skies and nearby trees. The silver owl is gone. Is that significant? If it is, I don't know why.

I breathe in a clean minty smell and hear distant footsteps. I turn to the path leading to Dovré, and Cas comes around the bend. *Cas.* That's what he asked me to call him. His full name is Casimir, and it suits him perfectly. I still can't believe Ailesse's *amouré* is someone so important. Actually, I can. He's the kind of person I've always envisioned for her.

"Hello again." Cas grins warmly and joins me on the bridge.

"Hello," I reply, trying to squash the sudden butterflies in my stomach. I can't think of him fondly when I'm about to deliver him to his death.

"I'm ready." He taps the hilt of a fine sword on his belt. A dagger is also holstered to his thigh.

"And the map?"

"Ah, yes." He removes a folded sheet of parchment from his pocket, passes it over, and holds up a lantern so we can study it together.

I unfold the map and examine the elaborate small-scale drawings on both sides. The first side shows a cutaway view of every level of the catacombs and mines. The second side is a bird's-eye view of the four main levels, each sketched in separate rectangles that are stacked in a column. Everything is labeled in the language of Old Galle, which I can't read. It takes me several moments to identify the paths I've already taken on the first and second levels. I didn't know any others existed deeper down.

"A few places appear to be chambers or larger quarries," Cas says. "We should search those first."

I can't stop staring at the fourth level. Unlike the angular tunnels above, the passageways here are serpentine, and the chambers on this level look more like inkblots than structured quarries. Maybe the fourth level is a web of caves. I point to a thicker line above a cavern that's so deep I don't know where it ends. "What do you think that is?" In the cutaway view of the map, the cavern's sides run off the bottom edge of the parchment. I flip the map over to see the bird's-eye view. Here, the thick line is a darkened strip running from one end of the cavern to the other.

"A staircase?" Cas suggests.

"No, stairs look like this." I set my finger on a rectangle filled with lines for steps. I scrutinize the slightly waving edges of the darkened strip. "It could be a natural bridge."

Cas leans closer, squinting at it. "Except it leads to a dead end."

"True," I reply, then notice tiny marks below the strip. Without my nighthawk vision, I wouldn't be able to see their ultra-fine lines and minuscule detail. They're symbols of a bridge and earth and full moon. Leurress symbols. I turn the map over and find the same marks by the bridge—it *has* to be a bridge, then. "Where did this map come from?"

"I don't know where it originated, but there's a chest in the library of Beau Palais that's filled with maps. We use them to plot strategy for small wars that break out across South Galle. A year or so ago, I found this one tucked inside one of the older maps." Cas scratches his neck. "So do you recognize something that will help us?"

I nibble on my lip. Tonight is a full moon, just like the symbol drawn next to the bridge. That doesn't necessarily mean that's where Ailesse will be—Bastien wouldn't know anything about that place, and neither would she—but I have a strong feeling I can't ignore. It's the same feeling I had when Odiva told me twice that Ailesse was dead, and somehow I knew she was lying. Now the feeling says I need to go there. "Yes," I answer.

As soon as I've spoken the word, the silver owl emerges from the forest and flies past me. I start to smile—she's confirming I'm right—but then she heads in a different direction than the ravine entrance of the catacombs. Is there a better way inside?

"Show me," Cas says.

My finger moves to point to the bridge, but it never lands on the parchment. I'm distracted by a distant trampling of boots—many of them. I clutch Cas's arm. "People are coming."

His brow furrows. "How do you know?"

I shake my head, flustered and nervous. All my life I've been forbidden to let people outside of my *famille* see me. "We have to hide."

"No, wait. Look." Cas watches the path to Dovré, and nine uniformed men come into view. "These are soldiers in my troop," he explains. "It's all right, Sabine. They can be trusted."

I take a closer look at each of them. The men have lanterns, like Cas, and several weapons among them. That makes me all the more distrusting. "Why have they come?"

"To rescue Ailesse." He frowns, confused by me. "She has three abductors, maybe more. I might be an excellent swordsman, but I'm not overconfident. We're going to need all the help we can get."

"No, they can't come with us." My voice is more abrasive than I intended. "I never agreed to that." The last thing I need is for an audience of sword-wielding men to witness their friend being slaughtered by Ailesse. Or worse, prevent her.

Cas crosses his arms. "Do you want to save Ailesse or not?"

"Of course I do, but we have to be smart. A barrage of soldiers will ruin our chance to attack by surprise."

"Surprise can't help us if we're greatly outnumbered."

I ball my hands. "If we make so much noise that they know we're coming, Ailesse will be dead by the time we find her."

Cas flinches when I say *dead*. His soldiers draw nearer to the bridge. He sighs and rakes a hand through his hair. "Where is she being held, Sabine?" He glances at the map. "Is it that place you thought was a bridge?"

I press my lips together and slightly avert my eyes. "No . . . the last time I saw her she was near the level right beneath the catacombs. Did you see how many tunnels are down there? You'd have to search for days before you found her, and by then she might be gone."

He considers me. "What are you trying to say?"

"I'm coming with you." I push my shoulders back. "And I won't tell you where we're going until we arrive. *And* I won't even take you there if we're going with *them*." I tip my chin at his soldiers.

Cas shifts on his feet. "Surely we can compromise. We have the same aim, after all."

I don't want to, but he's just as stubborn as I am. We can spend hours we don't have arguing about this, or we can find a middle ground on our terms. Even with all my graces, I can't incapacitate nine men before I take him captive.

I eye the map again and spot a zigzagging staircase close to the bridge. It leads up past every tunnel level until it reaches a marked entrance outside. It looks like it's a little over three miles away from here. "Ask your men to give us a head start once we reach the catacombs. The entrance where we're going isn't far from our final destination," I add, without pointing it out on the map. "It will give us a window of time to see if we really need the extra help."

He frowns. "Or it will give us an opportunity to be outnumbered and killed."

I shrug and stand taller. "That's a risk I'm willing to take to protect Ailesse. Are *you*?"

Cas rubs the side of his face, deliberating.

The soldiers reach us on the arched bridge, and I squirm, uncomfortable to be around so many men when I've only lived among women.

A young man with short-cropped hair steps forward, like he wants to speak to Cas, but then his gaze falls on me, and his brows lift.

Cas chuckles, prodding his companion's shoulder. "Yes, Briand, she's pretty. You can close your mouth now."

Briand blinks and composes himself. "We're, um, ready whenever you are." He bows his head, but his eyes drift shyly back to me.

Cas takes a deep breath. "Very well. I agree to your plan, Sabine." His beautiful smile melts all my frustrations with him. "Let's go and rescue Ailesse."

45
Bastien

I STAND IN THE TUNNEL and crank the wheel above the mine shaft until the last of the rope extends on the axle. I'm lowering Ailesse down to the level of the bridge first, to reserve her strength for ferrying.

It's pitch-black all around me. My lantern is hooked on to the end of the rope. It wasn't long before its light faded completely.

I wait a few moments and give the rope a tug. It's still taut with Ailesse's weight. Why hasn't she let go? I don't call her name. She wouldn't hear me.

I shift on my legs. I'm about to crank the wheel again to raise her back up, when the tension on the rope releases. She let go.

Or she fell.

My heart pounds. There's no way to tell until I'm down there myself.

I waste no time grabbing the rope and swinging into the shaft. I climb down as fast as possible. The rope is rough. After fifty feet, blisters start to form on my palms. After sixty feet, my muscles are on fire. I take controlled breaths and keep going. Seventy feet, eighty feet, ninety . . . The rope comes to an end. I secure my grip and look down. "Ailesse?" I shout. Sweat drips down my forehead. "Ailesse!"

"Bastien!"

Relief floods me. Her voice is muffled by thick air, but she can't be very far away. I notice a dim ring of light below—the end of the shaft.

"Jump when you reach the end of the rope!" she says.

I climb down a little farther until I'm hanging by the hook. I let go without thinking twice. I trust her.

The fall isn't long; I don't need to drop into a roll from the impact of landing. A moment after my feet hit the ground, Ailesse's hand weaves through mine. I kiss her before taking a look around us. "Do you see the bridge?" I ask. We're not closed in by tunnel walls anymore; this space is wider. She holds up the lantern. A few feet ahead, the edge of the ground falls away into a dark void.

"I think so." She leads me twenty or so yards around the curving edge of the pit. Solid circles representing the full moon are engraved on the ground along the way. Ailesse points to the symbol of the bridge over earth at the foot of a stone pathway that stretches across the void. The soul bridge. "I can't tell where it leads to or how far it goes into the darkness."

I'm about to suggest we walk across it together when I see an unlit torch in a sconce behind us. I cross back to it and rub the top of its wrapped fibers. They're coated in something sticky like pitch, but the resin smells strangely sweet. Whatever it is has kept stable for who knows how many years, decades, or even centuries.

Ailesse pulls out the candle from her lantern and hands it to me. I light the torch. The flame is strong and burns without smoking.

"Look, there are more." She points to two nearby sconces along the wall. As we light the torches inside them, we notice others and keep walking around the circular pit, lighting all of them until the ledge ends, about halfway around. At least we can see what's across the other side now—a curving, natural wall of stone.

It has to be about a hundred feet tall, where it blends into the cavern ceiling. The wall is pocked with boarded-up tunnel openings. Each marks different levels of the catacombs and mines above us—places that must have been carved out before people realized they'd drop off into this cavern. But the strangest thing is that no tunnel has been carved across the pit on *our* level.

"I don't understand." I scrutinize the thirty-yard-wide pit and the natural bridge that runs across it. "The bridge leads to a dead end." There's no wide ledge to stand on over there, like we have on this side. "What about the Gates of the Beyond that you said you have to open?"

Ailesse reverently gazes at the end of the bridge. "They won't appear until I play the siren song."

I nod like that makes perfect sense. I guess it will when I see them.

I study the bridge harder. It's five feet wide—much narrower than the land bridge I caught a glimpse of during the new moon. It's also five feet thick. Below the bridge is only air. It looks like wind or water whittled the rest of the stone away. Except there is no wind or water down here, and the rock is durable limestone, not sandstone. The thought of Ailesse standing on a bridge so thin and fragile-looking makes my pulse race.

"Do you think it's midnight yet?" I ask her.

"Almost."

"Are you ready?"

"Yes," she replies without the slightest tremble. "But you need to stay on the ledge. The Chained could catch you off guard and toss you into the pit."

I hate the fact that I can't see these monsters.

"Be careful with that black powder, too, or you might destroy the bridge."

I nod, begrudgingly removing the two packs from my shoulders. I set them fifteen feet back, against the far wall of our ledge. I hoped blasting the powder could help control the number of Chained on the bridge. I was going to ignite each cask, one at a time, whenever Ailesse called out that a Chained was nearby. But this ledge isn't far enough back from the bridge to be safe. If I caused an explosion, the bridge would blast apart. "What happens if some of the dead are thrown into the pit?"

She wrinkles her brow. "I'm not sure, but they'd survive the fall.

They'd climb back up, no matter how far they dropped."

That's comforting.

We walk back to the foot of the bridge, then stop and look at each other. Ailesse's face is bruised and scuffed up from our fight with the Chained man. Her umber eyes have brightened to amber in the torchlight, and her lips are a darker shade of rose from kissing me. She's never looked more beautiful.

I cup the back of her head and draw her mouth to mine. I kiss her longer than I should. I know we're short on time, but I'm reluctant to let her go. An ominous feeling builds inside me, like this might be the last chance I have to hold her.

Finally we break apart. "Be careful," I whisper, stroking her face. Tears burn in my eyes. I can barely hold them back.

She gives me an encouraging smile. "You, too." And then she's out of my arms, and the warmth of her body is gone. I feel like half of myself just walked away.

She steps onto the bridge, walks across it until she reaches the middle, and pulls the bone flute from her dress pocket. She closes her eyes for a moment, then straightens her shoulders and draws the flute to her mouth.

She looks at me one last time, gives me a wink, and starts to play.

It's a different song than the one that lured me to her, though this one is just as haunting.

My hands ball and flex as I glance around us, waiting for some sign of the approaching dead. "Maybe you can yell 'Chained' or 'Unchained' when each soul comes, so I'm aware," I suggest.

Her eyes lift to me, and she nods without a hitch in the song. The music soars on a high note, then lowers as it finishes the melody. Ailesse pockets the flute and stares at the dead end of the bridge.

"That's it?" I ask. "Don't you have to keep playing until they come?"

She shakes her head. "This isn't like a rite of passage. This song has more power, and the dead feel it more keenly. Wherever they are, they're already coming."

I gnaw at my lip and stare at the massive wall. "What about the Gates?" Maybe a secret tunnel is about to carve itself out of the stone, or the wall will vanish. But neither happens.

Before Ailesse can answer me, wind bursts up from the pit, and I startle backward. Specks of dust collect in the air. They gather together and form the shape of an arched door at the dead end of the bridge.

Ailesse laughs and flashes me a wide grin. I struggle to return it. The dust of the door is black, not limestone white, and I can't explain where the wind came from or how the dust continues to hover and swirl in a sheer veil. Everything about this place contradicts logic. I doubt even Marcel could make sense of it.

"Which Gate is that?" I ask.

"It's visible, so it must be Tyrus's Gate to the Underworld," Ailesse replies in a rush of enthusiasm. "The one at the land bridge is supposed to be made of water."

My brows tug together. I'm still caught on the word "visible." "So the other one is invisible?"

"Almost." She lifts on her toes and points to the right of the Gate of dust. "Do you see that silvery shimmer in the air?"

I focus, and a slight haze appears, like a smudge on a pane of glass. "A little."

"That's Elara's Gate, and the twirling shimmer above it is the spiral staircase to Paradise." She smiles even bigger. "*Paradise*, Bastien," she says again, like maybe I didn't hear her.

"Oh." That's my best response at the moment. My mind can't wrap around any of this.

My eyes travel to the high stone ceiling as I strain to see the shape of the stairs, but then I catch sight of something mysterious that I *can* see: a strip of dried clay that runs across the center of the ceiling. It's identical to the shape and size of the soul bridge directly below, but the clay has crumbled away in a few spots and reveals tight rows of wooden planks and dangling roots in the spaces between them.

I frown. Plants don't grow in the mines or the catacombs. Which means right above this cavern is the outside world—dirt, sky, fresh air. Someone's patched up a natural opening in the ceiling.

Ailesse clutches the pouch of grace bones around her neck and shakes her head. "I can't believe I'm here—that I'm actually seeing these Gates with my own eyes. They're even more wonderful than the ones I imagined at the land bridge."

I don't know what to say. I wouldn't call them wonderful. My father had to pass through a Gate like one of these.

She stiffens and gasps. "Do you hear that?"

I whip out my knife. "Where are they?"

"No, not the dead." She smiles. "Another siren song. It's coming from inside the Gates."

I lean a little closer to the pit. "I can't hear anything."

She blinks slowly, her gaze lost as she listens to music that doesn't reach my ears. "The deeper melody comes from the Underworld, but the descant rises above it from Paradise. Each part is so different, but they perfectly complement each other—one dark and one hopeful."

I watch her as she stands, listless like she's caught in a daydream. I clear my throat. "I'm sure all of this is amazing, but you need to get ready. A Chained soul could fly in here any moment."

"Souls don't fly," she replies absently. "That's a myth."

"Still, you—"

Her eyes dart past me, and she's instantly alert. "Chained!" she cries. "On your left!"

My knife swings, but I strike nothing.

"He's on the bridge now." She steadies her feet. "Stay back!"

She starts battling the Chained with a quick and varied series of kicks. I struggle against a fierce instinct to run to her side. She dodges blows I can't see. She ducks and cartwheels along the side of the bridge. I begin to relax, watching how focused and skillful she is.

Damn, she's beautiful when she fights.

"Your time here is over," she tells the Chained. She whirls around and drives her fist into the force of a tangible body. As she continues to attack, she pushes the soul back to the end of the bridge. She delivers a final kick, this one stronger than the rest, and the black dust scatters and re-forms into an arched door.

She turns to me, her brows lifted in shock. "I did it."

I grin. "Well done."

She rubs her arm. "It would be easier with a staff. That's how the Leurress are trained to ferry."

"You're doing just fine without one," I say. Then I notice she's panting, with beads of sweat on her forehead. She didn't tire this easily when she fought the Chained man in the quarry. But then again, moonlight and starlight were shining down on her through the aviary dome.

"More are coming!" Her eyes dart around the cavern. "All of them Chained. One from the shaft. Two from the tunnel."

The tunnel? I turn and quickly examine the wall behind my ledge. Sure enough, a tunnel leads out from a shadowy area next to the opening of the mining shaft. I race over to it, my knife raised, but a sharp blow to my stomach knocks me off my feet. "Bastien!" Ailesse cries. I fly backward and skid several feet across the ledge.

"I'm fine." I cough and push back up to my feet. But *she* isn't. From the way Ailesse twists back and forth—kicking, jabbing, punching—she's already battling at least two more Chained.

I sprint for the bridge. I'm barely on it when I bump into something. "What are you doing here?" a man's voice growls. "This isn't your fight."

I immediately plant my feet. Just as quickly, I slash my knife forward. My blade hits resistance, and I stab hard. The man hisses, drawing back. I keep striking. I parry, lunge, duck, and spin. I use every skill I've practiced, every varied formation, and force him backward. It seems to be working. I'm halfway across the bridge, and Ailesse has moved near the Gates.

She's only fighting one Chained now. The other she must have already ferried to the Underworld. I swing my knife again, but the air before me is empty. I hurry forward several steps, but I still can't figure out where my opponent went.

Ailesse makes a noise of exertion. She's whirling back and forth, battling in front of and behind herself. *Merde.* The man who left me is attacking her. I run, but she shouts, "Stay back, Bastien!"

I stop a few yards away, but I can't make myself leave.

"Please! I can handle these two." She's laboring for breath. Her face is flushed. "Get off the bridge!"

My blood pounds faster. Ailesse can't fight like this much longer. She needs to channel more energy. I look at my packs. "I'll be back soon! I'm going to blast apart the ceiling!"

She leaps over an invisible something and spares a quick glance at the ceiling. Her eyes widen. "Hurry!" She jabs an elbow behind her.

I race away, my knife swinging aimlessly in case any Chained attack. I need to ignite the powder casks before more get to Ailesse.

I grab my two packs and my lantern and sprint into the tunnel. Some of the Chained came in this way, so it has to lead outside. At any rate, I can't jump high enough to catch the shaft rope again.

Limestone bricks line the tunnel and lead to a staircase. My legs burn as I climb each zigzagging flight to the top. There must be twice as many steps here as there are in the three stories of La Chaste Dame.

The stairs end, and I see a hatch. The Chained have already pried it open. I look above—at a clear sky full of stars and the perfectly round moon. I let out a huge breath. "Thank you," I say to no one in particular.

I climb outside into a meadow surrounded by a thick forest. I'm standing in the middle of a circle of stones that barely rise above the wild grass. Some are engraved with phases of the moon.

My pulse races as I quickly rummage through the grass and search for the wooden planks I saw from the cavern. This is taking too long. Ailesse is probably fighting more Chained.

At last, I find a couple boards with dried clay squeezed between them. More are nearby. Soon I'm able to trace the long edge of the patched-up strip that matches the soul bridge below.

I set down my packs and remove the casks of black powder. I place three of them evenly apart along the strip. I uncork the fourth cask and spread a trail of powder that links each cask together, and from there to the edge of the meadow, several yards away.

I crouch and pull my candle from my lantern. My shaking hand makes the flame quiver. This could be disastrous. The explosion might crush Ailesse or break the bridge. But I have to risk it. She's not going to give up now. She needs a fighting chance to finish ferrying.

I take a steeling breath, roll to the balls of my feet, and lower my candle to the trail of black powder.

A brilliant flame ignites. It rapidly snakes toward the nearest cask.

I bolt for the forest and send a prayer to Ailesse's gods.

46
Ailesse

My muscles burn as I wrestle the last of the three Chained close to the swirling black dust. The man has an unrelenting grip on my shoulders. I slap the back of his elbows to stun him, and his hold on me weakens. I quickly hook my foot around his ankle and try to sweep out his legs. He doesn't budge. My pulse throbs through my head.

He grapples for my shoulders again. I twist before he can grab me, and shove him backward. He loses his balance, but doesn't fall. I grit my teeth and shove him again. He finally tumbles through the Gate.

I lean my hands on my knees and struggle to catch my breath.

Chazoure flares from the hole of the mining shaft. My stomach tenses. I straighten, tightening my fists. The soul drops to the ground. *No, no, no.* Not him. Not yet.

He leers at me. "I thought I'd find you here."

It's the man with the broken nose, thick arms, and chains crisscrossed over his chest.

The one I fought in the quarry. The one who invaded Jules's body.

I swallow hard. I'm too sapped of strength. And he's too vicious and powerful. How much Light did he steal from Jules?

His nostrils flare, but his brow twitches when he looks past me to the Gate of dust. Its lure brought him here. "You can't make me go to Hell. I don't belong there."

I lift my chin and square my shoulders. I won't let him see my weakness. "Prove it. Take off your chains."

He growls. He knows very well they're irremovable. "I'll kill you first."

He launches onto the bridge.

I tense to spring over him with my falcon grace. I'm standing right in front of Tyrus's Gate. If I'm quick enough, I can roll aside and he'll barrel through.

In mere moments, he's upon me. But he's veering toward Elara's Gate. I dive to block him, but even with my graced reflex, I'm too slow. He catches my leg. The sudden stop throws him off balance. He's going to fall and pull me with him through the Gate. I kick and thrash. Adrenaline pummels through me, but I still don't have the strength to overpower him. He doesn't let go. He steadies himself and drags me up to my feet. His meaty hands have a vise grip on my arms.

"You're the one who doesn't deserve Paradise." His breath is rancid. *Chazoure* spittle flies from his mouth. "Would you like to meet your *own* Hell? Look below." I don't. I know what I'll see—a torturous drop into nothing. He sneers. "I'll send you there."

He moves to hurl me off the bridge. I fight to anchor my footing with my ibex grace, but he's too strong. I fumble to unsheathe my knife. Just before the Chained throws me, I stab him in the stomach. He roars out in pain and releases me. I land ten feet back on the bridge, just shy of falling off the edge. My sixth sense weakly patters a warning, and I scramble to stand. The Chained is already running for me, his face ferocious.

"Goodbye, Bone Crier."

I'm going to die.

A deafening *boom* splits the air. The force drives me to my knees.

Boom! Boom!

The middle of the ceiling shatters apart. A storm of dirt and splintered wood rains down on me. I cover my head with my hands. Chunks of debris scrape my arms and back.

The bridge shudders beneath me. Fissures crack along the limestone. I frantically crawl forward, trying to reach the safety of the ledge.

The Chained hasn't fallen off the bridge. He shields his eyes from the settling dust and rubble and rises to his feet. A deep fissure snakes toward him, but suddenly freezes as the bridge stops quaking. Everything silences except my ringing ears. The Chained charges at me again. I scramble backward. My mind is still rattled with shock. I don't know what to do.

The last of the rubble clears. In that instant, a cool rush of energy sweeps into me. It radiates from the crown of my head to the tips of my fingers and the soles of my feet. My lungs expand. My heartbeat steadies. My blood surges with strength and Light. The sky has opened. The power of the moon and the stars reaches my bones and fires life into my graces.

I jump to my feet and bolt for the Chained man.

My fist connects with his jaw as we collide. His head jerks sideways. His hands grope out to strangle me, but I shove my knee into his gut and force him back again. He's the tiger shark in the lagoon. He's the bridge in view of Beau Palais. I welcome the challenge.

For every hit he gives me, I give him three. I leap over him and strike him from behind. When I receive a blow, I stumble back farther than I need to. It's a ploy. I'm drawing him closer and closer to the Gate of the Underworld.

He's so furious he doesn't notice. I play on that rage. I laugh when I dodge him. I prod instead of punch him. He's seething when I'm a yard away from the Gate. Energy pulses across my back, deeper than my sixth sense. The powerful lure of Tyrus's realm. I clench my jaw and refocus on the Chained.

"Ailesse!" A distant shout comes from above. My heart seizes. *Bastien.* I can't spare a moment to look at him. The Chained man is lunging at me.

I grab one of his arms. With all my strength, I swing him backward over my head and let go. The momentum casts him through the Gate. Black dust sucks him inside.

A dizzying breath of relief purges from my chest. I break into an exultant smile. The monster is gone.

"It's beautiful, isn't it?" someone whispers. I startle and whirl behind me. An Unchained young woman is on the bridge. She wears a brocade dress and a jeweled diadem. She drifts closer, tears flowing down her face. Her eyes are fixated on the near-invisible shimmer of Elara's Gate. "But I don't want to go," she tells me. "Please, don't make me go."

I touch her *chazoure*-glowing arm. "You'll be with loved ones who have passed on before you. They'll sing to you and ease your worries. They'll build you a castle made of silver and Light."

The young woman painstakingly pulls her focus from the Gate to me. "Will my mother be there?"

"Was your mother good?"

"She sacrificed everything for me."

"Then she will be waiting to embrace you."

The young woman gives me a trembling smile, but doesn't move forward.

"Listen closer to that beautiful song," I say, directing her to Elara's descant, the only siren song that an Unchained can hear from the Beyond. "It's meant to give you peace. Trust that feeling."

More tears streak down her face as she nods and inhales a deep breath. She wanders past me toward the shimmering Gate without any more reassurance.

"Ailesse, can you hear me?" Bastien yells, but the sound fades in my ears. It's eclipsed by the rising swell of the other siren song—Tyrus's song. Only the Leurress can hear both parts of the music.

Tyrus's dark and distinctive melody pulses from the Gate of dust and swallows the descant from Elara's Gate. The music almost has a masculine voice. I feel it murmur, *Cross over to me, Ailesse. See my wonders. Nothing in your world compares to mine.*

The Unchained woman's dress trails behind her as she steps across the threshold of Elara's Gate. Her *chazoure* body transforms into silver, and then she's nothing more than a translucent sheen twirling up the staircase to Paradise. It's breathtaking. But my eyes drift back to the churning black dust. I can't see anything past it, not even the stone wall.

I've been told a scathing river courses through Tyrus's realm. It boils the flesh off of sinners and runs red with their blood. The river parches dry when it reaches the Perpetual Sands, where those who murdered in life without the sanction of the gods may never quench their thirst. Past the desert, oath breakers and cowards are dragged by their chains to the Furnace of Justice, where they burn forever in an eternal fire. The ashes and smoke are said to form the great cape Tyrus wears around his shoulders.

The dark melody grows louder and quickens to the rhythm of my pounding heartbeat. *My realm is just as beautiful as Elara's,* the masculine voice whispers. *You could withstand my river. I would build you a barge of gold. I would shower you with water in my desert. The flames in my furnace would not burn your skin. They would bathe you in divine heat.*

My stomach quivers. Would Tyrus really keep me safe? He protected me when the ceiling shattered. I wasn't crushed. I didn't fall off the bridge either. My feet glide forward and bring me closer to the glittering dust. But what if he's lying? I stretch out my hand. An unshakable desire urges me to find out.

"Ailesse! Ailesse!" The words are nonsensical. They don't sing the language of the gods. I can't either, but I may learn.

My lashes bat slowly as I gaze past the dust into the blackness beyond. A hot breeze wafts to me from within and stirs the ends of my hair.

I take another step, lured to the dark call of Tyrus.

47
Bastien

"Ailesse!" I shout again. My heart pounds out of my chest. I stare down at her from the large rift I've blasted open. She's over a hundred feet below me and dangerously close to the swirling dust door. A few more steps and she'll be on the other side. "Get back, please!" She won't look at me. Can she even hear me? The song in her head must have grown too loud.

A strange breeze ripples through her hair and dress. She drifts another step toward the entrance to the Underworld. What will happen if she crosses through? Will she die?

I can't breathe. I don't know what to do. There isn't enough time for me to race down all the stairs and save her. "Ailesse, think! If you go in there, you can't ever come back." If none of the

Chained can, that much has to be true. "You won't see your *famille* ever again or your mother or your friend Sabine." My voice cracks. "You won't see me."

She freezes. I can't make out her expression, but her head turns, like she's trying to reorient herself. Finally, her face lifts to me. I drop to my knees and lean over the rift. "Stay with me. Don't look at the Gate again. Step away from it, and shut out the music. It's meant for the dead. You're not one of them."

She's still for a long moment. Then her hand covers her mouth. She quickly backtracks from the Gate.

The tension in my muscles releases. "Stay there!" I jump up to run for the hatch. But once I'm on my feet, I see a woman racing toward me.

Her speed is unnatural. *One of the dead*, I think. But I can't see the dead. I catch sight of her crown of bones. *Odiva*. My fingers flinch at the hilt of my father's knife. It's not too late to avenge him.

But could Ailesse forgive me?

"What is happening?" Odiva glances at the destroyed earth. "*Chazoure* is flooding here from everywhere."

"*Chazoure?*" I repeat.

"I followed the dead, you impudent boy," she snaps. "Ailesse— where is she?" Before I can answer, Odiva pushes me aside and stares down into the blasted rift. "A second soul bridge," she gasps.

I look with her and suck in a sharp breath. Ailesse is spinning and kicking at the air. *Merde*. Another Chained.

I can't think about revenge right now. I bolt for the hatch.

When I'm eight feet away, I collide with an invisible force. A man's voice growls and hurls me aside. I grunt as I hit the ground. His footsteps race toward the rift.

Odiva's black eyes narrow on me. A cunning grin spreads across her face.

What game is she playing? I spring to my feet and whip out my knife. "Aren't you going to help?" I run after the soul, blindly slashing the air. "He's going to jump through the rift."

"*They* are going to jump, you mean."

"Ailesse can't ferry three Chained at once!"

"Any Ferrier worth her bones can."

I keep attacking and striking nothing, racing toward her along the edge of the rift. I'm about to rush past when her hand flashes out and grabs my wrist. She yanks me close. The knife in my hand shakes as I try to pull away. Her grip is too strong.

"You can stop writhing about, Bastien," she says coolly. "All the Chained are with *her* now."

I look down through the rift. Ailesse moves twice as fast as before. The skirt of her green dress flares as she whirls, punches, and kicks. Nothing breaks her concentration, not even the lure of the Underworld.

Odiva drags me an inch closer. Her breath heats my face. "Do you love my daughter?"

My jaw locks. I'm sure about my feelings for Ailesse, but I don't know how Odiva will react. "Yes."

"And she loves you?"

I swallow. "Yes. She doesn't want to kill me anymore."

The corner of Odiva's lip curls. "She won't have a choice in the end."

Ailesse *does* have a choice. So do I. I've chosen *her*. Together, we'll find a way to survive the curse of our soul-bond. I broaden my chest. "Let me go. Let us have this year."

Odiva doesn't reply. She glances down at the rift again, and her raven brow arches. "She ferried them."

I look to see for myself.

Ailesse is standing still in the middle of the bridge, her body turned from the Gate of dust.

I blow out a sigh, but my relief comes too soon. Ailesse glances over her shoulder. And revolves. She faces the Gate.

No, no, no.

"Ailesse!" I shout. "Don't listen to the song!"

Odiva's mouth parts in shock. "No, Tyrus," she says under her breath. "Not like this."

Ailesse starts slipping toward the Gate. I desperately struggle against Odiva. "Ailesse, look at me! Please! Remember what I told you—you don't belong with the dead."

"She won't heed you," Odiva says. "The call of the Underworld is too powerful. If she had completed her rite of passage, she would have learned to resist what she desires."

My throat closes. I can't draw any air. I have to get away from Odiva. I might still have a chance to reach Ailesse in time. I'll pull her back from the Gate myself.

"Let me go, Bone Crier," I sneer. "We both know you won't kill me."

Odiva gives me a thin smile. "You forget I have the graces of five deadly creatures. I am devious, as well as resourceful." My pulse races as her eyes lower to my father's knife, then lift back to me. "The question is how much should I value your life?"

48
Ailesse

THE WHIRLING BLACK HOLDS ME in a tight embrace. Every inch of my skin prickles with heat. It's more wonderful than anything I've ever felt, even being wrapped in Bastien's arms.

I'm twenty feet away from the Gate of dust. I shake as I slip another five feet closer. I need to stop. I shouldn't go to the Underworld. It would mean my death.

Another rush of heat shivers through me. I close my eyes. I never want this feeling to end. The pull from the Underworld lifts me to my toes and makes them step forward. When I look again, I'm ten feet away. So close . . .

Too close.

I grit my teeth. Clench the ground with my feet. Tyrus's siren song throbs through all my muscles and bones. "I'm not as weak as you think," I tell him.

A drumbeat joins the music and pounds faster and faster. My pulse dances with it. All my nerve endings tingle. The song blares, races. I want it louder, blazing.

My chest lurches forward. I trip seven steps closer to the Gate. I'm three feet away now.

"No!" I hold my muscles rigid. "I don't want to die."

The lure builds into a fierce riptide no grace bone can give me strength to resist.

You have done enough, Ailesse, Tyrus sings without words, but my soul understands. *Come where your talent will be honored, where I will appreciate your Light.*

Ailesse, I need you! The sound of another voice startles me. It's beautiful and rich. Somehow I know it.

I glance at Elara's sheer and silvery Gate—just to the right of Tyrus's Gate—but when the voice calls again, it doesn't resonate from within her realm.

You have always wanted to be a Ferrier. Do not disappoint me!

It's coming from behind me. I start to look when Tyrus asks, *Is ferrying what you truly desired all your life? Or did you only wish to ascend the soul bridge to come closer to my kingdom? Now you can touch it for yourself. You can live here, Ailesse.*

Turn around!

Let go and come to me.

Tears of exertion blur my eyes. I'm torn between staying and going. The force of Tyrus's power channels into every space of my body. He wants me more. He can have me.

My head tips back in surrender.

I let go.

Something grips my arm. I can't move. The black dust has nearly enveloped me, but I'm held back. My blood burns. I'll kill whoever is—

I'm spun around. I'm staring into wide *chazoure* eyes. A girl without chains. "The boy says you don't belong there." Her voice is different from the others in my head. "And the beautiful lady says she can't fight all the Chained without you."

My brow furrows. Only some of her words make sense. I look past her.

In the middle of the soul bridge, someone in a midnight-blue dress and wearing majestic grace bones twirls and lashes, fighting four Chained at once. I gasp. "Mother!"

She can't look at me with all the dead surrounding her and more coming, but the tense line of her shoulders eases. "Take this one, Ailesse!" she calls. She strikes the flat of her palm into the man in front of her. He's thrown right at me. My mother's aim is exact.

Fierce instinct takes hold of me. Tyrus's siren song breaks. The Unchained girl lets go and passes through Elara's Gate. I rush toward the dead man.

I kick out his legs before he lands. He crashes to his knees. I haul him up and drive him backward to the Gate with unrelenting blows. I even gouge his eyes. He doesn't have a chance to fight back. *My mother is here.* I grin, even as the dead man curses me.

She came to help. She didn't allow me to die. She cares about me.

Warmth radiates through my chest. All my life I've dreamed of ferrying beside her, working together in perfect unison. That moment is here. Part of me wants the world to stand still so I can drink it in. But the stronger part—the part of me that's really my mother's daughter—won't stop to be sentimental. I fight the dead harder than ever.

I grab the man by the back of his *chazoure* tunic. I'm near the vortex of black dust now. I have to be quick. The Chained thrashes like a wildcat, but my grip is as strong as my tiger shark's jaws. I don't let go until I hurl him through the Gate. He cries out as the dust cloaks him from sight.

I hover nearby, staring at the spinning darkness. Tyrus's siren song returns and pounds through my head. *It's not too late, Ailesse. Come to me. I will not punish you. I will share my bounty.*

I square my jaw. I won't listen.

I run the other way. Too many souls swarm the ledge and bridge. They spider-crawl through the rift above and drop from the mine shaft. I rapidly scan the cavern for Bastien, but I can't see anything beyond streaks of *chazoure*.

Ten feet later, two more Chained confront me. I smirk and motion them forward. I attack with more vigor, but I still don't match my mother's talent. She's fighting five souls now. She doesn't even have a staff. My nostrils flare.

I hurriedly draw the two Chained backward to the Gate. One of them lunges at me. I strike his chest with the heel of my foot. The other barrels forward, and I sidestep him, jabbing his back with my elbow. My ibex agility keeps me balanced on the narrow bridge.

I turn to fight the first Chained, but he cuffs me hard in the jaw. I stumble backward, barely dodging a blow from the second one. I tighten my fists and attack faster, using every measure of my falcon speed. Once I have the advantage, I grab both souls by their chains and heave them through the Gate.

"Send more!" I shout to my mother.

She tosses me another Chained. A robust woman who immediately throws a punch at my face. I duck and ram into her stomach with my shoulder. With a sharp twist, I yank her around. She growls, thrashing as I drive her backward toward the Gate. I kick her off me and shove her into the black dust.

As soon as she's through, I bolt away to fight another Chained my mother thrusts at me. We ferry on and on like this until our movements become one fluid rhythm.

My chest burns with pride. She can't doubt my ability now. She must see how I'll be a worthy *matrone*.

The souls that are Unchained dart past us and run to the call of Elara's realm. Some are threatened by the Chained, but my mother and I help them break free.

I lose count of how many dead we ferry. A Ferrier's work can last until sunrise, if necessary. During the age of the plague, when death was rampant, my *famille* needed as much of that time as possible. But my mother and I must be nearly finished. The number of dead are starting to thin.

I throw another Chained through the Gate and look above me

to the rift Bastien blasted open. I shout his name, but don't hear anything back. My pulse beats out of time. Where is he?

My mother glances my way while she fights three Chained. My falcon vision narrows on the twitch of her brow. A sign of guilt? Did she find Bastien before he could return to me? I fight to breathe. "Bastien!" I cry again.

"I'm here!"

My pulse jumps. His voice sounds throaty and exhausted. He's standing on the ledge just past the foot of the bridge. He blindly battles a Chained with his father's knife while another one crawls headfirst down the cavern wall, ready to leap on him.

"Watch out!" I race to intervene, but my mother throws two more Chained at me. I scowl and fight them back toward the Gate as quickly as possible. "Above you, Bastien!" I call, though I can't see him anymore.

My hastiness makes me sloppy, and when I cast one of the Chained through, the second one grabs my dress. I'm dragged dangerously close to the swirling black dust. I grind my teeth and yank away just in time. The Chained tumbles through the Gate. I fall backward on the bridge from the force of our separation.

Well done, Ailesse, Tyrus's realm sings to me. *Now come and receive your reward.*

Reward? My limbs tingle, and I pull to my feet.

"Move back from the Gate, Ailesse!" my mother shouts. "You're too close!"

Vaguely, I hear the growls of several Chained surrounding her. She's too enmeshed in fighting to come for me.

My chest sways toward the Gate, but my feet root me to the ground. "I . . . can't go," I murmur into the hot breeze reaching out for me. "Bastien . . ." I frown and shake my head. *What about Bastien?* I can't remember what felt so urgent a moment ago.

Tyrus's siren song shivers through my body, a euphoric rush that promises more. *Where I am is a better place. It has greater power. You can do anything in my realm.*

"Ailesse!" A woman's voice. My mother again. What does she want now? "He is lying! Come back to me!" Her words are insignificant. They fade as the siren song blares louder.

"I want to fly," I tell Tyrus, my imagination running wild. "I want to breathe underwater."

I will give you that and more.

"I want . . ." My legs tremble. "I want love." Love has two faces. A blue-eyed boy. A dark-haired girl. But I can't remember their names.

"Do something, Bastien!" my mother cries.

My thoughts snag. *Bastien?* I almost know what that means. It doesn't stop my feet from slipping forward. The black dust undulates like beckoning fingers. What would it feel like to have that glittering darkness wrapped all around me? I lift my hand. I reach.

"Ailesse, no!" A new voice. Male. One that stirs warmth in my blood.

The drums beat harder, but I can't forget that voice. It doesn't come from the Gate. My sixth sense pounds up my spine and across my shoulders.

"Walk away from the Gate, Ailesse, or I will kill Bastien!" my mother yells.

Bastien. He's the boy I love. That's his name.

The siren song shatters. The black dust snaps at me like the jaws of a jackal. I jump backward and dodge the bite. Blood rushes to my head as I spin around. Two Unchained run toward me. I leap aside, and they race through Elara's translucent Gate. I look across the bridge. Three Chained fall off its side in streaks of *chazoure*. My mother delivers a powerful round kick and strikes the last soul standing. He screams and falls off the bridge with the others.

I gape at her. Those were the last of the dead, and she didn't even ferry them. She's staying close to Bastien with her hand at his back. He's unnaturally stiff—and he's no longer holding his father's knife. My heart stops. My mother is using it against him.

"What are you doing?" I dart toward them.

"That is far enough," she says calmly. I halt at once, ten feet away, fearing what she'll do otherwise.

Perspiration slicks Bastien's hair. His eyes are fever bright. He's been fighting the Chained just as hard as we have, but it's taken a greater toll on him. How can my mother reward him like this? "Let him go! He was helping us. Why are you—?"

"The Gates will not stay open much longer. The two years are at an end, and Tyrus has still not given him back to . . ." Her mouth creases shut, and she inhales a steadying breath. "This is my final chance, Ailesse."

My heartbeat quickens. She's not making any sense. What does all this have to do with Bastien? "Final chance for what?"

"To redeem myself." Her black eyes gleam. "I understand now. This is Tyrus's last requirement—my last act of reconciliation. I need to help you see it through."

I stop breathing. I glance at Bastien's pale face. "See what through?"

Her commanding gaze bores into me. "Your rite of passage."

49
Sabine

CAS AND I RACE DEEPER into the western part of the forest. The soldiers try their best to keep up with us. An hour ago, we heard an explosion in the same direction we're still headed. Cas said it was stolen black powder. We've been moving as fast as possible ever since.

Faint sounds of arguing drift to me on the night air. Even with my jackal grace, they're too distant to understand clearly. I can't tell who they are or what they're saying. What if one of them is Ailesse? I grab Cas's arm. "This is as far as the soldiers come."

He scans the ground around us. He doesn't hear what I do. "We've arrived at the entrance?"

I glance at the map. The entrance above the soul bridge is in a clearing, and we're still in the thick of the trees. But we have to be close. "It's only a little farther. We can't be more than a quarter mile away, if this map is drawn to scale. The cavern should be right below the entrance." I don't mention the long flights of stairs in between.

"Then the soldiers will come along until we reach it," Cas says.

"No." My chin lifts. "The soldiers will be close enough here."

He shifts on restless legs.

The breeze billows through my hunting dress as we stare at each other. I don't blink.

"Very well." He sighs and motions for Briand to join us. Cas surveys what sky we can see past the forest canopy above and places a hand on his companion's shoulder. "Do you see that pine—the tallest one?" He points at it. "If Sabine and I haven't returned by the time the moon touches the top of that tree, follow our trail and bring the soldiers."

The moon and tall pine are close to touching already. I frown at Cas. "That doesn't give Ailesse enough time to . . ."—*kill you*— ". . . be rescued."

"It's plenty of time if she is as close as you say. That's all I can risk without reinforcements."

I briefly close my eyes, hating this plan more and more. But I can't lose this chance. Ailesse is finally within reach. "Fine. Follow me."

Cas and I leave the others and press forward through the forest. He stays in step behind me, even though he's the one carrying the lantern. It doesn't matter. My nighthawk bone gives me vision in the dark to compensate.

Our surroundings brighten, and the trees around us thin to reveal a moonlit meadow. Burned sulfur reaches my nose before I notice curls of smoke rising off the ground.

Cas's brow furrows. "This is where the black powder exploded."

"Exploded what?" I can't see what's in the middle of the meadow—the surrounding wild grass masks it—but orange embers glow there.

He shakes his head. "That's what we need to find out."

I take his hand, and we race partway into the meadow before he pulls me to a stop. "Look." Cas points at a hatch that's flung open on rusted hinges. A staircase leads below. "This must be the entrance."

My pulse jumps. "We have to hurry."

"Wait, Sabine." He squeezes my hand. "This could be a trap."

It is. The back of my throat tightens. *For you, Cas.* I hastily glance away. He doesn't deserve to die.

My eyes land on hazy orange light cutting across the meadow. What I thought were burning embers is actually flickering firelight—from torches? It's coming from a jagged opening in the earth.

I drop Cas's hand and move closer. The opening runs deep underground. I'd need to stand right next to the edge to see how far down it goes. The bridge must be below.

"No, I won't do this!"

Ailesse.

I freeze at the sound of her desperate voice.

"Let him go, Mother!" she cries.

Odiva is with her?

"I'm not going to kill Bastien!"

My breath rushes out of me.

"What's wrong?" Cas comes to my side. He can't hear Ailesse like I can.

I shake my head. I'm sick with horror. "He's not the right boy."

"Pardon?"

I run for the open hatch.

"Wait!" Cas yells, chasing after me. "We need to exercise caution!"

"There's no time!"

My mother is trying to make my sister kill her *amouré*.

But it isn't Bastien.

50
Ailesse

My mother's brow arches at my defiance. "It is a full moon, Ailesse, and here we are on a soul bridge. True, you could kill Bastien anywhere, but this is more fitting, don't you think? You can do what you meant to do when you first laid eyes on him."

"Mother, I can't . . ." My chest seizes up. I'm desperate to get Bastien away from her. "I didn't *know* him then. I didn't *love* him."

"Love cannot always matter," she snaps, but her expression flickers with pain.

My teeth set on edge. "When does love *ever* matter to you?"

"You think I do not love you?"

"I know it. I understand what love is now." I meet Bastien's eyes.

They overflow with concern—for me, not himself, because that's who he is.

My mother's gaze thins. "I have loved deeply, child. I have sacrificed dearly for it. Why do you think—?" Her voice breaks. She swallows to compose herself. "I never wanted you to suffer as I have. I've done my best to protect you."

Protect me? She abandoned me. Her heart is glacier-cold. I've fought in vain all my life to thaw it. "If you really love me, you wouldn't ask me to kill my *amouré*."

"You should have never had an *amouré*. That is what I am trying to set right."

I shake my head in disbelief. She thinks I don't deserve love? "Let Bastien go, Mother. Honor my choice. You were once given yours when you met my father."

She bristles. "Your father was never the man I loved."

Her words are shards of ice in my chest. "*What?*" All my limbs go rigid as a sparkle of red at her neck catches my eye. A ruby lodged in the beak of a bird skull. I've seen that necklace once before. The memory tears across my mind.

Two years ago . . . my mother on the floor of her chamber beside a golden chest . . . a letter open on her lap—and the necklace pressed to her lips. I'd never seen her cry before, and it frightened me.

Now as I stare at her, my chest heaves with anger, even while my heart feels like it's shrinking. She holds Bastien in a shaft of moonlight on the bridge. I don't want her anywhere near him—or me. "You betrayed my father?"

She lowers her brows and jerks Bastien closer. He hisses as the knife bites his skin. "Kill him, Ailesse," she demands. "You cannot let your love for him destroy you, too."

My eyes burn. "You would really ask that of me after what you've done?"

"What does my past have to do with what's required of you?"

"It has everything to do with it! You've broken the rules of what we hold most sacred, and now you expect me to keep them. You expect me to *sacrifice* for them—to kill the person I love—when you didn't even love your own *amouré*." Revulsion courses through me. "Your rite of passage meant nothing. You broke your oath to the gods."

Her nostrils flare. "I have paid the price for that and more." She looks at Tyrus's Gate again, and her voice takes on a desperate edge. "Don't you understand? I must revoke what never should have happened. If I'd never met your father, you would not have become my heir—or even attempted to become a Ferrier."

"If you'd never met my father, I wouldn't have been born."

"But I am trying to save you, Ailesse! I have tried so very hard, for so very long, to save you."

"I don't know what this is really about, but don't pretend it's me."

Her eyes narrow. "I do not have time for this. *Kill him!*" She rattles Bastien, and his jaw muscle tenses.

My body flushes fiery hot, then cold. The drums of Tyrus's siren song beat louder. I shake as I struggle to drown them out. I glance at Bastien's father's weapon. "That isn't even a ritual knife."

"No." My mother withdraws another knife from a hidden sheath in her dress. "But this is."

I gasp. For one terrible moment I fear she's going to stab Bastien herself. Then I remember she can't. She wouldn't. It would kill me. Still, my pulse won't stop racing.

She lifts her chin high. "Show me your strength, Ailesse. You have prepared all your life to become a Ferrier. You always knew this would be the price." She extends the bone knife to me while she keeps Bastien's father's knife fast against his back. A bead of sweat rolls down his temple. "I have made my choices and suffered the consequences. You still have a chance for peace. Trust me, child. It will break your heart less to kill him now than to wait any longer."

Terrible pressure bears down on me. My legs quake harder as I look into Bastien's beautiful eyes. Loving him will lead to my death. I've always known that. Just like he knew loving me would do the same to him. He gives me a slight nod, asking me to save myself.

How can I?

The melody of the siren song resonates softer now, gentler. I hear its secret voice. *You have another choice, Ailesse. You could come to me first. Bastien will follow you. He will die when you do, and the two of you can be together in my kingdom.*

I pinch my eyes shut. That doesn't silence the music.

You could both be so happy.

My chest is a drum of black powder. My nerves are threads of flame.

I have to make this end.

I set my jaw. I imagine myself in the Nivous Sea. I'm turning around in the water to kill the tiger shark, even after Sabine asked me to give her up.

I walk forward and take the bone knife from my mother's hand. I stop trembling. Her eyes shine with pride. I've wanted her approval for as long as I can remember. My throat stings, but I swallow down my rising tears.

"I won't do this." My words are iron. My mother can't break them. Her grin falls as I step closer to Bastien and take his hand. "We'll do what you said," I tell him. "We'll find a way to break our soul-bond. And if we can't, then I'm prepared to die with you."

His brows quiver, but his eyes are a sure reflection of mine. He squeezes my hand and nods.

I turn to my mother. "You have no power over us. You can *never* make me kill him." I move to drop the bone knife over the edge of the bridge.

She isn't shaken. "Yes, I can."

In a flash, she grabs my wrist and secures my grip on the hilt.

"What are you doing?" I wrestle against her. "Stop!"

With graced strength, she drives the knife toward Bastien's chest.

51

Bastien

My heartbeat thrashes in my ears. I grab Ailesse's wrist. Throw all my muscle into stopping the bone knife. Its sharp tip trembles right over my heart. *Merde, merde, merde.*

I fight to pull it back. My head throbs, muscles burn. I can't make it budge. Odiva is too powerful.

My eyes find Ailesse. She's already looking at me. Her face is red. She shakes from exertion.

My throat tightens. I don't want her to see me die.

A frantic cry shudders through the air. "Stop!"

Someone's on the ledge. Odiva, Ailesse, and I turn our heads.

A dark-haired girl. The witness from Castelpont.

A boy my age races out from the tunnel behind her. He jerks to a stop once he sees us, eyes round.

"Sabine," Ailesse gasps without releasing any tension on the knife.

Sabine gives her a flash of a smile, then glares at Odiva. "You have the wrong boy."

My mind freezes. I stare at her blankly.

The boy scrutinizes me. "That isn't Ailesse's abductor?" he asks.

Sabine doesn't answer. She yanks him close, whips out another bone knife, and brings it to his neck. His lantern crashes to the ground. He struggles to break free, but his effort is just as pointless as mine.

"What are you doing?" he demands.

"Say another word, and I'll kill you." Her voice is cold and steady.

"Wrong boy?" Ailesse repeats Sabine's words. "What are you talking about?"

Sabine prods the boy a step forward. "This is your *amouré*, Ailesse."

"But you were my witness at Castelpont," Ailesse replies. "You *saw* Bastien walk onto the bridge."

"That doesn't necessarily mean he's your *amouré*," Odiva says. She isn't trying to drive the knife into my chest anymore, but she holds it there, resisting as Ailesse and I struggle to pull it away. "Any man could have stepped onto the bridge."

Ailesse looks at her mother and Sabine like they've both gone mad. "But . . . Bastien came when I played the bone flute."

"He wanted to kill you," Sabine says.

"He was *lured* to me. I saw it in his eyes."

Sabine shakes her head. "Any man would be smitten with you, Ailesse."

My heart beats faster. I size up the man in Sabine's clutches. Handsome. Clearly rich. But Ailesse's soulmate? Impossible.

Or maybe not . . .

My gaze drifts to Ailesse's auburn hair, tousled and wild from fighting. She's breathtaking. "It's true," I whisper.

Her eyes fill with hurt. "Why are you agreeing with them? That man isn't my *amouré*. You are. I don't care what they say."

"Isn't this what we want?" I ask. I wish we could have this conversation in private, without a knife in the grip of our hands. "If we're not soulmates, then death can't hang over us. We can be together in peace."

Ailesse falls quiet, searching my eyes. "But *you're* the one meant for me. I'll never love anyone else. Why would the gods—?" She tosses a scathing look over her shoulder at the only visible Gate.

"The gods have nothing to do with us." All I want is to hold her and kiss her and convince her I'm right. "We don't have to play their game." Is she listening? She hasn't turned back to face me.

"How can you affirm this boy is Ailesse's *amouré*?" Odiva asks Sabine. She's already looking at him with more approval than me.

Sabine doesn't answer. She stares between me and Ailesse in disbelief.

"Sabine," Odiva says pointedly.

She blinks twice. Clears her throat. "Cas, he . . . he heard Ailesse's song during the last full moon. He caught a glimpse of her as she was stolen away, and he's been searching for her ever since. I found him at Castelpont tonight."

Cas's mouth parts like he wants to say something, but he

doesn't, not with Sabine's knife at his throat. I take a harder look at him. He's vaguely familiar. It doesn't matter. I hate him. I don't care that he's done nothing wrong.

Odiva studies Sabine. Then, all at once, she releases her hold on the knife. Ailesse and I stumble backward and fall onto the bridge. I groan. My body can't take another beating tonight. I reach over to help her to her feet, but she bats my hand away. Her eyes are latched on to the Gate. She pulls up by herself.

Merde. Not again.

"Ailesse, wait!" I stand as she drifts toward it. "We're free now. You can't listen to—!"

A bright burst of pain strikes me in the back. A strangled cry rips out of me.

Ailesse finally spins around. Her eyes flare in shock. "Bastien!"

My legs give out. My body slams onto the bridge.

Ailesse is at my side the next instant. She falls to her knees and feels my back with shaking hands. "No, no, no . . . Bastien . . ." Hazily, I see her beautiful face. Tears pour down her cheeks. She pulls her hands away. They're covered in blood. My blood. She sobs harder. "Don't go, Bastien. Stay with me."

Nausea grips my stomach. I writhe and choke for air. I can't think past the burning pain.

Ailesse reaches around me. I cry out as something sharp tears from my back. My vision rocks. Its hilt. Its unwieldy blade.

My father's knife. Odiva stabbed me with it.

52
Ailesse

I DROP THE KNIFE, AND it clatters on the bridge. I gape as Bastien bleeds out faster. I shouldn't have pulled out the blade. I lean over him and kiss his brow again and again. I smooth his hair, forgetting my bloody hands. Tears flood my vision. "You're going to be fine," I promise. He looks anything but fine. His skin is as pale as the limestone beneath him. Tremors lurch through his body.

He fights to speak. "Ailesse . . ." His eyes start to roll back.

"Bastien!" I hold his face. "Stay with me! Please!"

His muscles go limp. His eyes shut.

"No, no, no." This can't be happening. I kiss his lips. He doesn't kiss me back. My head falls onto his chest, and I clutch him tighter. I can't breathe. Broken sobs won't let me. "How could you?" I shout at my mother.

She sweeps closer, glancing at Bastien with false pity. "Because this time I knew you would not die if I killed him."

I'm so horrified I can't speak.

"Sabine, bring Ailesse her true *amouré*." My mother stands tall. "Ailesse has a rite of passage to complete."

Sabine's mouth falls open. She doesn't move. I balk at my mother. How can she even suggest such a thing right now? Bastien is dead. Soon I'll see his soul and have to say my final goodbye— because of her.

A wildfire of rage ignites in my veins. I grab the knife and jump to my feet. I race toward her, my pulse pounding in my ears.

My mother holds up her hand. "Ailesse, think—"

"I hate you!" I swing the knife. She leaps over me. "Nothing excuses what you've done!"

She ducks my next attack. "One day you will understand. It was better to break your heart."

Her cruelty is revolting. "Because my heart means nothing to you?" I slash out again. She sidesteps me.

"Don't be irrational. I told you, I love—"

"Love isn't love if you never show it." I lunge at her. She strikes my forearm. My hand whips back from the force, but I keep hold of my knife. I swing for her again.

"Stop!" She kicks my legs out from beneath me. I tumble to the ground and slide to the edge of the bridge. I barely catch myself from falling off.

"I did what I had to." My mother sweeps a loose hair off her face. "You were never meant to feel my anger."

I scoff. "Were you so upset I wasn't good enough for you?"

"No, Ailesse." Her tone grows impatient. "I was angry with the gods. You were a constant reminder of what they stole from me."

Furious tears scald my cheeks. This is why she's been indifferent to me all my life? Because she loved another man instead of my father? I'm on my feet before I know it, faster than my mother for once. When I slash my knife out again, it cuts a deep line across her arm.

She sucks in a harsh breath and reflexively slaps my face. Hard. Stars burst before my eyes. I bend over, reeling.

"Stop it! Both of you!" Sabine shouts. Dazed, I turn my eyes to her. She's still on the ledge and holding Cas at knifepoint. "Ailesse, she's our mother."

I blink at her. *What did she say?* Dizziness racks my head. My ears are playing tricks on me.

"No!" Sabine cries a warning. Sharp pain lashes across the nape of my neck.

Acute weakness overcomes me. I stagger on my feet. My hand flies to my collarbone.

The pouch with my grace bones is gone.

"I am sorry." My mother wraps the pouch's cord around her hand, then steals my knife while I gape in shock—Bastien's father's knife. "I know of no other way to calm you. You are not yourself."

I lunge to grab back my weapons, but my knees buckle. I crash to the ground. My muscles shake from the strain of all my fighting tonight.

My mother drops the knife and kicks it backward. It spins toward Bastien's lifeless body and the blood pooling beneath him. My throat tightens as I hold back another sob. I need to ferry him to Paradise. His soul will rise at any moment.

"You must understand, Ailesse." Odiva kneels before me. "I was bound by a pact I made with Tyrus. I have tried my best to protect you, but he demanded terrible sacrifices of me."

My eyes water. "And am I one of them?"

She presses her lips together.

"Am I?" My heart struggles to beat. "Did Tyrus ask you to kill me?"

Her chin quivers. "Yes."

"Oh, Ailesse . . ." Sabine's voice carries my heartbreak.

I squeeze my eyes shut against deep-rooted pain. My darkest fears hiss through my mind:

You've never been enough for your mother. She doesn't need you.

I grind my teeth together. *No.* I refuse to listen to that voice any longer. I won't be a vessel for poison. I open my eyes and stare back into my mother's wretched gaze. Her hypocrisy is astounding. She's made me suffer because the gods stole her love, but she did the same thing by killing Bastien. I won't let her take away anything more from me.

With great effort, I rise to my feet. I steady my shaking legs. I have strength of my own. I'll use it without seeking to impress my mother. Without leaning on the graces I earned to make her believe in me.

A silver owl swoops in through the rift in the ceiling and circles around me. Her outspread wings shine in the light of the full moon.

I hear Sabine gasp. My mother's pale skin turns ash gray.

Confidence steels bone-deep inside me. I haven't seen the owl since she showed me a vision of Sabine before the last ferrying night. She's a sign of hope.

I roll my shoulders back. *I'll avenge you, Bastien.*

I'll avenge myself.

A sudden rush of adrenaline shivers through me. My hands tighten into fists. I slowly stalk toward my mother. "Get up if you dare to fight me."

She frowns. "Don't be absurd." She rises, and we stand face-to-face. "You have no chance to defeat me. Do not harm yourself by trying."

There she goes again, doubting me, trying to make me feel inferior. She's unprepared when I shove her with surprising strength.

She stumbles back and glances at the pouch in her hand with my grace bones. Her eyes grow wide. "How are you doing this?"

I honestly don't know. Maybe it's the silver owl. Maybe it's Elara's Light from the full moon pulsing stronger than ever inside me. Maybe it's years of pent-up rage and heartache. "Was Bastien your sacrifice, too," I demand, "or just a needless death?" I drive my palm into her collarbone. Her bear claw necklace stabs her skin. She's thrown back another three feet, still blinded by shock.

"You also wanted to kill Bastien once," she replies.

"Because you taught me there was no other way."

This time my mother is ready when I charge at her. Her leg

swings out with a vicious kick. I grab her calf before she strikes me, and twist hard. She flips over, and her stomach slaps the bridge.

The silver owl shrieks above me. It sounds like approval. Even Sabine doesn't cry for me to stop.

I stand over my mother. She scoots away, gripping her leg. "Killing me will not bring Bastien back to you," she says. "You will never know what tenacity that requires."

"I'm not going to kill you," I tell her, my voice sure and strong. "I'm going to take every grace bone you wear and cast them into the abyss. You'll never have power to hurt anyone again."

She swallows as I reach for her skull-and-vertebrae crown. "Wait! This is not necessary, Ailesse." She rises swiftly, keeping her weight off her injured leg. She glances behind her. The black dust is thinning. Her eyes fill with panic. "He hasn't come," she murmurs. "Tyrus still needs a sacrifice."

I harden my stare, daring her to try to send me through his Gate.

She gasps, suddenly looking past me. "Release Sabine at once!"

My heart pounds. I spin back. But Cas isn't threatening Sabine. She still has him in a firm grip and looks as confused as I am.

A sharp tug on my dress pocket jerks me off balance. I turn back around, and my mother grabs my shoulders.

"No!"

She hurls me backward several feet—but farther away from the Gate, not closer to it. My back strikes the bridge. My shoulder blade throbs as I lift my head and tense for another attack. But my mother doesn't move.

The bone flute is in her hands.

"I am sorry, Ailesse." Her black eyes shine with remorse, but her face is as hard as ice. She drops the pouch with my grace bones and races away, despite her injured ankle. She darts past Bastien and rushes toward the last swirling particles of Tyrus's Gate.

My breath catches. "Mother, no!" I spring up and bolt after her, my blood on fire.

The Gate is closing, but the siren song swells. I stiffen every muscle and cast up a wall against the lure of the Underworld. My heart twinges when I jump over Bastien's prostrate body, but I barrel onward, my speed blazing faster than ever. My mother is quickly within reach.

My arm stretches out for her. "Please, don't do this!" I shouldn't care if she leaves me—if she sacrifices herself for someone she loves stronger. But I do. Elara help me, I do.

I can't grab her in time. She pushes off the ground in a tremendous leap. Her hair is a river of darkness as she flies. Through the air. Through the dust. Through the Gate.

Dust blasts apart like she's broken through glass. It doesn't re-form into an arched door. It falls into the abyss in a rush of glittering black.

I crumple to my knees. "Mother!"

53
Sabine

I STARE AT THE WALL where the black dust swirled a moment ago. The shimmer of Elara's Gate has also vanished. My knife trembles against Casimir's neck. I can't release him, not even to wipe my tears. *Mother.* How can I feel such terrible heaviness? All my life, Odiva held a strong attachment to me. I never understood why—not until three days ago. There wasn't enough time to grow to hate her . . . or find a deeper place in my heart for her. And now she's gone, her last sacrifice in vain.

Ailesse slowly turns from the wall. One of her hands grips a fistful of hair at her scalp; the other hangs lifelessly at her side. Our eyes meet. I see her chin wobble. I ache to run across the bridge and let her cry on my shoulder.

"Let me go to her," Cas pleads, despite all the inexplicable things he's seen tonight. "Let me comfort her."

Before I can threaten him to keep quiet, Ailesse sighs and her eyes flutter closed. "Oh, Sabine . . . why did you bring him here?" No anger rakes across her quiet voice, just overwhelming fatigue. "Please, just take him away."

I frown. She wants me to leave? "But—"

She looks at Bastien and crumples to the ground, sobbing with fresh pain. "My mother killed him when she found out he wasn't my . . ." She buries her head in her hands, refusing to say "*amouré*."

Does she think Bastien's death is my fault? My chest burns with a sting of betrayal. "You have no idea how hard I've fought to . . ." I clamp my mouth shut and take a moment to rein in my frustration. "All I wanted to do was save you, Ailesse. I've been trying to save you since the night you were captured. I didn't know you'd had a change of heart."

She lifts her gaze to me. Her eyes are red. "Of course you didn't. I'm sorry. This isn't your fault, Sabine." But it is, even though I never meant to hurt her. "I know you were trying to save me. Somehow I . . . I saw you." Her brow wrinkles. "It was like a dream. You gave me hope when I needed it." Her mouth trembles into a smile. It's small and fleeting, but genuinely grateful. It eases the tightness in my chest.

Cas draws breath like he's going to say something, but I press my blade closer against his neck.

I don't know what to do about him anymore. If I let him go, Ailesse will still have to track him down later. "I realize this is a difficult time for you," I say tentatively, "but we need to take care of Cas—Casimir," I correct myself. I don't want her thinking I'm on casual terms with him. "This is your ritual knife," I add.

The pulse at Cas's throat jumps, vibrating along the bone blade. He grapples with the hilt to yank it away, but he can't outmatch my strength.

Ailesse isn't listening anymore. She stares at my shoulder necklace—her necklace. The golden jackal pendant suddenly weighs heavy. "You completed your rite of passage?" she asks. Disappointment etches across her face. Is she jealous? She's never been jealous of me. "You really killed your *amouré*?"

"No!" The thought is revolting, although I came close to killing hers. Now I wish I had.

She bites her quivering lip. "Then you've never met the person you're meant to love. Even if he wasn't chosen for you." She swipes away more tears. "I wish . . ." Her voice cracks. "I wish you could understand my loss. I need you, Sabine. I don't know how I can bear this alone."

My eyes blur as her tears stream faster. "You're not alone," I say gently, and wrench Cas's arm behind his back. "I do understand. It took everything in me to believe you weren't dead when Odiva told me you were."

Lines pinch between Ailesse's brows. "What?"

All the emotions that churned inside me over the past month return in full force. I fight to hold them back, even though Ailesse has always been the one to console me.

She shakes her head. "Oh, Sabine . . . I'm so sorry she hurt you like that." She doesn't mention how badly my words must be hurting her, too.

"My love for you may not be the love you're talking about," I say, "but that doesn't mean it's any less powerful." I take a steadying breath. "We're sisters, Ailesse."

She draws back. Studies me gravely. "What are you talking about?"

I lift a shoulder and try to smile. "Well, we do have different fathers."

A small laugh escapes her. "That isn't possible," she says, but I see her pain cut deeper as the truth settles. I silently curse myself. Why did I think this news might be comforting?

A quiet sound comes from the center of the bridge. A noise of pain.

Ailesse tenses in disbelief. Then her gaze floods with hope. "Bastien!"

She darts up and runs for him without watching her footing. Tiny fissures crack beneath her.

His eyes peel open. He rolls his head to see her.

The limestone groans. The fissures lengthen. Widen.

My heart rises up my throat. "Ailesse, move!"

She looks down. A deep clap of thunder rumbles. But there's no lightning.

The side of the bridge breaks away—a foot-wide sliver down the length of it.

Ailesse falls.

"No!" I cry.

I release Casimir and sprint as fast as I can. Bastien crawls for Ailesse, rasping her name.

She catches herself on a rough handhold off the side of the

bridge. I drop the ritual knife and snatch up the pouch with her grace bones. I don't stop running. The strange energy Ailesse had when she fought our mother is gone.

She drags her upper body over the edge of the bridge and braces herself on her elbows. She shakes, hanging by her folded arms. Her jaw is set. Her eyes are riveted on Bastien's.

Crack!

A two-foot chunk of limestone splits away from the bridge. It crashes against Ailesse's leg, and she screams. Her arms scrape and slide off the edge. By some miracle, her hands find purchase. She clings on by her fingers.

Blood rushes through my head. "Don't let go!"

Someone yanks Ailesse's pouch from my grip. I spin around and face Cas. His sword is drawn and dangerously close to my chest. "Are you going to steal this like her mother did?"

"Give those back! The bones strengthen her."

"Bones?"

There's no time to explain. "Please, she needs them!"

Ailesse releases a terrible cry of exertion. Cas and I jerk around. Her dress is torn away at her left leg. Trails of blood drip from her injured knee. She whimpers and tugs herself up, hanging by her elbows once more.

"Ailesse . . ." Bastien's voice is hoarse, but I hear him. Whatever he says is drowned by an oncoming battle cry.

Cas's nine soldiers storm in through the tunnel, their swords raised. One man has a nocked bow and aims at Bastien. "Don't shoot!" I say. "Cas, tell them to go! Ailesse needs my help!"

His face hardens. "Arrest Sabine!" he calls to his men.

He shoves past me. I chase after him. Bastien is closest to Ailesse and painstakingly crawls toward her.

Boots pounds and approach the foot of the bridge. "Stop!" I shout at the soldiers. "The bridge is too weak." The middle section webs with more fissures. "You'll break it!" I rush toward them to drive them away.

"I'm coming!" Cas yells to Ailesse.

The soldiers don't halt. I run straight for their pointed swords. Before they skewer me, I hurtle into the air and jump over them with my nighthawk grace. Their eyes widen with shock.

I land, turn, and quickly scan for Ailesse. She's completely dragged herself up onto the bridge. She claws toward Bastien. Her bloody leg streaks a path behind her.

The soldiers charge at me. I race several yards down the curving ledge to lead them farther away from the bridge. I allow the fastest man to catch up to me. I swiftly turn and leap over him. I draw strength and viciousness from the golden jackal and punch the man's back where his kidneys are. He grunts sharply. His sword fumbles from his grip. I dive for it, but another soldier kicks it away.

I scramble backward and check Ailesse again. She never reached Bastien. She's wrestling against Cas as he lifts her in his arms in a cradle hold.

I jump to my feet as more soldiers come near.

"Bastien!" A girl with straw-blond hair drops from an opening beside the tunnel. I gasp. She's the same girl I fought at Castelpont.

Bastien's face is disarmingly pale as he looks at her. Someone else falls through the opening. Bastien's other friend. His lantern snuffs out as he tumbles onto the ground.

A burly soldier rushes at me. I grab a torch from the ledge wall. I swing it against the flat of his blade. It flies out of his grip.

Bastien's friends are on the bridge and running toward him.

Two soldiers fan apart and lunge at me from my left and right. My torch windmills as I spin and kick and bash them away.

Bastien's friends haul him up into their arms. His arms hang limply. He strains to look back at Ailesse. She desperately mouths his name. Her beating fists slow and stop pummeling Cas. Her eyelids flutter sluggishly. Her leg hasn't stopped dripping blood. Her head falls onto his shoulder as she passes out.

My torch is knocked from my grip. A pair of rough hands comes around me. I thrash like an animal. Four more hands grab my limbs and force them still.

Jules and Marcel race off the bridge and carry Bastien into the tunnel.

I fight to free myself, but even my graced strength can't outmatch five men.

The blood from Ailesse's shattered knee soaks into Cas's sleeve. He smooths back her hair, walks off the bridge, and looks at me with cold eyes.

My lip is curled. My teeth are bared. My heart pounds wildly. The jackal in me wants to murder him. I thrive on the bloodlust.

"Take off her necklace, too," Cas commands his lead soldier.

Briand reaches for me. I vainly struggle as he unclasps the shoulder necklace. All my muscles turn to water.

My grace bones are gone.

The other soldiers let go. Briand hefts me up, carrying me as he follows Cas and his troop through the tunnel and up the long flights of stairs.

I'm still stunned by weakness by the time we climb out of the hatch. Briand sets me on my feet, but I struggle to stay upright. He's about to pick me up again when a flash of feathers streaks across my vision.

The silver owl swoops right in front of us and rasps shrilly.

I release an exasperated sigh. *What more do you want from me? I tried my best to save Ailesse.*

She wheels around and flies toward my face. Briand whips out a dagger.

"Don't!" I say.

The owl beats her wings back and dodges his swipe. She screeches once more, then soars away.

My mind clears in a sudden rush. I understand what she was trying to tell me: I *haven't* tried my best. And I don't need my grace bones to do so. My body is only in shock from losing them so suddenly. Even without them around my neck, I know what it is to be salamander-agile, nighthawk-quick, and jackal-strong.

A surge of hope floods my veins. I inhale a deep and sustaining breath.

I'll find a way to escape. I'll get back my grace bones, and I'll come for Ailesse.

I'll save her.

And this time I won't fail.

54
Ailesse

A STAB OF SORROW AWAKENS me. My eyes open to radiant light, but I shut them again. I fold my arms over the deep ache in my stomach. I haven't seen the sun in thirty days—the day of my rite of passage—and now I don't want to. My mother is gone. Bastien is gone. And I don't know whether or not he survived.

My hands tighten into fists. I can't lie here any longer. I need to find him.

I throw my blanket back and sit up. A shock of pain shoots through me. I suck in a harsh breath and hitch up the skirt of the nightdress I'm wearing. My knee has been wrapped in a linen bandage. *Merde.* I forgot about my injured leg. Hopefully it can still support my weight.

I press my lips together and slowly slide both legs off my mattress. I search for something to lean on, and take a long look around me.

I'm in a stunningly ornate bedroom. Even my mother's fur-laden chamber in Château Creux can't compare. The fireplace is a masterpiece of carved stone, the furniture shines dark and glossy, and scarlet tapestries cover the stone walls.

I scoot toward my bedpost and rise up on my good leg. I grab the back of a nearby chair and hop, hissing as it jostles my knee. From there, I brace my hands on a table for support. I hop slowly to the end of the table, then pause, staring at a tall window ten feet away. Between the table and the window is only empty space.

I inhale deeply and prepare for unavoidable pain. I take my first step on my broken leg.

A hundred knives pierce my knee. I shriek and collapse.

The door bursts open. Casimir. My nostrils flare. I look away from him and hold back another cry of terrible pain.

He picks me up and carries me back to the bed. "I wouldn't suggest jumping from that window. There's a hundred-foot drop to the river." He lays me down, and I wince as he gently prods my knee. "Please be careful. We haven't set the bone yet."

He pulls up a stool and sits beside me. I fight for breath as the pain gradually subsides. "What is this place?" I ask, glancing at the velvet canopy above me. "This isn't the room of a soldier."

"We're in Beau Palais."

My brows lift. "You live here?"

He nods like he's embarrassed. "I'm, um, the dauphin."

The prince? I don't believe him at first, but then my eyes stray to the fine clothes he's wearing, as well as a jeweled ring on his finger. "Why were you in uniform last night?"

He shrugs. "The successor to the throne must learn the art of warfare."

I'm at a loss for words. The heir of the kingdom of South Galle is my *amouré*? What are the gods thinking?

"Are you comfortable?" Cas's cheeks flush. "I asked my maids to change you into that nightdress."

I don't care about my clothes. "Where's Sabine?" I long to see her again, but my chest aches. She isn't the Leurress my mother preferred over me; she's the daughter my mother loved more than me. It isn't Sabine's fault, but it still weighs heavy on my heart.

Casimir scratches his light strawberry-blond hair. "What is the last thing you remember about her?"

I concentrate, but those memories are foggy. "She was battling your soldiers."

He nods and fidgets with his fingers. "She escaped."

I exhale with relief. That's something to be grateful for.

His expression grows soft as he gazes at me. "I couldn't take my eyes off of you on that bridge," he confesses. "Your fighting was incredible." His fingertips skim the corner of his lip. "Your power is connected to the bones in that pouch you wore, isn't it?" When I frown, he explains, "You grew weak after your mother took them away."

"How do you know what was inside the pouch?"

"Oh . . . I was safeguarding it for you."

"*Was?*"

He glances aimlessly around the room. "I'm afraid I lost it on the journey back to Beau Palais."

I study his stone-blue eyes, suspicious of everything he tells me.

He clears his throat. "Can you tell me about that dust storm your mother jumped through? I've never believed in magic, but what other explanation is there?"

I shrug a shoulder. "I don't understand it either."

Now Casimir is the one contemplating me. "I'm not your enemy, Ailesse."

Does he really believe we can be friends after last night? "I can't stay here."

"Your leg needs to heal."

If only I possessed Sabine's salamander grace. "I. Can't. Stay."

His jaw muscle flexes. "Because of Bastien Colbert?" He suppresses a scoff. "He's a wanted thief."

"I don't care."

Casimir's brow furrows at the steel in my voice. He opens his mouth to say something, then shakes his head and stares down at his hands. "Did you know my father is dying?" he murmurs and rubs his jeweled ring. "He'll be gone in a month—two at the most." He lifts his eyes to me. They're filled with heavy sorrow. "I'm his only heir. I'm not sure if I'm ready to be king."

I shift with an uncomfortable twinge of pity.

"Will you give me a chance, Ailesse?" he asks. "The same chance you gave to the boy who abducted you."

My stomach hardens. "Leave Bastien out of this." Casimir only wants me because he can't forget the siren song he heard a month ago. It should have lost its lure after my grace bones were dug up under Castelpont. Still . . . he is my *amouré*. The gods *want* me to give him a chance.

The gods have nothing to do with us. Bastien's words return to me. *We don't have to play their game.*

But I've already been sucked into one. I've lost my first battle of wills with Tyrus. I would have walked through his Gate if my mother hadn't thrown her knife into Bastien's back.

My throat tightens. I struggle to swallow the ache. The image of Bastien lying on the bridge and bleeding out is still seared in my mind. Have Jules and Marcel found a way to close his wound? I pray for the gods to spare his life, then I stop myself. I can't pray for Bastien anymore. I won't tempt Tyrus and Elara to make him suffer like the man my mother loved. He ended up in the Underworld, and I won't let the gods wrap Bastien in chains.

"Will you stay?" Casimir gently takes my hand. I'm stricken with guilt, so I don't pull it back. He doesn't realize I can never provide him with an heir. I refuse to even try. I won't allow myself to get close to him. He's fated to die in eleven months, but I will kill him sooner, before our soul-bond kills me.

I catch my callous thoughts. If I kill him, it would be the same as if I'd killed Bastien's father. How can I do that when Bastien and I clung to the hope that we could break our soul-bond—the bond I really share with Casimir?

I flex the muscles along my jawline. I won't give up until I discover it. My leg will heal, and when it does, I'll leave this place.

You're not missing from me, Bastien. I'm not missing from you.

I take a breath that fills every space of my lungs. I have to believe he's alive. I'll find a way for us to be together again—not underground, but somewhere we can walk under the moonlight and starlight, with no more dead pursuing us, with no more curse hanging over us.

Casimir brushes his thumb across the back of my hand, awaiting my answer.

I raise my eyes.

I whisper, "Yes."

55

Bastien

I HISS, BURYING MY HEAD in a pillow as Birdine jabs her needle into my back again. "How many stitches do I need?"

"Two more," she replies, matter-of-fact. "Three, if you keep squirming. I'm not a seamstress, you know. I don't have the steadiest hand."

Jules huffs and paces near the bed. We're in the room Birdine rents above a tavern in the brothel district. The catacombs aren't safe anymore. "You should have let me sew you up, Bastien."

I clench my teeth as Birdine cinches a knot in the catgut string. "I guess I wasn't keen on getting another raging fever." My voice is hoarse with weakness. "Or a scar matching the one on my thigh."

"What, you don't like puckered fish lips?" Jules smirks.

"Hilarious."

The morning sun beats into my eyes from a small window. I squint and painstakingly shift on the lumpy mattress. I want to go back to the darkness. I'd stab Odiva before she set foot on the soul bridge. Kill that bastard that took Ailesse.

I didn't recognize him at first, not in the soldier's uniform he was wearing, but his identity came to me soon enough. Casimir Trencavel. I suppress a bitter laugh. Ailesse's *amouré* is the damn heir to the throne.

Three knocks sound on the door. Then one. Then two.

Marcel's code.

Birdine bounces, and my stitches pull tight. "Careful," I groan.

She sucks in a sharp breath. "Sorry, Bastien."

Jules rolls her eyes and walks over to the door. She unlocks it, and Marcel struts inside with a satchel slung over his shoulder. He tips his head at Birdine, and her rosy cheeks blush even rosier. "Anyone hungry?" he asks cheerfully.

Jules shakes her head. "Are you ever in a bad mood?"

He purses his lips, giving it serious thought.

She sighs. "Never mind."

He sets his satchel on a small table and starts unloading the food—two loaves of rye bread, a wedge of hard cheese, and four pears. "No, I didn't steal this, if anyone's asking. Birdie used her hard-earned money to provide this meal for us."

Birdine beams and tucks a frizzy lock of ginger hair behind her ear. "Enjoy it while you can. I can't feed four mouths for long."

Jules ambles over and gives her a pointed look. "Go on." She wags her thumb at Marcel. Jules is tolerating Birdine since she's helping us right now. "Get something to eat. I can finish up here."

Merde. I bury my head in the pillow again.

Birdine and Jules switch places, and I prepare myself for a lancing stab. All I feel is a bee sting. I turn my head and raise my brows at Jules.

"What?" She pulls the needle through. "I can be gentle when I want."

There must be a first for everything. "So . . . how bad is it?"

She takes a heavy breath. "Well, you'll never walk again, and Marcel says the loss of blood you suffered will permanently damage your brain." The corner of her mouth curves. "But you'll live."

"Good thing I can wiggle my toes right now, or I might just believe you."

She ties a knot in the catgut string. "You're going to be all right. You just need to be patient while you heal. It's not going to happen overnight."

My chest sinks into the mattress. "By the time I'm able to fight again, Ailesse might be . . ." My raspy voice cracks, and I mash my lips together to make them stop trembling. "She's in worse shape than I am, you know. She can't just walk out of Beau Palais." Rumor has it the king will die soon. And if Casimir thinks he can make Ailesse his queen . . . I grab a fistful of bedding and squeeze tight.

Jules cuts the catgut with a pair of shears and places her hand on my shoulder. "Believe it or not, I want to rescue Ailesse, too. I owe her."

I take a closer look at my friend. Jules's eyes are sunken, and her skin's even paler than mine. "How long do you think that

Chained man was inside you?" I ask tentatively. Ailesse said the Chained can eat away a person's soul, steal their Light. "Maybe we can figure out how much . . ."

Jules's face hardens. She abruptly stands and tosses her braided hair behind her shoulder. "You're all stitched up now, Bastien. You should rest."

"But—"

She crosses her arms. "I don't want to talk about it."

I sigh and nod. "Fine." Jules probably can't even answer my biggest question—if someone can gain back the Light they lost.

Three knocks sound on the door.

Everyone in the room freezes.

One more knock. Then two.

Marcel's code. Again.

Jules withdraws a knife. Birdine scoots closer to Marcel. Marcel tries his best to look brave. I bolt upright, and my back wrenches in pain.

"Who's out there?" Jules calls, creeping toward the door.

No one answers.

She turns to Marcel. "Were you followed?"

"Would I know if I was followed?"

"Well, *I* would know if I was followed."

My head spins. *Don't pass out, Bastien.* I'm still dizzy from blood loss.

Rap, rap, rap.

Rap.

Rap, rap.

Jules throws me a questioning glance. I nod and ball my hands into fists.

She tightens her grip on the knife. Slowly unlocks the door. Cracks it open.

"*Merde!*" She jumps backward as a cloaked figure kicks the door wide.

Before anyone can react, a hand flashes out from the cloak. Seizes Jules's knife. Flings it across the room.

Thwack. The blade sinks into the wall right behind me. Adrenaline shoots through my limbs.

"I don't want to fight any of you," the visitor says in a distinctly feminine voice. One I recognize.

"Too bad." Jules lunges for her.

"No, don't!" I say, even though the visitor easily dodges her attack. "She's a friend. She's Ailesse's friend," I clarify. Jules's brow furrows.

The visitor takes three smooth steps into the room and draws back the hood of her cloak. Black curls spring around her face. Large brown eyes stare back at me. "Hello, Bastien."

I nod, struggling to stay upright. My back is on fire. "Sabine."

She lifts her chin. "I've come to tell you Prince Casimir has abducted Ailesse."

"Saw it with my own eyes." My jaw muscle tenses.

Sabine's hand drifts to her necklace of grace bones. She inhales a long breath through her nostrils. "I've come to ask for your help."

Acknowledgments

Dreaming up this story and crafting it into a polished book has been a wonderful and challenging adventure. I'm indebted and grateful to those who helped make it happen:

My agent, Josh Adams, who saw a spark of greatness in my long and rambling phone call about French folklore, star-crossed lovers, bone magic, and Ferriers of the dead.

My editor, Maria Barbo, who believed in Ailesse, Sabine, and Bastien from the start. You brought out their angst, demons, and desires with your signature magic. I trust you implicitly.

Stephanie Guerdan, Maria's brilliant assistant, who literally keeps us on the same page, adds wonderful editorial input, and performs a plethora of tasks behind the scenes.

My publisher, Katherine Tegen, and her fantastic crew at KT Books/HarperCollins. Thank you for giving me a home and continuing to support me.

The incredible design team: art directors Joel Tippie and Amy Ryan; and Charlie Bowater, who illustrated the breathtaking jacket art. I am absolutely smitten with the work you've all done.

My husband, Jason Purdie, for respecting my creativity and cultivating a home environment where it can run wild, and for continuing to inspire me with your theatrical talent.

My children: Isabelle, for her enthusiasm about this story; Aidan, for making me laugh during tight deadlines; and Ivy, for asking hard life questions that kept me grounded.

My French friends, Sylvie, Karine, and Agnés, who helped me feel seen when I felt lost and alone as a teenager, and who inspired my deep love for their country and culture.

My critique partners and besties, Sara B. Larson, Emily R. King, and Ilima Todd, for making my shark attack scarier, my world-building clearer, and my characters more relatable.

Bree Despain, for sharing firsthand knowledge and sensory details of her travels through the catacombs beneath Paris. One day I'll go exploring with you!

My French translator, Oksana Anthian, for tweaking my made-up French words until they sounded realistic and phonetically accurate.

My mother, Buffie, for assuring me the work would get done, and for providing me a quiet place in her home whenever I needed to escape in order to make that happen.

My writer father, Larry, who has already been ferried to the Beyond. I feel your love, help, and inspiration every day, Dad.

My writing friends, Jodi Meadows, Erin Summerill, Lindsey Leavitt Brown, Robin Hall, and Emily Prusso, for their pep talks, brainstorming, and laughter.

The best friends across my life: Jenny Porcaro Cole (high school), Colby Gorton Fletcher (mutual beauty school dropout . . . don't ask), Mandy Barth Kuhn (college), Amanda Davis (newlywed years), Robin Hall (past neighbor), and Sara B. Larson (writing life). Because this book is largely about best friends who would do anything for one another, I had to give a shout-out to all of you.

My nine siblings, Gavon, Matthew, Lindsay, Holly, Nate, Rebecca, Collin, Emily, and McKay. With our strikingly different personalities, it's pretty amazing that we all love each other and get along. Thank you for teaching me what a true *famille* is.

And to God, my steady rock and perfect deity. The gods in this book should take a lesson from You. Thank You for showing me how to love, grace by grace.

Don't miss the entrancing sequel
BONE CRIER'S DAWN

1
Sabine

"WATCH OUT, SABINE!" JULES'S LOW and scratchy voice calls from a mineshaft above. I barely have time to move aside before she drops into the tunnel. A rush of air hits Bastien's candle, and the flame sputters out. We're thrown into absolute darkness.

"*Merde,*" Bastien curses.

"Relax," Jules says. "Marcel always has a tinderbox in his pack."

"And another candle," Marcel adds.

"Excellent," Jules replies. "The thunderstorm is loud enough now. It's time to blow that wall."

We're in the mines beneath the catacombs close to Beau Palais, the castle where Prince Casimir lives, where he's holding Ailesse captive. Not for much longer. My heart beats faster.

Today, we rescue my sister.

A few seconds later, flint and steel strike together. The soft glow meets a candlewick and snaps into a brighter flame.

Bastien and I elbow forward for the candle. The alliance I've made with the boy who loves Ailesse—who she somehow loves in return—is tenuous at best. Just because he and his friends are helping me free her from her abductor doesn't mean I've forgiven them for also holding her captive.

"I'll do this myself," Marcel says.

"Wait!" Jules's eyes widen at her younger brother.

It's too late. He lowers the candle to the powder.

Whoosh.

Fire streaks an angry line toward the cask.

Jules yanks Marcel to his feet. Bastien spins and runs the other way. I shove him faster. Ailesse would never forgive me if he died.

We race until the dense atmosphere eats up all light and sound behind us. My nerves sting, waiting for the explosion. Did the fire burn out before it reached the cask? I glance over my shoulder.

BOOM.

A massive burst of flames zips toward us and throws me backward. I hit Bastien. We crash onto the ground. A second later, Marcel and Jules topple onto us. Chalky smoke and debris flash by. Sharp rubble scrapes against my sleeves. The chaos finally settles into fat flakes of twirling ash.

No one moves for a long moment. We lie in a tangle of legs, arms, and heads. Finally Marcel slides off our piled bodies, and his floppy hair bounces. "I may have misjudged the impact of the blast."

Jules groans. "I'm going to murder you." She rolls off and shakes dust and ash from her golden braid. "You better hope that sounded like thunder, or any moment now all the soldiers in Beau Palais are going to flood this tunnel."

We've been waiting for the perfect storm to mask the noise of the explosion, and as poor luck would have it, it fell on the same day as the new moon. Ferrying night. If this rescue attempt fails, I'll have to lead my *famille* on the land bridge myself and ferry the souls of the departed—the sacred duty of each Leurress, given to us by the gods of the afterlife, who we descend from. But I can't lead my *famille*. Ailesse is the only person alive who knows the song on the bone flute that opens the Gates to the Beyond. She was meant to be *matrone*, not me.

I scoot off of Bastien and offer a hand to help him up. He hesitates, then exhales and takes it. Despite our bickering, I want his assistance. We'll find Ailesse faster if we work together.

We stand side by side and stare into the hazy gray light shining in from the blasted hole. I inhale a deep breath. After fifteen long days, we finally have access to Beau Palais.

"Everyone ready?" Bastien cautiously rubs his back where my mother stabbed him. The wound is still healing. Only in the last week has he been able to walk without grimacing.

Jules nods and adjusts her cloak. I tighten my fists. Marcel settles into a comfortable position. He's going to serve as watch. If the tunnel is compromised, he'll light a small explosive filled with sulfur and pepper seeds. The stench will warn us not to come back this way. Meanwhile, Jules is going to guard our point of entry into the castle above.

Bastien waves Jules and me forward. The three of us advance to the end of the tunnel. I reach the wall first and climb the rubble. Through the blasted four-foot hole, I stare inside a dry castle well lined with river rock. Its construction isn't yet complete. King Durand, Casimir's father, commissioned it to replace a more vulnerable well outside the castle keep.

While Bastien and Jules have been spying in Dovré and gleaning these facts about Beau Palais, I've been forced to spend most of my time at Château Creux with my *famille*.

The Leurress are shaken by the news of Odiva's death. All I told them is our *matrone* died ferrying alongside Ailesse on an ancient bridge in an underground cavern. If they knew Odiva ran through the Gates of the Underworld to join her true love—my father, a man who wasn't her sanctioned *amouré*—it might spark anarchy. Once Ailesse comes back and rightfully replaces me as *matrone*, I'll let her decide what to reveal about our mother, and I'll retreat to the comfort of her shadow.

I leap to the opposite side of the well, grab an iron rung, and climb a ladder built for the well diggers. They're not at the castle today. No one labors during La Liaison except entertainers and those preparing food for the three-day festival.

We'd hoped to sneak in through the main entrance, but King Durand isn't holding a public celebration. According to rumor, he's too ill. But he was ill before Ailesse was taken captive, and the castle gates have only been locked since Prince Casimir brought her here.

Jules leaps onto the ladder after me. I envy the leather leggings she's wearing. My shoes keep tangling on the hem of my simple blue dress.

Bastien follows last, and the three of us rise sixty feet to the top of the well. It's covered by an iron grate, which scrapes loudly as we slide it off. A clap of thunder muffles the sound. For now, the rainfall doesn't reach us. We're in the tight quarters of the castle well tower.

I creep to the tower door and peek through a small window at the top. I can't see much of the castle courtyard beyond the pelting rain—even with my far-reaching vision, thanks to the power from my nighthawk grace bone—but I make out the blue-and-gold-striped awnings that line the perimeter. They provide shelter for a few servants who scurry across the wet cobblestones to reach the other side. One awning caps an arched passageway that leads inside the castle—the entrance we'll use.

Bastien removes his dusty cloak and tosses it over to Jules. Beneath it, he's dressed in the simple garb of a castle dungeons soldier. I also throw off my cloak and tuck a few stray black curls into my servant's cap. I slip my grace bone necklace beneath the neckline of the uniform dress Bastien stole for me and hide my bone knife in the sheath under my apron.

Bastien turns to Jules. "See you soon."

She sits on the rim of the well, still a little breathless from climbing. "Promise to keep your head, all right? If you can't pull this off today, don't be reckless. We'll figure out something else. We still have ten and a half months before—"

"This will work." He flexes his jaw muscle. "Come on, Sabine."

He slips out the door before Jules can say anything else.

I'm quick to follow. I don't wish to discuss the soul-bond between Ailesse and Casimir, either—the bond Bastien thought he shared with her until I discovered the truth. Now Ailesse has to kill Casimir within a year from the time the gods sealed their lives together, or she'll die with him. I'll make sure it happens before we leave the castle today. I'll hand her the bone knife and persuade her to save herself.

Bastien and I head through the rain for the arched passageway. We've committed to memory the map of Beau Palais he pieced together after conversing with a retired castle servant. "After three cups of tavern ale, the man was an open book," Bastien told me.

We shake off the rain once we're inside the castle. We're standing in a stone foyer that intercepts a long corridor running left and right. Straight ahead is the great hall. Servants mill about, setting gold plates and goblets on a few gathered tables. Garlands of vibrant late-summer flowers twirl around towering columns that support a vaulted ceiling. Blue banners embroidered with the gold sun symbol of Dovré—an homage to the sun god, Belin—hang alongside green banners with the tree symbol of the earth goddess, Gaëlle. I'm told *La Liaison* is held to invoke their joint blessing on the upcoming harvest.

Bastien and I share a quick glance and nod before we part ways. He heads left, and I head right. His direction leads toward the dungeons entrance, and mine accesses the staircase to the third level. Ailesse could also be locked in one of the royal apartments up there.

I've only taken a few steps when a handsome boy with strawberry hair walks around a column in the great hall, fifteen feet away. My body goes rigid, my blood cold—then scorching hot.

Prince Casimir.

He's wearing a burgundy doublet over a loose linen shirt and fitted breeches. A simple crown made from a thin band of gold wraps across the middle of his forehead.

He hasn't laid eyes on me yet, but I still can't force myself to move. Images from the last full moon crash through my brain: Casimir taking Ailesse's grace bones, carrying her away in his arms; Ailesse struggling against him while her injured leg dripped blood; me seeing them from a distance as I fought his soldiers; Bastien, also helpless, lying on the bridge and bleeding out from his stab wound.

"Can you add more wildflowers?" Casimir asks a female servant while surveying the garland draped around the column. "Ailesse is fond of them."

"Of course, Your Highness."

"I want everything perfect for when she meets my father tonight."

My mind snags on his words. *Flowers for Ailesse? A meeting with the king?* I glance at Bastien. He's taken cover behind a potted tree at the corner of the great hall and an adjoining corridor. From his deeply furrowed brow, he's just as confused as I am. How can Ailesse attend a dinner with Casimir's father? Isn't she locked away?

"I understand, Your Highness." The servant bows, and Casimir starts to turn in my direction. I jerk around, shuffle to the nearest table, and fuss with a place setting. I itch to hold the bone knife. If I could stab him right now, I would. But that would kill Ailesse. Their lives are woven together. She must be the one to wield the ritual blade and kill her *amouré*.

The prince's footsteps slowly clip toward me. My pulse pounds faster. I lower my head and pray to the goddess of the Night Heavens. *Elara, don't let him recognize me.*

"Pardon me, but are you new here?"

I stiffen, keeping my back to him. "Yes," I squeak.

"What is your name?"

I could run. With my nighthawk speed, I could make it to the third level before Casimir had a chance to catch me. If only I knew which room Ailesse was in. By the time I find her, he'll have the whole castle on alert. "Ginette," I murmur, feigning to be shy.

"Ginette, I am your prince and future king." Casimir's voice is warm and carries the charm that made me lightheaded when we first met. I had performed a proxy ritual to summon and kill Ailesse's *amouré*, expecting Bastien to come, but Casimir came instead, and for several wonderful and terrible moments, I thought he was my *amouré*, not hers. "You need not be afraid of me," he says. "In this castle, I treat my servants with regard."

A scoff rips out of my throat. "And how do you treat your prisoners?" My subterfuge is pointless. Whether I run or confront him now, he's going to discover me. "You can't win Ailesse with flowers and gold and false honor. She will always see you as her abductor."

My jackal hearing catches his soft intake of breath. "Sabine?" he asks.

I lift my chin and turn to face him. Casimir gazes back at

me with widened stone-blue eyes. I fight to keep the heat in my blazing stare. His restrained demeanor carries wisdom, depth, and strength. It makes it hard to remember he's the same person who felt entitled to steal my sister away.

"Where are you keeping Ailesse?" I demand. I pull out my hidden necklace and let my grace bones dangle, exposed, over the bodice of my dress. The three bones hang side by side—a fire salamander skull; a crescent-moon pendant, carved from the femur of a rare golden jackal; and the leg and claw of a nighthawk.

Two guards at the edge of the room take a step forward, but Casimir holds up a hand to stall them. He may not understand what I am—what Ailesse is—but he knows my bones hold power.

"Ailesse isn't my prisoner. I invited her to stay with me, and she agreed."

Lies. Ailesse would never consent to that. "Then tell her I'd like to pay a visit."

"You know I can't do that." His tone exudes a maddening level of calm. "You tried to kill me, Sabine. You are not welcome in this castle."

The golden jackal in me snaps. I whip out the bone knife beneath my apron. Casimir quickly draws a jeweled dagger. Our blades meet each other's throats at the same time. His dagger's sharp edge presses against the tendon of my neck.

"What would Ailesse think of you if you killed her sister?"

"No less than she'd think of you if you . . ."

An animalistic screech rings in my ears and drowns out the rest of his words. A small reflection appears in his pupils. A bird with a white heart-shaped face.

Somehow, as I'm staring at Casimir, the bird grows larger. I gasp. This is a vision. It has to be. I'm seeing the silver owl—the goddess Elara's bird. She hasn't appeared to me in her physical or transparent form since the night Casimir abducted Ailesse. Visions like this are unheard-of among the Leurress, but the silver owl has shown me two before, and both visions were in connection to saving my sister.

The owl grows to full size and hovers in front of Casimir with her wings unfurled. He can't see her; he's looking right through her at me. It's like she's protecting him.

I don't understand. The silver owl once wanted Casimir dead. She led me to kill the golden jackal, carve a flute from its bone, and use it to lure the prince during my proxy rite of passage. I could have killed him then without dooming Ailesse to die in return. The ritual would have protected her.

The owl beats her wings once, and my surroundings change. I feel the castle floor beneath me, but I see the cliffs overlooking the Nivous Sea above. It's the night of the last new moon. Ailesse is playing the siren song on the bone flute, trying to open the Gates of the Beyond.

She keeps playing. The harrowing melody floats to my ears and burns through my mind. I've remembered snatches of it before, but not every measure. Now all the notes pulse vividly inside me and plant deep roots. I doubt I'll ever forget them.

What's happening? I came here to rescue Ailesse, not see a memory, not learn a song. I came here to help her kill Casimir. Why isn't the silver owl helping me?

She beats her wings again. Now Ailesse is in the underground cavern on the fragile soul bridge. She moves toward the Gates of the Underworld with headstrong determination. I hear myself shouting for her to stay back, but she won't listen.

I blink and see Casimir again through the body of the owl. My bone knife shakes at his neck. Maybe the owl isn't protecting him from me. Maybe she's protecting *Ailesse* from me.

I could threaten Casimir, fight off his soldiers, find Ailesse, free her . . . but what if my sister shouldn't lead the ferrying tonight? She barely resisted stepping through the Gates of the Underworld last time. The only thing that distracted her was Odiva stabbing Bastien.

Perhaps . . . perhaps my sister is safer in Beau Palais. For now.

My eyes blur with infuriating tears. Casimir's brows hitch together. He doesn't know what to make of my reaction. For the longest time, all I've been trying to do is save Ailesse. Why am I prevented at every turn?

I pull the bone knife away. The silver owl disappears. I curse the goddess's messenger, but I've learned to trust her. She warned me about Odiva before I knew my mother's crimes. She led me to Casimir, who helped me finally find Ailesse. She'll help again when the time is right, when Ailesse's freedom won't lead to her death. She knows more than I do.

Casimir's dagger holds steady at my neck. He opens his mouth like he wants to say something, but his expression is torn between anger and pity. I harden my glare on him, even while my tears fall. I still hate him. My actions don't change that.

One of his soldiers clears his throat. "Shall we take her to the dungeons, Your Highness?"

The tip of Casimir's blade slides to lift my chin as he deliberates. He swallows. "Yes."

The soldiers advance. Casimir lowers his dagger down my neck. He's going to cut the leather cord of my necklace. With nighthawk speed and jackal strength, I grab his wrist and slam the hilt of my knife into his upper arm. His dagger tumbles from his grip. Before it clatters to the stones, I drive my knee into his gut. He buckles forward. I shove him to the ground and jab my elbow in his back. I pluck up his fallen dagger. The first soldier swings low for me. I jump over his blade and spring off Casimir's body. I bolt away before the second soldier can attack.

Casimir shouts my name. He's back on his feet and chasing after me. His soldiers follow. I run toward the long corridor, past Bastien's hiding place.

He shoots me a livid glance. "What the hell are you doing?" he hisses.

"Leaving. Tell Ailesse I know the siren song. I can open the Gates."